Chandrakanta

Chandrakanta

Devaki Nandan Khatri

PRABHAT
PAPERBACKS

Published by
PRABHAT PAPERBACKS
4/19 Asaf Ali Road,
New Delhi-110 002 (INDIA)
e-mail: prabhatbooks@gmail.com

ISBN 978-93-5266-738-3
CHANDRAKANTA
by Devaki Nandan Khatri

Edition
2018

Price
₹ 295.00 (Rupees Two Hundred Ninety Five only)

Translated by
Prof. (Retd.) Ram Bhagwan Singh
Prof. Chhote Lal Khatri

Printed at
R-Tech Offset Printers, Delhi

Dedicated
to
Smt Rajrani Khatri
Grand daughter-in-law of
Devaki Nandan Khatri

Preface

The publication of *Chandrakanta* in Hindi in 1888 caused quite a sensation in the Hindi belt. Its author Devkinandan Khatri became the most popular star and *Chandrakanta* — a household word. Its popularity prompted the people to learn Hindi to enjoy and appreciate the novel. Even after 128 years now, *Chandrakanta* still has its glamour and the old after-image. In fact, it is an imperishable work.

The popularity of *Chandrakanta* accounts for its combination of magic and romance, imagination and fantasy, superstition and the supernatural, ingenious tricks and tact, imaginary mechanical exuberance, suspense after suspense, battles and wars, truce and peace, espionage and revelation, conspiracy and its outcome, etc. It was written in an age when Lewis Carroll's *Alice in Wonderland* was published in 1865 and *Through the Looking Glass* in 1871. Both the writers have copiously made use of magic and fantasy. However, *Chandrakanta* is not a children's classic, it is everyone's choice as the main story is realistic and shows king's rivalry and superiority complex. For self-glorification, they sacrificed thousands of soldiers. The atmosphere smacks of deception and fraud, conspiracy and terror, servitude and helplessness.

The main story in *Chandrakanta* centres around the love and struggle of Prince Virendra Singh of Naugarh and Chandrakanta, the princess of Vijaygarh. He has to face a rival Krur Singh, the son of the Diwan of Vijaygarh. Krur Singh aligns with the king of Chunar, Shivdutt and raises obstacles between Prince Virendra Singh and

Chandrakanta, which ultimately unites the lovers, and Krur Singh dies. What attracts the reader most is the way the story is told in a series of episodes all interlocked. There are the *aiyars,* human beings with extraordinary capacity to run fast and fight, have knowledge of herbs and their medical application, are cunning spies and good musicians. Even more importantly, the *aiyars* can transmogrify themselves, i.e., completely change their appearance and take on the appearance of anybody, their voice, their manners and all.

Then there is the *Tilism* which is a hidden treasure constructed underground with ingenious safeguards and magical locks and entrances. In days of old, when a king had no heir, he consulted astrologers who predicted that there would be a prince illustrious enough to deserve his wealth. The king would then get a *Tilism* built and fill it with all his wealth. The *Tilism* had magical doors and fixtures, ferocious looking unearthly guards and layer after layer of safety. The key to the secret chamber lay in a book which was destined to go to the deserving prince and none else. He would ultimately break the *Tilism,* possess all the wealth and marry the princess. The *Tilism* reminds one of Ali Baba's secret cave but here there are caves under caves and a whole household with buildings, gardens, orchards, ponds, housemaids and furnishings.

The creation of *Tilism* and *aiyars* in the novel is all together new and different from other like creations in other literatures. Devakinandan Khatri's aiyar cannot only take on the appearance of any male or female, he can perform his or her role in all respects. He can fight, conspire and their astrologer can even foretell the future through his astrological device called *ramal.* The *aiyars* also act as a detective whose bag is equipped with magical herbs to etherise someone and revive his consciousness as well. Moreover, they are honest and loyal to their masters.

The novel *Chandrakanta,* though unique in its own right, was a tremendous feeder to public choice so long attuned to the stories of *Arabian Nights* and the contemporary trend of the detective novels like those written by Gopal Ram Gahmari and Kishori Lal Goswami. *Chandrakanta* is, at once, a detective novel, a fantasy and a realistic romance. On the one hand, the novel shows true and passionate love and, on the other, it shows its sustenance even at the cost of one's life as Kunwar Virendra Singh is going to kill himself jumping from the cliff having heard of the death of Chandrakanta. The novel also guards the reader against cheating and fraud. Appearances in many cases are only deceptive and intriguing. The author's skill lies in his super-duper art of creating a very complicated story charged with magic, suspense and coincidence. The main story of love and the pangs of separation is at times pushed back and forth to emerge as the all-motivating force. In passing, the writer presents the exotic beauty of the hills, forests, valleys and hideous caves which is, no doubt, a tribute to the imagination and fancy of Devkinandan Khatri. Today, he may be regarded as the fictional mother of Harry Potter.

Translators' Note

Translating an old classic entails upon the translator certain socio-cultural and linguistic demands. The story of *Chandrakanta* happens in our neighbouring state and poses no unfamiliarity. In fact, the core of the novel consists in its magic, mystery, suspense, fantasy and romance written at a time when the novel in Hindi was taking shape. In form though inchoate, it constitutes the triangle of love—meeting, separation and reunion of the heroine Chandrakanta and the hero Kunwar Virendra Singh.

What is characteristic of the novelist is the creation rather invention of *aiyar* and *tilism* having no parallel in any literature. Such concepts can only be explained and not translated. We have done as such in the glossary. Certain Arabic and Urdu words and phrases have been found their nearest equivalents in English. In narration, however, the original dialogues follow the old translation of naming the speaker each time he speaks. Today, we conveniently skip naming the speaker where there are only two speakers. Our attempt is at recreating the thrill and romance of the original text without interfering with the content and form. Though translated by two of us by inter-personal modifications, we have tried to minimise stylistic differences. We adopted the theory of close approximation of the text in target language without allowing any bizarre effect to an English reader. Our attempt has been to produce it as an enjoyable novel, as a pioneer Hindi novel reflecting the social and intellectual concerns of the time as Devakinandan Khatri himself wanted to say and the manner and form he chose fit for it.

Part-I

1

It's evening. The crimson sun is still peeping through the western hill. Virendra Singh and Tej Singh are sitting on a rock at a foothill facing a desolate field. Virendra Singh is barely twenty-one or twenty-two. He is the only son of Surendra Singh, the king of Naugarh. Tej Singh is the son of Jeet Singh, the *Diwan* of King Surendra Singh. Both are friends. Tej Singh is young, agile and sharp. With a *khanjar* (dagger) tied to his waist, a pouch in the side and a lasso in his hand, he is vigilant as he is talking to him. A horse is tied to a tree in front of them.

Kunwar Virendra Singh, desperate to see his love Chandrakanta, reveals his heart to Tej Singh, "Look brother, what love has made of me! You have carried my letters to her and brought hers to me several times which proves she loves me as passionately as I love her. Her and my kingdoms are just fifteen miles apart, still we are helpless to do anything. Even in this letter, Chandrakanta has written, "Come sharp by any means".

Tej Singh consoles him, "I can take you to her by all means. But her father, King Jay Singh has tightened the security around the palace. And his minister's son Krur Singh is infatuated with her. Your love for Chandrakanta is well known to him. He has alerted his *aiyars* Nazim Ali and Ahmad Khan to keep an eye on her movements. No doubt, Chandrakanta hates Krur Singh and the King too won't entrust his daughter to him. Still he is nursing his hope for her. Your love for her is a constant irritant to him. Through his father, he has informed Maharaja Jay Singh of your love for Chandrakanta. That's why, the king has turned against you and the palace is heavily guarded. Until I arrest the trouble makers, particularly his *aiyars*, it is not safe to take you there. First let me go to Vijaygarh and meet Chandrakanta and her dearest friend, Chapla. Except her, there is none to help me. I will come back after taking stock of the situation there and advise you what to do. We should not do anything in haste, lest we are arrested."

"Do whatever you think best. I count only on my sword, while you rely on both your bravery and *aiyari*."

"It is also known to me that recently Nazim and Ahmad have called on our King. I don't know what their motive was. Alas! I was not there at that time."

"The problem is they want to trap you and you want to trap them. God be with you. Anyway, now you go and arrange my meeting with Chandrakanta by any means".

Tej Singh got up and left for Vijaygarh on foot. Virendra Singh released the horse from the tree and rode off to his fort.

□

2

In Vijaygarh, Krur Singh is talking to Ahmad and Nazim in his parlour. "Look Nazim, Maharaja thinks how a king like him can accept his minister's son for his son-in-law. And Chandrakanta loves Virendra Singh. Now tell me what is the way out? If I kidnap Chandrakanta, where shall I go? Where shall I live? And what treatment would be meted out to my father? I think it would be better if we somehow arrest Virendra Singh and his aiyar Tej Singh and dispose them of in some secret place so that they are not traced for a thousand years and then at the right moment, kill the king and grab the throne. Only then I can enjoy my life at peace with Chandrakanta. But will the people accept me as a king"?

Nazim agrees with him and says, "In our court, the Muslims outnumber the Hindus. I can rope them in, to help you and make them swear that they will accept you as a king, provided you accept Islam once the work is done".

"It's done, by heart and soul".

"Then it's final. You write an agreement. I will show it to my Muslim brothers to ensure their support".

Instantly, Krur Singh wrote an agreement to accept Islam if he succeeds to become a king. Ahmad assures him, "Now it is our responsibility to take all Muslims in confidence. You need not worry about it. Of course, you must give us a promissory note that we would be appointed Ministers when you become a king. Then you will see the wonders of our *aiyar*".

Krur Singh also wrote a promissory note to this effect, which pleased them.

Nazim asserted, "We are now going to snoop around Chandrakanta to know what's going on between Virendra Singh and Chandrakanta. It's the right time as she would be in her garden talking to Chapla and narrating her pangs of separation from her love."

Having said this, they took leave of Krur Singh.

□

3

The sun is fading away. Chandrakanta, Chapla and Champa are strolling in the garden adjacent to the back of the palace. It was specially built for Chandrakanta's recreation. The soft smell of flowers mixed with slow breeze is refreshing. In the west, the cluster of mango trees and the sun rays filtering through the leaves create a splendid spectacle. Beds of flowers are fully watered and plants are washed clean. Beds of roses and jasmine are displaying their charm. A palatial building on one side and beautiful turrets on the other are creating a mesmerising landscape. Chapla who is a close confidant of Chandrakanta and a clever aiyar takes Chandrakanta on a stroll. While admiring the beauty of Chandrakanta, she is plucking fragrant flowers and giving them to her. All this hardly pleases Chandrakanta, who is nursing the pangs of separation from Virendra Singh. She is unwillingly taken to the garden by her friends to bring her some relief.

Champa, the friend of Chandrakanta, goes to the jasmine vine to pluck flowers to make a bouquet for Chandrakanta. Chandrakanta and Chapla slowly move to the fountain and sit down to watch the sight of water streaming down. Chapla wonders, "Where has Champa gone?"

"Must be hanging around somewhere".

"It has been more than two hours she is away from us".

"Look, she is coming".

"There is something different in her movement," observes Chapla.

Just then Champa came and gave a bouquet of flowers saying. "Look, what a beautiful bouquet I have made for you. Had Kunwar Virendra Singh been here, he would have appreciated my art and rewarded me".

Hearing his name, Chandrakanta suddenly turned pale. The past memories flashed in her mind and her lotus face faded. She started heaving and tears rolled down her cheeks. She sobbed, "I don't know what is written in my fate. I don't know what sins I committed in my past life that I am undergoing such suffering. I don't know what has obsessed my father? He says that he will keep his daughter unmarried. Virendra Singh's father tried to placate him for marriage but Kupath Singh, the father of wicked Krur Singh, has kept him in his control and the bloody Krur Singh is eying on me".

Chapla sensed the mischief and pressed Chandrakanta's hand to give her some hint to keep silent. Chandrakanta got the point and turned silent. While moving forward, Chapla dropped her handkerchief deliberately. When they crossed some distance, Chapla asked Champa, "Oh dear, please see if I have left my hanky at the fountain".

When Champa went to fetch the hanky Chandrakanta asked, "Friend, why did you suddenly stop me while I was speaking?"

Chapla said, "My dear friend, I got suspicious about Champa. From her gestures and words, it appears that she is no real Champa."

When Champa came back and handed the hanky to Chapla, she asked, "Did you do the work I assigned you last night"?

"Oh, sorry, I forgot to do that."

"But do you remember or have you forgotten that thing?"

"Of course, I do."

"If you remember it, tell me. Only then I will be convinced". Chapla grilled her.

Champa could not reply and diverted the talk. That made it clear that she was not Champa. Chapla did not show her suspicion; rather she took her away to share something and said, "My ear has been aching since yesterday. See if there is any foul smell coming out of it". Duplicate Champa was trapped. She smelt the ear and fell down in a faint. Actually, Chapla had stuffed some anesthetic powder in her ear. She called up Chandrakanta, "Come on friend, look at Champa". Seeing Champa lying unconscious, she said, "Are you sure, you are not mistaken? Or else you will feel sorry for it."

"Not at all". Chapla said firmly. She carried her on her back to the fountain. She asked Chandrakanta, "Throw water on her face fetching it from the fountain and I rub her face with it". Chandrakanta did so and Chapla rubbed it rigorously. In a short while, the face of Champa changed and Nazim was revealed. Chandrakanta turned red in anger and said, "How dare he do this impudence!"

"Now see, what I do with him". Saying this, Chapla carried him on her back to a small cellar in a corner of the garden under the turret. She lay him down and lighted a candle taking out from her bag. She also tied his hands and feet tightly behind the back with a rope. With a sniff of *lakhlakha*, she brought him back to his senses. Nazim sneezed and found himself imprisoned and helpless. Chapla started flogging him mercilessly.

Nazim started crying, "Forgive me. I committed a heinous offence. I will never repeat the same. I will never even think of it". But it fell to deaf ears and she kept on flogging, "Wait, wait. It's not enough for you. Why did you come here? To enjoy the fresh breeze in the garden? To take a stroll here? Didn't you know Chapla would be around? Son of a bastard, fraud. Did you do this by order of your father? See, I will also teach him a lesson. She unleashed another round of beating and then asked, "Tell me the fact. How did you come here and where is Champa?"

Nazim revealed the fact. Out of fear, he had to confess and he said, "It's I who had made Champa unconscious. I had left a bouquet of flowers with anesthetic powder in it on her way. She fell unconscious after smelling it. Then I put on her dress and hid her in a bower before coming to you disguised as Champa. Lo! I have said everything. Now please set me free."

"Wait. I'll free you". She gave him a few more terrible lashing and left him whimpering. Then Chapla asked Chandrakanta, "Please keep watch over him while I find out Champa. May be he is telling a lie".

Chapla reached near the jasmine vine in the light of a flint looking for Champa. She discovered her lying unconscious and naked in a bush. She brought her to consciousness with the smell of *lakhlakha* and teased her. "How are you? Got duped?"

Champa felt hurt, "How do I know *aiyari* would be played at this time in this place! I smelt a bouquet lying here and fell unconscious. I don't know what happened next. Alas! Who the hell made me unconscious and ripped off my clothes? They were costly". Chapla gave her Nazim's clothes to put on and asked her to follow. "Come with me, I will show you who did this mischief with you?" She along with

Champa came to the place where she had left Chandrakanta and Nazim. Pointing to Nazim, she told Champa, "Look, it is he who did you this favour". Champa got infuriated at Nazim and said, "Sister, allow me to administer a few lashes to release my anger". "Greet him with as many shoes or lashes as you can".

Champa gave him a full dose of flogging so much so that he started cursing Krur Singh, "Curse be with him who has brought me to such a pass". At last, having locked him in that cellar, they left for the palace. Nazim and Ahmad got an easy access to the garden as it was guarded by the Muslim guards.

□

4

Taking leave of Virendra Singh, Tej Singh reached Vijaygarh and began to look for ways to see Chandrakanta but found no way out as the watchmen were very vigilant and it was a moon-lit night. Had it been a dark night, he would have tried to climb up the palace by using his lasso.

At last, he went to a lonely place and disguised himself as a *chobdar* (mace-bearer). He reached the threshold of the palace where some *chobdars* and pawns were on duty. He told a chobdar, "Friend, I am also a servant of the Maharaja. I have been in his service as a peon for the last four months. Now I am at leisure. So, I walked to this place enjoying the moonlight. I got tempted to see you smoking *hukka* and thought to have one or two puffs with you. You must be aware how an opium eater feels at the smell of tobacco!"

They readily invited him, "Of course, you are welcome to have a puff with us". One of the *chobdars* offered him his *hukka*. Tej Singh politely said, "I am a Hindu, I can't take a puff from your *hukka*. Having said this, he took out the *chilam* from the *hukka* and started smoking."

Hardly had he taken in two puffs of *chilam*, he started coughing acutely and then said, "O *Miyan*, how bitter tobacco you smoke! I am used to taking the royal tobacco that the king uses. The man who tends king's *hukka* is my friend. He often gives me a little tobacco. I am so used to it that no other tobacco suits me".

Having said this, Tej Singh disguised as chobdar took out some tobacco from his bag and gave it to them saying, "Try it and say how it is."

They would not have even dreamt of smoking king's tobacco. So, everyone stretched out his hand and said, "Give me brother, by your grace, I too would smoke royal tobacco. You are very fortunate that you live with the king. You must be enjoying a lot". They took tobacco from him and prepared the *hukka* and offered it to Tej Singh who said, "You smoke first. After that, I will also take". They started smoking and gossiping. Very soon all of them felt giddy, and fell flat on the floor losing their consciousness.

Thus, Tej Singh easily got into the garden 'Nazarbag'. He saw a maid coming in that direction holding a light in her hand. Tej Singh quickly threw the lasso round her neck and pulled her down. Before she could speak a word, she was made unconscious with anesthetic powder. He dragged her to a recess. He lighted a candle and before a mirror disguised himself like that maid. Wearing her clothes, he reached near the place where Chandrakanta, Chapla and Champa were sitting along with a dozen maids chatting. Tej Singh disguised as a maid silently sat in a corner.

Seeing her, Chapla asked, "Ketaki, have you finished the job that I assigned to you? Why have you come back and silently sat here?"

The duplicate Ketaki replied, "Yes, I went to do the work. But on the way, I saw a scene and returned to report it to you".

"Tell me, what did you see?"

"First dismiss all the maids from here. I will confide it only to you and the princess". They were asked to leave. When only Chapla, Champa and Chandrakanta were left there, Ketaki said laughing, "I will tell you good news if you give me some reward."

Chandrakanta thought she might be having some news of Virendra Singh. The next moment she thought that she had never talked about Virendra Singh before Ketaki. Then what's the news for which she demands reward from me. At last, Chandrakanta said to Ketaki, "Yes, of course, I will reward you. Tell me, what is the good news?"

Ketaki insisted, "First, give me my reward, then I will tell you. Otherwise I am going."

Chapla could not tolerate Ketaki's whimsical behaviour and scolded her, "Ari Ketaki, what has happened to you that you are behaving so imprudently. I will give you a kick".

Ketaki retorted, "Am I weaker than you that you will kick me and I will leave you?"

It provoked Chapla and she rushed to pull her locks. Both got entangled in a wrestle. Incidentally, Chapla felt her breasts missing and she retreated with a shock.

The duplicate Ketaki teased her, "Why did you run away? Come, fight with me". Chapla took out her dagger and pointing it to her said, "O *aiyar*, tell me honestly who you are or I will kill you".

The duplicate Ketaki didn't reply. She just took out the letter of Virendra Singh and put it before Chandrakanta. Chapla also looked at it and seeing Virendra Singh's handwriting, she recognised that the duplicate Ketaki is Tej Singh as Virendra Singh will never send his letter to Chandrakanta through any other person than Tej Singh. Having thought about Tej Singh, whom she loved, she felt shy and kept mum with her head bent low. But she was full of praise for his skill and adroitness. And more, her love for Tej Singh got deepened in her heart.

Chandrakanta went through the letter very passionately and then turned to Tej Singh. "Tej Singh, he is fine, I suppose".

"What fine? He has stopped taking meals. His eyes have turned red and swollen because of weeping. His mind is lost in thoughts about you day and night. How can he have respite without meeting you! A thousand times I have counselled him but who listens to me. That day, I took your letter to him and today I had to come here again. He was insisting on accompanying me. Somehow, I persuaded him to stay back and asked him to let me go first to take stock of the situation and make necessary arrangement so that I can take you there safely. He saw the point and relieved me to come here with his reply to your letter".

Chandrakanta said with a sigh, "I am sorry, you should have brought him here along with you. I would have at least seen him. Here the two *aiyars* of Krur Singh are making such nuisance that I can't tell you. I have been persuading my father that they are my enemies. But he pays no heed to it as Krur Singh has taken him in his confidence. He has convinced my father with an exaggerated and distorted story of my meeting with Virendra Singh in such a way that he considers him upright and true. Krur Singh has been poisoning his ears. Now the King hardly listens to me. Of course, today I have got an opportunity to tell him a lot because my dear friend Chapla has arrested Nazim snooping on me in this garden. Tomorrow I will produce him before the King and ask him to see the true colour of Krur Singh. Even if he has been appointed to guard me, who has allowed him to come into the garden?

Chandrakanta told Tej Singh the whole story of Nazim's arrest and his being imprisoned in the cellar of the garden.

Tej Singh was surprised to listen to her deftness and fell in love with her. He thought a while and said, "Chapla did a good job, but she made a mistake".

Hearing it, Chapla was taken aback and wondered what lapse she had committed. As she could not make out she ultimately asked Tej Singh, "Tell me at once what went wrong?"

Tej Singh replied, "Didn't you know if Nazim was in the garden, Ahmad must be there, too. And why did you leave him in the garden? When you arrested him, you should have sent him to the lockup in the palace or produced him before the king at that very moment. Ahmad must have freed Nazim by this time".

Chapla was shocked and felt sorry for it, "Truly. It's a blunder. No one thought about it".

"Who else you think would have thought about it? You claim to be clever, being an *aiyar*. You should have taken care of it. Anyway, go and see if he is there or not".

Chapla ran to the cellar where Nazim was kept and saw the door open. There was no one in the cellar. Surely, Ahmad had released him and taken away. Repenting of her foolishness, she came back and confessed. "What to say, truly Ahmad has freed him."

Now Tej Singh started teasing her, "What a tall claim you used to make of your *aiyari*, cunning and intelligence! I am this. I am that. A low-grade third class *aiyar* has outwitted you!"

Chapla lost her temper and said irritatingly, "I am not Chapla, if I don't arrest both of them and whip them in this room".

"Tej Singh, your intelligence is now exposed. Now you will see how I arrest them and take them to my city".

Thereafter, Tej Singh told Chandrakanta and Chapla how he reached to them and where he had kept Ketaki after etherising her. He also said that he would not return her dress and costume as he would go out in it. He also cautioned them that no other than the three of them should know about this episode, otherwise the whole plan would be spoilt. Chandrakanta requested Tej Singh to visit her once in two or three days, "Your visit gives me confidence".

"Ok, I will do so". As he started to go, Chandrakanta said halting him, "Tej Singh, is it not in my fate to meet Kumar?" Saying this, her throat got constricted and she burst into tears. Tej Singh consoled her, "All this is being done to facilitate your marriage with him. How can we go on if you lose patience? Hold on Princess!"

Having consoled her thus, Tej Singh disguised as Ketaki took her leave and reached the gate where he saw a few guards regaining consciousness, some were half awake while others were still lying flat. Duplicate Ketaki scolded them, "Do you guard or just sleep? Why do you take so much opium that you keep dozing while guarding and when you sleep, you compete with the corpse. See, I will get you punished by complaining it to the queen".

The guards got stunned and started flattering her, "Forgive us Ketaki. Today we were duped by an unworthy orderly of the King. He made us smoke poisonous tobacco that brought us to this condition. That knave wanted to kill us, Allah saved us. You see, usually it doesn't happen. We got cheated today. We beg your forgiveness. If you ever see this again, punish us the way you like".

Duplicate Ketaki said, "OK you are excused today. But I warn you not to repeat this again". Saying this, she left and no one in fright dared to question where Ketaki was going.

□

5

When Ahmad, who was sitting on a branch of a tree, saw that Chapla had arrested Nazim and had gone into the palace accompanied only by Chandrakanta and Champa, and that Nazim was not with them, he guessed that Nazim would have been kept somewhere in the garden. He came down and started looking for him. When he reached near the cellar, he heard the cry of Nazim. He opened the gate of the cellar and went in. He unfastened Nazim and brought him out saying, "Hurry up, let us first get out of the garden and then tell me what happened with you".

Nazim and Ahmad came out. Nazim narrated the whole incident of being trapped by Chapla and whipped by her.

Ahmad says, "*Bhai* Nazim, as long as we do not capture Chapla, we won't succeed in our mission as she is very clever and she is gradually training Champa too. If she is not arrested, very soon her strength will be double as Champa will be fully trained to work for her".

Nazim concurs with him and says, "It's OK. But I can't do anything today. I just had a narrow escape. Of course, tomorrow we have to do this the first thing in the morning. Anyhow, we have to arrest Chapla and hide her in such a place which can't be traced and no one will suspect us".

They went on talking. Near the next gate of the palace, they saw Ketaki. Tej Singh disguised as Ketaki recognised them and thought it the right opportunity to play the sleight of hand with them and take them in custody, at least one if not both.

Ketaki (really Tej Singh) deliberately passed by Nazim and Ahmad tempting them to follow her. After a while, she turned back to scold them, "Why are you following me? Do what you are assigned". Ahmad replied, "What do you know, what we are assigned to do?"

Ketaki shot back, "I know everything. You better do what earns you Chapla's whipping. You have no hope at the palace where not even a single maid is on your side!"

They were taken aback and thought she could be of great help if she turned to their side and helped them.

Nazim was amused, "Listen Ketaki, *aiyari* is our profession. We are not afraid of being caught, beaten or killed. We are paid for it. We get reward in thousands for a simple act of favour. By God's grace, we get allies like you. It's good for you also to help us. We will give you your share".

"Listen! I don't risk my life for mere assurances. I go in for advance payment. If you pay me now, I will help you arrest Tej Singh tonight itself or you stay out. Do what you are doing".

They were amused to hear it. Nazim said, "If you get him arrested today, we will pay you what you demand".

"One thousand rupees. Not less than that. If you agree, show hard cash".

"Nazim, "how can I fetch you a thousand rupees at midnight! Of course, tomorrow I will certainly pay".

"Don't talk such silly things, I have already told you I don't believe in credit. Here I go".

Nazim stops her way, "Why do you get so annoyed? If you don't believe us, stay here. We will get back with a thousand bucks".

"Okay. One of you should stay with me and another one should proceed to fetch the money".

"All right. Ahmad will stay back with you".

Having said this, Nazim happily left for Krur Singh to get the money.

Ketaki engaged Ahmad in jejune talks for sometime. In the meanwhile, she offered him a few cardamoms and ate some herself, too. Ahmad was so happy at the prospect of imminent arrest of Tej Singh that he did not find anything wrong in it and ate the cardamoms. Soon, he felt giddy. He realised it was the work of an aiyar. He took out his dagger and attacked Ketaki without warning her. But she was alert enough to abort the attempt and grabbed his wrist. In a moment, Ahmad fell unconscious. Tej Singh tied his arms behind his back, packed him in his shawl and carried him on his back to Naugarh. He was walking briskly in excitement keeping in mind the possibilities of Nazim following him. Nazim went straight to Krur Singh to seek money. At that time, he was in sound sleep. Nazim woke him up as he arrived.

Krur Singh asked, "What's it that you are waking me up at dead of night?"

Nazim narrated the whole episode of sneaking into Chandrakanta's garden, being caught and beaten by Chapla, rescued by Ahmad and their chanced meeting with Ketaki on their way and negotiation for the arrest of Tej Singh for rupees one thousand. Krur Singh felt sorry for Nazim's arrest but sprang up in happiness over the news of the prospect of Tej Singh's arrest and said, "I am giving you one thousand rupees just now and accompanying you too". Having taken money from the chest, he accompanied Nazim. When they reached the place where he had left Ahmad and Ketaki, neither of them was seen there. Nazim was taken aback and burst forth, "We are duped".

"Nazim, what happened?"

"What to say? She was certainly not Ketaki but an aiyar who has deceived us and taken away Ahmad".

"Well done! You were already beaten by Chapla in the garden. Only Ahmad was spared there. Now he would be getting whipped somewhere. It's all over now".

Nazim searched for him for a while to overcome his doubt, but could not find anything. Ultimately, they left for home crying and cursing.

□

6

Having allowed Tej Singh to proceed for Vijaynagar, Virendra Singh came to his palace but was indifferent to any work. He either sat with his head drooping in the memory of Chandrakanta or talked to her photograph in loneliness, or wept bitterly lying in the bed covering his face.

If someone inquired, he made excuses. Virendra Singh's father Surendra Singh knew everything but he was helpless because the King of Vijaygarh was much stronger than he and had always ruled over him. Virendra Singh had asked Tej Singh to come back the same day while relieving him for Vijaygarh.

Virendra Singh waited for Tej Singh till midnight. When he did not turn up, Virendra Singh's anxiety shot up. Somehow he controlled himself and lay down on bed but his eyes remained fixed on the gate. Just before dawn, Tej Singh reached there carrying a sack on his back. Watchmen were perturbed to see him in this condition but could not utter a word in fear. Tej Singh went straight into his room and saw that he was still waking. Virendra Singh got up as he saw Tej Singh and said, "Hello brother. What's the news?"

Tej Singh recounted the whole story and handed over Chandrakanta's letter to him. He opened the sack of Ahmad and showed him saying, "This is the letter, and this is the gift".

Virendra Singh was very happy. Having read the letter several times, he touched it to his eyes and then said to Tej Singh, "Listen brother, hide Ahmad in such a place that no one knows of it. There will be trouble if Jay Singh comes to know of it".

"I have already planned for it. I am going to lock him up in the cave of a mountain that only I know".

Having said this, Tej Singh tied him back in the sack and sent for an aiyar named Devi Singh, who was a student, close friend and brother-in-law of Tej Singh and was no less an expert in the art of *aiyari*. When Devi Singh came, Tej Singh put the sack on his back and told Devi Singh, "Come along with me. I have an assignment for you". Devi Singh said, "*Guruji*, please give this sack to me, I'll carry it. It's not fair that you yourself carry it while I am with you". Ultimately, Devi Singh took that sack on his back and followed him.

Coming out of the city and passing through the meandering paths of the forest and hills, they covered around six kilometres and entered a dark tunnel. They saw some light after crossing some distance. Tej Singh stopped there and asked Devi Singh to put down the sack.

"*Guruji*, it's a strange place. If one comes here, it is difficult to get out". "Listen Devi Singh, except me, no one knows of this place. I have brought you here as you are my closest friend and you have to work a lot".

"I am your orderly, you are my teacher as you have taught me *aiyari*. I am ready to lay my life for you".

"Listen to me carefully and keep in mind what I say. Look at this door of stone. No one knows how to open it except me and my teacher who taught me *aiyari*. He is no more now. I am teaching you how to open it. You will lock in it the arrested persons so that neither anyone knows of them nor can they be freed. Here you don't need to keep prisoners tied. Just a loose fetter in their ankle is enough for safety. They can roam around slowly. You need not worry about their food because there is a small watercourse, a perennial source of water, and many trees of fruit and dry fruit inside it. Let us imprison this aiyar in it. Thereafter, you will seek one month's leave from the king pretending that you are not keeping well and you need change of climate. I will get your leave sanctioned. Then you go to Vijaygarh in disguise, stay there and snoop around to keep us updated about Vijaygarh. Whenever you get an opportunity, arrest the trouble-makers and bring them here to lock up in it.

Having briefed him thus, Tej Singh approached to the stone gate over which there was a big structure of a lion's face. Its mouth was big enough to let in an arm. Tej Singh asked him, "Insert your hand into the mouth and pull out its tongue". Devi Singh did so. He pulled out the tongue of an arm's length. As he pulled out, a sound burst forth and the door opened with a bang.

Both of them went in with Ahmad tied in the bundle. Devi Singh saw that it was a wide open place surrounded by a range of tall hills which no one could climb. In the midst of the hills, water was flowing out from a small spring and there were many trees of wild fruit making it a peculiarly pleasant place. The hills from top to bottom were densely covered with tall trees, wild fruit trees, shrubs and vines. Big mounds of stones looked like elephants, water falling from the hill created a pleasing sound. Rustling of trees when the wind blew, gurgling of streaming water and chirping of peacocks were all the more fascinating. Down below the stream which ran meandering from west to east had blackberries on both sides and ripe fruits were falling into that stream. The water of the stream was so clean that its bed was visible. At some places, the water was knee-deep, at others, waist-deep and even more. There were natural caves in the hill which looked as if God had made rooms for tourists to stay in. The hills around were sloppy and rather more spread out downside and the patches of clouds above were giving the joy of small tents. The place was so pleasant that one wouldn't get tired of it even if one spent years, rather one would feel happy.

It's morning. The sun came out. Tej Singh released Ahmad from the bundle and took out his pouch of *aiyari* and *khanzar* tied to his waist and put fetters around his ankle. Thereafter, he brought him to his senses. When Ahmad regained consciousness, and found himself in a pleasantly strange place, he believed that he was dead and angels had brought him to heaven. He started reciting Kalama. Tej Singh laughed at it and said, "Mian Saheb, you are my captive. Turn around." Ahmad turned to Tej Singh and was shocked to recognise him. He realised if he was not dead, he would die now. Ketaki's face flashed before his eyes; fear choked his throat so much that he could not utter a single word.

They left Ahmad near the spring at the same place and came out. Tej Singh asked Devi Singh to put the tongue in place which he had pulled out. Devi Singh did likewise. As the tongue collapsed in, the door closed. The two left for home through the same meandering path.

They returned to Virendra Singh in the forenoon. Virendra Singh asked, "Where did you go to lock in Ahmad that it took you so much time?" "We have locked him up in a cave at the hill. I will show you the place today. But now I think that Devi Singh should spend some time in disguise in Vijaygarh. It will help me a lot". Thereafter, he briefed him of his plan that he had shared with Devi Singh in that cave. Virendra Singh liked it very much.

They finished their daily chores, and went to the royal court. Devi Singh requested the King for leave on health ground. Devi Singh was dear to the King. So, he did not want to grant him leave. He said, "I will ensure your medical treatment here". However, on the recommendation of Virendra Singh and Tej Singh, he got leave. The court was adjourned. Virendra Singh along with the King went to the palace, Tej Singh along with his father Jeet Singh and

Devi Singh came home. He made the necessary preparation for the journey of Devi Singh and saw him off with some more suggestions.

Next day Tej Singh took Virendra Singh to the same valley where he had imprisoned Ahmad. Kumar felt very happy to see the place and said, "*Bhai*! This place creates many curiosities in my heart".

"I was more astonished when I first saw this place. But *guruji* satisfied me by telling so many things about this place that I will tell you later on".

Virendra Singh became more puzzled and insisted on knowing about that valley. Ultimately, Tej Singh narrated to him what he had learned from his *guruji* about it. Virendra Singh was pleased to know about it. They left for the palace. Kumar said, "*Bhai*! My courage has been boosted up now. I want to take on Jay Singh".

"Your courage is okay. But any haste on your part can put Chandrakanta's life at risk. Why are you so worried? See what happens. Tomorrow I will go there again to take stock of the situation in the enemy camp after Ahmad's arrest and the next time I will take you there". Virendra Singh sternly said, "No, I will definitely go there this time. Sitting idle like this does not behove a man. It's cowardice".

Tej Singh agreed, "It's OK. Come along. But you must do one thing, that is, to seek permission from the King to go for hunting for four or five days and pitch a tent on the border. Chandrakanta's palace would be just five miles away from there. There would be many advantages of it. Virendra Singh liked the idea and the plan was confirmed.

After a few days, Virendra Singh took eight days' leave for hunting from his father King Surendra Singh. He picked up a few well-trusted orderlies who had been deputed to his service and left for the journey. Just before evening, they reached the border of Naugarh and Vijaygarh and pitched their tent there. They stayed for the night. It was decided that Tej Singh would first go to Vijaygarh to take stock of the situation there.

□

7

Nazim was very sad on the arrest of Ahmad and Krur Singh was worried about himself for the fear of being captured by Tej Singh. He remained on constant alert but used to go to the court of Maharaja Jay Singh everyday and kept poisoning his ears against Virendra Singh.

One day Nazim counselled Krur Singh to kill his father Kupath Singh anyhow. After his death, Maharaja Jay Singh would naturally appoint him his minister (Wazir). The plan would be carried out speedily when he would be in power. Ultimately, he got his father poisoned. Maharaja mourned his death and for several days, court remained closed. The city too wore a mournful look on his death.

Krur Singh pretended to be in deep sorrow on his father's death and for twelve days, he laid out his separate bed. In the day, he used to cry for his father and at night, he sat with Nazim and thought how to meet Chandrakanta and arrest Tej Singh and Virendra Singh. During the same period, Virendra Singh pitched his tent on the border of Vijaygarh under the pretext of hunting. Nazim informed this to Krur Singh and said, "Virendra Singh must have come for Chandrakanta. Alas! Ahmad is not here. He would have been of great help. Anyway, let's see". Having said this, Nazim left for recce.

On the other hand, Tej Singh took leave of Virendra Singh and reached Vijaygarh. He learnt of the death of the minister and the mourning in the city. He returned to Virendra Singh with the news that Maharaja Jay Singh would appoint Krur Singh, his minister in two days after the lapse of *sutak* (mourning period after death). Virendra Singh said, "Look, Krur has killed his father for Chandrakanta. He can kill the King too. Such a man can't be taken for granted".

"It's true this wicked person, as far as possible, will also try his hand on Maharaja very soon. So, for two days, I will take stock of the court instead of going to Chandrakanta's palace. I will see if I get an opportunity in this course".

Virendra Singh said, "Not at all. Whatever may come, I will meet Chandrakanta today".

"Don't be in a hurry. Haste makes waste".

"So what! I will certainly go".

Tej Singh tried his level best to convince him. Separation from Chandrakanta made him lose the sense of good or bad.

He did not listen to him and got ready to go. At last, Tej Singh yielded, "Come along. What can I do if you are so obstinate? Come what may".

In the evening, they went out for strolling and told their orderlies not to worry about if they were late. Both of them went to Vijaygarh walking.

They reached near the Najarbag garden of Chandrakanta after sunset. The night was dark. So, they did not face any difficulty in making their way to the garden. Avoiding the watchmen, Tej Singh threw the lasso over the boundary wall and through it reached the garden. They looked around standing under a dense tree.

They saw a candle burning on a clean and smooth marble platform in the centre of the garden where Chandrakanta, Chapla and Champa were gossiping. Chapla was also keeping an eye around the place while talking.

On seeing Chandrakanta, Virendra Singh went hysterical. He started shivering and fell down unconscious. Tej Singh was not at all perturbed at it. He immediately took out *lakhlakha* from his bag of *aiyari* and brought him to his senses and said, "You should not create a scene in other's house. Now hold yourself and stay here. Let me first talk to them." Having said this, he went alone to see Chandrakanta, Chapla and Champa. On seeing Tej Singh, Chandrakanta burst out, "Where have you been for so long? Is this your loyalty? Even this time, you have come alone. Wah! Had it been so, you should have put on bangles in your wrists. Why do you boast of your manliness? If this is his love, why should I live?" Saying this, Chandrakanta burst into tears, she took hiccups. Tej Singh felt very nervous and said, "This is called childishness. You didn't even inquire about his well-being and started weeping. If this is so, I will fetch him instantly".

Having said this, Tej Singh went to the place where he had left Virendra Singh and came back with him to Chandrakanta. Chandrakanta was overjoyed to see Virendra Singh. They shared each other's pain and tears. Both wept bitterly to the extent that they swooned but regained consciousness soon. After a while, they talked love tempered with complaints.

Now see the turn of the situation. Wandering about and snooping around, Nazim also reached there. Seeing their happy meeting from a distance, Nazim felt heart-burning. He immediately returned to Krur Singh who found Nazim shaken and asked, "What's the matter? Why are you so upset?"

"O God! What I feared has come to pass. This is the right time to act shrewdly. Even now if you could do nothing, your fate is doomed".

"I can't make out anything of your words. Come to the point".

"The fact is only this that Virendra Singh has reached Chandrakanta and they are chatting in the garden right now".

Krur Singh felt crest-fallen for a moment on hearing it. The world looked gloomy and dark before his eyes. He was confined to his home in pretended condolence of his father's death for thirteen days. But this news threw him into frenzy. Immediately he stood up and rushed to Maharaja Jay Singh as he was, semi-clad and shaven head.

Maharaja Jay Singh was perturbed to see him like this and asked, "Krur Singh, I am surprised to see you coming here like this, breaking *Sutaka*, the thirteen-day condolence".

"Maharaja, you are my father. He gave me birth but I was brought up on your charity. When your honour is at stake, what use is my life and how will I be counted upon?"

'Krur Singh! Who dare damage my honour?' Jay Singh in rage.

"A small fry".

Jay Singh grinding his teeth, "Tell me quickly, who is inviting his death?"

"Virendra Singh".

"He can't dare face me. What to talk of dishonouring me! I do not get your point. Tell me clearly what's the matter? Where is Virendra Singh?"

"In the garden of your secret palace".

Maharaja's blood shot up and his body started shivering in anger. He ordered, "Cordon up the garden. I am coming there through the palace gate".

□

8

Virendra Singh and Chandrakanta are engaged in sweet talk; Chapla and Tej Singh are exchanging light banters and Champa, singled out, is looking at them. Suddenly, a coal-black man, from top to toe a black log of ebony, with red eyes, clad in loin cloth, leaping and jumping, appeared there and said, "The king is informed about you. O, my *Guruji*, you must listen to me." He disappeared as he had appeared. While going away, he dragged Champa by her foot to some distance and then left her.

Everyone was taken aback and scared to see the fiend. Champa screamed but Tej Singh immediately got up and said to Virendra Singh, "Hurry up! It's no time to stay put". He addressed Chandrakanta, "Don't mind our going away so soon. All of you must be sitting here till the King comes".

"What's the reason to hurry up? Who was that fellow whose words made you run away?" asked Chandrakanta

"There is no time to argue". Saying this, Tej Singh forcibly lifted Virendra Singh and came out of the garden with the help of lasso.

Chandrakanta felt shocked and with tear-filled eyes asked Chapla, "I don't understand what the mess is this. How scared I was to see that fiend! See, my heart is still beating fast. What have you thought?"

"It's not all clear. But it is certain that Maharaja is informed about Virendra Singh's visit here. He must be around".

Champa dropped in, "I don't know what enmity he has with me." Chapla laughed at it but she, too, was surprised at this prank. They kept on talking like this for some time. In the meanwhile, they heard the noise of men marching to the garden from all sides. Chapla said, "It seems trouble is round the corner; security guards have cordoned off the garden". Before she could finish the sentence, she saw Maharaja coming from the front. Everyone got up. Chandrakanta stepped forward and bowed down in salutation before her father "At this time, your sudden arrival..". Having said this, she kept mum.

"Nothing. I just wanted to see you, so I came here. Now you go inside the palace. Why are you sitting here? Dew drops are falling. You will fall ill." The king moved to the palace.

Chandrakanta, Chapla and Champa also followed the Maharaja to his palace. Jay Singh came to his room feeling ashamed of the whole episode and said to himself, "How Krur Singh falsely defamed my innocent daughter! Don't know what this idiot is up to that he so easily blamed her. If she comes to know, what will she think? Such a demon should not be encouraged, rather he should be punished so that such meanness is not repeated. Thinking thus, he ordered Hari Singh, a *chobdar* (mace-bearer) to fetch Krur Singh immediately.

Hari Singh reached near the garden looking for Krur Singh and saw him there along with many other men in siege of the garden. Hari Singh said to him, "Come on, Maharaja is calling you." Krur Singh got scared of the call and wondered if the thief was not caught. He had seen Maharaja going to the palace. He asked, "What is Maharaja doing?" He replied, "He has just come from the palace and is in rage. You are immediately summoned." Krur Singh was severely frightened to learn it and along with Hari Singh, he rushed shivering in fear to Maharaja.

On seeing Krur Singh, Maharaja burst out, "You bloody idiot, are you meant only for falsely blaming innocent Chandrakanta and disgracing me? What would these men surrounding the garden be thinking about her? You bloody idiot, donkey, scoundrel, how did you say that Virendra was in the palace?"

Maharaja Jay Singh's lips were trembling in anger and his eyes were blood red. Krur Singh stood aghast and spoke in panic, "This news was reported to me by Nazim who is currently detailed for the security of the palace".

Maharaja ordered, "Summon Nazim".

He was produced in a short while. Maharaja was so much in rage that he was unable to speak out clearly. He uttered in broken words: "Ye bloody! What news did you flash?"

He alone must be knowing in what a state of trepidation he was. He was hopeless of his life. He fumbled in fear, "I saw it with my own eyes, *hujur*. He might have escaped somehow".

Now Jay Singh could no longer restrain his fury and ordered, "Fifty lashes to Krur Singh and two hundred to Nazim be flogged. I am releasing you with this much. You would be beheaded if this is repeated in future. Krur Singh, you don't deserve to be a *wazir*".

The flogging started on both sides. Their cries ranted the palace but Maharaja's anger did not subside. When they were fully flogged and driven out of the palace, Maharaja went to bed but he was so agitated that he could not take a wink for the whole night.

Krur Singh and Nazim both came home and started quarreling. Krur said to Nazim accusingly, "Today my honour is sullied because of you. I lost the prospect of becoming *Diwan* in the future and am suffering the pain of being whipped, I alone know it. All this happened because of you".

Nazim replied complainingly "I am flogged for you, otherwise what have I to do with this? To hell with Chandrakanta and Virendra. What interest do I have to invite flogging?" Both kept on quarreling for hours.

At last, Krur Singh said, "Shame on us if we do not capture Virendra even after being punished this much".

"No doubt, Virendra will now visit the palace everyday because he has pitched his tent on the border only for this purpose. But I don't dare to take up another venture. If I see him again and after my reporting he escapes, I will certainly be killed," Nazim.

"Now we must do something that saves our life and enables the Maharaja to see Virendra in the palace".

After pondering over it for some time, Nazim said, "There is an astrologer named Pundit Jagannath in the court of Maharaja Shivdutt, the king of Chunargarh who is also an expert in ramal. He is so adept in playing ramal that one can ask him anytime where a particular person is, what he is doing or how he will be caught. He tells everything in no time. If you take him to your side and he comes and stays there to help you, the mission will be realised. Chunargarh is not very far from here. It's only about seventy kilometres. Let's go and by whatever means bring him here".

Krur Singh tied so many jewels in his waist band, called for two strong horses and left for Chunargarh with Nazim. He instructed the inmates that if Maharaja sends someone, tell him that I am very ill.

9

Virendra Singh and Tej Singh came out of the garden and proceeded to their camp. It was midnight when they reached the camp but Tej Singh had no respite. Having dropped Virendra in the camp, he left for Vijaygarh. Disguised as Ahmad, he went to Krur Singh's residence. Krur Singh had already left for Chunargarh. The persons on guard at his house were surprised to see Ahmad all of a sudden and asked him, "Ahmad, where have you been all these days?"

"I had been touring the hell. Now I have come back. Tell me where is Krur Singh?"

They told him the whole story, what had happened in his absence and said, "He has gone to Chunargarh. It would be better if you also go there".

Duplicate Ahmad said, "Yes, I am also going. I won't go home. Straight to Chunar". Having said this, he came back to his camp and narrated the whole thing to Virendra Singh and then he went to bed. In the morning, he got ready for Vijaygarh. He changed himself as a servant of Krur Singh, bare head, soiled face, soiled hands and feet, wailing and crying, he reached the court of Maharaja Jay Singh. Everyone was taken aback to see his condition. Maharaja instructed the Munshi (clerk) to ask, "Who is he and what does he want to say?"

Tej Singh in disguise related, "*Hujur*, I am a servant of Krur Singh. My name is Ram Lal. He has turned a rebel against Maharaja and has joined hands with the king of Chunargarh. When I forbade him to be disloyal to Maharaja, he beat me mercilessly and robbed me of my belongings. Alas! I am completely ruined. Not a penny is left with me. What shall I eat? How shall I reach my home? My sons will ask for my earnings of three years? They will ask, what have you brought from service to the royal court? What shall I give them? Have mercy Maharaja. Mercy, Mercy, Mercy!"

They consoled him with great difficulty. Maharaja burst out in anger, "Where is Krur Singh?" The mace-bearer brought the information, "He is very ill. He can't move".

Fake Ram Lal said, "Mercy Maharaja! He has also turned his side. He is telling lies. All Muslims are his friends. It demands serious investigation".

Maharaja asked his Munshi, "Go and see what the matter is". After a while, the Munshi came back to report, "Maharaja, Krur Singh is not at home and the inmates do not tell where he has gone".

Maharaja said, "He must have gone to Chunargarh. Okay. Summon any of his servants". Having got the order, a chobdar rushed to his home and brought in a hapless servant.

Maharaja asked, "Where has Krur Singh gone?" He did not answer correctly. Ram Lal again said, "Hail thee Maharaja! He will not speak the truth without being whipped". Maharaja ordered whipping. Immediately he revealed the fact that Krur Singh had gone to Chunargarh.

Maharaja Jay Singh was so furious on learning the facts about Krur Singh that it is difficult to describe in words.

He ordered:

1. All inmates – male and female – of Krur Singh's house must leave the state within an hour to save their life.
2. His house be plundered.
3. Ram Lal is allowed to take with him whatever cash from his property he can carry on his own. The rest is to be deposited in the state exchequer.
4. Ram Lal be given a job if he accepts it.

On hearing the order, Ram Lal first of all reached Krur Singh's house and asked the Munshi who went there to execute his orders, "First give me all the money that I can carry along and bless the Maharaja. That's all. Give me quickly. Don't torment me".

Munshi replied, "What a strange man; he is mad after his own end. Wait. Why are you in haste?"

Ram Lal started shouting "Mercy Maharaja! Munshi is not giving me money". Shouting thus, he moved to Maharaja. Munshi interrupted, "Take it, take it, where you are going. *Bhai* give him first".

Ram Lal quipped, "O, God! Had I not shouted, they would have siphoned off all my money."

Everyone laughed at this. Munshi had rupees two thousand placed before him and asked, "Take it and go". Ram Lal shot back, "Wonderful! Do you remember anything? What was the order of Maharaja? This much will just fill my pocket. What is there for me to carry?"

Munshi got irritated. He took Ram Lal to the chest of the treasure and asked him, "Take. Let's see how much you can carry!" In no time, he picked up ten thousand rupees. He kept cash on his head, stashed in his pouch, waistband, pockets and some even in his mouth and took his way. They all started laughing and saying, "Not a man; he should be considered a monster".

Maharaja's orders were executed, the house was plundered; women and men of his house ran off to Chunargarh, wailing and crying.

Tej Singh came to Virendra Singh carrying all the money and said, "Today I earned a lot, but friend, it is the money of a fiend. If you add something to it from your part, it will become pure".

"Tell me from where have you brought it?"

Tej Singh narrated the whole story. Virendra Singh said, "I am giving you whatever I have here".

Tej Singh added, "But the condition is that it should not be less than that because your status is much higher than his".

"Virendra Singh asked, "But from where shall I bring the money at this time?"

Tej Singh replied curtly, "Write a promissory note".

Kumar burst out laughing and took out a diamond ring from his finger and gave it to him. Tej Singh accepted it happily and said, "May God fulfil your desire! Now we should go back to our home because now I will go to Chunargarh. I must see what the son of the devil is doing there".

□

10

The news of Krur Singh's fall spread in the whole city. Maharani Ratnagarbha (Mother of Chandrakanta) and Chandrakanta also came to know of it. The princess and Chapla were very much pleased. When Maharaja went inside the palace, Maharani asked about Krur Singh in lighter vein. Maharaja replied, "He was a liar and wicked fellow, unnecessarily defaming our daughter".

Maharani raised the issue, "Why did you forbid Virendra Singh to come here? He is the same Virendra who used to come here and stay for several days since the time when Chandrakanta was not even born. After her birth, he used to play with her and this is how they gradually developed love for each other. In those days, it was hardly felt that you and Surendra Singh were two different persons or Naugarh and Vijaygarh are two different princely states. Surendra Singh used to follow your advice. At several times, you had said that Chandrakanta should be married to Virendra. This mutual understanding and love was spoiled by this villain Krur Singh and he created malice in your heart for each other".

Maharaja admitted, "I am myself surprised what befell my mind, how my understanding turned stony. I fail to understand what went wrong that turned me against Virendra. Alas! This Krur Singh had bewitched me. Now that he is away, I realise all this".

Maharani said. "Let's see what conspiracy he hatches at Chunargarh. Certainly he will provoke Shivdutt against us and create a new trouble".

Maharaja, "Well, we will see; God is our master. That wretch didn't spare anything to sabotage us".

Having said this, Maharaja went out of the palace. He was worried that someone must be appointed Diwan or else it won't work. Having thought over it for a few days, he appointed Haradayal Singh, a Deputy Minister (Nayab Diwan) as his Minister and gave him a robe of honour. He was very honest, dutiful, kind-hearted and unbiased. He had never hurt anyone.

□

11

Krur Singh was preoccupied with the sole aim of somehow killing Tej Singh and Virendra Singh and to ruin the state of Naugarh. He along with Nazim reached Chunargarh and appeared in the court of Shivdutt. He presented his gift to the king. Maharaja knew him well. He took the gift and asked about his well-being. Krur Singh said, "Maharaja, I will share my lot with you in private".

The court was adjourned. In the evening, Maharaja called him in his private chamber and heard him. He spoke as much against Maharaja Jay Singh as he could and added this also, "Nowadays, the army is in a very bad shape. The Muslims are with us. If you want, it is not difficult to conquer Vijaygarh, the daughter of Maharaja Jay Singh, who is unparalleled in beauty, will come to you".

By saying many such things, he fully provoked Maharaja Shivdutt. Ultimately, he said, "We don't need to wage a battle right now. First we will use our *aiyars*, then we will see what happens. I have six *aiyars*, out of which four *aiyars* and Pandit Jagannath, an astrologer are being dispatched for you. You take them along with you and see what they do. Later on, when required, I will rush there with my forces".

The *aiyars* were Pundit Badrinath, Pannalal, Chunnilal, Ramnarayan, Bhagwandutta and Ghasita Singh. Maharaja entrusted Pundit Badrinath, Pannalal, Ramnarayan and Bhagwandutta to Krur Singh and gave them necessary instructions.

In the meanwhile a mace-bearer came and reported to the king, "Maharaja, several complainants are standing at the gate. They say that they are the relatives of Krur Singh and that their houses have been plundered and they are driven away by Maharaja Jay Singh on hearing Krur Singh's flight to Chunargarh. What is your order for them?"

Krur Singh was shocked to hear it. Maharaja Shivdutt called them in and inquired about them. They narrated what had happened to them. Then turning to Krur Singh and Nazim, they said, "Ahmad, too, has come to you".

Nazim asked in surprise, "Ahmad! Where is he? He did not come here!" Every one of them said, "Strange! There he came to us and went away saying I am also going to Chunar".

Nazim said, "I got it. He must be Tej Singh. There is no doubt about it. He would have informed Maharaja; it's all his brewing".

Krur Singh started crying. Maharaja Shivdutt consoled him, "What was to happen, has happened. Don't worry about it. I will take revenge of it on Jay Singh. You stay in this city. The house in front of the common bath is given to you. Stay there with your relatives. The government will provide you financial help." As per Maharaja's orders, he settled down in the same house.

After a few days, Krur Singh appeared in the court and requested Maharaja for their movement to Vijaygarh. Everything had already been arranged. Maharaja dispatched the four *aiyars*, Pandit Jagannath with Krur Singh and Nazim. *Aiyars* got equipped with their tools. They took several kinds of clothes, the bags of *aiyari* slung across their shoulders and daggers in their sides. Jyotishiji also took his book, ramal, a few items of *aiyari* as he too knew a little bit of it. Thus, the gang of devils left for Vijaygarh. They also intended to go to Naugarh. Let us see where they go and what they do.

□

12

Virendra Singh and Tej Singh in the company of their men are sitting on the bank of Chandraprabha outside the palace and watching the beauty of the landscape.

Chandraprabha from one side and Karamnasha from another are flowing to meet in front of the palace. The width of the river is very wide, and there is a huge forest of Sal trees where thousands of peacocks and apes and other animals and birds add to the beauty of the forest with their respective chirrup. Kunwar Virendra Singh is sitting sad in the absence of Chandrakanta. The chirping of peacock pierces him like arrows, the chattering of apes comes as thunderbolt; the cool breeze in the evening is felt like hot wind of summer. He is silently watching the river and sighing sadly.

In the meanwhile, a saffron-clad *sadhu* with a Ramanandi *tilak* and a cymbal in hand is seen singing a song sitting at some distance.

Fickle Krur went to Chunar, brought four
Pandit god in his company, a qualified conniver
Beware of him, an extremely dangerous Ramal player
Why are you sitting carelessly, their challenge you must dare.

Tej Singh intently turned to him. That *sadhu* was also looking at him while singing. He took out his denture and showed it to him and went away.

Virendra is lost in thought of Chandrakanta. He knows nothing of it. He doesn't know who is singing and from where this sound is coming. He is gazing fixedly at the river. Tej Singh shook him by the arm. Kumar woke up with a start. Tej Singh asked, "Did you hear anything?"

Kumar replied in a puzzle, "What? Nothing. Say, what's it?"

Tej Singh said, "Get up. Move to your palace. I will tell you there confidentially". Virendra Singh got alert and stood up. They came to the palace and sat in the chamber. They are alone there. Now Virendra Singh asked, "Tell, what did you want to say?"

Tej Singh, "You already know that Krur Singh has gone to Chunargarh to seek Maharaja Shivdutt's help. Now listen what is the outcome of his visit there. Maharaja Shivdutt has assigned four *aiyars* and an astrologer to Krur Singh. That astrologer plays *ramal* brilliantly. Nazim is already there with him. Now they have grown in power; they will certainly create trouble. So, I request you to be very alert. Now I am going to take a call on them. I am confident that someone of them will surely come here and try to trap you. You must be cautious. Don't move away with anyone except me, neither eat anything given by anybody nor even smell perfume, flower, etc. offered by anyone. It won't be a surprise if one comes to you in my disguise. Keep this also in mind. This is how you will recognise me. Look at this mole in the lower pupil of my eye that no one knows. From today onwards, whenever I come to you at any number of times in a day, I will discreetly show you this mole as my identity. If I don't do this, take it as deception."

Many such cautions he gave to Kumar who listened to them very carefully and then asked, "How did you come to know all this?" Tej Singh replied, "Somehow I got to know. This will also be revealed to you at some time. Now I take your leave. If the king or my father inquires about me, tell him whatever you think fit to say".

Before dawn, Tej Singh equipped with tools of *aiyari* embarked upon his mission.

□

13

Chapla disguised as a male went out of the city for secret policing after midnight. Seeing clear moonlight, she was suddenly tempted to go to Naugarh and see Tej Singh. With this thought in mind, she moved to Naugarh. On the other hand, Tej Singh equipped with the tools of *aiyari* was on way to Vijaygarh. Incidentally, they came across each other on the way. Chapla recognised him and coming close spoke in her natural voice, "Hello! Where are you from?"

Tej Singh identified her with her voice and replied, "Well-done, what a right time to come across, otherwise I would have taken the trouble to meet you as I have to discuss with you some very important matter. Let us sit here".

They sat on a clean rock. Chapla asked, "Tell, what's the matter?"

Tej Singh, "You know that Krur Singh has gone to Chunar. Now listen what's going on there. Shivdutt has joined with Krur Singh who has four *aiyars* and one Pundit Jagannath Jyotishi for his help. Now they have got an edge and here we are only two. So, we have to be very alert. They have come here to take away Chandrakanta but if they do away with Maharaja Jay Singh, it won't be a surprise. I was coming to you to warn you of all these things".

Chapla asked Tej Singh, "Then, what should we do?"

"Let us do one thing. I will capture the new Diwan Hardayal Singh, impersonate him and work in his place. By doing this, the army and other servants will be under my control and I will be able to do a lot. You too should continue to work in the palace cautiously and meet me once in a day as far as possible. Since I will be working as Diwan, it won't be difficult to meet. Always come to my home, I mean to Hardayal's home, in your original guise. I will be living at his home in disguise".

Besides this, Tej Singh briefed her on so many other things. After a brief spell of light banter between them, Chapla went to the palace. Tej Singh spent the rest of the night in the same jungle and early in the morning became a perfume-seller, went roaming in the streets of Vijaygarh with bottles of perfume for sale. He kept roaming for the whole day and in the evening having got an opportunity, he approached Hardayal's house. He saw Diwan Saheb lying on his coach and a few friends sitting there and gossiping with him. There was silence inside and outside his house. Tej Singh carrying the bottles of perfume reached before him, saluted him and sat down there. He said, "I am a perfume-seller from Lucknow. Having heard your name, I have brought various exquisite perfumes especially for you".

He started making cotton wads of perfume and giving him one by one. Hardayal Singh was a kind-hearted man. He started smelling them and passing on to his friends. In a short while, Hardayal Singh and all his friends swooned on the ground. Leaving them behind, as they were, Tej Singh packed Hardayal Singh in a bundle and carried him on his back to Naugarh. He had covered his face with a piece of cloth. If anyone noticed him on his way, he would take him for a washerman and not suspect him.

He left the city and marching swiftly reached the same cave where he had locked up Ahmad. He opened the gate and went in. He left Diwan Saheb there in the same unconscious state, took out his official seal-ring from his finger, and his robe and came out. He did not consider it necessary either to fetter him or to bring him back to consciousness. He immediately returned to Vijaygarh and rushed to his house in the garb of Hardayal Singh.

At Hardayal Singh's place, it was time for dinner when a maid-servant came there to call him. She saw Diwan Saheb missing and his four-five friends lying unconscious. She was puzzled and all of a sudden cried out. Hearing her shout, servants and pawns rushed in; they were taken aback to see the situation. They looked for Diwan Saheb here and there but found him nowhere. Three-fourths of the night went by, his friends, who were unconscious, regained their senses and were perplexed to see their condition. The servants asked, "How did it come about? Where is Diwan Saheb?"

They said, "A perfume-seller came to sell perfume. By smelling his wads of perfume, we fell unconscious. We don't know where Diwan Saheb is. That's why, it is said that the company of the rich is always fraught with risk to life. We swear not to be in their company again".

They indulged in such wayward talk and it was getting dawn when Hardayal Singh was seen coming to them who was, in fact, Tej Singh. Everyone surrounded him and asked, "Where have you been?" His friends asked "Where has that bloody perfume-seller gone? How did we swoon?" Diwan Saheb replied, "He was a thief. I recognised him. So, I did not inhale his perfume deeply. Had I smelt, I too would have fainted like you. When I tried to catch him, he started running. I chased him in anger. But alas, he escaped".

In the meanwhile, a maid-servant asked: "Please take some food. No one in the house has taken a morsel. They all have been weeping till this time".

"It's getting dawn. I won't take a meal. I am tired, I want to sleep".

Having said this, he went to bed and his friends, too, went back to their homes.

In the morning, at usual time, he went to court in the official robe of Diwan and secretly tied the pouch of his *aiyari* in his waist. People on both sides of the aisle greeted him with raised hands. He, too, answered back their greetings by lightly nodding his head. He reached the court. Maharaja had not reached by that time. Tej Singh was familiar with the characteristics of Hardayal Singh. In the same manner, he sat at the designated place of Diwan and started executing his duty. In a short while, Maharaja also reached there. On getting the right opportunity in the court, he confided to Maharaja: "*Maharajadhiraj*, your servant has got firm news that the king of Chunar, Shivdutt Singh has helped Krur Singh and sent his five *aiyars* along with him to demean you. Not only this, he has also said that he will himself come with his army. It is a difficult moment because there is no aiyar in the government. Nazim and Ahmad are with Krur Singh. The Muslim forces are also aligned with them. Nowadays these *aiyars* must have been roaming around in the city in disguise to cause nuisance".

Maharaja Jay Singh said, "You are right. The conduct of the Muslims seems to be also indifferent nowadays. What arrangements have you made?" While they were talking, Diwan Saheb spotted a chobdar who seemed to be snooping around in the court. Diwan Saheb looked at him attentively. *Chobdar* got alert at this. Diwan Saheb pointing to him shouted, "Arrest that chobdar". Getting the order, the guards rushed to arrest him but he ran away so swiftly that no one could get at him. Had Tej Singh wished, he would have arrested that aiyar who had been there as a *chobdar.* But he had to conduct himself like Hardayal Singh. That's why, he did not move from his place. That aiyar ran away and those who went after him drew a blank.

Diwan Saheb said, "Maharaja, see, what I had said and what I was apprehensive of came true".

Maharaja got scared of the scene. He adjourned the court and went to his parlour along with the Diwan. He asked Hardayal, "What should we do? That wicked Krur has turned a powerful king against me. We can't match Maharaja Shivdutt in any way".

"Maharaja, I again submit that we don't have any *aiyar* in our government. Nazim and Ahmad who were with us have aligned with Krur. No one can meet the challenge of aiyar without aiyar. They are very shrewd and dangerous. It's not a big thing for them to kill four to five hundred men. So, we must appoint an honest aiyar. But this can't be done all of a sudden. It is learnt that Tej Singh, the son of the Diwan of king Surendra Singh, has emerged as a great *aiyar*. I hope that if Maharaja wishes and asks for help, Tej Singh will not deny because he has reverence for Maharaja in his heart. So, what if Maharaja has prevented Virendra Singh's entry. Even now king Surendra Singh's affection for Maharaja is the same as it was?"

Having listened to him a Maharaja pondered a while and said, "You are right. Surendra Singh and his son Virendra Singh both are deserving. There is no doubt that Virendra Singh is brave and knows politics well. He is able to counter an army of ten thousand soldiers with one thousand men and even his sharpness can't be questioned. It is as you say but I have greatly offended them and for which I am ashamed of. I feel shy in seeking their help besides this who knows how much annoyed they are of me. Yes, you go and see them. If they have some grievances against me in their hearts, wash them off and bring Tej Singh. Then we can expect something".

Hardayal Singh said, "It is appropriate Maharaja. I will go myself and do this work. Maharaja may kindly write a brief letter to Maharaja Surendra Singh and give it to me with your ring-seal. Then I will manage the thing. I won't have anyone; rather I will go there alone".

Maharaja liked Hardayal's opinion. He himself wrote a letter and sealed it with his ring and handed it to him. Hardayal Singh taking leave from Maharaja, came to his house but didn't go onto the female quarter and remained outside. He asked for his meal there. After lunch, he thought of communicating everything to Chapla before leaving for Naugarh. Chapla came to him in the evening. Hardayal Singh narrated the whole thing to her in private and showed her the letter that Maharaja had given to him. Chapla was very happy to see it and said, "Hardayal Singh will come to your side. He is very gentle. Now you go and accomplish this task soon". Chapla lavishly praised his sharpness and hope sprouted in her heart that now meeting of Virendra Singh with Chandrakanta would be facilitated.

Fake Hardayal made his way to Naugarh and on his way, he changed himself into his original self.

□

14

Naugarh and Vijaygarh are mountainous states with dense forests. Chandraprabha and Karmanasha rivers flow meandering through those mountains. There are so many naturally carved beautiful caves and passes in these mountains. Among the trees, *teak, tendu, vijaysar, sanai, korya, go, khaja, peyar, jigna, asan,* etc., besides jungle tree like *parijat* found in great number in these mountains are strangely interesting. At one moment, you are in a village, you cross a mile and you will be trapped in a dense forest; no path to be located through which you have come and which way to go out. During the rainy season, its condition is amazing. You will come across ten watercourses in a span of two miles.

Among the animals found here are antelope, deer, leopard, bear, ravine deer, ape, monkey, etc. At times, lions are also seen but not in the rainy season because their living places get damaged by the overflooded rivers and watercourses and they go up the higher hills. Deer are not found at the top of the hills but are seen in numbers in valleys. Guinea fowls and peacocks are found more than other birds. The important thing is that these beautiful mountains are still very much intact and worth visiting.

The *aiyars* who came in company with Krur and Nazim made their base in this interesting forest instead of the city and decided that they would carry out their work separately and whenever needed, one would call another to assemble in the forest by blowing the whistle. Badrinath who was the cleverest and most intelligent of these *aiyars* suggested that everyone in different disguise should first enter the city, observe the men and the maid-servants of the court and the palace, even the queen, familiarise themselves with their faces, conduct, behaviour and learn their names so that when they change their faces to do *aiyari*, there should not be any mismatch in their guise as well as conduct with the originals. Everyone liked this idea. Nazim told them everyone's name and as far as possible he helped to identify them. These *aiyars* in disguise entered into the palace and observed everything. But they could not carry out any trick of ayari because of Chapla's alertness. They were also not inclined to play any trick before they were fully prepared for it.

When they got fully acquainted and well prepared, they started playing *aiyari.* Bhagwandutta donned the face of Chapla and went to Naugarh to trap Virendra Singh. He reached the gate of the room where Virendra Singh was relaxing and said to the gate-keeper, "Go and inform Kumar that Chapla from Vijaygarh has come to see him". He informed Kumar. It was late at night. Kumar Virendra Singh lost in the memory of Chandrakanta was fancying thousands of ways to meet her and was heaving intermittently when the gate-keeper reported, "*Prithvinath*! Chapla from Vijaygarh is waiting at the gate. What do you order?" Kumar winced at the name of Chapla and happily said, "Fetch her in quickly". Accordingly, Chapla appeared before him. Kumar got up to greet Chapla and made her sit by his side and started talking to her. He inquired about Chandrakanta. Chapla said, "She is fine but for the anguish of your memory, she has no problem. She keeps harping that you are so unkind; you never inquire if she is dead or alive. She got so disturbed that she sent me to you and gave me two pears peeled off and sliced with her own hands for you and adjured you to eat them". Virendra Singh was happy to listen to her talk.

Kumar, deep in Chandrakanta's love as he was, got easily deceived and could not differentiate between right and wrong. How could he dishonour Chandrakanta's vow! He instantly picked up a piece of pear and as he was going to bite, he saw Tej Singh coming there. Tej Singh noticed that Virendra Singh was sitting there and before him, Chapla was also sitting there, some pieces of pear were laid before him and one in his hand. He got flared and forewarned in loud voice, "Don't take it in your mouth".

Virendra Singh stopped and said, "Why? What's it?"

Tej Singh asserted, "I have counselled you a thousand times while leaving but you don't remember anything. Has ever Chapla visited here! Did you recognise if she was Chapla or an *aiyar*? Just you saw a whore and indulged in sweet talk".

Virendra Singh blushed at being so reprimanded by Tej Singh and looked up to duplicate Chapla. Realising that she was trapped, she took out her dagger and charged at Tej Singh. Virendra Singh also realised that she was an *aiyar* and having seen her attacking Tej Singh, he leaped forward, caught her hand with the dagger with one hand and with another held her waist and lifted her in the air. He wanted to dash her against the ground so that her backbone and ribs may be crashed. But Tej Singh forbade him, "OK, OK. Don't throw him. He will die. This is what *aiyars* do. Hand him over to me". Virendra yielded and dropped him on the ground lightly and having tied his arms behind the back handed him over to Tej Singh. He forcefully stuffed his nose with anaesthetic powder to make him unconscious, kept him aside in a bundle and resumed his talk.

Tej Singh advised him, "Let bygones be bygones. Henceforth, don't get cheated". Kumar was so embarrassed that he could not answer it and enquired about Vijaygarh. When Tej Singh related the whole development and showed him the letter that Maharaja Jay Singh had written to King Surendra Singh, Kumar's happiness knew no bounds and hugged him blissfully and said, "Do fast whatever is to do". Tej Singh consented, "Don't worry. Everything will be done". This is how they kept on talking for the whole night.

It was getting dawn when Tej Singh carried the bundle containing that aiyar on his back to the same cave where he had locked up Ahmad. He opened the door and went in. He walked to the spring and saw Ahmad lying flat alongside a watercourse and Hardayal Singh was sitting with his head bent on a rock beneath a tree. Seeing Tej Singh, he stood up and asked, "For what fault of mine have you imprisoned me?" Tej Singh answered smilingly, "Had you committed any offence, you would have been fettered as you might have seen Ahmad. You have not made any offence. Your detention for a day served my purpose a lot. That's why, I did such an insolent act. I beg your forgiveness. Now you are free to go to anywhere you like. I am your orderly. In Vijaygarh, you are the only fair, honest and upright person. That's why, I seek your help".

Hardayal Singh replied, "Tej Singh, you know well I have always been friendly to you and Kunwar Virendra Singh and I have no problem in serving you people. I was myself stunned why Tej Singh captured a friendly person! First I did not realise how I came here whether dead or alive. But when I noticed Ahmad, I learnt that it was your doing. Tell me what did you do after detaining me here and now in what way I can help you".

"I did not go inside your female quarter. This you can take for granted," said Tej Singh. Hardayal Singh replied, "I regard you more than my son. So, what even if you had gone there. Anyway, tell me the fact".

Tej Singh showed him Maharaja Jay Singh's letter and returned his robe that he was wearing and told him everything. "Now you keep your official robe and go to the court with this letter and ask the king for me to accompany you. Otherwise the *aiyars* who have come from Chunar will ruin Vijaygarh and Maharaja Shivdutt will conquer Vijaygarh. I will go there with you and arrest those *aiyars*. You must take care particularly of two things. First keep the Muslims at bay and deploy the Hindus as far as possible. Second, always take care of Kunwar Virendra Singh and regularly praise him before Maharaja so that he calls him too for help".

Hardayal Singh pledged, "I have always been a well-wisher of you people. I will do more than what you have said".

Tej Singh opened the bundle and put a loose shackle in his legs. He took away his bag of *aiyari* and dagger from his waist and brought him to his senses. He washed clean his face and then recognised him as Bhagwandutta. Being an *aiyar*, he knew all *aiyars* and they, too, knew him well.

Tej Singh left him by the side of a watercourse and came to the door along with Hardayal Singh. He stopped there and sought his permission, "You may kindly allow me to etherise you for a moment. I will bring you back to consciousness outside the cave".

Hardayal said, "I have no problem. I don't want to see the way in this cave. It's meant for you. What will I do of it?"

Tej Singh made him unconscious and, then bringing him back to senses outside the cave, said, "Now you put on your robe and accompany me". He did so.

In the city, he parted ways with Tej Singh and went alone to the court of king Surendra Singh. The king greeted him warmly and inquired about him. Having briefed him about the latest development in Vijaygarh, he gave him the letter of Maharaja Jay Singh. With due respect, he took the letter and passed it to his Wazir (Minister) Jeet Singh to read aloud. He read the letter aloud. Surendra Singh was happy to listen to the letter and said looking at Hardayal Singh, "My state belongs to Maharaja Jay Singh; he is welcome to call anyone he likes. I have no objection. Tej Singh will go with you".

He instructed Jeet Singh to extend warm hospitality to Hardayal Singh and adjourned the court.

Diwan Hardayal Singh enjoyed hospitality for three days and was very much pleased. On fourth day, Diwan Saheb sought his permission to leave. The king gave him jewels and gold in farewell and sent Tej Singh with necessary instructions.

They reached Vijaygarh with elaborate provisions and reported to Maharaja in his evening court. Haradayal Singh handed over the letter of reply to Maharaja and elaborated his visit lavishly praising Surendra Singh. Maharaja was pleased to know all this and issued him the appointment letter. He asked Hardayal Singh to make necessary arrangement for his accommodation and take upon himself the responsibility of his hospitality and comfort.

When the court was over, Diwan Saheb arranged for him a decent accommodation and deployed chosen guards and orderlies who were all Hindus. Next day, Tej Singh reported in the court of Maharaja and was given a chair beside Hardayal Singh.

□

15

It is well known that Tej Singh is familiar with all the *aiyars* of Maharaja Shivdutt. Now Tej Singh wanted to identify the four *aiyars* sent here. So, on the second day in the evening, he disguised himself as Bhagwandutta whom he had locked in the secret cave, and went out of the city into the jungle roaming here and there but didn't find anything. It was rainy season, a dark night and cloudy sky. At last, he climbed a hillock and blew the whistle. In a short while, all the three *aiyars* and Pundit Jagannath assembled there and said to Bhagwandutta who was standing there: "Why didn't you go to Naugarh? What did you do? Returned empty-handed?"

Tej Singh recognised everyone and replied, "Yes, I couldn't do anything there because of Tej Singh. If any of you accompany me, we can achieve something".

Pannalal remarked, "Okay, tomorrow I will go with you. Tonight, let's go with our plan in the palace".

Tej Singh, "All right. But I am very hungry right now. I must eat something so that I can focus on the work. If you have anything, give it to me".

Jagannath, "Whatever we have is anesthetic. If you buy something from the market, we will eat together and break up".

Bhagwandutta said, "Okay. Come someone along with me". Pannalal accompanied him. They left for the city. Pannalal advised him on the way, "We should change our face because Tej Singh came to this city yesterday and knows all of us. He may come across".

Bhagwandutta thought that if he changes his face, he may be caught while applying colour. "It's needless. Who comes at night?"

Bhagwandutta's refusal put him under suspicion and Pannalal stared at his face but in the darkness of night, he could not recognise and at last blew his whistle. They were approaching the city and *aiyars* were far away. So, they could not listen to his whistle. Tej Singh, realising that he is doubted and there is no need to delay, grabbed his neck under his arm. Pannalal took out his dagger and a scuffle broke out between the two. Finally, Tej Singh thrashed him on the ground, tied his arms behind the back, etherised him and packed him in a bundle and then carried it on his back to the city.

He reached his quarter in his original face, locked up Pannalal in a room. Having passed necessary instructions to the guards, he made his bed at the gate of that room and slept. In the morning, he produced him in the court.

Ramnarayan, Badrinath and Jyotishiji were waiting there for them to come and have dinner. But the situation was different here. They apprehended that the two might have been arrested. But they had not thought that Bhagwandutta was a duplicate.

That night they could not do anything. But, in the morning, they set out in disguise for search operation. First they went to the court of Maharaja Jay Singh and saw Tej Singh going to court and ten to fifteen soldiers following behind him with Pannalal as a captive. The *aiyars* also followed them to the court.

Tej Singh along with Pannalal and others reached the court that was in session. He saluted Maharaja and took his seat. The captive was produced before him. Maharaja asked, "Tej Singh, who is he?"

He answered, "Maharaja, he is one of the five *aiyars* who have sneaked into the state from Chunargarh. He is arrested and brought before you for the sentence that befits him".

Maharaja attentively looked at him with a sense of happiness and asked, "What's your name?"

He shot back, "Makkar Khan alias Aiyar Khan".

Maharaja laughed at his impudence and reply. He ordered, "It's enough. No need to ask further. Imprison him and place under heavy security". On getting the order, guards handcuffed him and fettered his legs and took him to jail. Being pleased, Maharaja rewarded Tej Singh with a hundred gold coins. Tej Singh saluted him and kept the coins in his bag.

Ramnarayan, Badrinath and Jyotishiji were watching all this in disguise. When Pannalal was sentenced to be imprisoned, they also came out and made a clever plan. Badrinath went aside and changed himself as Tej Singh.

Ramnarayan and Jyotishi ji put on the guise of guards and went to the guards who were taking Pannalal to jail. They called out: "Stop! Maharaja has issued another order for this wretched *aiyar* because I requested him that his friends will anyhow release him from jail. If I keep him in my custody, it would be better as I have arrested him and he won't escape from my custody. So, you hand him over to me".

The guards knew that he was arrested by Tej Singh. So, they did not refuse him and left him to his custody. Duplicate Tej Singh took him to the forest. The guards returned to the court to report. The court was in session as usual and Tej Singh was also there. The guards were taken aback and stopped reporting. Tej Singh asked, "What's the matter? Have you put that aiyar behind the bar?" The fear-stricken guards pleaded, "You yourself took him away from us." Tej Singh got startled and said, "What! I have been here since then".

The guards were shocked; they could not answer and stood immobile like a statue. Maharaja turned to Tej Singh and asked, "What happened?"

Tej Singh replied, "Maharaja, an *aiyar* played his trick. He took on my face and took Pannalal away".

Maharaja was greatly annoyed with the guards. But Tej Singh pleaded "Maharaja, they are not at fault. *Aiyars* are like this; they deceive even the smart ones, what to say of these guards".

On his request, Tej Singh pardoned them but he felt disappointed for quite some time on their having escaped.

Badrinath and others reached the jungle with Pannalal, sat beneath a tree and asked about the whole story of his being captured. Now they learnt that Bhagwandutta was also arrested by Tej Singh and was in his custody. They all asked Pundit Jagannath, "Find out through your ramal where Bhagwandutta is".

Jyotishi ji played his *ramal*, counted something and said, "Undoubtedly, Bhagwandutta is also captured by Tej Singh and is kept in a cave four miles north from here".

They made for the cave. Jyotishi ji with the help of *ramal* arrived at the cave and went in and when the light flashed, he saw the door but didn't know how to open it. Jyotishi ji once again played his *ramal* and, after calculating, said, "This door is linked to a *tilism* and ramal can't work in *tilism*. We have to find out some other way to open it. They came out of the cave and looked for an opportunity to play *aiyari*.

□

16

One day Tej Singh went out of Vijaygarh for spying. Before evening, he went far away roaming about. He spotted Virendra Singh sitting beneath a tree with his horse tied to a tree. Before him, an antelope was lying dead and fire was burning. When he reached near, he saw some pieces of meat on leaves.

He noticed Tej Singh coming and called out, "Come brother, Tej Singh, you are so much engaged in Vijaygarh that you did not inquire about me. Have you completely forgotten me?"

Tej Singh grinned, "In Vijaygarh, I am doing your work, not my father's!"

"Of course, your father's."

Saying this, Kumar burst out laughing. Tej Singh didn't answer it and sat down beside him laughing. Kumar asked, "Did you see Chandrakanta?"

Tej Singh replied, "Sorry, I was so busy with my work that I could not see her. Meanwhile, I captured an *aiyar*. Maharaja ordered to put him behind bars but before he could be taken to jail, his friend got him released on the way deceiving the guards by donning my face. Since then, no one has been arrested".

"They are proven devils," said Kumar.

"Everything else is as usual. Badrinath has also come with them from Chunargarh. He is very shrewd. If I am afraid of one person, it is him. Anyway, it will be seen.

No problem. Tell me what you are doing here! No one in company," said Tej Singh.

"Today, in the morning, I, taking along some men, left for hunting. Till noon, we kept wandering about to no avail. At last, I saw this antelope passing before me. I chased for long and, in this course, all my men were left far behind. It is now that I could shoot it with an arrow and it fell down dead. I was very hungry. So, I thought of roasting it and eating. While sitting, I saw you coming from this end. Now you roast it yourself. I had some spices that I have rubbed to these meat pieces after properly washing them. Now you prepare the stuff. We will eat together. But hurry up. I have not taken anything for the whole day.

Tej Singh quickly prepared the meat and by the side of a spring where clean water was flowing, sat with Kumar to eat. Virendra Singh wiped off the spices before eating the meat. Tej Singh asked, "Why are you wiping the spices?"

"Light spice gives me better taste". Having taken two to three pieces, Virendra took sufficient water from the spring on his palm and said, "It's enough. I am satiated. It's difficult to eat much after a whole day fast".

Tej Singh replied, "Whether you eat or not, I won't spare it, it's very tasty. Having taken it as much as he could, he washed off his hand and mouth and said, "Let's go. I will accompany you to Naugarh and then turn to Vijaygarh". "Come," Virendra Singh said and climbed his horse. Tej Singh followed him on foot.

After walking some distance, Tej Singh said, "I don't know why my head is reeling".

Kumar shot back, "You have overeaten; it's causing heat". As he crossed a little distance, he felt dizzy and fell in a faint on the ground. Virendra Singh jumped from the horse-back, tied his hands behind the back and bundled him tightly before carrying him on his back to Vijaygarh, holding the bridle of the horse. Having gone a little far, he blew his whistle that echoed far and wide in the jungle. In no time, Krur Singh, Pannalal, Ramnarayan and Jyotishi ji assembled there.

Pannalal exclaimed with joy, "Well done Badrinathji! You have done a great job. The greatest catch! What's left? It's over". Krur Singh leaped in happiness. Badrinath, who was till now disguised as Virendra Singh, put down the bundle and said to Ramnarayan, "Take this horse to Naugarh and leave it near the stable from where it was stolen. They will fasten the horse themselves". Accordingly, Ramnarayan rode the horse to Naugarh. Badrinath again put the bundle on his back and made his way to Chunargarh giving necessary instructions to the *aiyars.*

It was the routine of Tej Singh to go to the court of Maharaja Jay Singh everyday and to take his seat after saluting him. For a day or two, Maharaja saw Tej Singh's chair vacant and then asked Hardayal Singh, "Nowadays Tej Singh is not seen here. Have you seen him?" Diwan Saheb submitted, "No, I too haven't seen him. I will inquire about it and report". When the court was adjourned for the day, Diwan Saheb went to Tej Singh's quarter. Not finding him there, he questioned his servants. They said, "He has not been here for several days. We searched for him but could not trace him".

Hardayal Singh was stunned to hear it. He went to his palace and thought what to do. If Tej Singh was not traced, it would be very disgraceful. By any means, he must be traced. Ultimately, he sent his men in different directions to look for him. He also sent a letter to the Diwan of Naugarh, Jeet Singh with an instruction to the bearer to return with its reply to the court next day. The bearer reached Naugarh in the evening and went straight to Diwan Jeet Singh's home. He was informed about his visit. Diwan Saheb called him in. The bearer saluted him and passed him the letter. He read the letter attentively. He believed it for sure that Tej Singh had come into the hands of *aiyars*. He sent the bearer back with the reply 'He is not here'. He sent many of his spies here and there to find him out. Next day, Diwan Jeet Singh reported to the king Surendra Singh in the court, "Maharaja, yesterday a man from Vijaygarh came to me with a letter of Diwan Hardayal Singh. He has sought information if Tej Singh is here or not because for several days, he has not been in Vijaygarh. I have written in reply that he is not here".

The king was astonished to learn it and asked the Diwan, "Tej Singh is neither here nor there; where has he gone? Is it that he has got into the hands of *aiyars* because some of the *aiyars* of Maharaja Shivdutt have reached Vijaygarh and Tej Singh had gone alone to counter them?"

Diwan Saheb replied, "As far as I understand, he has certainly been trapped by the *aiyars.* Anyway, things will be clear in two to four days".

Kunwar Virendra Singh was also sitting there in the court to the right side of the king. He begged, "If you permit me, I will go in search of Tej Singh". Diwan Jeet Singh turned to him and, with a smile, replied, "No one can question your courage and, valour but we should think that when Tej Singh, who is by profession an aiyar, got into the trap of *aiyars,* will you take this risk? What's the need? You know it well if an aiyar arrests another, he does not kill him but just keeps him in custody. If Tej Singh has come into their hands, he will be in jail. He will somehow come out of it because he is an expert in his art. One who practises *aiyari,* however clever he may be, will get trapped sometime or the other. Then why worry about it? Have patience for five to ten days. See what happens. If he does not come back, you can do whatever you want to".

Virendra Singh countered him, "Yes, you are right but it is necessary to find him. It is not proper to sit idle in this assumption that he is clever and he will come out of it on his own".

Jeet Singh said, "True because of your love for him, you are so worried. OK, it will be seen".

King Surendra Singh intervened, "At least send someone to trace him".

Diwan Saheb answered, "Many spies have been dispatched to trace him". The king and Kunwar Virendra Singh turned silent but they remained grief-stricken. Next day in Vijaygarh court, Maharaja Jay Singh again asked Haradayal Singh, "Did you get any information about Tej Singh?"

Diwan Saheb replied, "There is no information yet. Maybe in Naugarh. I have sent a man there, he must be coming. Then we will know".

They were talking while the man reached there with the reply.

Hardayal Singh read the letter and reported with regret, "Tej Singh is neither in Naugarh". This is the reply of his father.

Maharaja asked "Have you taken any action to trace him or not?"

"Yes, many of the spies have been dispatched".

Maharaja was very sorry about Tej Singh. He went to his palace after adjourning the court. In course of a chat with Maharani, he referred to her the case of Tej Singh and said, "This is called turn of fate. Krur Singh has already been creating nuisance here. Tej Singh came here for help but now he has gone traceless for several days. It will embarrass me before Surendra Singh. When I think of Tej Singh's conduct, talk, skill and his cleverness, I get overwhelmed. He is a very worthy chap. I have never seen his face sullen".

Maharani, too, expressed her sorrow over Tej Singh's lot. Incidentally, Chapla was standing there. Hearing this account, she rushed to Chandrakanta. She wanted to narrate the condition of Tej Singh but she got overwhelmed and failed to relate. Taking note of her condition, Chandrakanta asked, "What's the matter? You are looking so pale, say something". As she opened her mouth to speak, her throat got choked and tears dropped from her eyes and she could not answer. Chandrakanta was even more perplexed. She repeated, "Why are you weeping? Speak out".

Ultimately, Chapla controlled herself and could barely utter, "I heard Maharaja speaking that Tej Singh was captured by the *aiyars* of Maharaja Shivdutt. Now it would be difficult for Virendra Singh to visit her as Tej

Singh was his backbone". While saying this, she burst into tears. Chandrakanta realised that Chapla loves Tej Singh. She started thinking that it is good for her too. But she felt very sorry for Tej Singh and Chapla. Then she told Chapla, "Are they making all-out efforts to release him? Will he be released by your weeping? If you can't do anything, I will do something myself. Champa was sitting there listening to their regretful talk. She proposed, "If I am allowed, I will go in search of Tej Singh". Chapla intervened, "You are not competent for it yet".

Champa retorted, "Why? What am I lacking in? Can't I do *aiyari*?"

Chapla replied, "Yes you can do but you can't match those who have arrested a veteran aiyar like Tej Singh. Of course, if princess orders me, I will go". Chandrakanta said, "Does it require my order? If your effort could release him, you would be able to refer to it for the whole life. Don't delay, now go". Chapla cautioned Champa, "See, I am going. But several *aiyars* have infiltrated. No new nuisance should happen in my absence. Well then, whatever happens will be seen, but you must be on full alert in the security of the princess. If you commit a mistake or any trouble comes upon the princess, I will not see your face for the whole life". Champa assured, "You take it for granted that I will always be vigilant".

Chapla, having equipped with the tools of *aiyari* and some jewels and clothes of southern style, left in search of Tej Singh.

□

17

Chapla was not a simple girl. Besides beauty and elegance, she had strength too. It was an easy job for her to take on two to four men and overpower them. She was adept in weapon craft and martial arts. She was endowed with several qualities besides the art of *aiyari*. She was skilled in singing, playing musical instruments and dancing and was fond of making fireworks. What to say more, there was no art that she did not know. She was creamy white with a well-built body. Her hands and feet looked so tender as if one could kill her with the strike of a flower. Whenever she needed to go out, she used to either distort her beauty or disguise herself deliberately.

Now it's evening; rather the night has advanced a bit. The full moon is out spreading its beam. Chapla armed with the *aiyari* bag in her side, lasso and a dagger tied to her waist, is marching through the forest in her original guise. She is so lost in the memory of Tej Singh that she is hardly conscious of her body. She is unconscious of why and where she is going, what lies before her – stone or a pit, a river or canal – just moving on bare feet. Tears are rolling down her cheeks; all her clothes in the front are drenched. She stumbles at every little distance and her toes are bleeding. But she is unaware of it. There was a canal ahead but she took no note of it and fell in it with a thud and got her head injured and bleeding, her clothes got drenched in it. Then she came to realise that she was on a mission to trace and free Tej Singh. Words of repentance gushed forth, "Oh dear, I forgot you, forgot my duty to get you released. It's a punishment for this". Now Chapla got alert and realised where she was. After pondering a lots, she realised that she had lost her way and was in a terrible jungle. For a moment, she got scared but then controlled herself. She turned back from that dangerous canal and thought that there was no doubt in it that Tej Singh was captured by the *aiyars* of Maharaja Shivdutt and they must have certainly taken him to Chunargarh. First I should search for him there. If he is not found there, then I will look for him elsewhere".

Thinking thus, she looked for the route to Chunargarh. After wandering till midnight, she found the route and proceeded straight to Chunargarh through the mountainous track. When it was about dawn, she turned herself into a male security guard. Unmindful of bath or meals, she kept on crossing the distance. Ultimately, by the evening, she reached Chunar, hungry and thirsty. She had pledged to herself that she should neither eat nor drink until she had discovered Tej Singh. She did not take rest anywhere. She kept on wandering and looking for him here and there. All of a sudden, an idea flashed in her mind. She turned herself into Pannalal and went to the residence of Ghasita Singh.

It is already known that four out of six *aiyars* had come to Vijaygarh and Ghasita Singh and Chunnilal were left at Chunar. Ghasita Singh stood up to see Pannalal and, after greeting, asked, "Pannalal, say who have you brought this time?"

Pannalal said, "This time I haven't got anyone. I have come just to ask if Nazim is here or not. He is traceless".

"He hasn't come here".

"Then who has captured him? Now there is no *aiyar* there".

"I can't say if there is any other *aiyar* there or not. Only Tej Singh was popular who was arrested. At this time, he must be weeping in the lock-up of the palace".

"Anyway, no problem. It will be discovered. Now I must go. I can't stay". Saying this, fake Pannalal left. Chapla felt relieved thinking that Tej Singh was discovered and was very much there. She would free him by any means. She came out into an open field, sat on the bank of the Ganges and having taken some dry fruits and Ganga water, felt relaxed. She changed herself into a female singer. Chapla needed no makeup to look beautiful. She was herself so beautiful that she could outweigh thousands of beauties. But she had to change her face so that no one could recognise her. When she was equipped with everything, she went to the back of the palace with a flute in her hand and sat at a clean place and started singing *Birha* at a high pitch and then played the same song on the flute.

It was late midnight. Shivdutt was engaged in pleasant talk with the queen. All of a sudden, they were drawn to the melody of a song. They stopped short and paid attention to the song. After a while, sneaked in the music of a flute, the number of which was clearly recognisable. Maharaja felt uneasy, immediately he called a maid-servant and ordered her, "Tell someone to bring immediately that singer whose voice is pouring in from down the palace".

The guards rushed out and saw a tender body singing. Seeing her face, they got non-plussed. After some time, they said, "Maharaja has called you to the downside of the palace. He is desperate to listen to your song". Chapla did not deny, she followed them to the palace and started singing. Her song made him impatient. He could not restrain himself and ordered, "Take her to the public auditorium and arrange for light. I am coming there". Maharani intervened, "By voice, it seems to be a woman, what's the problem if she is called in the palace." Maharaja said, "First let's see her and then what's required will be done. If she is worth visiting here, she will be placed at your service, too".

As per order, everything was arranged. Maharaja took his place in the public auditorium. Chapla bowed her head in salutation. Maharaja saw a woman, exquisitely beautiful, white colour, wearing dark gray sari, embroidered light green blouse in southern style, one end tucked behind, open locks arranged with the help of back pins, a small golden flower tucked in, a big vermillion mark on the forehead, beautiful filigree ear-rings in the ears, nose-ring of Saraja, a *tikka* of gold and a necklace with a string of bells in the neck, unknotted bracelets with a set of black bangles, tasseled waistband in the waist and anklet in the legs standing before him with a charming elegance. Ornaments are of little worth. What is devastating is her well-built physique. When he observed attentively, he found a small mole by the side of her chin that was further enhancing the glamour of her face. Maharaja got spellbound and forgot his loving queen. He spoke out, "Wonderful! Beyond description!" He was transfixed. He said, "Come, sit here." Chapla swaying her waist walked to him, saluted and sat near him flirtatiously. Maharaja came under the spell of her beauty.

He couldn't say much, kept gazing at her face and then asked, "Where are you from? Who are you? What do you do? For a woman like you, to wander alone in the dead of night puts me in surprise". She replied, "I am from Gwalior, a Patlapa Katthak dancer. My name is Rambha. My father was a great singer. I fell in love with a man who got annoyed over a trifle and went away. I am wandering in search of him. What should I do? I often go to the royal courts. I may find him there as he is also a versatile singer. So, it's not unlikely that he might be in some court. I was singing to relieve my tension when your highness sent for me and I am here before you". Maharaja remarked, "Your voice is very sweet. Sing something for me". Chapla said, "Maharaja, you did a great favour to this worthless being by making me sit near you and honoured this servant. If you want to listen to my songs, call in the accompanists of your court. If they accompany me, my singing will be worthwhile. However, I am ready to sing in any way". Maharaja was very much pleased to hear it and ordered, "Accompanists be summoned". Servants rushed to the accompanists and served the summon. They were perplexed to think. What had occurred to Maharaja's mind at the third quarter of night! But helplessly they had to come. When they saw a slice of moon before them, they were pleased. They came faded, but now they bloomed. Quickly they got ready with their musical instruments, Chapla started singing. Lo and behold! Singing with the musical accompaniment and the audience, the spell of the last night stupefied Maharaja, the accompanists were also amazed. They had to use all their expertise. It was an untimely concert, even then a good number of people assembled there. In just two *Darbari* (courtly) songs, it was dawn. After singing a *Bhairawi*, Chapla requested, "Maharaja, it is morning now. I am tired of yesterday's journey as I travelled a long distance. If you permit me, I may go now". Maharaja winced at her words. He looked around, it was really morning. He took out a chain of pearls from his neck and gave her in reward and said, "My heart is not yet fully filled with your songs. Stay here for a few days before you go". Rambha replied, "If Maharaja is so pleased with this servant, I have no objection to staying on".

Maharaja commanded, "Make proper arrangement for the stay of Rambha and arrange for a public show tonight. Everything was arranged accordingly. A beautiful house with attendants was provided to Rambha.

There was a public assembly tonight. The gentry were assembled. Rambha too appeared and sat down after saluting. There was none in the assembly whose eyes were not turned to Rambha. Everyone was heaving. They were talking among themselves only this, "O goodness! What an innocent face! Have you ever seen such a beauty?"

Rambha started singing. Everyone was spell-bound like a statue. Having sung a song, Rambha urged, "Maharaja, once I sang a song in the assembly of king Surendra Singh of Naugarh, it was superb. Such rapture at the song I could not create again. The reason was that his Minister's son Tej Singh accompanied me with his flute. Oh! I will never forget that concert. Two to four days back, I again went to Naugarh. I learnt that he was missing. Then I too did not stay there. Immediately I turned back". Saying this, Rambha got stuck. Maharaja had already lost his heart to her. He said, "Nowadays he is in my jail. But the problem is I can't release him and he will never play flute in captivity". Rambha replied, "If he is told about me, he will certainly accept it. Moreover, if he is called in a particular way, he will undoubtedly accompany me, otherwise he won't listen even to me, he is very stubborn." Maharaja asked, "What's that method?" Rambha elaborated, "First a Brahmin should be sent to call him and he should not be more than twenty. Second when he brings him, no one should be with him. If there is a threat to his escape, his legs should be fettered. It doesn't matter and, third, the flute should be of high quality".

Maharaja remarked, "It's not a problem". He looked around and found a Brahmin boy, Chetram of this age. He ordered him to bring Tej Singh with him and commanded Mirmunshi, "You go and tell the guards not to obstruct in fetching Tej Singh here. Yes, he must be kept in fetters".

Having got the order, Chetram got up to fetch Tej Singh and Mirmunshi informed the guards of Maharaja's order. They dispatched Tej Singh alone. Tej Singh immediately sensed that a friend of his must have reached there. That's why, he has so cleverly called me here on such conditions. Happily he went along with Chetram. When he came to the assembly, he saw the strange spectacle. He saw a very beautiful woman sitting and everyone gazing at her. When Tej Singh reached in the centre of the assembly, Rambha called out, "Come, Come Tej Singh. Rambha has been waiting for you for long! How can I forget the flute that you played in Naugarh !"

Saying this, Rambha turned to him and shut her left eye. Tej Singh knew that she was Chapla. He said, "Rambha, you have come! Even if death stares in my eyes, I will die only after playing flute on your song because how can I find a singer like you". Maharaja was surprised to listen to their talk. But he was obsessively waiting for Tej Singh to play his flute and Rambha to start singing. A high-quality flute was placed before Tej Singh and he started playing. Rambha too began singing. Now the mood it created was beyond praise. Maharaja was astounded. Others' condition was not different.

Having accompanied to a song, Tej Singh put down the flute. Maharaja asked, "Why, play more". Tej Singh replied, "Enough, I play only one music in a day, not more than that. If you are so eager, you can listen tomorrow". Rambha added, "Yes Maharaja, this is the problem with him. King Surendra Singh, whose servant he was, repeatedly asked him but he did not comply with it and stopped after playing a single music. What's the problem, you may listen tomorrow".

Maharaja thought what a strange person he is! What does he intend to get out of it. Alas! He is not in my court. Rambha, too, having said so many placating words, stopped singing. A craze remained in everyone's heart. With regret, Maharaja suspended the assembly and Tej Singh was sent back to jail in company with the same Brahmin, Chetram.

Maharaja got addicted to the song of Rambha on the flute of Tej Singh. Again the concert was organiseds the next day and the same Brahmin Chetram was sent to bring Tej Singh to the assembly. On that day, too, Tej Singh put down the flute after playing for a song. Maharaja was left unsatisfied and he ordered for a full assembly the next day. Next day again, the assembly was held, everyone took his seat before time. But Rambha finding an opportunity changed herself into Chetram and reached the jail an hour before the schedule. The guards were aware that Chetram comes alone to take Tej Singh; this was the order of Maharaja. They unlocked the cell, took out Tej Singh, fettered him and handed over to Chetram. Chetram (Chapla) made his way with him, unfettered him having crossed some distance. Now free, they took their way to the forest.

Chapla cast aside her assumed guise and came into normal form. Tej Singh lavishly praised her. Chapla responded with a blush, "Don't embarrass me because I don't consider myself as clever as you are hailing me. Above all, there was no personal motive in rescuing you. I did this for Chandrakanta's sake".

Tej Singh replied, "Alright, why should you be concerned about me? Needy I am that I became your accompanist! What my ancestors had not done, I had to do". Chapla burst into laughter and said, "Forgive me! Don't say so". Tej Singh said, "Well, no forgiving. I won't leave you without charging my fee".

Chapla: "What do I have to give!"

Tej Singh: "Whatever you have is enough for me". Chapla, said, changing the topic "Well then, what do you say? Should we go empty-handed or show some magic of our hands to Maharaja Shivdutt?"

Tej Singh, "I intend so. But as you say". Chapla; "We must do something".

Having deliberated for some time, they chalked out a plan and went to another dense jungle to execute it.

□

18

Now let us turn to the soiree of Maharaja Shivdutt. Maharaja Shivdutt had already taken his seat. When it was getting late for Rambha to come, he sent a mace-bearer to call her and asked Chetram, a Brahmin to bring Tej Singh. After a while, the mace-bearer came back and reported that Rambha was not at her place and had gone somewhere. Maharaja was amazed as he had developed fascination for her. He felt a sense of regret for Rambha in his heart and ordered to launch a manhunt for her. In the meanwhile, Chetram returned and informed that Tej Singh had escaped from the jail. Maharaja was shocked to learn it. The whole assembly was stunned to know that a beautiful singing girl came and befooled all of them. Ghasita Singh and Chunnilal *aiyars* opined, "Maharaja, certainly he was an aiyar who came and got Tej Singh released in this way."

Maharaja said, "It's OK. But whatever she did, she deserves a reward" *Aiyars* too listened to her songs. They were present in the soiree. Had they lost their wits that they did not recognise her? Shame on your being called aiyar". Having said this, Maharaja in grief and anger left the assembly and went to his palace. The audience also left for their homes. This news spread throughout the city like fire in the jungle. Everywhere it was the talk of the day.

Next day when Maharaja in fury came to the court, chobdar reported, "Maharaja, the singer that had come here was really a woman. She got Tej Singh released in the guise of Chetram. I have just seen them in that *saal* forest".

Maharaja was astonished to hear it and ordered that a large contingent of force be sent to arrest them. But chobdar urged, "Maharaja, they can't be arrested in this way; they will run away. Of course, if Ghasita Singh and Chunnilal come along with me, I will show them from a distance. They should arrest them by their *aiyari*". Maharaja liked the idea and commanded them to accompany the mace-bearer. He took them to the place where he had spotted Tej Singh but no one was there. Ghasita asked the chobdar, "Where to look for them, now?" He retorted, "Is it necessary that they should be sitting beneath this tree since then? Look around, they may be somewhere". Ghasita replied, "Ok. Then go ahead".

They started looking around here and there. In the meanwhile, they saw a milkmaid carrying milk in a small wicker basket on her head. Chobdar asked her, "Have you seen a man and a woman around?" She said, "Yes, yes my cowshed is there in that jungle where I have so many cows and buffalos. I have just sold milk of two paisa to them and the rest milk I am carrying to the city for sale". On hearing this, chobdar offered her four paisa as reward but she refused and said, "I don't accept money for free. Of course, if you buy milk for four paisa, I will be spared of going to the city and will feel obliged to you". The mace-bearer added, "No problem. You give us milk". The milkmaid put down her basket and gave him milk. The mace-bearer asked the two *aiyars*, "Come, you too should take it". They replied, "We don't want".

He remarked, "As you wish". The mace-bearer drank milk and then said to the two *aiyars*, "Wah! How tasty is the milk? You have been taking milk in the city everyday, try this today and feel the difference". On his insistence, they also took milk and paid her four paisa.

Now they resumed their search for Tej Singh. After a while, chobdar said, "I don't know why my head is reeling". Ghasita Singh added, "So is mine". Chunnilal fell down before speaking out a word. After this, the mace-bearer and

Ghasita Singh too fell flat on the ground. The milkmaid had not gone very far. Seeing them falling, she ran to them. She brought the mace-bearer back to his senses with the smell of *lakhlakha*. That mace-bearer was Tej Singh. He put on his original form after getting back consciousness. After tying their arms behind their back, they put them in two separate bundles and Chapla carried one and Tej Singh the other on their back to Naugarh.

□

19

When Chapla went to Chunar to rescue Tej Singh, Champa thought there were so many *aiyars* of Chunar there and she was alone. She must do something lest they should wreak havoc. She must employ a mechanism in which there should be no fear of *aiyar* and they may comfortably enjoy sleep. Keeping this in mind, she prepared a solution. When everyone including Chandrakanta went to bed Champa mixed that solution into water and smeared it on the floor two yards around the gate and slept under Chandrakanta's bed with peace of mind. The feature of this solution is that when it is applied on the floor and the floor gets dry, it bursts like crackers if one steps on this floor. But one cannot detect it by seeing that the floor is coated with anything. For the whole night, Champa slept peacefully. No one came into that room. In the morning, she washed off that solution with water. Next day she applied a different trick. She made a clay head looking just like Chandrakanta, put it on her bed resting on the pillow where she used to sleep. She put some clothes in place of her body and covered it with a light shawl, but the face was kept uncovered, the room was lighted and the floor coated with the same solution. She requested Chandrakanta to sleep in a different room. Chandrakanta got the point and went to bed in a different room. The floor around the gate of the room where Chandrakanta was sleeping was also coated with the same solution. There was a small room beside the room in which the clay head was kept on the bed. Champa blew out the lamp and slept there.

After midnight, there came the sound of cracker from the room where the clay head was kept. Hearing it, Champa instantly got up and rushed out. She bolted the gate from behind and started shouting. So many maid-servants gathered there and one of them informed Maharaja that thieves had broken into Chandrakanta's bedroom. Maharaja himself rushed to the spot and called five to ten soldiers who were guarding the palace. When they all assembled there, the door was opened. They saw the two *aiyars* Ramnarayan and Pannalal inside. The soldiers went in to capture them but they took out their daggers and charged on the soldiers. Four to five soldiers got injured but ultimately they were overpowered. Maharaja ordered to keep them in jail and had the details from Champa. She told him of her whole enterprise. He was overjoyed to hear it and rewarded her. He asked, "Where is Chapla?" She replied, "She is ill." Maharaja didn't ask any further and retreated to his retiring room. In the morning, the *aiyars* were produced in the court. He asked, "What's your name?" Pannalal tersely replied, "Sartod Singh." Maharaja felt angry at his insolence and said, "They are wicked. Not the least scared. Anyway, take them back to jail and keep strict vigil on them." Accordingly they were sent to jail.

Maharaja asked Hardayal, "Any information about Tej Singh?" Hardayal Singh answered, "Not till date. If these *aiyars* are beaten black and blue, they may disclose something".

Maharaja said, "It's O.K. But Tej Singh will feel annoyed at their beating. It's not the practice. Anyway, wait for Tej Singh for a few more days and then whatever is required will be done. But take care of one thing. Our forces must be ready as it won't be a surprise if Shivdutt attacks us".

Hardayal Singh, "I am conscious of it. Only one thing I want to ask but that I will do in privacy".

When the court was adjourned, Maharaja called Hardayal Singh in his private chamber and asked, "What's the matter?"

He replied, "Maharaja, Tej Singh has repeatedly told me and even Kunwar Virendra Singh and his father have asserted that all Muslims here are aligned with Krur Singh. As far as possible, they should be dropped from the royal service. I also observe that it is true. I seek your order in this regard".

Maharaja, "All right, I was about to tell you the same thing myself. Anyway, now I tell you to gradually drop out the Muslims from sensitive positions".

Hardayal Singh, "Very good. It will be executed". Having said this, he took leave of Maharaja and went home.

□

20

Maharaja Shivdutt Singh sent Ghasita Singh and Chunnilal to capture Tej Singh and adjourned the court. He went to his palace but his heart was so intricately locked in the locks of Rambha that he could not get out of it. He didn't even talk to his queen in a cheerful mood. She asked, "Why do you look so dull?" He replied, "Nothing, just the effect of overnight waking". She further put a question. "You have promised that you will bring that female singer inside the palace to sing for me. What happened to it?"

"She befooled us all and fled away. Whom should I ask to sing for you?" Maharani Kalavati was greatly surprised. She asked, "What's the matter? Tell me clearly".

"I am not myself right now. I can't speak much". Saying this, Maharaja moved to his special room and lay on bed recalling the memories of Rambha and thinking who Rambha was. "There is no doubt about it that she was a woman. Why did she rescue Tej Singh? Was she in love with that person as she referred to. Alas! You wounded me, Rambha. Did you come for this sake! What to do; I don't have your whereabouts. Where to look for you?"

He could not sleep for the whole night in desperation and thinking of Rambha. In the morning, he came to the court and inquired about Ghaseeta Singh, Chunnilal and Tej Singh. He was informed that they had not come back yet. Maharaja felt more unhappy to hear it. He was listening to the appeals of all but remained engrossed in memory of Rambha. In the meantime, he saw Badrinath, Nazim, Jyotishi ji and Krur Singh. They saluted him and sat down. Their languid faces deepened his distress. But he did not ask anything in the court. Having dismissed the court, he went into his private chamber and called them in. They went in and after paying due respect sat down. Maharaja asked, "Tell me, what did you do in Vijaygarh?"

Pundit Badrinath replied, "The only development is that Bhagwandutta was arrested by Tej Singh and Pannalal and Ramnarayan were very cleverly entrapped by a woman called Champa. We escaped. Among them, only Tej Singh was arrested and sent to you. Nothing else was done".

Maharaja added, "Tej Singh, too, was rescued by a woman. She deserves punishment, but alas, I don't know who she was. She did take away Tej Singh and it seems she preyed on Chunnilal and Ghaseeta Singh while fleeing away. They went in search of them but haven't yet returned. Helping Krur has incurred only loss to me. Now you should find out who was that woman who made me impatient by singing to me. She cheated all of us and fled away with Tej Singh. Her beautiful face is still flashing before my eyes. Nazim immediately responded, "*Hujur,* I know, she must be Chandrakanta's friend, Chapla. This is no one else's job". Maharaja asked, "Is Chapla more beautiful than Chandrakanta?"

Nazim replied, "Maharaja, Chapla is no match to Chandrakanta. But, next to her, Chapla is the most beautiful woman in the world and she is in love with Tej Singh". Having learned this, Maharaja was stunned for a while and then said, "Whatever may come, as long as I do not get hold of Chandrakanta and Chapla, I will have no respite. It'd be better I should write a letter to Maharaja Jay Singh for them".

Krur Singh said, "Maharaja Jay Singh will not honour the letter".

Maharaja asserted, "What's harm in it? If he does not honour the letter, I will conquer Vijaygarh". Having said this, he sent for his chief clerk. When the clerk came, he ordered, "Write a letter to Jay Singh on my behalf, asking him to marry Chandrakanta to me and give Chapla in dowry". The clerk wrote the letter accordingly on which Maharaja put his seal and gave it to Pundit Badrinath and said, "You alone will carry this letter to him. Only you can realise this mission". Pundit Badrinath had no objection and immediately rushed to Vijaygarh.

□

21

Next day when Maharaja Jay Singh was taking report from Hardayal Singh in the court whether Tej Singh was discovered or not, Tej Singh appeared there carrying a big bundle on his back. He put down the bundle in the centre of the court and bowed to Maharaja. Maharaja Jay Singh was very much pleased to see Tej Singh and asked him to sit down. When he took his seat, Maharaja inquired, "Where have you been for so many days? We were very much worried about you. Diwan Jeet Singh too would be worried as I had inquired about you there also".

Tej Singh reported, "Maharaja! This servant fell into the hands of the enemy. Now, by your grace, I am released and while coming here, I picked up two *aiyars* from Chunar".

Maharaja was very happy to know and in reward gave him his bracelet that he was wearing on his wrist. He informed, "Here also Champa trapped two *aiyars* in the palace who were sent to jail. They should also be sent there". Having said this, he looked at Hardayal who ordered guards (pawns) to unfasten the bundle. Guards opened the bundle and Tej Singh brought them to consciousness and asked the guards to lock them up in the same jail where Ramnarayan and Pannalal were lodged.

Tej Singh requested Maharaja, "Everyone in Naugarh would be worried to hear of my arrest. If you allow me, I would go and see them".

Maharaja consented, "Yes, of course, you must go there. Go, but come back soon". After this, Maharaja ordered Hardayal Singh, "You, too, go to Naugarh along with him taking gifts on my behalf".

"Very good," saying this, Hardayal Singh prepared the gift hamper, took some men and left for Naugarh along with Tej Singh.

When Chapla reached the palace, Chandrakanta felt overjoyed to see her and hugged her. After a while, she inquired about her well-being. Chapla related the whole story. For some time, Chapla and Chandrakanta continued light-hearted talk. The princess informed her of Champa's cleverness and said, "Your trainee has also arrested two *aiyars*". Chapla was pleased to hear it and embraced Champa who was standing there and applauded her.

On the other hand, Tej Singh, who was on the way to Naugarh, told Hardayal Singh, "If we reach there in the morning at the time of court, it will be better as, at that time everyone will be there."

Hardayal Singh liked the idea and they all stopped for a day and next day in the morning they reached the court direct. Virendra Singh was sitting by the side of the king who felt so happy to see him as if he had got the treasure of both the worlds. Hardayal Singh bowed to the king and prince Virendra and met Jeet Singh on equal terms. Tej Singh laid his head at the feet of king Surendra Singh. The king lifted his head with love. Then he touched his father's feet and took his seat beside Virendra Singh. Hardayal Singh presented the gift hamper and a dress for Kunwar Virendra Singh, which he was made to put on there. King Surendra Singh was very happy and Kumar's happiness knew no bounds. The king asked him about his arrest. Tej Singh narrated the whole sequence of his arrest and his release and also added, "While escaping from there, we captured two *aiyars* who are behind the bars in Vijaygarh." The king became very happy to learn it and gave him several things in reward and said, "You must go immediately to the palace and meet everyone and your mother. Only she knows what trauma she has been undergoing because of your absence". Tej Singh accordingly moved to see everyone. The king entrusted the responsibility of Hardayal Singh's hospitality to Jeet Singh and adjourned the court. Tej Singh having met everyone in the palace went to Kumar Virendra Singh's chamber. Kumar happily took him in his arms and when they sat, he teased, "You have narrated your arrest story honestly but you inserted some lies in your account of release. Now speak the truth, who got you released?" Tej Singh praised Chapla whole-heartedly and honestly related the story of his release with the help of Chapla. Kumar said, "Congratulations!" Tej Singh replied, "First I will congratulate you, then only it will befit you to congratulate me". Kumar just laughed. For a few days, Tej Singh happily spent his time in Naugarh. But Virendra Singh kept on reminding him to arrange his date with Chandrakanta. Tej Singh continued consoling him.

After a few days, Hardayal Singh requested Maharaja in the court, "So many days have passed since this servant has come here. It must be causing a lot of inconvenience there. It would be better if you permit me to take your leave. Maharaja had asked me to bring Tej Singh with me on return. Now as you wish". "Very good. Take along Tej Singh". He presented a robe of honour to Hardayal Singh and sent Tej Singh with him.

While leaving, Tej Singh called on Kumar. Kumar saw him off saying, "I need not say more. You can see my condition". Tej Singh comforted him profusely and left for Vijaygarh. They reached the same day. Next day both of them appeared in the court and took their respective seats after paying obeisance to Maharaja. Maharaja asked Tej Singh about the well-being of king Surendra Singh, which he very intelligently reported.

In the meantime, Badrinath also reached there with a letter of Maharaja Shivdutt. He blessed the Maharaja and gave him the letter which was forwarded to Diwan Hardayal Singh to read out. While reading the letter, his face turned red. Maharaja and Tej Singh were looking at his face. From his face, they learnt that there was something offending in the letter. After reading it, he urged that it should be read out in private. Maharaja said, "O.K. First arrange for Badrinath's stay and then come to me in the parlour along with Tej Singh".

Maharaja adjourned the court and went to the palace. Diwan Hardayal Singh made necessary arrangement for Pundit Badrinath's stay and went along with Tej Singh to Maharaja. They saluted him and took their seats. Maharaja asked Hardayal to read out Shivdutt's letter. Hardayal requested him to read it himself. Maharaja went through the letter. His eyes turned blood shot in rage. He tore the letter to pieces and said, "Tell Badrinath to leave the place at once, and treat it as a reply". For a while, Maharaja remained lost in some thought and then said in a low tone. "When Krur Singh left for Chunargarh, I thought at that very time that he would create mischief as far as possible and ultimately this is what has happened. Anyway as long as I am alive, his dream is not going to fulfil. But you, too, should make all-out arrangement".

Tej Singh with folded hands submitted, "There is no doubt that Shivdutt will now charge at us. That's why, it is necessary to prepare a strong army with necessary war equipment in advance. Though his intention was apprehended already when he had sent his *aiyars* here, now it goes beyond doubt".

Maharaja said, "I know it well that Shivdutt has thirty thousand soldiers and we have only ten thousand. But shall I be scared of it?"

Tej Singh said, "Ten thousand soldiers of Maharaja and five thousand of my king, the total comes to fifteen thousand men. It's enough to wipe out such cowards. Now you may kindly send Diwan Saheb with a letter to Naugarh along with me. I will bring the army here, or if Maharaja likes, Kunwar Virendra Singh can also be sought for and the charge of the army can be given to him. Then see what happens".

Diwan Hardayal Singh added, "*Kripanath*, I also agree with him".

Maharaja said, "It's all right. But my heart does not allow me to give charge of war to Virendra Singh. However skilled he may be in warfare, he is like my son. How can I ask him to fight in a war and why will Surendra Singh accept it?"

Tej Singh said, "Maharaja, do not think about it. It is not possible that Maharaja goes for war and Virendra Singh will retire at home. His heart will never accept it. King Surendra Singh is brave, not a coward. He will not let Virendra Singh sit back at home. Rather, it won't be a surprise if he actively takes part in the battle himself".

Maharaja Jay Singh was overjoyed to listen to Tej Singh's talk and ordered Diwan Hardayal Singh, "Write a letter to king Surendra Singh elaborating Shivdutt's audacity and the reply I gave to it and ask him for opinion. On receiving his reply, we will do whatever is necessary. Tomorrow you will take this letter to him personally and come back the same day because there is no time to delay". Haradayal Singh wrote the letter accordingly, Maharaja gave his seal on it and dispatched him immediately. Diwan Saheb taking leave from Maharaja set for Naugarh. He reached there before evening and went direct to Diwan Jeet Singh. On receiving the news, Diwan Jeet Singh came out to receive him. He took Hardayal Singh to his home and asked about the present situation. Haradayal Singh related the whole development. Jeet Singh reacted in anger, "Nowadays Shivdutt has gone hot-headed. He takes us lightly. Anyway, we will see. No problem. You can meet the king in the evening". Hardayal Singh along with Jeet Singh went to see king Surendra Singh in the evening. Kumar Virendra Singh was also sitting there. The king offered them seats and inquired about Maharaja. Hardayal Singh handed over the letter to Maharaja Jay Singh. The king read it himself. He got too furious to speak a word and passed on the letter to Kumar Virendra Singh. Kumar read it thoroughly. He too felt the same. In anger, his vision turned hazy and for a while, he was lost in thought. Next moment he requested his father with folded hands, "I have a passion for war and this is our duty too. It's an opportunity, I don't want to miss. So, I request you to allow me to take the force to Chunargarh. I will arrest Shivdutt before he could attack Vijaygarh".

King Surendra Singh said, "There is no need to act in haste. First you go to Vijaygarh. *Kshatriyas* love war more than their father, son, brother and nephew. That's why, setting aside my affection for you, I order you to take along all the forces to help Maharaja Jay Singh and earn laurels." Then turning to Jeet Singh, he said, "Proclaim this order by the beat of drum in the army that they have to get ready by night. And that in the morning, they have to march to Vijaygarh under Kunwar Virendra Singh". Thereafter, he told Hardayal Singh, "Stay here for tonight. Tomorrow you should move taking along the forces and Kunwar".

Jeet Singh took Hardayal Singh to his residence and Kumar went to his chamber and engaged himself in the preparation for battle. He didn't realise how time fled away in the pleasant thought of marching to battle and to meeting Chandrakanta.

□

22

By morning, Kumar got ready dressed in armour and equipped with arms went to the palace to seek his parents' blessing on the movement. Maharaja had already briefed the queen in the night. They were pleased to see Kumar bow down before them to seek their blessing. The queen took him in her arms. Moving her hands on his back, she said with tearful eyes, "Go my son, add to the glory of brave men and uphold the honour of *Kshatriya's* clan by triumphing over the enemy. It's the religion of warriors that in the event of war, they don't care for their parents or about personal comfort. So, march on to the path of duty. May the enemy not see your back in the battle!"

Taking leave from parents, he came out and saw Diwan Hardayal Singh ready. He rode off followed by his forces marching like waves of the sea. When they reached near Vijaygarh, Kumar got down from his horse and said to Hardayal Singh, "In my opinion, I should halt my army here in this jungle, arrange everything properly and then move to the city".

Hardayal Singh agreed, "Very good. I will go in advance and intimate the king of your arrival and then come back to receive you". Kumar said, "Fine! You go". Hardayal Singh reached Vijaygarh and went to Maharaja to inform him of Kumar's arrival. He said, "Kumar along with his army has his camp two miles back." Maharaja was very happy to learn it and said, "It's good for the army. But Virendra Singh must be offered hospitality here. Take along all the courtiers from here to welcome him and bring him here".

As per order, Hardayal Singh took along some courtiers to welcome Kumar. Tej Singh also got the news and rushed to Virendra Singh and shouted from a distance, "Welcome!" Kumar was very happy to see him and inquired about him. Tej Singh said, "It is fine whatever it is. The rest will be set right".

Saying this, Tej Singh took up the arrangement of the military camp. Meanwhile, Hardayal Singh along with courtiers reached there, formally welcomed him and related what was ordered to him. Kumar accepted it and well-adorned he mounted the horse and rode off in company with a hundred soldiers to Vijaygarh to see Maharaja. The news spread out in the whole city that Kunwar Virendra Singh has come in support of Maharaja and at this time, he is going to the palace. Men and women assembled on their respective terraces of the homes before time and crowds gathered on both sides of the road to watch the procession. Everyone's eyes were turned to north waiting for the cavalcade. The news reached the king that Kumar is to arrive shortly at the palace. Maharaja informed the queen. She joyfully went up the high balcony of the palace along with Chandrakanta, Chapla and other women to witness Kumar's cavalcade. Maharaja too went up the roof top of the public hall. In a short while was seen dust rising in the north. As it came close, they saw some cavaliers marching in. As time passed, everything became clear.

Some of them were wearing armours; the setting sun rays falling on their iron shield reflected on the scene. Holding lances and flags in their hands, carrying shield and sword, they were looking very brave in bold rapture of youth. Ahead of them, a beautiful and strong horse, decorated with jewellery and saddled with embroidered clothes was showing flirtatious gesture. Kumar Virendra Singh was riding on it. He was wearing a steel helmet to which a long plume of huma's feather was attached, and was dressed in precious robe with steel jacket over it. Light-skinned body, big eyes and bright red cheeks. A garland of large size emeralds was hanging round his neck. Armlets were also made of emeralds whose brightness reflecting on his face was doubling his beauty. His waistband was studded with precious diamonds; his costly boots were so studded with pearls that leather was not visible. Armed with shield and sword, dagger, arrows and bow, mace hanging in the case of the saddle and lance in hand, he was marching ahead. His strength, youthfulness, courage and dignity reflected from his face, which inspired love in the heart of friends and fear in the enemy. The best part was that the hundred cavaliers accompanying him were of his age. The city got crowded. Whosoever looked at Kunwar, his or her eyes got dazzled. When the queen saw Virendra Singh coming so regally and awe-inspiringly after a long gap, her love for him got multiplied hundred times. The words gushed out of her, "If there is a bridegroom worthy of Chandrakanta, it is Virendra Singh. What may come I will make him my son-in-law". Chandrakanta and Chapla were also watching from another window. When Chapla looked at Chandrakanta, she blushed. She lost her heart and the picture of Kumar got fixed in her eyes. She hoped that now she would be able to see him at close quarters. On the other hand, Maharaja was also spellbound.

By this time, Kumar reached the threshold of the palace. Maharaja could not restrain himself and came down from the rooftop. As Kumar stepped into the palace, Maharaja too reached there. Virendra Singh touched his feet. Maharaja took him into his arms and holding his hand ushered inside the palace. The queen stepped forward to greet him. Kumar touched her feet. Her eyes filled with tears of love. With great pleasure, she asked him to sit down. Maharaja too sat down. On the left side, the queen took her seat. Maid-servants in fine dresses and jewels were gathered around to attend on him. He looked down across the room as if his eyes were searching for someone. Chandrakanta too was looking at him from the corner of the door. She was anxious to meet him but was helpless. For some time, Maharaja and Kumar remained in the palace. After that, Maharaja stood up and went to the hall of audience along with Kumar. He assigned a beautiful room to him by the side of his special retiring chamber. Taking leave from Maharaja, he went to his room. Tej Singh also came there and spent some time with him in jest. Kumar was disappointed for he could not see Chandrakanta in the palace. He slept thinking how to see her.

In the morning when Maharaja went to court, Virendra Singh having finished his bath and prayer put on court's robe, jewel-decked turban on the head went to the court in company with Tej Singh. Maharaja offered him a chair studded with jewels and precious stones by his side. Haradayal Singh presented before him the letter of king Surendra Singh that he had written in reply to his letter. Maharaja was very glad to read it. After a while, he ordered Diwan Saheb to organise a market for Kumar's army and make complete arrangement of food grains. There should be no problem to anyone. Kumar said, "Maharaja, goods have come together".

Maharaja said, "Do you think this state belongs to others? What if goods have come? They too will be used when needed. Now I entrust you the responsibility of the combined forces. Do as you think best".

Kumar turned to Tej Singh and said, "Go and form two companies of my forces consisting of two thousand soldiers each and deploy them on the two sides of Vijaygarh. And the rest one thousand soldiers should be spread across the ten-kilometer area in ten small units of hundred soldiers each. Make necessary arrangements for tent. Dispatch detectives and spies all around. Tomorrow after the inspection of Maharaja's forces, decision will be taken for their deployment".

Having got the order, Tej Singh set off. Maharaja felt even more comforted to see this arrangement and his togetherness. Hardayal Singh was ordered to make this proclamation by drum beat in the forces that tomorrow will be their parade. In the meanwhile, the spies of Maharaja came and after saluting him, informed that Shivdutt with his thirty thousand forces had set off for attack. In two to three days, they will reach here. Kumar asserted, "Don't worry. I will see. Move on to your duty".

Next day, Maharaja Jay Singh and Kumar came riding an elephant to inspect the parade. Hardayal Singh had minimised the strength of the Muslims; even then, one thousand Muslim soldiers were left in the army. Kumar was happy to watch their parade but frowned at the sight of Muslims. Maharaja read his face and asked in a whisper. "Should we remove them?" Kumar replied, "No, they will turn to the side of the enemy if they are sacked. I think it would be better to send them first on the front to counter the enemy. An artillery battery along with some of our soldiers will be placed behind them. If they play foul or try to run away, artillery fire from behind will wipe them out. This fear will make them fight bravely; they will prefer to die fighting to losing their life for not". Maharaja liked this idea very much and appreciated his intelligence.

When Maharaja turned to go, Kumar asked, "I want to go on hunting if you permit me".

Maharaja replied, "OK. Don't go far and return before evening". Saying this, he asked the mahout to make the elephant sit down. Kumar got down and mounted on a horse. Following Maharaja's indication, Hardayal Singh dispatched a hundred troopers along with him. Kumar left for the hunt and reached a dense forest where he shot down two antelopes with his arrow. As he was reaching his prey, Tej Singh reached there. Kumar asked, "Have you arranged everything that you are here?" Tej Singh answered, "Is it possible to arrange everything today, something is done today and the rest will be completed tomorrow. At this time, I felt that I should take a round of that cave where Ahmad was locked up. So, I have come to ask you if you would also like to go there".

"Yes, I will go". He turned his horse to that direction. Tej Singh followed him. He ordered the soldiers to go back to the camp with the two hunted antelopes. Kumar and Tej Singh reached the cave and went in. They passed through a dark tunnel and came into a lighted space, where they saw the door. Kumar got down from the horse. Now Tej Singh asked him, "Can you open this door or not?" Kumar returned, "Why not, what art is involved in it!" Saying this, he pulled out the tongue from the lion's mouth and the door opened. Tej Singh complimented. "Well, you remember". Kumar said, "Am I to forget?" They went in and strolling round reached near the spring. They saw that Ahmad and Bhagwan dutta were sitting on a rock and chatting, fetters in their feet intact. They rose to their feet seeing Kumar and bowed down to salute him and said, "Now our offence should be forgiven". Kumar said, "Yes, have patience for a few days".

Both of them kept on strolling, plucking and eating fruits for some time. Tej Singh averred, "We should go now; it's getting late". Kumar consented and they came out. Tej Singh said, "You have opened this door, now you should lock it up also". Kumar closed the door saying, "Okay, I am locking it up myself". Kumar mounted the horse. When they reached near Vijaygarh, Tej Singh said, "Now you may go. I will joint you after taking stock of the forces". Kumar agreed, "Okay, you may go". Tej Singh turned to another side and Kumar came to the palace, went into his room and took a rest. Late at night, Tej Singh came to Kumar. Kumar said, "Tell, what's the update?" Tej Singh reported, "All arrangements have been made according to your instruction. The whole day I did not get even an hour's leisure to see you". Virendra Singh burst into laughter. Till noon, you were with me and still you say that you could not meet me!" Tej Singh got alarmed and remarked, "What do you say!"

Kumar retorted. "What to say, didn't you go with me to that cave where Ahmad and Bhagwandutta are locked?"

Now Tej Singh's face turned pale, he stared at Kumar's face and Kumar was also surprised to notice Tej Singh's condition.

Tej Singh questioned, "Please tell me where I met you, how far I went with you and when I came back". Kumar narrated the whole sequence of events. Tej Singh lamented, "You have turned the table. I am not so sorry for the escape of Ahmad and Bhagwan dutta. But the secret of the door is revealed to others is a matter of greater concern". Kumar reacted, "I don't understand what you say".

Tej Singh remarked in anguish, "Had you understood me, you would not have been deceived. If not, then try to understand now that the *aiyars* of Shivdutt duped you and learnt the secret of the cave. Certainly, it is the work of Badrinath and not of anyone else. The astrologer tells him everything with the help of *ramal*.

Kumar was shocked to know it and repented of his mistake. Tej Singh consoled, "What has gone is gone; no use repenting it. I am going now. Prisoners would have escaped. I will go and rearrange the lock".

Kumar asked, "What arrangement will you make for the lock?" Tej Singh replied, "There are other locks also in that door which are stronger than this but they consume lots of time in locking and unlocking but now I will do it".

Kumar inquired, "Will you show those locks to me?"

Tej Singh, "Not now. As long as we do not conquer Chunargarh, I will not tell. Such a blunder may recur". Kumar replied. "Okay. As you wish".

Tej Singh left for the *tilismi* cave at that very moment and came back before dawn. In the morning, Kumar woke up and asked Tej Singh, "Tell me the condition of the cave". He replied, "The prisoners have escaped but I have rearranged the locks". They took a bath, breakfast and got ready for the court. Having reached there, they saluted the king and took their seats. The spies gave the information that forces of Shivdutt have come closer, they are just twenty kilometers away.

Kumar requested Maharaja, "Now the time has come that the Muslim soldiers should be sent to the forefront to counter the enemy". Maharaja said, "Okay. Send them". Kumar asked Tej Singh, "Dispatch our one artillery unit behind these Muslim forces". He further added, "Instruct the artillery unit to finish them off if they do any mischief". Tej Singh along with Hardayal Singh left to execute the order. Maharaja suspended the court and went to the palace taking along Kumar. Both took lunch together and after that Kumar went into his room. He kept pining but even today he couldn't see the face of Chandrakanta though Chandrakanta saw him clearly from behind a cover.

□

23

In the evening, Virendra Singh went to see Maharaja. Maharaja made him sit by his side and began talking to him. In the meantime, Hardayal Singh and Tej Singh also reached there. Maharaja took report. They informed that forces have been sent to take on the aggressors. They started discussing battlecraft and their strategy. Half the night passed in this discussion. Suddenly some chobdars rushed in and reported, "Maharaja, some men were seen sneaking out of the secret palace. Taking them for enemy, the guards hit them with arrows but they escaped despite being wounded".

On listening to it, Maharaja fell into a pensive thought. Kumar and Tej Singh were also surprised. By then, they heard the sound of weeping coming from inside the palace. Their attention turned to the cries. The sound of weeping and crying was going up to the extent that the whole palace was filled with deep commotion. Maharaja, Kumar and others turned white-faced. Just then some maid-servants came running in who could barely utter while weeping that someone had chopped Chandrakanta and Chapla's head and run away with them". This news pierced them like an arrow. Maharaja fell unconscious for a moment saying "Oh....!" Kumar turned pale. Hardayal Singh started weeping and Tej Singh was dumbfounded. Maharaja controlled himself and seeing Kumar's alarming condition, took him in his arms and rushed to the palace holding his hands. He saw commotion everywhere. Maharani was weeping over the body of Chandrakanta; her head was injured and bleeding. Maharaja too fell on her body. Kumar didn't have even that strength to enter. He fell on the gate itself, his teeth lock-jawed, face turned pale like a corpse.

The bodies of Chandrakanta and Chapla were lying there, heads were missing. The room was littered with blood everywhere. Everyone was in deadly shock. Maharani was saying while weeping, "Alas! Dear, where have you gone?

How cruel was his heart that slashed your throat! Alas, Alas! Now what is the use of my living. The whole trouble was for you and you are not alive. What does the state mean now?" Maharaja lamented, "Now Krur's heart must have got cooled. Shivdutt had his desire fulfilled. Tell them to come now and rule Vijaygarh, "We will go with our daughter".

Suddenly, Maharaja's eyes turned to the gate and saw Virendra Singh lying and his head bleeding. He rushed to Kumar and felt his pulse missing, no life in the body. He took his hand to his nose and felt that his breath was running cold.

Now Maharaja cried out even more loudly, "A disaster befell! For us the state of Naugarh was also wasted. We had in mind that we would go to forest handing over the state to Virendra Singh but alas! Destiny didn't like even this. *Arrey*! Someone rush to Tej Singh and fetch him here quickly. He must look after Kumar. Alas! Alas! I too have to die in this house now. I think King Surendra Singh will also lose his life in this house! Alas, what I was thinking just now and what has befallen! Oh God, what have you done?"

In the meantime, Tej Singh came and saw Virendra Singh lying and Maharaja weeping beside him. Whatever life was left in Tej Singh, it gushed out to see the scene. He sat beside the corpse of Virendra Singh and shouted, "Kumar, I don't want to weep because I don't want to live in this world now. I will happily follow you". Saying this, he took out his dagger and was about to stab in his stomach when a man jumped across the wall and held his hand.

Tej Singh saw the man who was painted in vermillion colour from top to toe. He recited a song:

Why do you lay your life? Listen to me attentively
Take all this for imposture
Learn the fact by observing the body carefully
Rise, make prudent inquiry
Find out who played this aiyari.

Having said this, he ran away showing his teeth, leaping and jumping.

□

Part-II

1

Everyone saw that man, but everyone was surprised to think, who he was, how he came and what he said! Tej Singh called out loudly, "Silence! Silence! I have discovered; it's all *aiyari*. In reality, princess and Chapla both are alive. These are not their bodies."

Everyone was astonished at this and silence gripped there. They stopped weeping and turned to Tej Singh. The queen ran to him and said, "Son, tell me quickly what the matter is. How do you say Chandrakanta is alive? Who was that fellow who suddenly jumped into the palace?"

Tej Singh replied, "I don't know who that man was but it is discovered that Chandrakanta and Chapla have been kidnapped by the *aiyars* of Shivdutt and their artificial bodies are kept here so that we take their death for granted and do not look for them".

Maharaja said, "How do you know these bodies are artificial!"

Tej Singh answered, "It's not a big deal. Come to the body, I'll show you." Maharaja along with Tej Singh and the queen came near the corpses. Tej Singh put out his dagger and chopped Chapla's leg and showed it to Maharaja. Is there any bone in it?"

Maharaja observed it closely and said, "OK. It's artificial. Thereafter, he observed the body of Chandrakanta in the same manner and didn't find a bone in that too. Now everyone learned that it was the case of *aiyari*. Maharaja lamented, "All right, I have learnt that Chandrakanta is alive but she has fallen into the hands of the enemy. Is this less woeful?" Tej Singh, "No problem. Now what has happened has happened. I will soon find out Chandrakanta and Chapla." They felt a bit comforted but Kumar Virendra was still lying unconscious. He knew nothing of it. Maharaja was worried that he must be brought to consciousness. A doctor was called in. They all tried in many ways but Kumar did not regain sense. Tej Singh too tried his art but to no avail. Seeing this, Maharaja was very much scared and asked Tej Singh, "What should we do now?" After thinking over it for some time, Tej Singh said, "Kumar should be taken to his room. I will treat him in solitude". Maharaja tried to lift him himself but Tej Singh lifted him in his arms and turned to his room. Maharaja also followed him but Tej Singh requested, "You should not accompany me. He will be treated alone". Maharaja stopped there. Tej Singh carried Kumar to his room, laid him on the bed, shut all doors and windows and spoke in his ear, "Chandrakanta is not dead; she is alive. Look, the *aiyars* of Maharaja Shivdutt are taking her away. Run quickly, seize her, otherwise they will run away with her. Is this called bravery? Fie! Chandrakanta is being kidnapped by the enemy and you don't speak even after seeing it. Ram! Ram!"

As these words fell into his ears, he opened his eyes and said with a shiver, "Hey! Who is kidnapping her? Where is Chandrakanta?" Saying this, he looked here and there and saw Tej Singh sitting. He asked, "Who was just saying that Chandrakanta is alive and the enemy is running away with her?" Tej Singh answered, "I was saying and it is true. Princess is alive but the enemy has kidnapped her and in her place, a synthetic body was kept there and the red colour was sprinkled here and there, so that we take princess for dead and neither chase the enemy nor search for her".

Kumar said, "You are deceiving me. How do I know that the body is artificial?" Tej Singh replied, "I will just make you believe". He opened the gate of the room and saw Maharaja standing there, tears rolling down continuously.

He asked Tej Singh, "How is he?" "He is fine, back to his senses. Come and see". Maharaja went in. On seeing him, Kumar rose to his feet. Maharaja embraced him. He asked, "How is your health?" Kumar replied, "I am fine". Some maidservants also dashed there who were sent by the queen to take stock of the situation. Tej Singh asked a maid-servant to bring the hand and the leg that he had chopped off from the corpses. The maid-servant went back running and brought them. Tej Singh showing them to Kumar, asked, "See, is the body artificial or not? Where is the bone?" Kumar was convinced, "OK, but they have done great mischief". Tej Singh remarked, "Anyway, what they had to do, they did. Now let us do what we have to".

The sun rose over the sky. While Maharaja, Kumar and Tej Singh were talking among themselves, Hardayal Singh reached there and saluted Maharaja. He pointed at him to sit down. Diwan Saheb took his seat. Others were asked to go away. Hardayal Singh asked Tej Singh, "I have heard that it was an artificial corpse which was taken for Kumari's body?" Tej Singh replied, "Yes, it's true". Then he elaborated the whole story. After this, Diwan Saheb informed, "And see the disaster! The news of Kumari's death saddened everyone. Government servants who heard about it rushed to the door of the palace, crying and wailing. Consequently, security at the place where the *aiyars* were imprisoned got relaxed. Having got the right opportunity, their *aiyar* friends charged at the prison, wounded the guards and the *aiyars* broke loose".

Tej Singh, Kumar and Maharaja were stunned to hear this news. Kumar rued, "We are caught in the deep sea. All his *aiyars* are let loose. Princess and Chapla are kidnapped; it's terrible. I can't bear it anymore. We will move today and avenge the enemy". While they were talking like this, a chobdar came to report, "A spy has come with the news of the war. He is standing at the gate. Your order for him?" Hardayal Singh asked, "Bring him here". The spy was brought in. He said, "The Muslim forces were sent to counter the enemy. By the time they reached there, the enemy had moved eight miles inward. At the time of face-off, they started running away. At this, artillery unit fired from behind in which one-fourth of them were killed. Then, they could not dare to flee and fought bravely to the extent that they killed around one thousand enemy soldiers. At last, they were done away with. If immediate reinforcement is not sent the artillery forces will meet the same end".

Kumar immediately ordered Hardayal Singh, "A reinforcement of 5,000 forces be immediately sent to the front and also dispatch tent for us. We will set out for the same at noon". Hardayal Singh left to dispatch the forces. Maharaja told Kumar, "I will also accompany you to the battle-front".

Kumar said, "What's the hurry? You should be here, look after the affairs of the state. I am going. Let me see how brave Shivdutta is! You need not trouble yourself".

After a brief talk, Maharaja went inside the palace. Kumar and Tej Singh too rose up to get ready. First of all, Tej Singh got up, and ordered the proclaimer to drum-beat the order, "It is proclaimed in the whole city that anyone who cherishes for Dantarwir should report to Tej Singh immediately". Accordingly, the proclaimer left to do the job. Everyone was surprised at what Tej Singh had ordered.

□

2

Maharaja conducted the court at the usual time. Kumar and Tej Singh were also present. Today's court was very dull and dejected, but Kumar got the permission to set out for the battle and left the place. Maharaja too out of humour left the court and went into the palace. Though it was made clear that Chandrakanta and Chapla were alive, but where, in what condition, comfortable or tormented, such thoughts kept everyone from the queen to maid-servants regretful. Everyone was tearful; no one cared for food, only Chandrakanta was in their thought. When Maharaja went inside the palace, the queen asked, "What are you doing for Chandrakanta". Maharaja replied, "Tej Singh has gone in search of her. Who else is more competent to be sent? Virendra Singh too has taken leave of me for setting out to the battlefield. Let us see what happens".

□

3

A little shaft of the fading sun is still left. In a field covered with green grass, 15-20 chairs are kept and only three men– Kunwar Virendra Singh, Tej Singh and Fateh Singh are sitting. Other chairs are vacant; to their east, hundreds of tents in semi-circles are pitched. In the centre, it is the platoon of Virendra Singh busy cleaning their arms. Canons are standing in big tents and they seem well-equipped and maintained. In the south, there is a stable where high-quality horses are fastened and they are neighing. A little ahead of it is the stable of elephants where huge-shaped elephants are standing, tied with shackles. In the west are the band party, tunnel diggers, mountain blowers, spies, and stock of supplies in their respective camps. Kumar told Fateh Singh, "I think my tent would be pitched by the early morning in the field of Lohara to challenge the enemy". Fateh Singh complied, "Yes, of course, by the morning, it would be ready. Our forces will move much before dawn and in the morning, they will reach there. The day after tomorrow, our valour could be seen. We were upset sitting vacant for so many days". They were talking like this when Devi Singh well-adorned as *aiyar* was seen coming there and saluted Kumar and Tej Singh. Kumar was overwhelmed to see Devi Singh and embraced him. Tej Singh also hugged Devi Singh and asked him to sit. Fateh Singh, the army chief, greeted Devi Singh. When Devi Singh sat down, Tej Singh started praising him. Kumar asked, "Tell us what you did before coming here?" Tej Singh intervened, "Listen, his achievements from me. I'll tell you in brief". Kumar said, "OK, tell us". Tej Singh started, "When you were sitting in the garden of Chandrakanta and a ghost came there and recited 'Your king is informed, listen my teacher', on hearing it, I forced you to move from there. That ghost was he. In Naugarh too, he broke the news about Krur Singh's movement to Chunar and of bringing *aiyars* from there by playing tambourine. When the mourning of Chandrakanta's death was thick in the air of the palace and you were lying senseless, it was he who informed me that Chandrakanta and Chapla are alive. Then I rose to recognise, otherwise the whole family would have been ruined. This much work he has done. It was to call him back that I asked to make that proclamation in the morning because he has no whereabouts". On hearing it, Kumar patted his back and said, "Well done! I have no words to praise you. You have saved two houses". Devi Singh remarked, "Of what worth am I that you are praising me so much. Praise me after accomplishing my all tasks. At this time, we should think of rescuing Chandrakanta. If we are late, then who knows her life may be at stake. Besides this, we must also see if we are too engrossed in search of Chandrakanta, the result of the battle could be damaging". Kumar asked, "Devi Singh, tell me where is Chandrakanta?" Devi Singh replied, "I don't know where Chandrakanta is. Of course this much information I have that Nazim and Badrinath have kidnapped her and Chapla. It will be discovered if we try". Tej Singh said, "Now, all *aiyars* of the enemy are at large. They are nine and we are just two. Either we search for Chandrakanta and Chapla or be with the army to safeguard Kumar. It's really a tough time". Devi Singh responded, "No problem, everything will be done. Now, we should move to face Shivdutt. We will think of rescuing Kumari there itself". Tej Singh said, "We have taken leave of Maharaja. We will move a little before dawn. The advance party has already departed".

They kept on talking until mid-night. After that, Kumar went to his tent. Tej Singh's tent was beside Kumar's where Devi Singh and Tej Singh slept for the night. Forces were patrolling all around and the sound of patrolling was audible. A little before dawn, a canon was fired. After a while, military band started playing; preparation for the movement was done and the forces moved on slowly. When they went ahead, Kumar mounted an elephant surrounded by many cavaliers. Tej Singh and Devi Singh were equipped with their kits of *aiyari*, walking on foot sometimes forward, sometimes backward, sometimes beside Kumar. Before noon forces of Kunwar Virendra Singh reached before Shivdutt's where the forces of Maharaja Jay Singh were in position. The battle was at rest and all Muslim soldiers had been killed. Tents had already been pitched there, platoons were stationed as per procedure. When everything was arranged, Kunwar Virendra Singh organised a court in his tent and ordered the Munshi, "Write a letter to Shivdutt stating that it seems nowadays you have become hot-headed who needlessly under the instigation of a worthless Krur has waged a war against Maharaja Jay Singh. It is also learnt that your *aiyars* have kidnapped Chandrakanta and Chapla. It would be better to send back Chandrakanta and Chapla with due respect to Maharaja Jay Singh. You should go back with your forces, otherwise you will have to repent. When our brave soldiers flash their swords in the battlefield, you will not find a way to run away".

Mir Munshi wrote the letter accordingly. Kumar asked, "Who will carry this letter?" Devi Singh responded with folded hands, "Please, allow me to carry this letter because I have a great desire in my heart to talk to Shivdutt". Kumar said, "It's not good for you to go alone". Tej Singh intervened, "Don't worry. Let him go". Ultimately, Kumar agreed and gave him his dagger which Devi Singh received and saluted him. He put the letter in his pouch and touched the feet of Tej Singh and left.

No one in the forces of Maharaja Shivdutt Singh recognised Devi Singh. He saw from a distance a richly embroidered huge tent. He went straight to the threshold of his tent and asked the guards, "Inform your king that an *aiyar* of Kunwar Virendra Singh has brought a letter for him. Go, hurry up!" Then and there, a guard rushed in and informed Maharaja Shivdutt. He ordered, "Let him come". Devi Singh went in and saw that Maharaja Shivdutt was sitting on a gold-studded throne. On his left, Diwan Saheb was sitting and on both sides, several great warriors donned in richly ornamented dresses were sitting in silver chairs. The weak would be frightened at a mere look. Beside them, *aiyars* were sitting in Neem chairs. Aamir and other rank-holders were sitting according to their hierarchy. A number of mace-bearers were standing cross-armed. It was an awfully intimidating royal court. Devi Singh without saluting anyone stood in the centre and looked around the court and then moving forward placed the letter before Maharaja. Maharaja Shivdutt shot into rage and said, "How dare a mosquito face an elephant! Virendra Singh is still a milk-sucking child". Saying this, he tore the letter into pieces. At this, Devi Singh's eyes reddened with anger and he said, "Disaster consumes the victim's sense". Devi Singh's words hit Shivdutt like an arrow and he said, "Arrest this insolent fellow!" Many chobdars rushed to Devi Singh. He took out his dagger and finished 2-3 chobdars. He quickly took out a ball from his pouch of *aiyari* and struck it on the ground. It made a huge explosion, the court trembled and Maharaja shuddered so much so that his turban on which a diamond was studded fell on the ground. Devi Singh leaping forward, picked it up and jumped out of the tent. Everyone was taken aback, no one could do anything.

Shivdutt vented all his fury on *aiyars* who were sitting there at that time. "It's a shame on your *aiyari* that a simple *aiyar* of the enemy dishonoured us before you!" Badrinath replied, "Maharaja, we are *aiyars*. We enter alone into a crowd of thousands and perform our work. But ten *aiyars* don't pounce upon a single man. It is against our rule. So many great warriors were sitting there, what did they do?" Shivdutt replied Badrinath with a silence. He later added, "Okay, I'll see them tomorrow!"

□

4

Devi Singh came back to Kunwar Virendra Singh carrying Maharaja Shivdutt's crown and narrated the whole incident. Kunwar burst into laughter and said, "Well, it's an auspicious beginning!" Tej Singh added, "It's more auspicious for me as I produced a worthy disciple". Saying this, he took out the diamond from the turban and put it in his pouch. Kunwar told, "What will you do with it, what use is it for you?" Tej Singh replied, "Its name is 'Jewel of Fateh'. The day your marriage procession is taken out, I will march ahead with a flag in Maharaja Shivdutt's guise wearing it on my head". Kumar laughed at it, but at the same time, two drops of tear flashed from his eyes which he wiped quickly with his hankie. Tej Singh realised it was for Chandrakanta's separation. He too was worried about Chapla and instructed Devi Singh, "Listen Devi Singh, tomorrow fighting will certainly take place. So, it is necessary for an aiyar to remain here and even more important to search for Chandrakanta". Devi Singh said to Tej Singh, "You remain here to take care of the army. I am going in search of Chandrakanta". Tej Singh said, "No, you are not well familiar with the hills of Chunar and I hope Chandrakanta must be there. So, it would be better that you stay here and I go in search of Kumari". Devi Singh said, "As you wish". Tej Singh addressed Kumar, "Devi Singh will be with you and I am going. You must be careful and do not make any haste in battle". Kumar said, "OK, go. May God help you!" It was evening while talking, rather it was getting dark. Tej Singh stood up and, equipped with the necessary items of *aiyari*, he set out to a dense forest.

□

5

"Where could have they kept Chandrakanta, in a good room or a dark room? What food they would have served her? What would she be doing except weeping! Would she be conscious of food and water? Her face would have turned pale in grief and mourning. They would be pestering her for her consent. I wish she would not have committed suicide in vexation". Kumar was lost in the whirlpool of such thoughts and couldn't sleep for the whole night.

When it was getting dawn, drum-beat from the side of Maharaja Shivdutt's army was heard. It was felt that the enemy was getting ready for the assault. Kumar got up and washed his face. In the meanwhile, a messenger came to inform him that the enemy camp was getting ready for the attack. Kumar said, "Our camp should also get ready quickly". On getting the order, *Harkar* (announcer) rushed to the camp. By this time, Kumar finished his bath and prayer. Forces of both sides had taken their position. Labourers had levelled the ground. Kumar too reached the battle-ground riding his Arbi horse and said to Devi Singh, "Shivdutt should be proposed that it's not good to shed blood of so many men. Those who are proud of their bravery should come and fight with me one by one. It will settle the matter quickly. Shivdutt Singh regards himself as Arjun; I am ready to face him. Why should these poor, innocent soldiers lose their life?" Devi Singh said, "It's very good. I am going to fix it just now". He moved forward towards the ground and tossed his shawl in the air 2-3 times. On seeing it, Badrinath from the camp of Maharaja Shivdutt rushed out to Devi Singh and said, "Hail thee Maya!" Devi Singh also responded, "Hail thee Maya!" Badrinath asked, "What makes you call the *aiyar*?"

Devi Singh, "I have to tell you one thing".

Badrinath, "Tell."

Devi Singh, "In your army, who are in greater number, men or women?"

Badrinath said, "No face of a woman is seen here."

Devi Singh, "Is there anyone brave in your camp or they are just making poor soldiers scapegoats and watch the show?"

Badrinath said, "We are packed with brave soldiers."

Devi Singh said, "You sound like saying that they are worthless."

Badrinath said, "This will be proved only in the battlefield."

Devi Singh said, "Then, why don't you ask them to show their valour by fighting one by one? This will yield the result quickly and save the life of hapless soldiers. Our Kumar says that Maharaja Shivdutt is very much confident of his bravery. He should come and fight with him. Either he wins or Kumar will be the ruler of Chunar. The matter will be settled in no time."

Badrinath said, "Our Maharaja will never back out on this. He will crush your Kumar in a trice."

Devi Singh said, "I too know that his fingers are very sharp. Then, ask him to accept the challenge."

Badrinath turned back to his camp and reported the whole thing to Maharaja Shivdutt. On listening to it, Maharaja Shivdutt turned furious and said, "This child of yesterday wants to fight with me!" Badrinath averred, "It is just his spirit, his courage. There is nothing to be annoyed at; as far as I understand, he is right". Hearing it, Maharaja Shivdutt kicked his horse and galloped to the ground. He lifted his lance and waved it, Having seen it Virendra Singh spurred his horse and reached in front of Shivdutt and challenged him, "You pat your back yourself and say that you are brave. Are brave men pilferers, too? Did you dare to take away Chandrakanta by fighting bravely? Shame on such bravery!" Virendra Singh's words pierced Maharaja Shivdutt's heart like an arrow. He couldn't answer. Filled with anger, he forcefully discharged his lance on Kumar. Kumar jerked it with his lance in such a way that Shivdutt's lance slipped out of hand and fell away.

Seeing it, foes and friends from both sides alike shouted 'bravo! bravo!' Shivdutt flared up and taking out his sword rushed at Kumar. Kumar replied with his sword. They continued fighting till noon. In the afternoon, Shivdutt's horse got injured and fell down. Maharaja Shivdutt too suffered several injuries. Jumping from his horse, Shivdutt tried to strike Kumar's horse. But Kumar sensing his intention vaulted out of the saddle and coming forward hit Shivdutt's wrist so forcefully that his sword fell down on the ground, which was quickly picked up by Devi Singh. Maharaja Shivdutt realised that Kumar was superior to him in all respects. If this fight continued for a while, he would be either killed or captured. Keeping this in mind, he signalled his army to charge at Kumar. Suddenly, Kumar was surrounded by his enemy. Seeing this, Kumar's forces waged a counter-attack. Commander Fateh Singh and Devi Singh managed to reach near Kumar and started flashing sword and dagger. Both the forces were set against each other and a fierce fight started.

The great warriors of Shivdutt tried to kill Kumar but they could do nothing. Many of the enemies were killed at the hands of Kumar. In the evening, beating retreat was played and the fight came to a halt.

Kumar came to his tent, but he was very tired. Commander Fateh Singh was also injured. Everyone went to bed at night.

Maharaja Shivdutt consulted his Diwan and Commanders to decide what to do now thinking that "the army of Virendra Singh is much smaller than ours in numerical strength but their courage disheartened us as we have incurred a heavy loss in this fight. In my opinion, we should attack Kumar's army at night". Everyone liked this idea. A little before dawn, Shivdutt stormed Kumar's camp with his 500 soldiers. Chaos was created there. In the darkness of the night, it was difficult to distinguish between foes and friends. Kumar's soldiers mistook theirs for the enemy and attacked them. The news reached Virendra Singh who quickly came out of his tent. Devi Singh distributed fire crackers (Mahtab) to burn. This Mahtab was developed by Tej Singh. They made the battlefield lighted like day. Now what was the problem? It was not a big deal to kill 500 men.

By the morning, 500 soldiers of Shivdutt were killed but Kumar by that time had lost 1,000 soldiers, which saddened him very much and he did not stop the fight in the morning.

Again both the forces were engaged in close fight. Kumar quickly took his bath, performed his prayer and put on his armour and entered into the enemy camp. Heavy fighting was going on. No one cared about his body. All of a sudden, from north-east corner, some army troopers were seen marching forward. They were led by a cavalier adorned in rich dress and riding an Arbi horse. They were around 500, galloping forward to the battlefield. By the dress and decoration of the leader, it seemed that he was the commander. His face was covered with a scarf and his troopers had also covered their faces. This troop attacked the forces of Shivdutt from behind and killed them in great number. When the army of Virendra Singh saw that the enemy was attacked by another troop also, they got more spirited. The forces of Maharaja Shivdutt could not withstand the double attack and ran away. Kumar got an edge and chased the enemy spiritedly for four kilometers. And, finally, they declared their victory and came back to their camp but they were surprised about the veiled troopers who helped them at the right moment and then went back to the direction from which they had come. Anyone extending a little help to the other claims his obligation on him; but they didn't even come to tell us. It's a matter of great gallantry. They thought a lot but could not understand it.

Maharaja Shivdutt's warehouse and camp property were seized by Kumar. When Kumar was at peace, he asked Devi Singh, "Can you tell me who were those veiled cavaliers?" Devi Singh replied, "I don't remember anything but bravo! This is called bravery!" In the meanwhile, an informer came and informed that the enemy after running away some distance had halted at a place and were preparing for a fresh attack.

□

6

Taking leave from Kunwar Virendra Singh, Tej Singh went out of the army camp in search of Chandrakanta and Chapla. He wondered where to go, where to search for? There is no point in looking for them in the enemies' camp because they will never keep Chandrakanta there. So, it would be better to move to Chunar and he left for Chunar and reached there next day early in the morning. He started wandering here and there in disguise. He stopped at different places and tried to get some clue but to no avail. He could get no information of Kumari. At night, Tej Singh changed his face and entered the fort and started searching here and there. Then getting an opportunity, he covered himself with a black cloth and climbed up roof-top of the palace with the help of lasso. It was midnight. He looked around from the top. There was complete silence but the area was lighted. Tej Singh climbed down to a hallway and looked around. There was a big room before him which was beautifully decorated with portraits and other decorative items. There wasn't much light; just two candlesticks were burning and a lady was sleeping on a high couch in the centre of the room. Several women were also sleeping on the floor around her couch. Tej Singh stepped forward and blew out the candles one by one, only one candle was left in that room. Now Tej Singh moved to that room, standing at the gate and saw woman's face very clearly. The whole body was covered with a shawl but the face was open. As she was resting on one side, some part of her face was hidden in the velvety pillow. Her fair complexion, redness on the cheeks, on which a lock of hair was lying, looked very beautiful. There seemed a scar of some wound near her eye but even that seemed very pretty. Tej Singh got convinced that she was certainly the queen of Maharaja Shivdutt. Having thought for a while, he took out from his pouch a pen and an inkpot and wrote on a piece of paper, "I don't know why I am tempted to see Chandrakanta at this time. What may come, I am going to see her. I have come to know her whereabouts and its route".

Thereafter, he moved closer to the bed and took *lakhlakha* (anaesthetic powder) to the nose of the queen that made her unconscious. Tej Singh checked by putting his finger before her nose. She was breathing in unconsciousness. He quickly tied her in a bundle and left behind the note that he had written under the pillow and came out from there with the help of lasso and opened the window which was facing the river Ganga. He ran away to the hill. He went very far and gave an additional dose of *lakhlakha* to the queen and concealed her in a mountain pass. Thereafter, he came back to the gate of the palace and hid himself in a corner there.

□

7

Now it was getting morning. When the maid-servants in the palace woke up and saw their queen missing; they got panicked and looked for her all around but could not find her. Lots of commotion started. Search operation was launched all around but there was no trace. The news spread outside; everyone was very worried. Maharaja Shivdutt along with 10 to 15 cavaliers rushed back to Chunar from the battlefield. As he entered the palace, he was informed that the queen was missing. He was shocked to learn it; it was a double setback. He hurriedly went inside the palace and saw commotion all around; the sound of wailing was coming from all corners.

At this time, Maharaja Shivdutt was in a peculiar condition. He was not in his senses. He had left behind his forces and his *aiyars* after instructing them and himself rushed to Chunar where he saw this situation. At last, in a depressed mood, he went to the bed of the queen and sat weeping there. Incidentally, he saw the corner of the piece of paper under the pillow. He opened it and saw something written on it. It was the same note which was written by Tej Singh and left there. Reading it, so many thoughts came to his mind. First, it didn't seem to be written by the queen. Her handwriting was not so clear. Then who wrote it? And if the queen had written it how did she know where Chandrakanta was kept? Now what to do? I don't have any *aiyar* here to send in search of her. If I send someone else to the place where Chandrakanta is locked in, the secret would be exposed.

He kept on thinking like this. Ultimately, he came to the conclusion that he must visit the place where Chandrakanta was kept, whatever may befall. There is no problem if I go alone to see her. But I must go in the evening and not in the day. Having thought of this, he came out and sat down silently in the public hall taking neither food nor water. He didn't tell anything to anyone but many of his men had already left in search of the queen without the order of Maharaja.

Evening was closing in; Maharaja asked for his horse, and riding it he went out of the palace in the eastern direction. It was getting dark but it was a moon-lit night. So, everything was clearly visible. Tej Singh was hiding beside the door of the palace. Having seen Shivdutt going alone on the horse, he started following him. He followed him for six kilometres but Maharaja didn't get a hint of it. Now Maharaja led his horse to a dry canal. As he moved forward, the canal got deeper and deeper and on both the sides, there was a very fearsome forest of tall teak and *asaan* trees. The voices of wild animals were horrible. As he moved forward, the slopes got deeper and the canopy of the trees on both sides of the canal touched one another.

He continued moving like this for two kilometres. Now moonlight was not at all visible in the canal as trees on both sides were interlocked. The canal looked like a tunnel. Maharaja's horse was moving slowly because of darkness and rocky terrain. Tej Singh moved forward and came closer to Maharaja. All of a sudden, a little light was seen at some distance. Tej Singh thought that this was the end of the way and it proved right. When he reached near the light, he saw a small cave which was guarded by tall and brave soldiers holding naked swords in their hands. They were around twenty. The inside view was also clear enough to see two women sitting on a rock. Tej Singh recognised them as Chandrakanta and Chapla but their faces were not clear.

Seeing Maharaja, the guards recognised him. One of them moved forward to hold the horse. Maharaja got down from the horse. The guards lighted two torches and in the light, Tej Singh saw the faces of Chandrakanta and Chapla clearly. Chandrakanta's face was getting pale, hair dishevelled and head injured. She was sitting on the ground leaning against a rock, stupefied and mud-stained and Chapla was sitting beside her leaning against the rock with her hand on Chandrakanta's head. Some food items were kept before them from which it seemed that they had not been touched. Their eyes seemed so hopeless that they moved Tej Singh to tears.

As Maharaja came, he looked here and there and also where Chandrakanta was sitting. He looked all around but he could not find anything of his purpose because he had come in search of the queen. He was pinning his hope on the note that he had found from the bed of the queen but to no avail. He didn't ask anything from anybody. He didn't even look at Chandrakanta properly and turning back then rode off to the palace. The guards were surprised at his sudden arrival and departure in this manner but who could ask him? No one dared. When Tej Singh saw Maharaja turning back, he thought of hiding there, but he could not hide himself because the canal was narrow and there was no way to climb it up. Ultimately, he had to come out of the canal. He ran out of the canal before Maharaja and hid himself on one side. Maharaja came out of it and left for the city.

Now Tej Singh began to think how to rescue Chandrakanta and Chapla alone from here. "It's not the right time to fight but what to do? If I go there, disguised as Maharaja and do something, it won't be right because Maharaja has just left from here. If I apply some other trick and it does not work, the enemy will come to know of it and shift Chandrakanta to a different place. Then it will become more difficult. It's better that I go back to Kumar and bring some men from there because it won't be proper to go alone through this canal and attack the guards."

Thinking like this, Tej Singh moved to Vijaygarh. He continued walking for the whole night and next day at noon, he came to Virendra Singh. Kumar hugged him and anxiously asked, "Did you get something?" Kumar felt elated at his reply 'Yes'. He dispersed everyone. Only Devi Singh, Fateh Singh Commander and Tej Singh remained there. Kumar asked him to narrate the whole development. Tej Singh related everything and said, "Had it been to rescue someone else, I would have played my trick. If it had gone wrong, I would have escaped. But it was the case of Chandrakanta who is very tender. Neither I can bundle her with my own hands nor I can think of inflicting any pain on her. Our attempt shouldn't go waste. I have just come to take along Devi Singh and I will return just now. I know that you have defeated Maharaja Shivdutt. There won't be any problem to you in the absence of Devi Singh." Kumar said, "Devi Singh should go and I will also go with you because the battle is not going on here and in any way Fateh Singh is here. There won't be any problem." Tej Singh replied, "Okay, you too come along." Hearing this, Kumar got ready in a moment. He gave necessary instructions to Fateh Singh and by the evening, he set out. Kumar was riding the horse. Tej Singh and Devi Singh were walking on foot. On the way, Kumar narrated the whole story of his victory over Shivdutt and also about the masked cavaliers who helped them at the very right moment.

It was a moon-lit night. The path was clearly visible. They had travelled about 8 kilometres when they saw on the way Pundit Badrinath alone. He too saw Kumar and saluted him as he came near. Kumar laughed in reply. Devi Singh said to Badrinath, "Why are you on the side of that coward, traitor and thief. Come to our court and see how lion-hearted and fair is our leader!" Badrinath answered, "You are very much right and one day it would be possible but as long as I don't settle the matter with Maharaja Shivdutt, how can I side with you and even if I do, will you people trust me! After all, I am also an *aiyar!*" Having said this and saluted Kumar, he quickly took another route to a dense forest and disappeared. Tej Singh said to Kumar, "This encounter with Badrinath on our journey is not good. Now he will certainly be on the lookout for where we are going." Devi Singh added, "Yes it is undoubtedly a bad beginning." At this, Kumar's heartbeat shot up and he said, "What should we do now?" Tej Singh advised, "At this time, no other plan can work. Of course, we should give up the jungle trail and move through open plains. This will help us see if someone is following us." Kumar said, "Okay, you lead us."

Now they moved from the jungle to the plain and kept looking back to see if someone was following them. For the whole night, they kept on walking smoothly. At dawn, they relieved themselves near the canal and performed the morning rituals and again set out. By the first quarter of the day, they reached a big forest from where that canal, which led to the cave where Chandrakanta and Chapla were kept, was just 4 kilometres away. Tej Singh said, "We should spend the day in this forest and move forward in the evening because it would be better to operate at night." They took shelter under a huge teak tree. For Kumar, they laid out a saddle cloth and they put a long rope around the neck of the horse and tied it to a tree so that it could graze grass easily. The whole day passed off in talks and planning. When the sun set, they resumed their journey. In a short while, they reached that canal. First, they stood on their toes and looked around. When they heard no one's footsteps, then they entered into the canal which is looking like a tunnel.

Kumar was surprised to see this canal and exclaimed, "How terrible!" Slowly they moved forward. When they reached the other end of the canal where Tej Singh had seen candles burning, they saw complete darkness there. Tej Singh felt a sudden anxiety over this new turn. At last, they reached the gate of the cave where Kumari and Chapla were kept. They saw several men lying senseless on the ground. Now Tej Singh took out something from his bag and lighted it, which made it clear that all the guards which he had seen earlier were lying dead. They entered into the cave and found Kumari and Chapla missing from there; of course, their ornaments were lying there in pieces and the place was blood-stained. Kumar couldn't bear it. He fell on the ground saying 'Alas!' and started weeping. Tej Singh consoled him, "Why are you so desperate! God who brought us here will take us to Kumari also." Kumar sobbed, "Brother, now I have lost all hope of meeting Chandrakanta. She must have died." Tej Singh, "Never, had it been so she too would have been lying among them." Devi Singh added, "I think Badrinath has played his game." Tej Singh replied, "It doesn't seem true. Even if we take it for granted that Badrinath has played his game, who killed these guards. It is very strange. I am unable to comprehend anything. Anyway, there is no problem; this mystery will also be revealed. Now we must leave this place."

It's better not to describe Kunwar Virendra Singh's condition. Having consoled him a lot, they carried him out of the canal. Devi Singh made a point, "We should rush to the place where you have kept Shivdutt's queen." Tej Singh said, "Let's go." All three went there and saw that queen Kalawati was not there. This added to their anxiety.

It was more than midnight. They sat thinking what went wrong. All of a sudden, Devi Singh said, "*Guruji*, I have got an idea which will help me solve this case. You just wait here, I am going to investigate. If possible, I will bring the relevant proof also." Tej Singh said, "Go, you do some commendable job; we will be here in this jungle."

Devi Singh disguised himself as a rural pandit and set out. Chunar was not far from here; he reached there in a short time. He saw from a distance a soldier walking on patrol. He approached him with a phial and told him in vernacular showing a gold coin, "I will give you this coin if you tell me what this perfume is made of. I am from the countryside. A perfume-seller came and showing me this perfume, asked if you can recognise this perfume, I will give you 5 gold coins. I am a village folk, what do I know. What it is made of. So, overnight, I rushed here. By god's grace, I saw you. You are from the royal court. You must have seen so many perfumes. If you tell me about it, I will leave for my village just now. I have promised him to reply in the morning." He felt very happy to listen to Devi Singh and to see the gold coin in the light of the candle burning in a nearby shop. He thought in his heart what a fool he had come across. You are getting a gold coin for free, take it; whatever you feel, tell him. Will he come tomorrow to take it back? Thinking this, he took the gold coin and kept it in his pocket and said, "It's not a big issue, I will tell you." He opened the cap of the phial and smelled. What was left now, he fell flat on the ground as he sniffed. He lost his consciousness. Devi Singh tied him in a bundle and carried him to Tej Singh. He said, "He is the guard of the palace. We should first inquire from him. If it does not work, we will think of another plan." He brought that guard back to senses. He was amazed to see how he landed there. He saw Devi Singh as a village pundit standing there. On the other hand, he saw two more brave men. He wanted to say something when Devi Singh asked, "Tell us where your queen is? Hurry up." Even though his hands and legs were tied, he asked, "Who are you to ask about the queen? What do you have to do with it?" Tej Singh stood up and gave a kick saying, "Will you tell or question me!" He started speaking, "Maharani has been missing for several days. She is traceless. There is uproar in the palace. I don't know more than this."

Tej Singh said to Kumar, "Now it will take several days to unravel the mystery. You should go to your army camp. I will engage myself in the search." Kumar replied, "Now I will not go to the camp." Tej Singh said "If you do so there would be great trouble. If Shivdutt comes to know of it, he will immediately resume the battle. Maharaja Jay Singh will be frightened to know of it and your father will wilt to learn it." Kumar insisted, "Whatever may come, when Chandrakanta is not alive, why should I care what goes in the world." Tej Singh persuaded him by all means that he should not behave like this. If he loses patience, they will also get disheartened, and won't be able to do anything. Ultimately, Kumar agreed, "Okay, let me stay with you till tomorrow. If she is not discovered by that time, I will go back to the army camp and will attack Chunar. I will wage a war and you look for Chandrakanta." Tej Singh said, "All right, it's done." All this happened so confidentially that the guard could not get a whisper of it.

Tej Singh fastened him tightly to a tree and said to Devi Singh, "You stay here with Kumar. I am going to collect information." Devi Singh replied, "Okay, first you go." Tej Singh asked several questions from Devi Singh and went to the palace in the guise of the guard.

□

8

The jungle in which Kumar and Devi Singh were sitting was very dense. It was not easily accessible to anyone. Kumar and Devi Singh were sitting on a clean rock and talking. It was getting morning when someone threw a pebble from the west that dropped near Kumar. They turned to that direction in surprise. At that very moment, another pebble landed there, though it didn't hurt anyone. Devi Singh shouted loudly, "Who is throwing stone stealthily; why don't you come out?" A voice came and replied, "The jackals who speak in the language of lion are killed from a distance." On hearing it, Kumar flew into anger. He immediately clutched the hilt of the sword and rose to his feet. Devi Singh, holding his hand, said, "I am going to arrest and fetch him here just now. What is he?" Saying this, he went in the direction of the voice. As he moved forward, one more pebble was thrown. Devi Singh quickly followed. He saw a man but because of darkness in the dense forest, he couldn't see his face. Having seen Devi Singh coming towards him, he threw one more pebble at him and ran away. Devi Singh ran after him but he disappeared in those dense trees circling here and there several times like a fox. Devi Singh began searching for him here and there. The night went by and it became a sunny day but there was no trace of that man. Ultimately, having lost hope, Devi Singh returned to the place where he had left Kumar. He saw Kumar missing from there. He looked around but could not find him. He rushed to that soldier whom he had tied to a tree but he was also not there. He got unnerved and his eyes were filled with tears. He sat on the rock holding his hand on the head and began thinking, "Now what to do, where to search, where to go? If I move far away while searching for him and if Tej Singh comes and doesn't find me, what will befall him?" Having taken all this into consideration and looking around for a while, he came back to the original place and kept waiting for Tej Singh. In between, he rose to his feet and went around searching several times but to no avail.

□

9

Tej Singh in the guise of that guard reached the gate of the palace. The guards on duty there saw Tej Singh coming and asked, "Jay Ram Singh, where had you gone? Some disturbances were reported in the security here. Badrinath ji had come on inspection. He was deeply annoyed to learn that you had gone somewhere and he himself went to look for you. He hasn't come yet. It is for you that he expressed his annoyance on us." Tej Singh replied, "I fell ill. My bowel was upset, so I went to the field. I had several motions, so I got late. Again I am having bowel movement. Brother, life is first and foremost. Whether one is annoyed or pleased, the call of nature cannot be ignored. I am going again. I will be back in a while." Having said this, the duplicate Jay Ram Singh escaped from there.

Through this talk with the guards, Tej Singh learnt that Badrinath came there and had gone in his search. So, he got alert. He thought if Badrinath came while he was there, he would recognise him. That way it was not good for him to stay there. Ultimately, after going some distance, he changed himself into a beggar and sat by the side of a road waiting for Badrinath to return. After some time, he saw Badrinath coming there followed by Nazim, carrying a bundle on his back. He was followed by the same guard in whose costume Tej Singh had come there.

Tej Singh was surprised to see Badrinath coming in that style. He thought in his heart that it was not a good sign. I had tied this guard to a tree who is trailing behind them." Kumar and Devi Singh were also sitting there. Without making some trouble, they could not have got hold of this guard. Certainly, something went wrong there. Nazim must be carrying in his bundle either Kumar or Devi Singh, but it's not the time to intervene because there is none to help me here. Keeping this in mind, Tej Singh kept sitting silently there. When they went inside the palace with the bundle, Tej Singh made his way in the direction which he had left Kumar and Devi Singh behind. Devi Singh was sadly sitting there on the rock and thinking. Tej Singh reached there. Seeing him, Devi Singh ran to him and fell at his feet and spoke in frustration, "*Guruji*, Kumar got into the hands of the enemy."

Tej Singh sat on the rock and said, "Anyway, tell me clearly what happened." Devi Singh narrated the whole incident. Tej Singh commented, "See, nowadays our star is running in rough weather. I have challenges on all fronts but what to do. On the one hand, Chandrakanta and Chapla are in deep trouble. I don't know in what condition they are. I was worried about them and now Kumar is trapped." For some time, both Devi Singh and Tej Singh kept talking and then they stood up and moved in a particular direction.

□

10

Virendra Singh, in mournful mood, is sitting, leaning against the door in which iron bars are fitted. The room is inside a special palace of Maharaja Shivdutt in the fort of Chunar. Virendra Singh is handcuffed and his feet are fettered. Several women on guard having daggers tucked in their waist are moving around. Kumar is murmuring, "Alas! We learnt about Chandrakanta but it's of no use. First we discovered that she was kidnapped by Shivdutt but what to say now, where to go! O Chandrakanta! where are you? These fetters and prison do not trouble me as much as your abduction. Alas! If I am convinced that you are safe and have reached your parents, I will be happy to die in this captivity without food and water. But as long as you are not traced, this life seems a nightmare. Oh! What would be your condition, where should I search! This shackle at this time seems to me like salt rubbed on a wound. How much better it would have been had I been wandering in search of Kumari from forest to forest, thorns pricked in the feet, feet bleeding, deprived of food and water. Oh God! You did nothing. You should have taken into account my courage on the path of love, how strong I am. You have crippled me. Alas! You have given me birth and every comfort. Do you feel pleasure in giving me pain and misery?"

While prattling like this, tears from Kumar Virendra Singh's eyes were rolling down his cheeks and he was heaving. It was about midnight. The room in which he was imprisoned had a decorated courtyard in front of it where four or five candles were burning. When Kumar got very upset, he lifted his head and looked up in that direction. At one time, 5 to 7 maid-servants came in from one side and lighted several candles in multi-shaped glasswares, creating a day like brightness. Thereafter, in the centre of the courtyard, a precious mattress was spread and all maid-servants stood looking towards the gate as if they were waiting for someone to come. Kumar was looking at them intently because he was very much surprised to think why he was kept at a place inside a palace where men were not allowed in and what Maharaja Shivdutt was going to gain from it!

After a while, Maharaja Shivdutt was seen coming there with great pomp. Virendra Singh was astonished to see it. He was puzzled, kept watching fixedly. He saw Chandrakanta on the right side of Shivdutt and Chapla on the left walking slowly hand in hand and sat on the mattress which was laid out in the centre. Chandrakanta and Chapla sat on either side of Maharaja in close physical contact. Chandrakanta and Kumar have been close since childhood but today the beauty and elegance of Chandrakanta were so exuberant that Kumar had never seen it before. Betel leaf-box, perfume pot and other luxury items were placed before her.

Seeing this, blood shot into his eyes and he thought, "What is this! Chandrakanta is so happily sitting beside Shivdutt and showing romantic gestures. What's the matter? Love for me is vanished from her heart and love for parents has also evaporated and that too she is doing all this before me. Does she not know that I am lying as a captive in this room before her? She must be knowing. Just look! She is looking sidelong at me and grimacing. Along with her, what has happened to this Chapla who was in love with Tej Singh and who put her life at stake to rescue Tej Singh from Maharaja Shivdutt's captivity? At that time, she didn't fall in love with Shivdutt and today she is sitting like this beside him at par with Chandrakanta, her mistress.

Oh God! Women are unpredictable; it's a blunder to rely on them. Alas! Have I been destined to fall in love with such a woman! A girl of such a great lineage and so mean act! Alas! Now my life is worthless I will certainly shed my life. But should I leave Chandrakanta and Chapla alive for Shivdutt? Never. It's true that brave men do not raise their hand against women but now I don't have to show my bravery. I don't have to stand before anyone in the world. So, I need not think about all this. Now it is better that I should kill these two women and then commit suicide. Tej Singh will certainly stand by me. Let us fix this trouble once and for all.

In the meanwhile, Chandrakanta put her hand around Maharaja Shivdutt's neck flirtatiously. Virendra Singh could not bear it. He broke the handcuff with a strong jolt. In the same enthusiasm, he kicked open the door and dashed to Shivdutt. He grabbed the sword lying there, drew it and slashed Chandrakanta's head. The head fell apart and the body started throbbing. Before Maharaja Shivdutt could recover, he cut Chapla into two pieces but did not attack him.

Maharaja Shivdutt got up but this sudden spurt of force and agility in Kumar unnerved him. He could not even utter a word. His whole manliness vanished. He kept standing and staring at Kumar.

When Kumar was standing with a blood-dipped naked sword in his hand, Tej Singh and Devi Singh appeared before him with a thud. Tej Singh called out, "Well done, bravo! Nicely controlled yourself." After having said this, he quickly put his lasso around Maharaja Shivdutt's neck and pulled him down. Shivdutt was already getting worse. As his throat choked, he fell down on the ground. Devi Singh hurriedly tied him in a bundle and put him on his back. Turning to Kumar, Tej Singh said, "Come along with me. Don't talk anything else. I know well your condition at this time." At that time, there was no man except the maid servants. Having seen this kind of bloodshed, some of them fell unconscious and the rest kept mum, just staring with a fixed gaze and these people made their way.

□

11

Kumar's mood changed. He got rid of the thoughts he was gripped with. The concern for parents, the thought of Vijaygarh, craze for battle, friendship with Tej Singh have all disappeared with the death of Chandrakanta and Chapla. All three came out of the fort. Devi Singh carrying the bundle of Shivdutt was marching ahead, keeping Kumar in the middle followed by Tej Singh. Kumar was oblivious of where he was going. By evening, they reached in a dense forest where on Tej Singh's command Devi Singh put down the bundle and cleaned a rock with his shawl for Kumar to sit, but he kept standing, staring at the ground stupefied.

Tej Singh felt flustered to see such condition of Kumar. He was thinking how he will survive. Strange is his condition. His face has turned pale, body senseless and eyelids motionless and pupils of the eyes transfixed in the ground. What has happened! Has he too died along with Chandrakanta! Why is he standing! Tej Singh forced him to sit down by pulling his hand but his knee did not bend and fell flat on the ground, head got injured and started bleeding but his eyelids remained wide open, pupils motionless and breathing intermittent.

Now Tej Singh lost hope of Kumar's life. He tried to control himself but burst out weeping. Seeing this, Devi Singh too couldn't help joining Tej Singh. While weeping, Tej Singh called out, "Alas! Kumar, have you really left this world! Alas! Under what influence of evil spirit you fell in love with Chandrakanta whose consequence is this? Now I come to realise that this was the length of your life". While Tej Singh was crying like this, a resounding voice came from a side: "No, Kumar's life is not short. He has a long life. No one is born in this earth who can kill him. His love for Chandrakanta didn't take place under evil influence, rather it was an auspicious occasion and its result would be fabulous. He will be married to Kumari and will rule over Chunar. Not only this, he will also conquer some other states. He will have two brave sons from Chandrakanta who will be more gifted and will earn greater name. What is it that you are wailing for?"

Tej Singh and Devi Singh stopped crying and looked here and there. Tej Singh thought, "Ah! Who is he! Who has spoken these words which can breathe life into the dead! What words! Who is there to kill Kumar! Kumar will have two brave sons! How pleasantly strange! Here Kumar is breathing his last. We must find out who he is!" Tej Singh and Devi Singh started looking around but couldn't find anything. A voice came again, "Look here!" Tej Singh looked straight towards the voice and saw Pundit Jagannath, the astrologer, climbing down the tree.

Pundit Jagannath came close to Tej Singh and said, "Don't be surprised. These good words are mine. It need not be thought why I am talking in favour of you despite being loyal to Maharaja Shivdutt. You will come to know shortly the reason behind it and you will treat me as your true friend. First, we will treat Kumar and then we will talk."

Pundit Jagannath in the presence of Tej Singh and Devi Singh searched the herb and plucked it. Its leaves were triangle-shaped and flowers were sky blue and stalk was white in colour with rough scale. He smashed the herb in his palm and put two drops of juice into his eyes and ears and put the dregs on his palette. He tore a piece from his shawl and bandaged his injured head and sat waiting for his recovery.

Within half-an-hour, the colour of Kumar's eye started changing, eyelids dropped down to cover the eyeballs, gradually his limbs began showing movements, he sneezed twice or thrice and with this, he came back to his senses and sat down. Having seen Pundit Jagannath along with Tej Singh and Devi Singh sitting around him, he asked, "What had happened to me?" Tej Singh narrated the whole thing. Kumar prostrated before Pundit Jagannath and said, "Maharaja, why have you shown so much grace on me? Tell me, I am getting suspicious."

Pundit Jagannath said, "Kumar, it's all the *Maya of God*. Now I want to live with you. Maharaja Shivdutt is not worth sacrificing my life for him. He is not the connoisseur of men, not the admirer of the wise. Living with him is like spoiling one's merit. He never admires the virtue of a virtuous man. He is very much selfish. If someone commits a mistake, he immediately turns against him, however virtuous he may be. Besides this, he is a very wicked person. No righteous person would like to live with such a man. That's why, I have turned away from him. If I work for someone, I will work for you. I haven't seen an admirer like you. I have been looking for the right opportunity for several days to prove my genuineness and become your friend because howsoever I may plead, it is difficult to win confidence of other *aiyars*. Today I got this opportunity because it was the day of dire misfortune for you which was brought to you by the deceit and cunningness of Maharaja Shivdutt." Having said this, he turned silent.

The last statement of Pundit Jagannath astonished them. All three came closer to him. Tej Singh said, "Yes, Jyotishi ji, tell us openly why did Shivdutt deceive us?" Jyotishi ji said, "It is the rule of Maharaja Shivdutt that whenever he wants to do something big, he consults me. Whether I advise him for or against the plan, he follows his own dictate and meets disappointment as well. On several occasions, Pundit Badrinath also felt annoyed that when you have to do of your own liking, why you ask Jyotishi ji. Tonight what trick he played on you I had objected to it, but he didn't pay heed to it. And the result — Ghasita Singh and Bhagwandutt lost their lives. I will narrate the whole story openly only when you promise that you will keep me in your fold as an *aiyar* or a friend." Having heard this, Kumar looked at Tej Singh. Tej Singh said, "Jyotishi ji, I would be very happy to have you in my fold but first you will have to take pledge of your genuineness."

To dispel doubts from the mind of Tej Singh, Jyotishi ji held his sacred thread in his hand and took oath of his righteousness. Tej Singh got up and hugged him and inducted him into his fold. Kumar took out a costly string of pearls and put it around his neck. Jyotishi ji said, "Now listen from me why Kumar was locked up inside the palace and the reality behind the bloodshed last night."

"When you left from your army camp in search of Kumari, Badrinath spotted you on the way. So, he reached there before you to shift Chandrakanta to a different place. When he entered into that cave, he saw that Kumari was missing from there and he returned empty, handed. Then taking along Nazim, he left in search of you and finding you there in the jungle where he played his *aiyari*. It was Nazim who was throwing pebbles and Devi Singh chasing him by then Badrinath who was already there to disguise as Tej Singh made Kumar unconscious, I don't know how, and took him to the palace with the sole intention to eliminate his love for Chandrakanta from his heart, so that he should neither look for her nor fight against Shivdutt. That's why, Bhagwandutt and Ghasita Singh who are of our age were made Chandrakanta and Chapla whom you killed and rest of the story you know well."

Hearing his talk, Kumar jumped into ecstasy. He said, "Alas! What a terrible design it was! What a treachery! Now I have learnt that Chandrakanta is alive but I don't know where she is. Anyway, it will be known, too."

They all made a serious deliberation on the situation and resolved to take following actions: 1. Maharaja Shivdutt should be locked in the cave where *aiyars* were kept earlier and double lock should be put in because the secret of first lock that opens by pulling out the tongue from the mouth of the lion was revealed to Pundit Badrinath. But the secret of second lock was known to none except Tej Singh. 2. Kumar will go to Vijaygarh because as long as Maharaja Shivdutt is in his custody, war will not resume. However, for security purposes, some forces should be retained on the border. 3. Devi Singh should accompany Kumar and live with him. 4. Tej Singh and Jyotishi ji should go on in search of Kumari.

Subsequently, they dispersed for their assigned jobs.

□

12

At noon, two girls were sitting on a clean rock by the side of a watercourse. Both of them were wearing dirty, torn saree; their mouth smeared with soil, open hair lock, very dusty feet, bewildered and troubled faces. It was a fearsome forest all around, the sound of wild animals was coming. Whenever the wind blew forcefully, the rustle of trees made the forest even more fearsome.

Before these two girls on the other side of the watercourse, a leopard came down to drink water. They saw the leopard but it could not see them because they were sitting behind a thick rose-apple tree.

One of them who was more tender got scared to see the leopard and whispered to the other, "Dear friend, see if it does not come across this side." She said, "No friend, it will not come across and if it tries to come, I will shoot it with these arrows which I have seized from the guards on the watercourse whom I killed. We have two hundred arrows and we both are archers. Take an arrow and mount it on your bow strength." Both got ready with their bows but it did not warrant. The leopard having taken water climbed up the hill and disappeared before them. Thereafter, they began talking like this:

One – Chapla, "Do you recognise where we have come to, which forest is this and which way leads to Vijaygarh?"

Chapla – Kumari, "I am unable to identify it. Rather driven by the urgue to run away, I don't know in which direction I have come. I don't know where Vijaygarh is, where did I leave behind Chunar and what is the route to Naugarh? I spent my life living with you in the palace or wandering within the area of Vijaygarh. I have never been to these forests. Of course, I know the straight route from Chunar to Vijaygarh. But I did not take that route as the enemy forces nowadays are camping there. So, I took a jungle route lest we should be spotted by someone. Anyway,

God is almighty, one or another route will be discovered. I have some dry fruits in my pouch, take them and have some water; then we will see what to do.

Kumari, "Leave it for some other time. Who knows for how many days we have to suffer! It's a very dense forest. Let us pluck some plum and gooseberry and eat; though it does not sound well, but we have to bear it."

Chapla, "As you wish."

Both Chapla and Chandrakanta stood up and went up to the ridge of the watercourse and started strolling here and there. Strolling under the shed of trees and plucking and eating wild plums, they reached near a deserted, dilapidated building by afternoon. It seemed to have been built by some great king but now it was in a worn-out condition. Chapla said to Chandrakanta, "Sister, you sit at this broken gate of the building. I am going to have some fruits, then we will sit here and eat together. Thereafter, we will enter the building and see how it is. As long as we do not find the route to Vijaygarh, this ruined building will be our refuge. We will bear with it. When a traveller or a herdsman passes through it, we will ask the route to Vijaygarh and then we will move."

"It's okay. I am sitting here. You go and pluck some fruits, but don't go far."

"I won't go far. I will be here within your view". Saying this she went to pluck fruits.

□

13

Chandrakanta was sitting alone there and getting nervous. She thought while Chapla was plucking fruits, she should have a look at this ruined castle because however dilapidated it may be, it seems to have its own unparalleled glory in the past.

She got up and went inside. The entrance was intact and strong, though the door was missing. However, a visitor would say that there must have been a wooden or iron gate at this entrance.

Kumari saw that it was a huge rectangular building. The central structure was worn out but the enclosed space around it seemed intact. She moved forward and reached the gallery. The roof was broken but the pillars were standing. Piles of stones were strewn here and there on which she was walking slowly. There was a field in the middle of it. Kumari began to see attentively. It clearly seemed that earlier it was a garden because beds of marble still existed. Small watercourses which might have been used to sprinkle water were still safe. Many fountains were seen out of order. They were covered with a sheet of soil. A huge crane of stone was seen in the centre of the garden. Kumari inched forward to observe it closely, to see its artistry and its finish. She began praising the artist who had made it. The crane was made of white marble and placed on a waist-length large pillar of black granite. Its legs were not seen. It seemed as if it was sitting on the pillar with its belly. The circumference of its belly would be not less than 30 feet. Its long beak and wings were made with such fine artistry that she could not help praising the artist repeatedly. She was tempted to see the crane from a closer distance. She drew near it. As she reached there, the crane opened its mouth. She got scared to see it and hurriedly turned aside. Now the crane spread out its wings.

Chapla had made her very bold. Sometimes when the context demanded, Chapla used to say that there are no ghosts and spirits in this world, magic and mantras are all stories, whatsoever it is, it is *aiyari*. Kumari has also come to believe this. That is why, when the crane opened its mouth and spread out its wings, she did not run away in fright. Had any other tender woman come across this situation, she might have died of fear. When she saw the crane spreading its wings, she turned back. There was a rock behind the crane on which she incidentally put her foot. As she put her foot, the crane shook once and quickly turning to Kumari swallowed her in mouth and turned back to its position, rolled up its wings and shut its mouth.

□

14

In a short while, Chapla came back with a basket full of fruits. She saw that Chandrakanta was not there. She looked around, but she was nowhere. She wondered if she had gone to that ruined house. She went in keeping this in mind. Kumari had gone there unhesitantly but Chapla was taking steps cautiously looking around carefully and examining everything. As she entered into the gate where she saw verandas on both sides there were piles of bricks and stones and at some places roof was broken but paintings on the wall and statues of stones were looking new.

Chapla looked at the statues with surprise; none of the statues was in full body. Some didn't have the heads while some were without legs. In some, hands were amputated, while, in some others, upper part of the body was missing. The faces of these statues were strangely dreadful. As she moved forward, she saw heaps of clays and stones on which wild plants had grown up. While having passed through them, she reached near the field and saw from a distance the crane which had swallowed Kumari.

She stopped looking around and rushed straight to that crane. The crane opened its mouth. Chapla was amazed, she retreated. The crane closed its mouth. She thought what to do now? It looks to be a work of great *aiyari*. Its secret must be discovered. This ruined place seems to be an old *tilism*. 'First I must find out Kumari, lest she should have been trapped in it'. Keeping this in mind, she moved from there and started looking for elsewhere.

It was enclosed by boundary wall from all sides. There were several verandas and dilapidated rooms and few rooms were intact as well. She started looking into them from one side. First she reached in a veranda measuring eighty meters in length, and roof was broken in the middle. There was a pile of clay and lime in the centre, so many bones were strewn around, and there were cobwebs and dust all around. Many small plants of peepal and other trees had grown up on the pile of soil. She saw a small room on one side of the veranda. When she went in there, she found a well. It was pitch dark inside.

What is inside this well? Why this room seems cleaner than other places! The well, too, looks clean. Usually, in old wells, plants are overgrown which is not the case here. It sends out some inaudible sounds, as well. To discover it, she took out some lumps of camphor from her pouch of *aiyari,* lit it and then dropped in the well. They lighted the well and it became clearly visible that it was wider in circumference at the base and clean and dry. In place of water, a clean white bed was laid on which an old man was sitting. His beard seemed very long but his face was not visible as his head was bent. Before him, there was a wooden cot on which colourful flowers were kept. Chapla got scared to see this scene. Still she checked herself and sitting on the mouth of the well began contemplating but she felt at her wit's end. The pieces of camphor also burnt out and there was darkness once again.

There was a passage connecting that room to another veranda. Chapla took that route and reached there and witnessed a scene far more dreadful than this. It was superior to previous veranda in garbage and hips of bones which may be of donkeys. Crossing over them, she reached in the middle of the veranda.

She saw a marble platform of a man's length with nine beautiful steps to climb over it. A man was seen lying on a wooden cot on it. He seemed to be reading something from a book in his hand, but it was not seen clearly because of its height. She was thinking if she should climb up the platform or not. Will it cause any trouble? Should I put my foot on the stairs? Thinking this, she put her foot on the marble slab of a step. It resulted into an explosion of sound and the marble slab opened like a box throwing her away on the ground with a jerk. She got up regaining her balance and saw that the marble slab that had opened up like a box came back to its original position.

Chapla began thinking while standing aside that "this dilapidated building is a strange spectacle. It must have been built by some great *aiyar*. It is difficult to stroll in this building; a little mistake can take one's life. But I have nothing to worry as Chandrakanta who is precious than my life is somewhere trapped in this building. It is very important to find her out. No matter if I lose my life, I will never go away from here without finding her out. Let me see what sorts of *aiyari* have been done in this stair and platform." Having thought for some time, she put a slab of nine kg on the stair. As this stair had thrown away her foot, it threw away the slab with a resounding thud.

Chapla tried putting a slab on each step, and each time it repeated the same miracle. What is there on the platform must be examined. While having this thought, she started working on a different plan. She gathered lots of bricks and stones near the platform and ascended on them. She saw that a man of around thirty years was lying with a book in his hands on a marble seat. On close examination, she discovered that the man was a marble statue. When Chapla put a small pebble in his mouth, the statue behaved like a human being. It removed the pebble with his hand and brought it back to the same position. Thereafter, Chapla put a pebble on its foot, which it dropped by shaking its leg. Though Chapla was very clever and bold, the miraculous spectacle of this statue frightened her and she quickly turned away. Now she moved to another direction. She reached yet another veranda adjacent to it and noticed an underground room in the middle of the veranda. There was a staircase to climb down and a double panel door in the front which was open at that time.

Chapla thought while standing there if she should go inside or not. She was worried if the door was closed behind her when she went down the cellar and she might get stuck in it. So, she thought it better to test it first by throwing into it a flat piece of stone. If it closes by the entry of a man, it will certainly shut up when the stone piece falls in. Then it would be difficult to examine it by going inside it. Therefore, something should be done to obstruct the closure of the door or better the gate should be broken apart if possible.

Chapla went to the door and tried to break apart the gate but she couldn't because the panels of the door were made of iron. They were not hinge-based, rather the pivots in the centres of the planks were fixed deep in the ground.

Chapla unfastened the lasso from her waist, made it fourfold and tied its one end tightly with the door-plank and another end with a pillar in the same veranda near the door. Then she threw a slab of stone from a distance. As the slab dropped in the cellar, a peculiar sound started emanating as if the wind was blowing powerfully from a furnace. At the same time, one panel of the door shut suddenly, another also got pulled in but could not break loose from the lasso with which it was tied. It remained stretched ajar. Chapla thought, "No problem. I learnt that this lasso will not allow the door to shut. Now I should step inside it fearlessly and see what happens." With this resolve, she entered the underground room.

□

15

Champa was not sitting idle. She too had come out of her home in search of Kumari. When so many days lapsed and there was no trace of Chandrakanta, she took orders from the queen and set out. She went on tracking from forest to forest and mountain to mountain, but could not locate her. Tired of several days' journey, she sat under a tree in the forest, thinking now where to go, where to search for her because she had promised the queen that without consulting Virendra Singh and Tej Singh, she would discover Kumari. But no expectation was fulfilled by now and without accomplishing the job, she would not go back to Vijaygarh. What might come, she would not deter.

While Champa was sitting under a tree, four men in uniform were seen coming towards her. They were equipped with sword and shield and carrying a short sword in their hands.

Looking at Champa, they talked something among themselves, which she could not overhear as she was at a distance, but she kept gazing at their faces. Sometimes they looked towards Champa, sometimes they talked and laughed among themselves, while at others, they looked back standing on their toes. It seemed they were waiting for someone. In a short while, they drew near her from all four sides and sat down behind the trees.

Champa got alert thinking who they were, why they had surrounded her and what was their intention. "I should not stay here." She got up and took her way but they did not let her go. They surrounded her and said, "Where are you going? Wait. Our master is coming here shortly. Wait till he comes. We will take you to him and request him to keep you as a servant. You will be happy there. How long will you be wandering in the forest!"

"Since I don't need a job, I need not wait for your master to come. I can't stay back."

"No, No. Don't be in a hurry. Wait. You will be happy to see our lord. You would never have seen such a handsome youth. Rather, we will try to get you married to him."

"Be in your senses while talking or else I will set you right. Don't treat me like a lonely woman. I can deal with ten men like you."

They were amazed at it. They looked up to one another's face. Champa proceeded again. One of them caught her hand. What was left then? Champa quickly drew her dagger and wounded two of them and ran away. The rest two men chased her but she escaped.

Though Champa ran away, her feet did not support her. She stumbled against a stone and fell down. She was so heavily wounded that she could not get up. In the meanwhile, the two chasers reached there. Before they could utter a word, they saw a convoy of around 200 merchants coming there. They were led by an old man with long white beard, having black complexion, brown eyes and about eighty years old. Clad in costly attire wearing sword and shield and a spear in hand, he was riding a dark baby horse along with a young man of not more than 20 years who was riding a Nepalese chariot (tangan) with great pomp. In beauty and dress, he looked like a prince. They were escorted by a number of cavaliers and some foot soldiers and at the end, their stores and tents were being carried on some camels. There were a few palanquins too, which were surrounded by guards wielding match lock guns. The two men who chased Champa shouted at the top of their voice, "This woman has wounded our two men....!" Before they could say anything, some men surrounded Champa, seized her dagger and handcuffed her.

That old cavalier, about whom we can say that he would be the chief of the convoy, pointing to one or two of his men said, "We will pitch our tent in this jungle. It seems to be a less-troden area because there is no track visible on the ground."

The tent was pitched and in a small ridge tent-captive women who were being carried on palanquins were kept. Hapless Champa was also thrown among them. When the sunset, a candle was lit in that small ridge tent. Two maid-servants came there and asked the women if they would cook their food themselves or would they have readymade food. They replied, "We will have readymade food." But two of them said, "We will not eat anything." The two maid-servants went away saying in reply, "See how long you remain on fast." One of them was Champa herself and another one was a very tender and beautiful woman, who continued weeping and sighing intermittently. Champa was sitting near her. First quarter of the night went by; dinner was served to all except the two who had refused. After midnight, silence dawned. Only the footsteps around the tent were heard. Champa understood that the guards were moving around the tents. Champa started talking to her in low voice. Champa said,"Who are you and how did you fall into their hands?" Woman said, "My name is Kalavati. I am the wife of Maharaja Shivdutt. When Maharaja went on war, I was sleeping on the ground in pangs of his separation. I don't know anything. When my eyes opened, I saw myself in their custody. What else should I say? Sister, who are you?"

"Oh! You are the queen of Chunar! In this condition! Oh God, you are gracious! What should I say? If you are the wife of Maharaja Shivdutt you must be knowing Chandrakanta. I am her friend. I was wandering in search of her when they captured me."

While they were talking to each other in low tone, a voice was heard from outside – "Who is there? Run away, run away, escape." Maharani was scared but Champa remained unaffected. The whole night passed away in talks. Neither of them slept. It was getting morning when the two maid-servants wielding swords in their hands came there and said, "Come, one by one you go to toilet in the field." Other women went out but Champa and Maharani remained seated there. No one insisted on it. When the day ascended to its first quarter, the old chief of the convoy reached there along with an old woman. The old woman said, "Is this all or there are still more?" Chief said, "At this time, this is all. If you are in favour, we will have more." The old woman said, "You just see how many women I bring. Yes, now tell me how much will I get for each type of woman?"

Chief said, "See, they all are of one type. This type of woman will fetch 10 rupees. (Pointing to Champa) If you bring this type of woman, you will get 50 rupees. (Pointing to Maharani) If they are so beautiful, you will get complete 100 rupees. Understand?"

Old woman said, "Yes, I got it. How did you get them?"

Chief said, "This, who is the most beautiful was found in a cave. She was lying unconscious and this (Champa) was caught at this place itself. She had killed my two men. She is very wicked."

Old woman said, "Her wickedness pips from her face. If three or four such women come here, your convoy will go to heaven."

Chief said, "There is no doubt about it! And these women, they have been caught from different places in different manners. One is from Bengal. My lad started living in her neighbourhood and trapped her in his love affair. These four have landed here for lust of money and the rest I have bought from their mother, grand-maternal mother or their successors. Now let us come, we will talk in our tent. I am an old man. I can't keep standing for so long."

Old woman said, "Come."

When they left from there, the women abused them a lot, "Look at this wretched. She is planning to trap even more women. I don't know from where he got this old woman. She looks devil. She says, "See, how many women I trap." Oh God, are you kind towards them also? No one knows how many houses this witch will ruin!" Champa looked to that old woman very attentively and then kept thinking for half-an-hour, but Maharani kept weeping — "Alas! What will be the condition of Maharaja in the war, how will he be, how sad he will be calling me to mind!" She murmured this while weeping.

Champa consoled her, "Maharani, hold on, don't lose heart. I am confident, if God wills, we will be released very soon! What can I do? I am handcuffed. If somehow my hands are freed, I will give them a taste of their villainy. I am helpless as these fetters cannot be opened; they can only be cut asunder which is very difficult here."

This is how they spent their day wailing and sobbing. Evening came. The old chief again came to that ridge tent where women were kept. He was accompanied by the same old witch, the bundle of trouble, and a young beautiful woman.

The old woman said, "Compare her. Is she number one or not?"

Chief said, "She is not number one but certainly number two. You opened your account with fifty rupees today. There is no doubt about it."

The old woman said, "Anyway, let it be fifty. Does it require any investment? Tomorrow again I will pick up someone. Come."

At that time, they were whispering very slowly. No one heard them but Champa guessed something by the movement of their lips. This new woman seemed very happy, her hands and feet were unfettered. She was immediately served food. She too savoured the whole food gleefully. She used to laugh and crack jokes to see other women dull and wailing. Champa thought aside, she is a terrible thing. She is unconcerned about her being trapped. There is something wrong in it.

□

16

The night passed away like last night. All women were sent to the field one by one with the maid-servants in the early morning to relieve themselves. Maharani and Champa did not go even today. Champa asked Maharani, "Have you eaten anything or not since you fell into their hands." She replied, "In the hope of meeting Maharaja, I am keeping myself alive by taking something in every second or third day. What can I do? Nothing is in my hand."

In a short while, two men came to the tent and informed them, "Both of you come out. Today it is the order of our Chief that all women are taken out to the field and seated under trees so that they can have open air of the field and their health is not affected in captivity." Saying this, they took them out. The women who had already been in the field were sitting under a fat and dense mahua tree. They, too, went there and sat down. Champa started looking around.

It might be mid-day. The same old woman, who had brought a woman yesterday, reached there with a young and more beautiful woman. The old Chief warmly welcomed her making her sit beside him and sent that young woman to the place where other women were sitting. Champa closely watched her. Ultimately, she broke her silence and looking up in the sky, said in code words, "*Mee samagata*. (I recognised you)." The new woman looked to her face. After a while, looking down to her toe and rubbing it with her hand, she said, "*Champkala chat men baaprophasa* (You will be alive if you keep mum)." Thereafter neither of them opened their mouth.

It was evening. All women reached the same ridge tent. At night, dinner was served. Everyone except Maharani and Champa took their food. The two women who were newly trapped enjoyed themselves.

It was late night, silence dawned and the tent was being patrolled all around. A candle was burning in their tent. All women were asleep, only four were awake – Maharani, Champa and the two new entrants. Champa, looking at the two, said, "*Kadaak mee teti, no se paro phesto*. (Break open my shackles or I will get you arrested by revealing your secret)." One of them replied, "*Timaye ko*? (What will happen to you!)." Then Champa said, "*Rani men sengi*. (I will side with the queen)."

They took out some sharp tools from their waistband and silently cut her handcuff and fetters. Now Champa was free and smiling.

It was midnight. Suddenly that tent was surrounded by a large number of men. The noise of uproar, "Kill! Capture!" was being heard. Gun-shot was also heard. All women were convinced that it was an attack of robbers and the fight was going on. There was commotion. Women in the tent were running helter-skelter. Maharani in panic started calling "Champa-Champa" but she could not locate Champa anywhere. The two newly inducted women reported, "It seems Champa has escaped. But you should not panic; they are your servants who have attacked. I am also your servant. Don't take me for woman. I am going to fetch a palanquin for you which will be ready somewhere around." With this they went out.

The outcry of men subsided on the three sides of the ridge tent in which women were kept. The fight was continuing only on the fourth side where so many tents were located. Two masked men came there with a palanquin and having made Maharani sit in it, they went away. The night passed off and the sky became clear. Champa and Maharani had already left but other women were sitting in the same ridge tent. Their faces had turned pale in panic. They were looking at one another's face. In the meantime, Pannalal, Ramnarayan and Chunnilal reached the door of the ridge tent with a palanquin which was curtained with gold-embroidered satin cloth. They put down the palanquin outside the tent and went in and began properly observing all women and asked, "Two women from among you are not seen. Where have they gone?"

Every woman was scared. No one was telling anything. Panalal retreated, "You shouldn't be afraid. We are not robbers. This attack was carried out just to get you released. Tell where those women are?" Now they felt a bit relieved. One of them said, "Not two but four women are missing, of which two women were captured yesterday and day before yesterday. They went out after telling a woman that she should not be afraid. We are your servant. We are bringing a palanquin, then we will take you. Thereafter, a palanquin was brought, sitting in which she went away. The fourth had escaped first of all."

Pannalal lost his wits; he looked at Ramnarayan and Chunnilal was amazed. Ramnarayan said, "All right, having comforted Maharani, we went out in search of you to fetch the palanquin. We called you by blowing the whistle and then we were coming here with this palanquin but who is the other person who brought a palanquin and carried away Maharani before us? They are rightly saying that Champa had left much before when we were in the tent disguised as women and the fight was going on outside." Maharani called out in fear 'Champa!' At that time, she was not there but I don't understand what was the case! Let us come out; we should count the palanquins of these slave traders if they are in the same strength or less. Take out these women also." All women rushed out in fear. They saw blood strewn all around and at some places, dead bodies were also seen. The old chief of the convoy and his handsome son were sitting under a tree tied with fetters. Ten men with naked sword were guarding them and hundreds of handcuffed men were sitting under other trees. All the tents were ravaged.

Pannalal, Ramnarayan and Chunnilal went to the place where so many palanquins were kept. Ramnarayan said to Pannalal, "See, they are sixteen, earlier we had counted seventeen. It means that Maharani was carried away in one of these palanquins. But who carried her away? Chunnilal, you go and call Diwan Saheb here. He is sitting there in the army camp."

Chunnilal came back with Diwan Saheb. Pannalal said, "See, our four days' labour was spoiled. They had pitched their tents three stations away from Vijaygarh. We halted this old chief by promising to supply him women, so that he should not move away and then informed you. You also came here with your full strength and despite this much bloodshed, we missed Maharani and Champa. Champa managed to escape by acting wickedly. She asked us to cut open her fetters, otherwise she would reveal their secret that they are men and that they have come to cheat and then we will be caught. Finding no way out, we cut her fetters and getting an opportunity, she immediately escaped but who took away the queen?"

Diwan Saheb was also puzzled at what had happened and said, "Give severe beating to these trouble-makers including their old chief and ask whether it is their mischief!"

Pannalal intervened, "When the chief is in your custody. I don't understand how they can kidnap Maharani. You take away these slave traders and the army and also look after the affairs of the state. We are again going in search of Maharani. We have taken it upon ourselves."

Diwan Saheb along with prisoners and their stores left for Chunar. Pannalal, Ramnarayan and Chunnilal went in search of the queen, talking among themselves.

Pannalal said, "Look, what is the fate of Chunar nowadays! On the one hand, Maharaja is trapped, on the other, Maharani is traceless. Even when she was discovered someone befooled us and took her away."

Ramnarayan said, "Brother, we worked hard for it but in vain. With what hardship we could locate them; how many strategies we employed to keep them engaged in the forest for two days! We didn't let them move away. We ran to Chunar and called in Diwan Saheb with forces; we fought with them, lost some of our men but in dividend, we earn disgrace as on the first day."

Chunnilal, "I was very happy that Champa would be in our hands but she turned out to be craftier. How had she recognised us and blackmailed us to cut open her fetters? She is very cunning. Has she had done all this?"

Pannalal said, "No. Champa cannot carry away Maharani in a palanquin alone."

Ramnarayan said, "Having engaged us in this search, Pandit Badrinath, along with Ahmad and Nazim, has gone to release Maharaja from captivity. Let us see what honour he earns."

Pannalal said, "What credit do we have to give to Chunar and listen to their achievements and see what glory they have earned! If we could not find out Maharani, what face will we have to show off there?"

Ramnarayan said, "Enough. We have learnt that the person, who so smartly kidnapped Maharani today, is really our master. Now we should start farming in this jungle, bring our family and settle here. It's difficult to find out Maharani."

Pannalal said, "Well done, what courage! What an incarnation of Pinik!"

They went to some distance talking like this and fixed a point to reassemble and parted ways.

□

17

Pandit Jagannath is sitting with Tej Singh in a huge canal that passes through a dense forest. Beside them, a simple palanquin is laid, curtain rolled in and a woman sitting inside is talking to Tej Singh. She is Kalavati, the queen of Maharaja Shivdutt. Champa is standing behind it, keeping a hand on the palanquin.

Maharani said, "I am not ready to go to Chunar. I don't want kingdom. My heaven lies at the feet of Maharaja. If he is in custody, fetter my legs and put me at his feet."

Tej Singh said, "No, I don't say that you should go to the prison where Maharaja is kept. If it pleases you, then go to Chunar. We will take you there safely. There was no need to bring you here. Jyotishi ji has praised your fidelity to your husband several times and said that Maharani will be in great pain in the absence of Maharaja. Considering this, we brought you here, otherwise we went there just to rescue Champa. Now, you tell me, should I send you to Chunar or to Maharaja because you cannot reach Maharaja except through me and who knows how long he will be in prison."

Maharani said, "You have been so kind to me. Really no one can take me to Maharaja as quickly as you can. Send me to him just now, don't delay, I will be obliged to you."

Tej Singh said, "But you can't go there like this in a palanquin. I can take you there after making you unconscious."

Maharani said, "This too is acceptable to me. By any means, take me there."

Tej Singh said, "Okay, take this phial and smell it."

Maharani was deeply in love with her husband. Tej Singh asked for her head as a condition to take her to Maharaja. She would have accepted that too.

Maharani unhesitatingly inhaled the phial and fell unconscious. Jyotishi ji said, "Now take her to the same cellar. As long as you don't come back, I will wait for you in this jungle. Champa should also go back to Vijaygarh. We are already looking for Kumari Chandrakanta, why should she trouble herself!"

Tej Singh said, "Champa, Jyotishi ji is right. You go back home lest you should again fall into trouble."

Champa said, "As long as Kumari is not discovered, I will not go back to Vijaygarh. I fell into the hands of these slave traders and I escaped from there on my own. You didn't have to trouble yourself for it."

Tej Singh said, "You are right. We do not say that we rescued you. We wandered to this place looking for Chandrakanta and looked into the slave traders' tent in her search. We didn't find her but saw Maharani and you trapped in it. When we planned to rescue you, we saw Pannalal, Ramnarayan and Chunnilal endeavouring to free Maharani from them. We decided to move aside and let them work. This was to help us to free you easily and so it happened. By your intelligence, you escaped from there and we took Maharani away. Anyway, let it pass. Now you tell me, if you don't go back home, what will you do? Where will you search? Let it not happen that we discovered Kumari and went back to Vijaygarh and you kept wandering here for months."

Champa, "I am not such a fool, rest assured."

Tej Singh was rendered helpless and had to leave behind Champa on her own discretion. Jyotishi ji stayed back in the jungle and Tej Singh carried Maharani in a bundle on his back to that cave where Maharaja Shivdutt was kept. Champa also took her own way.

□

18

After the departure of Tej Singh, Jyotishi ji was left alone. He began to think that through ramal, he should try to find out where Chandrakanta and Chapla were. He opened the bag and started throwing ramal and making calculations. He did it minutely for about three hours. Suddenly, there was a radiance of joy on his face and a smile on his lips. Instantly, he tied ramal and ran towards that cave where Tej Singh was carrying the queen. An aiyar as he was, he did not lag rather sprinted as fast as he could.

Tej Singh was striding along the path. He had hardly gone 15 km when he heard from behind, "Stop! stop!" He turned back and saw Jyotish Jagannathji coming very fast. He stopped, became a bit apprehensive to think why he was running after him!

When he came closer, seeing laughter on his face, Tej Singh felt assured and asked, "Why, why are you running after me?"

Nothing, just I will also accompany you to that cave.

Why so?

Not here, I will tell you only there.

Tej Singh said, Then at the gate, you will have to be blind-folded because when Badrinath had discovered the secret of the first lock from Kumar by fraud, since then I have set another lock which was already there but we did not use it out of lethargy because it takes time to lock and unlock it. I have decided not to disclose the secret of this lock to anyone.

Jyotishi ji said, I won't be blind-folded and will surely enter that cave. You will have to take me on your own.

Funny! Let me know a bit!

Great fun! I will show you Chandrakanta there!

What? Tell me the truth!

If I prove false, kill me and bury me in that cave.

Well said! If I kill you, you will not be harmed but I will be liable for punishment to kill a Brahman!

Jyotishi ji suggested, "I tell you the way how to escape the punishment to kill a Brahman."

What's that?

Not difficult at all, first become a Muslim and then kill.

Tej Singh burst out laughing to hear Jyotishi ji and said, "Well brother, go on, what to do, it is a must to obey you."

Next day in the evening, these people reached the cave. In front of Jyotishi ji, Tej Singh began to open the lock. First of all inserting his hand into the mouth of the lion, he pulled out his tongue. Thereafter, he began to open the second lock.

On both sides of the door, two stones were set along the wall. Tej Singh vehemently kicked the stone on the right side. With a sound, the stone sank into the wall along the earth. A snake was seen coiling on a small platform, Tej Singh caught its neck and spun it round in the air twice and the door opened. Carrying the bundle of the queen, Tej Singh and Jyotishi ji went in and closed the door from inside. On the left side in the wall, there was a hole, inserting his hand in it and Tej Singh did something which Jyotishi ji could not see.

Jyotishi ji asked, "What's in it?" Tej Singh replied, "There is a bar turning which the stone gate is closed, the one I had kicked. From this hole, only that stone can be shut but not opened. To open that, one has to repeat the process that was applied outside the door".

Shutting the door, they proceeded further. Having reached a field, they opened the bundle carrying the queen, brought her back to consciousness and said, "Come along with me, I will take you to the king." The queen went on along with them, Tej Singh asked Jyotishi ji, "Tell me, where is Chandrakanta?" Jyotishi ji said, "I never came inside this cave before. So, I am not familiar with the places inside, you go ahead, search for Maharaja Shivdutt, Chandrakanta will also be visible".

Walking around in search of Maharaja Shivdutt, they came to that canal. Suddenly, they saw Maharaja Shivdutt standing on a stone on the other side of the canal looking upward.

Seeing Maharaja, the queen was frenzied. Without asking how deep was the canal or how to cross it, she immediately jumped in. There wasn't much water, so she crossed it and running with tears fell at the feet of Maharaja Shivdutt. Maharaja lifted her and embraced her. By then, Tej Singh and Jyotishi ji also crossing the canal came to Maharaja Shivdutt.

Seeing Jyotishi ji, Maharaja asked, "Why, how did you come here? Did you also fall into the hands of Tej Singh?" Jyotishi ji replied, "No, why should I fall into his hands? No doubt, out of kindness, he had included me in his company. Now I am in favour of Virendra Singh and have nothing to do with you."

Hearing the words of Jyotishi ji, Maharaja came into a tantrum. With red eyes, he began to stare at him. Jyotishi ji said, "You are unnecessarily showing anger, what will you gain from it? I am where I like. It is proper to live with him who cares for. You think yourself and remember what bitter words you had used for me. That time you did not even consider that I am a brahman. Now why do you look at me with red eyes?"

Hearing Jyotishi ji, Maharaja Shivdutt lowered his head and gave no reply. Just then there came a fine call, "Tej Singh!"

Raising his head, Tej Singh looked in the direction the sound had come from. He saw Chandrakanta and spontaneously tears welled up in his eyes. Alas, how she is looking, her hair is dishevelled, her rose-like face has faded, her body looks dirty, clothes are tattered, on a hill standing outside a cave, she is calling 'Tej Singh! Tej Singh!'

Tej Singh ran in that direction and wanted to reach the princess climbing the hill, but he could not make it, found no passage, he struggled a lot but failed. Being helpless, he flung the lasso to climb up. But that could not cover even the one-fourth distance. He borrowed Jyotishi ji's lasso, and tying them together, flung again. It did not even cover half the distance. He tried all sorts of efforts but to no avail. Being helpless, he called and asked, "Princess, how did you come here?"

Tej Singh's words reached the princess clearly but the princess's voice being thin could not reach Tej Singh's ears clearly. The princess gave a reply which was not clear. However, it seemed, "fate.... rescue!"

Tej Singh felt perturbed that he could not talk to the princess well. But there was no help. She said something more but that was not intelligible; it just appeared that someone was speaking. Tej Singh called again, saying, "Don't worry, I'll find out some way so that you may come down". In reply, the princess said nothing. There was a tree nearby, having big and thick leaves. She plucked a leaf and from a pointed stone, wrote something on it and tearing out a stripe from her saree, she wrapped the leaf with a small stone and threw it with such calculation that it fell in water near the bank of the canal. Tej Singh found it out and untying the knot looked carefully at the writing on the leaf. It read, "You first go and bring Kumar here."

Tej Singh showed that leaf to Jyotishi ji and said, "You please stay here. I will fetch Kumar here. Till then, you think out a plan for Kumari to come down". Jyotishiji replied, "All right, you go and I will think out a strategy."

The Maharani also saw all this but she could not know what the princess had written and where did Tej Singh leave for. Nevertheless Maharani felt very sorry at the helplessness of the princess and kept looking on in that direction. Tej Singh went out of the cave and, setting a double lock, set out for Vijaygarh.

□

19

Ever since princess Chandrakanta disappeared from Vijaygarh and war was fought against Maharaja Shivdutt, not only Maharaja Jay Singh and the ladies of the palace were unhappy, but all the subjects of Vijaygarh were unhappy and the city was enveloped in gloom.

When having dispatched Tej Singh and Jyotishi ji in search of the princess, Kunwar Virendra Singh returned to Vijaygarh with Devi Singh, all were hopeful that princess Chandrakanta might be coming with them but, when from Kumar Maharaja Jay Singh heard the whole story, he felt even more troubled. He became happy to hear of the arrest of Maharaja Shivdutt, but when he heard about the disappearance of the princess from the canal, he was totally disappointed. Diwan Hardayal Singh and others fully consoled him saying that even if the princess may be in the Netherlands, Kumar will surely discover her, still Maharaja did not feel assured. In the palace, the condition of the queen was even worse, she had given up eating, drinking and talking; she just wept and recalled the princess all the time.

For several days, Kumar stayed in Vijaygarh. In between, once he went to Naugarh and met his parents but he always felt ill at ease, he saw unhappiness everywhere.

One night when Kumar was lying in his room, the door was closed, half the night had passed, he was thinking something in separation from Chandrakanta, sleep evading him, he had an inkling of somebody speaking rather uttering the word 'princess'. Instantly getting up from the bed, he came to the door and setting his ear close to the door started eavesdropping. He could hear, "I tell you the truth, you believe it or not. Previously, I was fully convinced that Kunwar Virendra Singh has true love for the princess. But now I have known that but for the desire to possess the kingdom of Vijaygarh, he has no love for the princess, if he had true love, surely the search...".

As Kumar heard only this much, the guards heard footsteps of some thieves. They stopped talking and shouted, "Who's there?" But they found none. Kumar kept sitting near the door for long but he heard nothing thereafter, he only knew that the guards were talking among themselves.

Kumar became even more perturbed, began to think that when guards and gatekeepers feel that Kumar is not the real lover of Chandrakanta, surely Maharaja must be having the same belief, rather the Maharani in the palace must be having the same impression. Now it is not good for me to stay in Vijaygarh, but I am not even willing to go to Naugarh because if I go there, people will feel even more firmly that the love for the princess was false. Where to go then and what to do? Thinking like that he spent the whole night.

Today, Kumar disposed of his daily routine and lunch in a hurry. Two to three hours might have passed, he called for his horse and rode out of the palace. Several people came up. Kumar did not take them but Devi Singh stuck to him. Kumar dissuaded him again and again but he went on following him. Kumar galloped the horse so that Devi Singh might be left behind but Devi Singh was an expert in *i*. He also had the habit of running. Hence, he did not lag behind. The hilly path being rugged and uneven, even Kumar's horse could not run as fast as he wanted. Devi Singh got tired. Kumar also had pity on him. He thought in his heart that he loved him so much. So long as he was alive, he would not desert him. It was not proper to harass such a man deliberately. At last, Kumar stopped his horse and looking towards Devi Singh laughed.

Devi Singh said panting, "Well, let me know your plan, haven't you gone frenzied?" Kumar got down from the horse and said, "All right, let the horse loose to graze and listen to my intention." Spreading the saddle cloth for Kumar Devi Singh, let the horse loose and sitting beside him asked, "Now tell me, what were your thoughts behind going out of Vijaygarh?" In reply, Kumar told the whole story of the night and said that if he could not find out the princess, he would not go to Vijaygarh or Naugarh.

Devi Singh said, "It is a mistake to think so. How can you find out more than us? Tej Singh and Jyotishi ji have already gone in the search. I may also go if you order. You can't do anything. If you don't like to go to Vijaygarh without finding out the princess, then go to Naugarh and live there. When she is discovered, come back to Vijaygarh. Now you have come close to your house." After thinking Kumar said, "Is my house closer than Vijaygarh from here? I have come a long way."

Devi Singh said, "No, you are mistaken. Nobody knows in what mood you went on riding your horse without caring about the direction. But I know it very well that Naugarh is just five km away from here and see that big peepal tree that stands near the cave in which Maharaja Shivdutt is caged. (Seeing Tej Singh coming) *Arre,* where from is Tej Singh coming? Look, he must have discovered something!"

Tej Singh was seen coming from a distance but Kumar could not help advancing towards him. Tej Singh also saw the duo and Kumar striding towards him, he ran to him. Impatient Kumar just asked, "Is there any news?"

Tej Singh, "Yes."

"Where?"

"Come along, I will show you."

Hearing it Kumar embraced Tej Singh and cheerfully said, "Let's see."

Tej Singh, "Ride on your horse, why do you fear, I was just going to call you, but why are you sitting here?"

"Ask Devi Singh about it, first let's go there."

Devi Singh readied the horse and Kumar rode on it. Tej Singh and Devi Singh in the front and Kumar following them reached near the cave in a short time. Tej Singh said, "Now, I open the lock before you but you must beware, lest *aiyars* may discover it cheating you". The lock was opened and the three men went in. Quickly they reached that stream where Jyotishi ji was sitting. Pointing with his index finger,

Tej Singh said, "Look up, Chandrakanta is standing there."

Chandrakanta was on the high hill. Seeing Kumar from a distance, she became anxious to meet Kumar. It was the same with Kumar. Without thinking about the passage, he got ready to climb up, but what could be done. Tej Singh said, "Why do you fear? Had there been a path upward, where was the need to bring you here? I could have taken the princess to you."

Both of them were staring steadfastly. Kunwar Virendra Singh began to see the princess and vice versa. Both of them had tears flowing from their eyes. They could do nothing as it was a very difficult situation. For whom he left his home, got ready to sacrifice his life, thousands of lives were lost, who appeared after months of disappearance? Today it was not possible even to talk to her, not to speak of meeting her. Only they must be experiencing their feelings in such moments.

Looking at Jyotishi ji, Tej Singh asked, "Why, have you thought of any way out?" Jyotishi ji replied, "So far no way out has come to mind, but I must say at least that without taking any big action, it is difficult for the princess to come down. The way she has come, the same way she will go out. There can be no other way. I had also consulted ramal and even that indicates the same thing. Therefore, let us ask the princess in any manner which way she had come here. Only then we can do something. This is a matter of *tilism* and not fun."

Tej Singh liked the idea and called the princess saying, "Please don't panic. The way you wrote on a leaf and threw it down, similarly write in brief and tell us the way you had reached there."

□

20

When Chapla stepped down into the cave, a large room came to view which had only door frames and no panels. At first, Chapla looked at it minutely and then went in. As soon as she stepped in, an iron plate fell with a thud from the middle of the upper door frame. Amazed Chapla looked back and found the door closed. She began to think – is this a room or a mouse trap? Its door is very much like a mouse trap. What to do now? There was no way out visible, it was totally dark, pitch dark! In the dark, Chapla began to move around and grope.

While moving around, one of Chapla's feet fell into a ditch and simultaneously there was some sound and the door opened. Moonlight also entered the room. This was not the door which had closed earlier, rather it was a different one. Moving closer, Chapla saw that this door too had no panels. At last, through that door, she came to a garden out of that room. She saw that there were different colour flowers in small flower plants. On one side, through a canal water was being sprinkled in the garden, but the flower beds were not regular. In the front, there was a twelve-pillared structure. Walking slowly, she reached there.

This structure was made of black stone. The roof, floor, pillars, all were made of black stone. In the middle, there was an 18" red square platform placed on a royal marble seat. Chapla looked at it, the words engraved on it were – "This is, whoever is entangled in it, he can never go out. No doubt, if somebody breaks it, he can free all the captives and possess all the wealth. The man who breaks it must have enough strength, otherwise it is a futile exercise."

As Chapla read it, she was convinced that her death was imminent. She regrets. "The path I have come in, I can never go out that way. The door of the room has closed. It proved useless to tie the outer door with the lasso, but perhaps, that door may be open through which I have come into this garden". Thinking thus, Chapla again moved towards that door. But there was no trace of it. Even it was not clear where that door was. Again he returned to that twelve-pillared structure and approached the royal seat. She had an impulse to lift that stone. If I get a chance by any means to go out, I will carry it with me and show it to the people. She bent down to lift the stone but as she touched it, she felt a sensation in the body and felt dizzy and, finally, she fell down unconscious.

Chapla lay unconscious so long as it was day. By the evening, she came to her senses. She got up, went to the canal, washed her hands and face, felt relieved. There were many grape-vines in that garden but in her nervousness and sadness, she ate nothing. Again she reached the same twelve-pillared structure. It was night and the structure started shining. As the night advanced, the brilliance of the structure went on increasing. The roof, wall, floor, pillars – all were shining, every nook and cranny was visible now, even part of the garden in the front looked bright.

To know how it is shining, Chapla stroked the floor, the walls and the pillars, but she could not understand anything. She could not sleep because of fear, surprise and disappointment, she kept awake whole night. At times, she stroked the wall, or going near that royal seat, looked minutely at that stone touching which she had gone unconscious.

The day broke, again Chapla began to walk in the garden. She reached near that wall under which the canal ran to this garden. She began to think, "The wall is not very wide, even the mouth of the canal is open, I can go out through it. There is sufficient space for one to pass". After thinking a lot, Chapla decided on it, she stepped into the canal with her clothes on, and decided to reach the other end of the wall. She made it, i.e., she went out of that wall. Taking her head out of water, she found the canal wider here than in the garden. She came out of water and saw high hills under which this canal ran and under the wall, it reached the garden.

Chapla dried her clothes in the sun, the *aiyari* bag was not wet because its cloth was waterproof. When she was fully furnished, she moved straightaway. High mountains on sides, a watercourse between them, *parijat* trees on the sides on way to climb the hill, even if one climbs a length, he will have to come down. Chapla started near the watercourse. By mid-day, she covered about 10 km, there was no passage to go ahead because another hill stood in the way and the water rushing down from that hill met the canal below. There was a veranda below that hill about 10 yards long and 1 yard wide. Seen minutely, it appeared that it had been cast from the hill. In the middle, there was a stone snake whose mouth was open and could accommodate a complete man. In the front, there was also a large marble stone installed on the earth.

Chapla moved closer to see the snake. As she stepped on the marble stone, the snake started breathing air and in a short while, it breathed in so fast that Chapla could not hold her feet stable on it and she was dragged into its belly and got unconscious.

When Chapla regained consciousness, she found herself in a room which was narrow. Only ten to twelve men could sit in it. Beside the room, there was a staircase to go up. Chapla sat surprised for some time. Different kinds of thoughts crossed her mind. She was puzzled to think what the matter was. At last, Chapla controlled herself and through the staircase went up. The door automatically shut upon her and there was no way to go down. She began to look sideways. High hills on all sides. In the front, there was a small cave which was not very dark because it had light from the front side.

Being helpless, Chapla entered that cave. At a small distance, she found a small verandah. Having reached there she found that Chandrakanta was sitting with lots of big leaves before her and was writing on them with the point of a stone. She looked down and found that the hill was steep low, no way to step down. Below that Kunwar Virendra Singh and Jyotishi ji were looking up.

Princess Chandrakanta heard the footsteps of Chapla. She looked back and recognising, got up and said, "Wah friend, you've reached on time. Look, all are standing below. I find no way to reach them. I hear their voice but nobody hears me. Tej Singh has asked me by which way I have come to this place and I am writing the reply to it on this leaf and now I will throw it down".

Chapla looked around very cautiously. When she found no way out to climb down, she said, "No need to write on leaf. I will shout out to them. They will clearly hear my voice. First tell me, were you swallowed by the crane or have you come by any other way?"

The princess said, "Yes, that crane had swallowed me which you might have seen in that ruin, maybe he had swallowed you, too!" Chapla said, "No, I have come by another passage, first let me give them the whereabouts of that ruin, then we will talk so that they arrange something to free us. So far as I think, it seems we will remain entangled here for several days. Anyway, we will see what happens.

□

21

Kunwar Virendra Singh and others saw from below Chapla coming to the princess. From above, Chapla called, "The cave in which Shivdutt had imprisoned us, about 14 miles to the south in an old ruin. There is a very heavy stone stork who had devoured the princess. Our life can be saved only if that is broken, there is no other way out to our release. I went into that *tilism* very carefully. Still I got enmeshed, when you go, you must look at that very cautiously. I don't know which side of Chunar that cave is, we were imprisoned by that rogue Shivdutt".

Everybody heard Chapla very clearly. Kumar got into a tantrum at Maharaja Shivdutt, and drew the sword to strike him. The wife of Maharaja Shivdutt sitting by his side was witnessing all the drama, now seeing Kunwar Virendra Singh drawing the sword, ran then and there and fell at the feet of Kumar and said, "Kill me first because as a widow, I cannot live a life worse than that of a corpse!" Tej

Singh caught hold of Kumar's hand and with his pleadings, pacified him. Kumar told Tej Singh, "If you consider it fit and proper and there is no harm in it, bring in the parents of the princess and show the princess so that they feel a bit assured. Tej Singh said, "It will never be, don't regard this cave as ordinary, whatever we should say, everything will be told to him, Now we should think how to release the princess. Let us go and tell Maharaja Jay Singh everything take him to that ruin which Chapla has described".

Saying this, Tej Singh told Chapla, "Look, we are going to that ruin. Nobody knows how much time it will take to break that *tilism*. You should be consoling the princess and see that she has no trouble of any sort. What to do, we can't find any way out to send you clothes and eatables, etc".

Chapla replied from above, "Nothing worrying, there will be no problem about food because there are several fruit trees around here and also small streams running from the hills. You people should work very cautiously. I have learnt that this *tilism* cannot be broken without Kumar. But you people also should not desert him, be very careful!"

Leaving Maharaja Shivdutt and his wife in that very cave, Kunwar Virendra Singh, Tej Singh, Devi Singh and Jyotishi ji, all the four people came out from there. They double-locked the cave. Then to convey the message, Kumar sent Devi Singh to his parents at Naugarh and also told him, "From Naugarh, you must return to Vijaygarh tomorrow itself. We are going there and will go elsewhere only when you come back". Hearing it, Devi Singh left for Naugarh.

Since morning, Kunwar Virendra Singh was absent from Vijaygarh. He had gone away without telling anyone. So, Maharaja Jay Singh was very unhappy and had sent several spies all around to search for him. By the evening, these people reached Vijaygarh and saw Maharaja. Maharaja said, "Kumar, you go away like this at your sweet will without telling me. That gives us very much pain. Don't do so".

To this, Kumar gave no reply but Tej Singh said, "Maharaja, such was the need that Kumar had to go early in the morning. At that time, you were at rest. Therefore, he couldn't talk to you". Thereafter, Tej Singh narrated the whole story of going to Chunar at battle, abducting the queen of Maharaja Shivdutt, searching for the princess in the cave, meeting Jyotishi ji, the details about slave traders, seeing the princess and Chapla in that cave and hearing from her the story of the *tilism*, etc. And, in the end, he also said that they were going to break the *tilism*.

Maharaja was awfully surprised to hear such details and said, "No doubt, you people have done a good work, rather beyond capacity. Now you are preparing to break the *tilism* but that is located in another's territory. Even if the king of that territory is under your captivity, still you should go fully prepared. It would be fine if I go with you too". Tej Singh replied, "No need for you to take the trouble. We'll take a small army, that'll be enough". Maharaja said, "All right, I needn't go but I must go to see the *tilism*". Tej Singh said, "As you please". Maharaja ordered Diwan Hardayal Singh, "Half of my army and Kumar's full army must be ready by tonight. Tomorrow they will march towards Chunar".

As ordered, the Diwan arranged everything. Next day, Devi Singh also came back from Naugarh. With all the preparation, they marched to Chunar to break the *tilism*. Diwan Hardayal Singh was left behind at Vijaygarh.

□

22

It took four days on the way. On the fifth day, the army reached the border of Chunar. When the Diwan of Maharaja Shivdutt heard about it, he became nervous as Maharaja Shivdutt had already been arrested and now nobody had the courage to fight. With several presentations he appeared to see Maharaja Jay Singh. Having got the information, Maharaja sent word, "No need to see us. We have not come to conquer Chunar because the day your Maharaja was caught by us, we had conquered Chunar. We have come on another business, don't think of anything else".

Being helpless, the Diwan had to go back, but he came to know that they had come on a particular business. Till today; nobody knew about that, rather nobody had seen that ruin. Today, it became popular that there is a *tilism* which Kunwar Virendra Singh will break. Several spies were sent here and there to find out that *tilism*i ruin. Tej Singh and Jyotishi ji also engaged themselves. At last, it was discovered. Next day, everybody along with the army pitched their camp in that forest in which that *tilism*i ruin was located.

□

23

Maharaja Jay Singh, Kunwar Virendra Singh, Tej Singh, Devi Singh and Jyotishi ji went to walk inside that ruin. As soon as they entered they were convinced that it was a *tilism*. They entered from each side and examining minutely each and everything, they, reached the stork in the middle. They had already heard from Chapla that the same stork had devoured the princess. Therefore, Tej Singh did not allow anybody near that; rather approached himself. As Chapla had handled this stork, Tej Singh also handled it in the same way.

Maharaja was puzzled to see the activities of this stork like opening its mouth, spreading its wings, lifting things from behind and gulping them. Everybody saw these things and started admiring it full of wonder. Thereafter, he came near that cave into which Chapla had entered. Seeing the panel of the door fastened with rope, Tej Singh understood that it must be Chapla's doing and this lasso also must be hers because at one end, the name of Chapla is engraved.

But fastening this door proved useless as after entering it, Chapla could not come out.

Looking at the well thoroughly, he came to that platform on which a man of stone was sleeping with a book in hand. Like Chapla, Tej Singh was also taken in. Just stepping on the ladder going upward, the stone above with a loud sound opened like a panel and Tej Singh fell down with a thud. Kumar laughed seeing him fall but Devi Singh got into a tantrum. He began to say, "All this nuisance is due to this man who is sleeping on this platform. I'll take care of him". Saying this, he gave a sound slap on his head. As the slap struck, the stone man got up, opened his mouth and wind started blowing as from a furnace. In no time, there was a loud noise and the whole building started shaking. It seemed there was an earthquake, everybody became unnerved. Jyotishi ji said, "Get out of this building. There is no time to stay".

Everybody fled away from this veranda to another veranda. While fleeing, nobody could keep his foot steady because of the earthquake. Standing out of the ruin, they began to look in that direction. They saw the whole building shaking. It lasted for two hours; till then, the shaking of the building in the ruin did not stop.

Tej Singh told Jyotishi ji, "You find out from ramal and astrology how and by whose hands this *tilism* will be broken". Jyotishi ji said, "Wait till today and think whatever you like. At night, I will find out everything from ramal and then we will do whatever seems desirable. But it will take several days. It is not proper for Maharaja to stay. It is better for him to go to Vijaygarh". Everybody liked the idea. Kumar told Maharaja, "You had come just to see this ruin which you have done. Now you go. It is not proper for you to stay here".

Maharaja was not willing to go to Vijaygarh, but on everybody's insistence, he agreed. Leaving half the army of his own and half the army of Kumar, he took the rest with him and marched to Vijaygarh.

□

24

Throughout the night, Jagannath Jyotishi was engaged in throwing *throughout* and making calculations. Kunwar Virendra Singh, Tej Singh and Devi Singh also sat nearby. Considering all, Jyotishi ji said, "From *ramal*, it transpires that the way to break this is engraved on stone and even that stone is buried somewhere in this ruin. Searching for it, we should dig it out, then we will know. Having performed daily routine and eating our meal, we should walk about in this. Surely that stone will come to light".

Free from all works they entered the cave during noon. Walking about, they reached that platform on which the stone man was sleeping and Devi Singh had given a slap. Again that man was found sleeping there.

Jyotishi ji told Tej Singh, "Look here, there is a heap of bricks. Chapla might have collected them and riding on it would have seen this man. You also climb on it and observe minutely. What is written in the book in his hand?" Tej Singh did accordingly and saw getting on that heap of bricks. It was written in the book —

8 panel — 5 nos.
6 hands — 4 fingers
Aggregate — 0 — total correct measurement.

Tej Singh told Jyotishi ji that such and such was written in the book but it does not transpire what it means. Jyotishi ji said, "The meaning will be clear. You just copy the writing on paper". Tej Singh took out paper-pen-inkpot from his bag and copied what was written in that stone book.

Jyotishi ji said, "Now we should see walking around whether there is in this building any pole or platform having eight sides or panels". Everybody now began to search for an eight-panelled pole or platform. Walking around, they reached that veranda where there was a cave. They found a pole having eight folds. The one end of the rope was tied to the door of the cave and the other end was tied to that pole. There was no shed over that pole. Jyotishi ji suggested that its length should be measured by hand. Tej Singh measured it to be six hands, 10 fingers. Devi Singh also found it six hands, 5 fingers length. Then Jyotishi ji measured and found six hands and 10 fingers length. Finally, Kunwar Virendra Singh measured it and found six hands, 4 fingers length.

Jyotishi ji was pleased to say, "Lo, this is that pole described in the book and under it 'total wealth', i.e., that stone having the formula to break the *tilism* engraved on it is buried. It has come to light that this *tilism* will be broken at the hands of Kumar, because in that book, which we have copied, its measurement is written six hands, 4 fingers, which means Kumar's. And it seems that this *tilism* will be won by Kumar alone. Now we should unfasten this lasso which is tied to the pole and the door.

Tej Singh unfastened the lasso, Jyotishi ji looking towards Tej Singh, said, "Now everything has tallied, 8 sides and the measurement six hands, 4 fingers. Look at this. On this side, it is the number 5. What remains is 'correct measure break'. Here Kumar's measurement is correct and he will break it".

Kunwar Virendra Singh picked up a very heavy stone and raising it high up, struck the pole so hard that the entire pole shook up. He repeated it two to three times until the pole got weak and loose. Then Kumar pressed it to his side and pulled out. When the pole was uprooted, an iron chest emerged which was locked. With great difficulty, the lock was broken. Inside there was another chest locked up which was broken. Then came out another chest. Thus, one after another, seven chests emerged. In the seventh chest, they found a stone with something written on it. Kumar took it out and read, "Work carefully, don't make haste to break the *tilism*. If you are Virendra Singh, this wealth is meant for you".

"Towards the stork's mouth, the marble stone on earth is in reality no stone; rather it is batter made. Uproot it and grinding it fine, mix it into syrup and smear it all over the stork's body. That is also made of batter. It will melt away in just two hours. Smash all the wires–wheels and parts beneath it. Downward you will find a room which would have been lighted as a result of the dismantling of the stork. From that room, there is a passage leading to the well in the eastern veranda. There again an old man made of batter holding a book in hand will be seen. Take the book from his hand but don't snatch it all of a sudden, otherwise you will be cheated. First hold his right arm. He will open his mouth. Fill his mouth with camphor. In a short time, he, too, will melt away. Then take the book. All the pages are made of birch leaves. Do as has been instructed in the book — Vikram".

Kumar read it out and everybody listened to it. For a complete hour, they all spoke highly of the maker of the *tilism*. Nobody said anything else. Thereafter, it was decided that as a little day time was left, they should go and take a rest and tomorrow after daily rituals, they will turn to the *tilism*.

The news spread far and wide that in the Chunargarh area, there is *tilism* in a in which princess Chandrakanta and Chapla have been enmeshed and to release them and break the Kunwar Virendra Singh along with his army has camped at the place.

What is *tilism*? What is called *tilism*? How does man get entangled in it? Why will Kunwar Virendra Singh break it? To understand and see these things, many people from far off places were gathered where Kumar had pitched his camp. But out of fear, nobody dared step into the cave. All saw from outside.

Kumar's camp men saw a few horse-riders in disguise, the news of which was communicated to Kumar.

Taking Badrinath, Ahmad and Nazim along, they went out to get Maharaja Shivdutt released. Plucking out the tongue from the lion's mouth in the cave, they wanted to open the door but failed because Tej Singh had double-locked it. When nothing worked, they returned to Vijaygarh and were thinking about *aiyari* when they heard the news about Kunwar Virendra Singh. They came back to the same spot. Pannalal, Chunnilal and Ramnarayan also gathered at the same spot and they all began to think of raising obstacles in breaking the *tilism*. In this pursuit, they started moving about incognito around the camp.

□

25

Next day having performed daily routine, Virendra Singh, Tej Singh, Devi Singh and Jyotishi ji again entered that cave carrying syrup with them. Read once again what was written on that stone which was pulled out yesterday and as per instruction started work. At the gate outside, rather all round the ruin, there was strict vigilance.

Approached the stork, pulled out the white stone buried in the earth, stepping on which the stork opened his mouth. Underneath there was another stone. Grinding the white stone, fine-dipped it in syrup and smeared it all over the stork's body. In no time, the stone partly melted and started flowing and its aroma began to spread. In two hours, the stork melted away. The pole on which it was sitting also melted down. The room below became visible in which there were steps to go down where several wires and parts were equipped with. All were broken and all the four people went down and reached that well where an old man was sitting with a book in hand. On the front side, they saw on a stone platform stone flowers of different colours.

Just as they held the arm of the old man, he opened his mouth quickly taking camphor from Tej Singh. Kumar filled his mouth with it. For an hour, these people kept sitting there. Tej Singh had already lighted a thick flame. When the old man melted, the book fell on the earth and Kumar picked it up. Its cover with some writings on it was also made of birch paper. Kumar read it. The words were —

"Pick up these flowers, too, they will serve your *aiyars*, their merits are also described in this book. Read this book at the camp, and don't do any other work today".

Very cheerfully, Tej Singh picked up those flowers six in number. From that well, they came to the room and slowly walked out.

A little day was left when Kunwar Virendra Singh reached his camp. It was decided to read the book at night but Tej Singh was in a hurry to know the merits of the flowers. He told Kumar, "This time read the merits of these flowers, read the rest at night". Kumar said with a laugh, "When all *tilism* will be broken, the merits of these flowers will be read". Tej Singh placated a lot. At last, being helpless, Kumar opened the cover. At that time, there was none other than these four people. The rest were sent away. Kumar began to read —

Merits of Flowers

1. Rose flower: If ground in water, it is taken, he will be immune against any type of senselessness for seven days.
2. Jasmine flower: If ground in water, it is dropped in a well for twelve hours, the water of that well will work as an anaesthetic, whoever drinks it, will fall unconscious, it will take half-an-hour to take effect.

   Having read the merits of just two flowers, the three began to jump out of joy. Kumar closed the book and said, "That's all, no more reading!"

   Now Tej Singh started imploring with folded hands to read the book further saying after all the benefits will go to him, they were just his order bearers. After joking for some time, Kumar resumed reading —
3. China rose – Ground in water, take it not to feel hungry for four days.
4. Oleander (Kaner): Ground in water, wash your feet with it to have relief from fatigue and sloppishness.
5. Chrysanthemum flower: Ground in water, its application to the eyes makes one see in the dark.
6. Pandanus flower: Ground in oil, its application protects from cold, ground in water, it protects from

sun, ground in betelnut water, its application will make a man without any zeal and enthusiasm for seven days.

Tej Singh very happily put these flowers in his bag. Devi Singh and Jyotishi ji begged for them, but they were denied even to see them.

□

26

Getting these flowers Tej Singh became as happy as perhaps never before in his life. Already he was super duper in *aiyari*, today these flowers added a new feather to his cap. Who can equal him now? No doubt, one thing was missing, *lopanjan* or some formula he did not get in this *tilism* so that he could be invisible to others. And it was good, otherwise his *aiyari* would not have brought him laurels. Because if a man had something to make him invisible, then he would have no use for his *aiyari*. Being invisible, he could do whatever he wanted.

The four spent tonight awake. The whole night was spent admiring the, merits of flowers, reading the *tilismi* book, planning to go to the *tilism*, etc. The day broke, quickly they performed the daily routine work and eating something, got ready to go to the *tilism*.

Kumar told Tej Singh, "Lifting the book from my bed, carry it along. There I will read again before doing anything". Tej Singh went in to take the book, but there was no book. He saw under the bed and all round but there was no trace. At last, he asked Kumar, "Where is the book? It is not on the bed".

Hearing it, Kumar felt nonplussed. Came running to the bed, searched thoroughly but the book was traceless. Saying 'alas!' Kumar plunged on to the bed, got disheartened, had no hope of meeting Chandrakanta. Now where did the book go which contains the strategy to break the *tilism*? Tej Singh, Devi Singh and Jagannath Jyotishi ji also felt nervous. For two hours, nobody spoke a word. Thereafter, a rigorous search started. Throughout the camp, there was a big hue and cry, saying that the *tilismi* book was lost from the camp of Kumar, security was tightened, people were sent in all directions, in search of the book.

Tej Singh told Kumar, "Don't lose heart. I promise that I will surely catch hold of the thief. If you feel disheartened, all will feel humbled. No work will be done". After much persuasion, Kumar got up from the bed. Just then, a guard came in with a peculiar message. With folded hands, he reported, "One of the guards deployed at the *tilism* for vigilance has come, who says that there are signs of several people inside the *tilism,* but since there is no permission to go inside, they can't have definite information". He is waiting for your order.

As soon as Tej Singh heard this news, he got ready to go to the *tilism* to find out the truth. He told Devi Singh, "You also accompany me, let's see, what's the matter". Jyotishi ji said, "I will also go". Kumar himself got up. At last, all the four set out for *tilism*. General Fateh Singh was standing outside. Kumar also took him along. As they entered, they heard sound of people crying. A few steps further, they knew that there were several people. They went on following the sound. They reached that verandah in which, on a platform, a stone man was sleeping holding a book in hand.

They saw that the stone man was sitting and pressing Pundit Badrinath with both hands and Badrinath was crying. Pannalal, Ramnarayan and Chunnilal were trying some strategy to free Badrinath but to no effect. They were extremely unhappy to lose the *tilismi* book, but here seeing the condition of Badrinath, they all burst out laughing. The *aiyari* looked back and saw that Kunwar Virendra Singh along with his three *aiyars* and General Fateh Singh was standing.

Tej Singh challenged, "Very well, no doubt, as you sow, so do you reap. You enmeshed innocent Kunwar Virendra Singh, you are being punished for it! God is justice-loving.

Why Pannalal, why do you get entangled willingly? Leave him as he is and go, enjoy yourself!"

Pannalal said, "Is it possible for us to leave him in such condition? Now, we are here, you do as you please". Going to Pundit Badrinath, Tej Singh said, "Pundit ji *Pranam*! How are you? Had you come to break the *tilims*? You should have first freed your king! Anyway, perhaps you thought that breaking the *tilism,* you could possess all the wealth and become king of Chunar yourself!"

Devi Singh went a step further and said, "Brother Badrinath, when you break the *tilism*, give me too a little bit of it. Don't grab all alone!" Jyotishi ji added, Badrinath ji, your stars are unfavourable now. You will have peace only when you hand over that book to us which you people have stolen in the night".

Badrinath listened to all but did not answer back to anyone. Pannalal, Ramnarayan and Chunnilal broke away, leaving Badrinath alone and told Kumar, "For God's sake, save Badrinath by any means!"

Kumar replied, "What can we do, we know nothing about *tilism,* the book I had got from *tilism* reading which I could break the *tilism* has been stolen by you. Had that been with me, reading that I would have devised to free him. Well, if you give me that book, surely Badrinath can be released from this adversity".

Hearing it Pannalal looked askance at Badrinath. He also gave some hint. Pannalal told Kumar, "We have not stolen that book. Otherwise, we would have surely given in such dire circumstances. Now either get Pundit Badrinath free by any means or give us orders to go out to arrange some food for him or even more. So long as your book is not recovered and you do not break the *tilism,* let Badrinath remain in the same helpless condition. Till then someone from among us be permitted to go in and come out for feeding someone".

Devi Singh said, "Pannalal, now tell me if Badrinath remains in captivity like this. You will surely arrange for his food, but if he has to answer the call of nature, what will you do? Where will you dump that excreta? Or will that heap remain inside him?"

Pannalal gave no reply to it. Tej Singh said, "Listen to me. *Aiyars* know *aiyars* very well. If Kumar does not give orders for you to go and come, I give you orders to come and protect Badrinath in whatever way possible. You people have harmed us a lot, stolen our *tilismi* book and now you are smiling. Now all of you are under our control. We can do whatever we like with whomsoever. If not in a simple way, by using force we can capture the book, but no, I give you up and caution you strictly to keep the book safe, I will not rest without recovering it and that without arresting you".

Hearing the words of Tej Singh, Pundit Badrinath got into a tantrum and said, "You are talking tall, finding me helpless at this hour! I will call it your bravery when you perform some *aiyari* after my release and you get the upper hand! Are you the only aiyar in the world? I tell you boldly that I have stolen your *tilismi* book but without arresting or torturing someone from us, you cannot get it. Your audacity that without arresting *aiyars* and giving them freedom to go out and come in, you get the book will not work. If you succeed to do it, since that day, we will belong to you and leaving Maharaja Shivdutt, we will serve Kumar. I tell you that I will not give the book and get free from here".

Tej Singh replied, "I also swear an oath that if I don't get the book without arresting you, I will never talk of *aiyari* and getting my head tonsured, go out to another country! I, too, have to settle my score with you in one go".

Tej Singh and Badrinath both took an oath on it. Poor Kunwar Virendra Singh just looked on but said nothing. Taking Devi Singh and Jyotishi ji away, Tej Singh said something in their ears and that very moment, the two went out of *tilism*. Then Tej Singh went near Badrinath and said, "We are going now. You may send Pannalal, Ramnarayan and Chunnilal wherever you want and plan a strategy for your release. The guards are being instructed not to object to your companions going in and coming out".

Along with Kumar, Tej Singh reached his camp and found Jyotishi ji sitting there. Tej Singh asked, "Why Jyotishi ji, did Devi Singh go?"

Yes, he did.

Did you see anything just now or not?

Yes, I have discovered, but there is one disaster after another.

What's that?

Jyotishi ji, "From ramal, it transpires that book has passed from their hands and till now it has not been placed anywhere. Let's see, what Devi Singh does. It would have been better had I accompanied him".

Tej Singh, "Then why are you waiting? Go, I will also do my part".

Hearing it, Jyotishi ji immediately left from there. Kumar said, "Let me also know what you people have decided, what you are doing and why you have let them go. I will surely say that this time being presumptuous, you have spoiled the chance, otherwise they were in our trap".

Tej Singh said, "You have not understood my purpose as yet. Surely, I will take the book from them and more as much as possible, I will make them our followers. Otherwise, how far will this *aiyari* work everyday? *Aiyars* never desert their master and accept subservience except on insistence and ill fame". Kumar said, "It is another bother. God forbid, if you are defeated and Badrinath gets released, then will you desert me?"

Tej Singh said, "No doubt, I'll desert you and never appear before you".

Kumar said, "Then you ruin me and ruin yourself. A good friendship maintained. Alas, what to do now? At least tell me where have Devi Singh and Jyotishi ji gone?"

Tej Singh said, "I will not tell you now. But you don't be afraid. God willing, everything will be all right and our relationship will not break. Please wait, I am going somewhere for two hours".

Kumar, "All right, go".

Tej Singh departed from there. Fateh Singh was also let go. Now let's see what they do and who wins.

□

27

After the departure of Tej Singh, Devi Singh and Jyotishi ji, Kumar sat listless for long. Different kinds of thoughts crossed his mind, a little pat sound and he turned to the door to see perhaps it might be Tej Singh or Devi Singh and when nobody was seen, he was plunged in thought keeping his hand on his cheek. When a quarter day time was left and none of the three *aiyars* came back, Kumar became restless and came out of the camp.

Seeing Kumar going out of the camp, many courtiers came before him. The camp of Commander Fateh Singh was nearby. Hearing of it, he also came out putting on his outfit and stood beside Kumar. Kumar told Fateh Singh, "Let's have a walk, but none else will go with us!" Saying this, he went ahead. Fateh Singh forbade them, so nobody came along. When walking together the two went away very far from the camp, Kumar held Fateh Singh's hand and said, "Listen Fateh Singh, you are also my friend. We grew up and studied together, nothing is hidden from you, Tej Singh also likes you very much. Today I feel very depressed. Now it is difficult for me to live because I don't know why Tej Singh insisted with Badrinath and let out a thief from our hands. God knows what happens now? Whether we get the book back or not, the *tilism* is broken or not, I get Chandrakanta or not or whether she dies pining in the *tilism*".

Fateh Singh, "Don't worry at all. Tej Singh is not a fool. He has insisted on something and that is all right. All *aiyars* will turn to your side. I also know today's happening. He has made very good arrangement. He has also entrusted a work to me and I have done that. Let's see what happens".

While talking, they went away very far. Suddenly, they saw some women who were not very far off. They stopped talking and began to see the women from behind the trees.

They were around twenty women holding the reins of their horses. They were coming in the same direction. Though all of them were very beautiful, but the one who was leading them was the most vivacious and tender. She might be fifteen years of age. From her dress and jewellery, she appeared to be the daughter of a king. She was bedecked from head to foot with gems, her each and every limb comely and proportionate, her face was shining like a rose from a distance. The other women were also extremely beautiful wearing valuable clothes.

Kunwar Virendra Singh started staring at that woman who was leading them. Even in such troubled times, Kumar burst out — "Wah, what proportionate hands and feet. Many of her features tally with those of Chandrakanta. Even the gait and delicateness are like hers. She has a book in hand from which it appears that she is educated".

The women came closer. Now Kumar had a chance to see them thoroughly. Where they were hiding behind the trees was not visible to others. The woman who was coming ahead of them, whom we may address as princess stopped while walking. Opening that book, she began to look at it and spontaneously tears started flowing from her eyes.

Kumar recognised that it was the same book, because on its cover in golden block letters, the words written were *Tilism*. He began to think — "This book was stolen by *aiyars*, Tej Singh has gone in search of it. How could she chance upon this book? Who is she and why does she weep looking at this book?"

[]

Part-III

1

A young girl with a book in her hand was leading some women. Let us call her the forest girl so long as we do not know her whereabouts. Walking slowly, she reached close to the cluster of trees behind which Kumar Virendra Singh and Fateh Singh were hiding. She stopped and looked back. Another woman with a young man holding a photo proceeded past the flower girl who took the photo from her and gave her book in return.

The forest girl heaved a sigh, her eyes filled with tears. Kumar also saw the photo and stared at it until the girl went away far off. He started talking to Fateh Singh, "Well, Fateh Singh, do you know her?"

"I know nothing about her, but I can guess she is a princess".

"I am sure, it is the same book in her hand which we had found in the *tilism* and was stolen later by Shivdutt's *aiyars*. Tej Singh and Badrinath had an encounter for the same book and our *aiyars* are still looking for the same".

"But, how did they find the book?"

"It's a puzzle, no doubt, but perhaps you didn't notice a more puzzling thing".

"No, what's that?"

"It's my photo which the girl had taken from the other woman."

Then it's really more surprising.

"I am myself in a fix and don't know what's all this".

"Anyway, let's follow them wherever they go".

"Okay.

Kumar and Fateh Singh proceeded in the direction of those women. They had hardly taken a few steps when somebody called them from behind. Turning back, they saw Tej Singh. They stopped and seeing him nervous and upset they asked him, "Why are you white-faced?"

Tej Singh was so sorry that he uttered only that he was parting with them forever. His throat choked and tears rolled down his cheeks. Seeing this, Kumar also became restless but he could not understand why Tej Singh was so upset.

Fateh Singh was equally agonised. With his handkerchief, he wiped the tears from Tej Singh's eyes and asked him, "Please tell us something, why are you so much disturbed? Why will you go away from us forever?"

Tej Singh said patiently, "You see, we failed to regain the *tilismi* book and there seems to be no chance of getting it back. So, I must own the responsibility and leave you all".

Before Kumar Virendra Singh and Fateh Singh could say something, they saw Devi Singh and astrologer Jagannath walking towards them. Jagannath ji yelled loudly, "Tej Singh, don't worry. You didn't get the book nor did they. It has happened as I had said before, a third person took away the book".

Now Tej Singh heaved a sigh of relief. Kumar said, "Bravo, you wept yourself and made us weep. I saw who had got the book, but before I could narrate the story, you were weeping already". Saying it, Kumar looked in the direction the women had gone but could see nothing. Tej Singh asked nervously, "Who was holding the book? Where is that person?" Kumar replied, "How can I say where she is? Let's go she might be seen that way. O God, our problems are multiplying one after another".

They slowly moved on with Kumar leading the three *aiyars* and Fateh Singh in the direction the women had gone. But Devi Singh and Jyotishi ji felt puzzled to think that when Kumar had seen who was holding the book, why had he not snatched it. It occurred to him several times to ask Kumar but finding him himself restless and puzzled, Tej Singh did not ask him anything. Kumar searched for an hour, but the women were not traceable. At last, he felt frustrated and stood under a tree.

Tej Singh asked him to clear the facts but Kumar refused to speak on the spot. However, he said to say everything at the camp.

All of them reached the camp. Kumar asked them to first to go to the *tilismi* ruins to see Badrinath. He himself moved towards the ruins and all *aiyars* followed him. Hardly had they set foot on the threshold of the ruins that they saw before them Pundit Badrinath, Pannalal and others coming towards them. Kumar was surprised. He said, "Look, they are coming our way. How come! How was Badrinath released?" Tej Singh was equally surprised. Devi Singh wondered whether they had got the book. If so, it would be a bigger problem. But Fateh Singh was unruffled. He said, "Don't worry. So far they haven't got the book, though I can't say if they get it hence because the book was seen in other's hand only a short while ago".

Meanwhile, Badrinath and others came closer.

Pannalal yelled, "Oye Tej Singh, haven't you been defeated?"

Tej Singh, "How can I be defeated?"

Badrinath, "Why not? We got free without giving the book".

Tej Singh, "We've recovered the book. We don't care how you managed your release. Recovering the book is our victory. Now, you should join our camp leaving Maharaja Shivdutt".

Badrinath said, "Show me that book and I'll change my loyalty here and now".

Tej Singh, "Why don't you show the book yourself? If you don't have it, it means it is with us".

Badrinath said, "That's all. We are sure from your talk that you haven't got the book; rather it has gone to a third person. Until now, we were not sure".

Devi Singh said, "But then tell me who was defeated?"

Badrinath said, "None".

Kumar said, "Now, tell me how you got released?"

Badrinath said, "Only God released me. We did not plan anything. Pannalal just placed a stick on the head and the stone man caught the stick and released me. That's way, I got free. He is still holding that stick in his hand".

Kumar said, "Well said, both of us were saved".

Badrinath, "I really want to be with you, but I am helpless. I can't be disloyal. There must be same reason for disloyalty. Now allow me to go".

Kumar said, "Yes, you may go".

Jyotishi ji said, "Anyway, whether you join our camp or not, but stop *aiyari*".

Tej Singh said, "Bravo, Jyotishi ji, after all, you are still a Ved-worm. Why should we be afraid of *aiyari*. Let them do their best".

Pannalal said, "We'll see. Let's go. Hail maya!"

Tej Singh said, "Hail maya!"

Badrinath and others left the place. Kumar also didn't go to *tilism*; rather made for home. At night, all *aiyars* and Fateh Singh met at Kumar's place. The gatekeepers were instructed not to allow anybody inside. Tej Singh asked Kumar, "Now tell me who was holding the book, who that person was and why you did not try to get the book".

Kumar replied, "That I do not know who that person was but whoever that person was, she couldn't be more valuable than Chandrakanta nor less valuable in any way. Her beauty prevented me from snatching the book".

Tej Singh feels puzzled, "What can be the relation between Chandrakanta and the book?"

Kumar said, "What can I say, I'm in a fix". (He heaves a sigh)

Tej Singh said, "You're in a fix. I can't understand why". (Looking towards Fateh Singh) He says, "You were yourself with him. You can clear the facts. He sighs more and speaks less. He falls in love again and again one after another".

Fateh Singh related the whole story. Tej Singh was puzzled who that woman was and when she had first met Kumar and loved him and had procured his photo.

Jyotishi ji threw ramal several times but couldn't get a clear picture. He only said that she was a princess. They all stayed for the whole night but achieved nothing. At last, it was decided that they should find out that woman by any means.

All of them made for their camp to rest. But the memory of that forest girl kept Kumar awake. At one moment, he recalled her lovely face and at another, her tearful eyes. Thus, sighing and changing sides, he spent the night. It was an hour past sunrise but Kumar was still in bed.

Tej Singh came and saw Kumar had wrapped his face with the sheet which was wet with his tears. It was clear that Kumar was pining for the love of the forest girl. So, it was not proper to give any advice. He called, "Are you awake or sleeping?"

Kumar, "No, I'm awake".

"Then, why didn't you get up? It's your routine to bathe and pray in the morning. What happened today?"

"No, nothing". Kumar got up and hurriedly performed the morning chore. He had his meal. Tej Singh and others also ate and got ready to look for those women in the forest. Kumar offered to join them. All tried to dissuade him saying that his presence could cause an obstacle in the search. But Kumar rejected their advice and said that he would also take Fateh Singh with him so they would be free to search while he would roam about with Fateh Singh. Tej Singh again tried to advise him saying that the *aiyars* of Shivdutt might entrap him but Kumar dismissed his advice. At last, all along with Kumar and Fateh Singh proceeded to the forest. Kumar and Fateh Singh were left at a place in the forest and the three *aiyars* departed separately in search of those women. Now, Kumar Virendra Singh started talking with Fateh Singh, but all the talk centred round the forest girl.

□

2

While Kumar Virendra Singh and Fateh Singh were talking a comely flower girl holding a hamper of wild flowers passed Kumar unconcernedly as though nobody was around. She was heard saying, "Today I was delayed making flower ornaments. Now the princess must be very angry. I'm afraid how she will treat me".

Both of them heard those words. Kumar told Fateh Singh, "It appears that she is the flower girl of that very lady. We had better ask her. "Fateh Singh called her. She looked back in surprise. Fateh Singh called her again from the gesture of his hand. Shaking with fear, she came to them. Fateh Singh asked, "Who are you and who are you carrying these flower ornaments for?"

She replied, "I am a flower girl. I can't say who I serve and for whom these flower ornaments I am carrying. Please excuse me. I am very poor, you won't get anything by killing me. I pray with folded hands, please spare my life".

Saying these words, the flower girl started crying and entreating for life. The basket of flowers was lying in front emitting loud smell in the air. In the meantime, a man in mask appeared and, turning to Kumar, said, "Don't get entrapped in her snare. She is an aiyar, in a few moments, the smell of these flowers will make you senseless".

Hardly had the man in mask spoken those words that the flower girl tried to escape running but Fateh Singh then and there caught her hand. The stranger went away. Kumar told Fateh Singh, "I don't know who this man is and why he came to do us good'. Fateh Singh replied, "It is difficult to find out the man's motive because he is hiding his identity. Anyway, it is not safe to stay here. Had this man not come, we would have been entrapped."

Kumar said, "You're perfectly right to say that. Now, let's go and take her with us. There we'll ask her who she is". Kumar returned to his camp with Fateh Singh and then said, "Now ask her name". Fateh Singh was sure that the aiyar would not tell her real name. So, he said, "Look, I'll find out the real identity of this."

Fateh Singh arranged hot water and washed the face of the aiyar, who turned out to be Pundit Badrinath. Now, Kumar asked, "Tell me, what should we do with you?" Badrinath replied, "Do whatever you think proper".

Kumar told Fateh Singh, "You guard him. When Tej Singh comes, he will decide his fate". Fateh Singh took Badrinath to his camp. Tej Singh, Devi Singh and Jyotishi ji came back late at night and proceeded to Kumar's camp direct. Kumar asked, "Is there any news?"

Tej Singh replied, "No news, our whole day was wasted".

Kumar replied, "It will be found out in a day or two. Here, I have arrested an aiyar".

Tej Singh replied, "Oye, who is he? Where?"

Kumar replied, "In the custody of Fateh Singh, call him to see who he is".

Devi Singh was sent to bring in Fateh Singh with the aiyar. When Tej Singh saw the face of Badrinath, he was overjoyed and asked, "Now, what's your design?"

Badrinath replied, "The same as before".

Tej Singh replied, "Will you leave Shivdutt or not?"

Badrinath replied, "Why should I leave Maharaja Shivdutt?"

Tej Singh replied, "Then you'll be arrested".

Badrinath replied, "Let it happen".

Tej Singh replied, "Don't think that your companions will free you. My prison is not so easy".

Badrinath, "Your prison is already known to me. Imprison me if you like".

Devi Singh replied, "What a fearless man!"

Tej Singh asked Fateh Singh to have strict watch over him. It is night now, he'll be sent to prison tomorrow.

Fateh Singh called his policemen and entrusted Badrinath to them. Just then, a *chobdar* came and handed a letter to him saying that a man in mask is standing outside who has given this letter for Kumar. Tej Singh looked at the envelope which read:

To the lotus-feet of Kumar Virendra Singh

Tej Singh handed the letter to Kumar who read it:

"For whom I sacrificed rest and riches,
That callous one is indifferent to me,
Leaving the palace, I will become a yogi,
And bask in the heat of separation.

—A bereaved one".

His eyes welled up with tears while reading. His throat choked with emotion, he said, "Bring in the letter-bearer". The *chobdar* complied and reported that the man had already gone away.

One can realise how much sorry Kumar would have felt. He gave the letter to Tej Singh who also read it and said, "From this letter, it appears that it has been sent by the same girl we had been searching for. And more, it is clear that she is also over head and ears in love with you. You need not be so unhappy".

Kumar replied, "This letter has fanned the fire of love. Now I am more obsessed with thoughts about her. Anyway, now you people go and take rest. We'll see what happens tomorrow".

□

3

Tonight hanged heavier on Kumar than the yesternight. He read the letter again and again. Got up in the morning, performed his routine work and got ready to go to the forest. Tej Singh was called in. Today again Tej Singh dissuaded Kumar from going to forest but Kumar did not agree. Then Tej Singh plucked one of the *tilismi* flowers and grinding it with water, gave it to Kumar and Fateh Singh to drink. Then he said that nobody could make them senseless now. However, there was no guarantee against adduction.

Kumar said with confidence that nobody could ever abduct him.

The five people entered the forest. At a distance the three *aiyars* departed leaving Kumar with Fateh Singh. Kumar Virendra Singh and Fateh Singh went on walking here and there. After they had covered considerable distance, they saw two people coming on horseback. When they were close, one man got down from the horse, put something on the earth and mounted the horse. Kumar proceeded towards them. When he was close to them, they said," Take this book and the letter." They rode away.

Kumar saw that it was the same *tilismi* book. It had a letter on it and pen, paper and inkpot on one side. Very happily, Kumar lifted that book and told Fateh Singh, "It is not understandable why both the riders went away leaving this book but from their tone, it appears that they were women. Let me see what is written in the letter". He opened the letter and read.

"I have emotional attachment with you and the one you love that poor soul is entangled in *tilism*. If she faces any trouble, you will be aggrieved. I regard your happiness as my happiness. With this feeling, I hand over this book to you. Break the *tilism* and free Chandrakanta but don't forget me. I charge you in the name of one who you love most. Write your reply to the letter and place it on the spot you have lifted the book from".

Reading the letter, Kumar wrote a reply immediately –

"From the very moment I saw you holding that book,

I am eager to see you. I'll feel fortunate the day we meet. But it's a pity that you have an aversion to my face.

–Yours Virendra"

Kumar placed the reply on that very spot. The two riders were standing at a distance. Kumar waited for them for a long time but they did not come close. When Kumar moved away a bit, one of them came and lifted the letter and went out of sight in no time. Kumar came back to his camp with Fateh Singh.

At night, Tej Singh also came back and met at Kumar's camp. He said, "Today also I could not trace anything, though we saw a few persons in mask roaming about. I tried to locate them but failed as they moved very cleverly. But tomorrow I am sure to find out who they were".

Kumar said, "Look, you could find nothing but I did such *aiyari* that the lost thing was recovered. See this *tilismi* book". Saying this, Kumar placed the book before Tej Singh.

Tej Singh, "Your *aiyari* is already known to us but please tell me how you got the book".

Kumar narrated the whole story how he had got the book and then showed the letter and told him about his reply to the letter.

Jyotishi ji said, "Why not, after all, she belongs to a high family. It also appears from the letter that she is fully familiar with the state of Kumar but we have no clue about her".

Kumar replied, "Tej Singh should feel ashamed of himself that though a big aiyar, he couldn't trace out a couple of women".

Tej Singh replied, "I'll surely trace out and amply please you but now that the book has been recovered, we should dispose of the *tilism* work".

Kumarv replied, "Will they be waiting till then?"

Tej Singh replied, "Don't you care about Chandrakanta now?"

Kumar replied, "Why not? The love for the princess is running in my veins but you too should consider how much true is her love for me. Here you are considering Chandrakanta better than me".

Tej Singh replied, "I don't mean that you don't care about her but is also important to us".

Kumar replied, "We'll do likewise. During daytime, we'll work to break the *tilism* and find out those people in the night time".

The night passed as usual. Next morning, after daily routine work, Kumar Virendra Singh, Tej Singh and Jyotishi ji entered the *tilism* keeping the book in hand. They started breaking the *tilism* as per instruction in the book.

It was already written in the book that the *tilism* breaker must come out of the *tilism* an hour before dusk and stop breaking.

□

4

Having entered the *tilismi* ruins, first they went to that spot where a stoneman lay on a stone platform. Kumar started breaking the *tilism* right from here.

Five feet away from the platform towards the head of the stoneman, Kumar dug the earth with his own hands. A yard deep there was a white stone with strong iron rings attached for lifting it. Catching hold of the ring, he lifted the stone. Now, there seemed to be a cellar with descending stairs.

Tej Singh lighted a flare and all of them went down in that light. They saw a broad, open room meticulously neat and clean. In the middle, there was a marble puppet holding a nail in one hand and a hammer in another.

Kumar took the nail and hammer from the hands of the puppet and as he inserted the nail in the left ear and hammered it, the lips of the puppet started moving and it seemed that the puppet was singing.

It lasted sometime. Suddenly the puppet split into two sides and a rose plant, eight inches long, came out of its stomach. The plant had a few flowers and a key was hanging from a stem along with a bronze leaf with something written on it. Kumar read it.

"This plant has been manufactured from spices by our physician Ajayab Dutta. The fragrance of rose will be spreading far and wide at all times. The physician has placed this unique plant here as a present for you to keep in your court".

Kumar was overjoyed to read it and, turning to Jyotishi ji, said, "I've got such a wonderful thing. See, even at this hour, what sweet scent is oozing out of these flowers.

Tej Singh repiled, "No doubt about it".

Devi Singh repiled, "It shows wonderful craftsmanship".

While Kumar was talking, one side door opened. In the dark room, so far, they had seen no sign of any door or opening but as the door opened, it was flooded with light. The flare was put off and they came out from that door. They saw a small, beautiful garden. It was the same garden in which Chapla was seen earlier.

As per instruction in the *tilismi* book, Kumar fastened a rope to the lock connecting the puppet's stomach. Holding the rope by hand and dragging the lock, Kumar went round the garden. Moving through the flower beds, the lock stuck to the ground near a fountain. All of them stopped there. As per Kumar's instruction, they started digging the earth. Hardly had they dug two or three feet when Jyotishi ji said, "Now just an hour is to dusk. We should be out of the *tilism*".

Kumar lifted the lock and all the four people passing through the room went upto that veranda where that stoneman was sleeping on a stone platform and digging towards his head, they found a rock. They covered the cellar with that rock. Then they shut the lock.

All the four people came to Kumar's camp. Taking rest for a while and then informing Kumar Tej Singh, Devi Singh and Jyotishi ji made for the forest in search of the forest girl. It was roughly two hours to dusk.

The three *aiyars* had already covered a short distance when they saw someone in a mask. Devi Singh and others stalked him hiding behind trees. That horseman turning westward was going to Chunar direct. He stopped many times on the way, looked back and moved on.

The sun had set. The dark night spread its wings. The dense forest in the dark looked hideous. Now the three *aiyars* followed the sound produced on dry leaves by the footfalls of the horse. After an hour, they reached the edge of the forest.

The masked horseman got down from the horse. Many horses were tied there. He also tied his horse there. There was a stack of grass on one side. He put some grass before the horse and walked on foot.

Stalking that masked man, the three *aiyars* reached the bank of the Ganga. From a distance, twc shafts of light appeared on the surface of water. It seemed that two moons had descended on the Ganga water. The white light showed on water. When they came near, they saw several beautiful women sitting in a decorated boat. In the middle, on a seat a tender young girl, very imposing, was sitting. Her moon-like face was shining from a distance. And two lights on both sides were burning.

On reaching the bank, the masked man sounded a whistle loudly, which was responded to by a similar whistle sound from the boat. Two of those women in the boat got up and untied a dinghy, connected the boat, brought to the bank and took the masked man in.

Now the three *aiyars* started talking among them.

Tej Singh said, "How nice these women look sailing between the two shafts of light!"

Devi Singh replied, "Jyotishi ji these fairies might fly away with you. Then we'll lose a friend from our group".

Tej Singh repiled, "As far as I think, it is the same group that Kumar had sighted".

Devi Singh repiled, "Certainly".

Jyotishi ji repiled, "Then why not swim to them? You are afraid of water like an old opium addict".

Devi Singh repiled, "Then what have we gained from your company? We had heard high praise of you that Jyotishi ji is this and that; he is a wheel, a giant but, in fact, nothing. You can't trace an ordinary group".

Jyotishi ji repiled, "What the hell can I say! These people seem even more clever than me. All of them have changed their names. When I try to find out their real names, strange names turn up instead. Someone is bereaved one, another one is *yogini*, *bhutani* and *dakini*. Now, tell me, shall I accept them as real names?"

Tej Singh repiled, "Why did they change their names?"

Jyotishiji repiled, "Just to befool us".

Devi Singh repiled, "Well, leave out their names, find out their homes".

Jyotishiji repiled, "When I consult ramal about their homes, I am told that their homes are in water. Shall I accept that they are water bodies, in other words, fish?"

Tej Singh repiled, "It's all right. You are to see whether they are water creatures or not".

Jyotishiji repiled, "Friends listen, the four elements — air, water, earth and fire are a hindrance in the functioning of ramal. If someone wants to outwit an astrologer or ramal, he can do so by manipulating these four elements. The astrologer will fail, the almanac and *patra* will become a white elephant".

Tej Singh repiled, "How? Tell us clearly so that we may also understand it. Such knowledge will stand us in good stead".

Jyotishi ji repiled, "I'll tell you but, at the moment, do what you have on hand. Let's swim".

Tej Singh repiled, "Okay".

These three *aiyari* started swimming to the boat. Tying the *aiyari* bag to the waist and depositing their clothes on the river bank, they landed in water. But hardly had they gone two or four feet that they heard a whistle from behind and the flare on the boat was extinguished. Now it was totally dark, the boat was eclipsed from the view. Devi Singh spoke, "See the result of our swimming."

Tej Singh replied, "It seems all very mischievous."

Jyotishi ji replied, "I had already warned that it was most disastrous to all of us. Now you have realised the truth of my words. These people have nullified all our efforts".

Devi Singh replied, "Let's return to the bank. They have outwitted us. It seems somebody on the bank was keeping watch. When we were swimming, he must have whistled. It became dark. Everything must have been pre-planned".

Jyotishi ji replied, "Why did the bloody bore sound the whistle after we had landed into water. Had he whistled before, we wouldn't have wet".

The three *aiyars* came to the bank to find that their clothes were gone.

Devi Singh replied, "Jyotishi ji, congratulations! Our clothes are missing! Oh, if I find any of them, I'll eat him alive".

Tej Singh replied, "I appreciate them. Their *aiyari* was superb".

Devi Singh replied, "Why not? Praise them more and more so that if any of them is listening at the moment, he will be soft to you and will not trouble you".

Jyotishi ji replied, "What more trouble can they inflict! They've even left us naked".

Tej Singh replied, "Let's go to our camp. This time we can't do any other thing".

It must be past midnight when those naked aiyar-victims proceeded towards their camp.

□

5

After Tej Singh, Devi Singh and Jyotishi ji left, Kumar Virendra Singh kept waking the whole night waiting for their return. As night advanced, Kumar felt more and more worried. It was almost dawn when the three *aiyars* returned. Tej Singh opined that they should go naked and finally they reached naked.

Kunwar Virendra Singh was awake, the flare was on. He was taken aback to see the strange appearance of those *aiyars* and asked, "What's this?" Tej Singh only said, "First look at our appearance and we'll relate the rest later".

Then they put on their clothes. By now, it was clear day light. Kumar asked Tej Singh, "Now, tell me, what problems did you have to face?"

Tej Singh replied, "We were so badly cheated that we will remember our whole life".

Kumar replied, "What's that?"

Tej Singh replied, "The one you are over head and ears in love, who we are madly looking for, undoubtedly loves you as much but we don't know why she's hiding herself and for what purpose".

Kumar replied, "Did you find out anything?"

Tej Singh replied, "Not to speak of anything, we saw with our own eyes, that's why we were given such harsh punishment. She also has several super *aiyars*. Had we known before, we would have been more cautious".

Kumar replied, "Say clearly so that I may understand".

Tej Singh narrated the whole story, Hearing it, Kumar started laughing and told Jyotishi ji, "They have also cheated your *ramal*".

Jyotishi ji replied, "Don't ask anything. They are a bundle of cheats".

Kumar replied, "If you could not understand their trick, you should have considered whether it was some *aiyari* on the part of Shivdutt".

Jyotishi ji replied, "No, Shivdutt's *aiyari* has nothing to do with them; rather they don't even have the scent of it. I have considered it thoroughly".

Tej Singh replied, "That's the only relief".

Jyotishi ji replied, "Today we'll go in the day time to investigate things".

Tej Singh replied, "How will we do the breaking then?"

Kumar replied, "It doesn't matter if we stop work for a day".

Tej Singh replied, "That's why, I say that your love for Chandrakanta has gone down".

Kumar replied, "Never, nothing in the world do I love more than Chandrakanta. But I don't know why I feel anxious to know about the forest girl, too".

Tej Singh replied, (Laughing) "All right, first we have to take aiyar Badrinath to the cave. Then we will do another thing, lest he should be stealthily released".

Kumar replied, "Take him to the cave this very day".

Tej Singh replied, "Okay, just now I am taking him there. Depositing him, I will come back overnight. The distance of 25 miles is nothing. Till then, Devi Singh and Jyotishi ji may go in search of the forest girl".

Tej Singh's opinion was accepted. He got ready after the daily bath and prayer. He fed Badrinath mixing anaesthetic powder in his food and when he became senseless, he tied him in a bundle and carried him on his back to the forest. Kumar sent Devi Singh and Jyotishi ji in search of the forest girl.

Tej Singh reached the cellar by the evening carrying Badrinath in a bundle. By inserting his hand in the lion's mouth, he pulled his tongue and then opened another lock, but the door did not open. Now Tej Singh was flabbergasted. He tried again and again but the door remained shut. He sat down to think but could understand nothing. At last, being helpless, he returned with the bundle, carrying Badrinath on his back.

□

6

In search of the forest girl, Devi Singh and Jyotishi ji had hardly gone some distance when they met a rider in mask who called them and said, "Where are you going, Devi Singh? Your trick will not work with us. Only yesterday you were treated properly. You were forced into water and we snatched away your clothes. Now, do you want to be arrested? Wait for a few days, we'll teach you *aiyari,* then you will see".

Hearing the words of the rider, Devi Singh was puzzled at heart but, looking towards Jyotishi ji, said, "See, this rider will teach us *aiyari*. He cannot even show his face out of shame".

Maskman replied, "What will Jyotishi ji see, he also must be feeling ashamed as we have nullified his *ramal*. He played ramal several times but could not trace anything".

Devi Singh replied, "If you stay in this area, we'll certainly find you".

Maskman replied, "I'm sure to stay here. Will see you everyday but will not let you find me".

While talking, Devi Singh very cleverly jumped and removed the mask from the face of the rider. He saw that the whole face was daubed with vermillion. So he was not recognisable.

The rider very swiftly snatched away the turban from Devi Singh's head and throwing a letter before him rode away. Devi Singh felt ashamed. He picked up the letter. On the envelope the words were:

"Kunwar Virendra Singh"

Jyotishi ji told Devi Singh, "We don't know where they come from but I think all in their group are *aiyars*".

Devi Singh (puts the letter in his pocket), "No doubt about it, see every time we are humbled. I had thought that by unmasking him, I could know his identity but he was so clever that under the mask, his face was coloured".

Jyotishi ji, "Anyway, we'll see to it later. At the moment, we have to go to the camp because we should first deliver the letter to Kumar and see what it has. Had there not been Kumar's name on the envelope, we might have read it".

Devi Singh replied, "Yes, let's go. First let's hear what the letter says. Only then we will think of further action".

Both of them returned to the camp and briefing Kunwar Virendra Singh at his camp, handed the letter to him. Kumar read as follows:

"Whatsoever may happen, I will not appear before you until you agree in writing to the following terms:

(i) Chandrakanta and I are married the same day or the same occasion.

(ii) I should not be rated lower than Chandrakanta because I am equal to her in all respects.

If you don't write an agreement to this effect, I will go to my house tomorrow itself. Moreover, I tell you without my help, you may try for a thousand years but you will not get Chandrakanta".

Kumar's love for the forest girl was of the highest order. His love for the forest girl was not any less than that of Chandrakanta but reading the letter, he felt squarely worried. He began to think how it can be possible that he is married to both Chandrakanta and the forest girl on the same occasion. Will she ever agree to it and will king Jay Singh allow it! Besides, what's this that without her help, I can't meet Chandrakanta. However, as it is, without the forest girl, it is difficult for me to live. I'll surely write an agreement as she says and will consider the rest later on. Princess Chandrakanta will surely agree with me.

Kumar showed that letter to both Devi Singh and Jyotishi ji. They were also puzzled to read what the forest girl had written and what the reply should be.

For the whole day and night, Kumar was engaged in thinking what reply to give to the letter. Next day, at dawn Tej Singh also turned up carrying on his back Pundit Badrinath in a bundle.

Kumar asked replied, "Why did you return?"

Tej Singh replied, "What can I say, everything went haywire".

Kumar replied, "Why?"

Tej Singh replied, "The door of the cellar did not open".

Kumar replied, "Has anybody shut from inside?"

Tej Singh replied, "No, there's no locking arrangement inside".

Jyotishi ji replied, "There must be either of the two things — either a new man has come who has upset the lock or Maharaja Shivdutt has played some trick from inside".

Tej Singh replied, "Why will Shivdutt create more problems for himself by locking the door from inside? It will only harm him and not help him in any way".

Kumar replied, "Maybe, the forest girl might have played a trick".

Tej Singh replied, "Your thinking is strange. What can be the connection between the forest girl and the cellar?"

Kumar replied, "You don't know. She has written to me that I can't meet Chandrakanta without her help. She has also written two other things. I am in a dilemma what to say in reply and why it is that I will need the help of the forest girl. But now I have become suspicious to see you come back undone".

Devi Singh replied, "I also think it's all her making".

Tej Singh replied, "If the forest girl wanted to create some mischief for us, she wouldn't have returned the *tilismi* book to us. Look, what's written in that letter which has come with the book!"

Jyotishi ji replied, "You're right to say so".

Tej Singh to Kumar replied, "Well, give me the letter in which the forest girl has written that without her help you can't meet Chandrakanta".

Kumar handed the letter to Tej Singh. On reading the letter, Tej Singh was immersed in thinking what could be the matter. He was at a loss. Kumar said, "You people know how much the love for the forest girl has affected my heart. I don't have peace even for a moment without seeing her. Then what is the harm in writing the agreement as demanded by her. When she is pleased, she will surely let out the secret".

Tej Singh replied, "Do what you think right, poor Chandrakanta will not object but Maharaja Jay Singh will never agree that both the marriages are performed in the same pavilion. Who knows who she is, who is her father and where she comes from?"

Kumar replied, "She has also written in the letter that she is in no way inferior to Chandrakanta".

While such talks were going on, an orderly announced, "A sepoy is standing outside, who wants to say something". Kumar ordered to bring him in. When the man appeared, everybody saw that he was a strange man. Short in height, black complexion, tight *pyjama* with lace, a bamboo basket-type hat and having a sword and shield. He bowed to Kumar in salutation".

Everybody found his appearance funny and laughable but suppressing his laughter, Tej Singh asked, "Who are you and where you have come from?" The young sepoy said, "I am god and have come from the assembly of giants. I want from Kumar reply to the letter which was given to Devi Singh and Jagannath – Jyotishi ji by a rider yesterday".

Tej Singh replied, "Now, how did you know the names of Jyotishi ji and Devi Singh?"

Young man replied, "I know Jyotishi ji since the day he was born in this world and Devi Singh is my old disciple".

Devi Singh replied, "O brute, when did I become your disciple?"

"Do you insult me?"

Young man replied, "Rather you are insulting me as you show no respect to your guru".

Devi Singh replied, "It appears death has brought you here".

Young man replied, "I am death myself".

Devi Singh replied, "Shall I punish you for your impudence?"

Young man replied, "I am not a puny man's messenger. I have been sent by one to whom you will bow your head hundred times in a day".

Devi Singh wanted to speak further but Tej Singh stopped him and said, "Keep quiet, it seems that he is either a fool or an aiyar. Being yourself an aiyar why do you from at an aiyar's joke?

Young man said, "If you don't understand even now, I'll call in Champa to convince you".

All people present laughed at the words of the young man. Still they were puzzled who the man was. And the irony was that all the men of the forest girl knew everything about us whereas we could not even know them.

Tej Singh started scrutinising the face of the man. He said, "Why do you stare at my face, I am not an *aiyar*, I have not coloured my face. Bring in hot water and wash my face. I have not become dark today. I have been black for four hundred years".

Tej Singh burst out laughing and said, "Whoever you are, you're all right. I am not to examine you further, had there been a man from the enemy camp, I would do so, but no need to doubt you. Whether a fool or an aiyar, you are from the friend circle".

Hearing this, he bowed in salutation and looking towards Kumar said, "Please give me the reply because I have to cover a long distance. Kumar wrote on the back of the letter – I accept everything from the bottom of my heart". Then he stamped it with his ring and handed it to the young man. Taking the letter, he went away.

□

7

Today, it was too late almost mid day talking to the young man and writing the letter. Tej Singh revived Badrinath and posted him on patrol duty. He said to Kumar, "You perform your daily routine and then we'll think what to do. No work was done during the last two days".

Kumar dismissed the court and after bathing and prayer, sat in the camp. Fateh Singh and the *aiyars* came. Before they discussed anything, the orderly announced, "An old woman is standing at the gate and wants to say something. She refuses to talk to us. She says she will tell Kumar whatever she has to tell because it concerns him".

Kumar said, "Bring her in promptly". The orderly ushered in the old woman. At first sight, Tej Singh burst out, "Is this the court for devils and *jinns*?"

The old woman heard it. With her eyes shot red with anger, she turned towards Tej Singh and said, "Now I'll say nothing, I'm going back. It's nothing to me. Kumar will have to pay for it". Saying this, she went out of the camp. Getting a hint from Kumar, the orderly brought her back amicably.

That woman had a peculiar face. She would be about seventy years of age, hair partly white, majority of teeth missing but two large front teeth protruding two inches outside lined with tobacco and plaque. The ring and brass trinklets completed her dress.

Tej Singh asked, "What do you want?"

Old woman replied, "Let me first breathe free. But why should I talk to you? Whatever there is, I'll say only to Kumar".

Kumar replied, "Okay, speak to me, what do you have to say?"

Old woman replied, "I'll surely say to you. It's for your good". (coughs)

Devi Singh replied, "Now she will cough for an hour. Then she will open her month".

Old woman replied, "Again, another man has interfered".

Kumar replied, "No, no, nobody will disturb you".

Old woman replied, "There's something I'm going to tell you for your good hearing which you'll be overjoyed. But I also want something in return".

Kumar replied, "Sure, I'll certainly please you".

Old woman replied, "Kumar, first you swear that neither you nor your men will interfere with me and nobody will think of beating or arresting me".

Kumar replied, "When it is in my interest, why will anybody beat or arrest you?"

Old woman replied, "Okay, it's all right but I fear because I have done something for you which you would not have done in a thousand years. Because of this I fear that out of resentment, your *aiyars* may harass me".

Hearing the words of that old woman, all people were stunned and began to think what great feat this woman has worked that she is giving herself airs. At last, Kumar took an oath that neither he nor his men would mind whatever she says. Then she rejoined, "I can tell you the whereabouts of that forest girl and also give you a clue to meet Chandrakanta by breaking the *tilism* in a few minutes".

All present were delighted to hear the old woman.

Kumar said, "If so, tell me right now who is that forest girl and how to break the *tilism* in a few minutes".

Old woman said, "First, let it be clear about my reward".

Kumar said, "If your words are true, you'll get what you want".

Old woman said, "Then swear on it".

Kumar said, "All right, but let me know what reward do you want".

Old woman said, "Nothing more, only that you marry me. Whenever you may marry Chandrakanta and the forest girl, but you must marry me today because I have been in love with you for a long time. In fact, while trying to meet you, I have grown old. Only today I have got an opportunity that you are in my clutch. Now, be quick. Otherwise I'll lose my youth and you will repent thereafter".

Hearing the words of the old woman, Kumar turned red with anger and his *aiyars* also got angry but they felt helpless. Had Kumar not taken the oath, they would have treated her like a donkey.

Tej Singh asked Jyotishi ji, "You tell me, is she an *aiyar* or as she looks? Had Kumar not taken an oath, we would have found out the fact by any means".

Jyotishi ji put his hand on his nose and, examining the sound, said, "She is not an *aiyar*, she is what she looks." Now Tej Singh was even more angry and told the old woman, "Now, go away from here. We have already honoured Kumar's oath so that we did not say anything to you. Now, if you take time to leave, I'll get you mauled by dogs. What a drama is this! Such witches falling in love with Kumar!"

The old woman said, "You will repent if you don't value my words. I'll upset all your plans. Have you not seen what a lock I have fitted in that cellar that you couldn't open. And, at last, you had to return carrying Badrinath in a bundle. Now I'll go and free Maharaja Shivdutt and then create a fuss".

Saying these words her eyes red with anger, she went out of the camp. At a hint from Tej Singh, Devi Singh also followed her.

Kumar said, "Tej Singh, this witch is a bundle of troubles. She says she had locked the cellar".

Tej Singh said, "I fail to understand what the matter is".

Jyotishiji said, "If her words are true, a terrible misfortune has cropped up before us".

Tej Singh said ", "The truth of her words will come out if Shivdutt is freed. If it so happens, I'll surely kill her".

Jyotishiji said, "Such a person must be killed".

Tej Singh said, "Kumar has not sworn that nobody will touch her for the whole of her life".

Kumar (Breathing long), "Alas, I had to see such a day!"

Tej Singh said, "You don't worry. Just see what we do".

Devi Singh is stalking her, he will not return without tracing her identity.

Kumar said, "These days your *aiyari* has rotten. You couldn't trace that forest girl, how can you trace the witch now!"

Such a remark cut Tej Singh to the quick. But he said not a single word and went out of the camp.

After these people left, Kumar was alone. Different thoughts crossed his mind, now Chandrakanta's helplessness and arrest in the *tilism*, then the delay in breaking the *tilism*, or not getting the exact information about the forest girl and at times the witch's proposal to marry him, etc. He was plunged in regret and pain. He was very sad and unhappy. At last, the day was over and evening set in.

Kumar called in Fateh Singh and asked him, "Where is Tej Singh?" He replied, "Don't know anything for certain, but has gone somewhere with Jyotishi ji".

□

8

Devi Singh followed the old woman. Till day long, the old woman went on and on. He also chased her. At night, she reached the narrow pass of a small mountain between high hills on both sides. While passing through the pass at one point, she entered a cave with such a small opening that only one man could enter. Devi Singh thought that might be the abode of that witch. He sat under a tree. He kept sitting for the whole night, but that old woman did not come out of that cave. In the morning, he, too, entered the same cave.

The cave was totally dark. Devi Singh went on fumbling. By touching the sides with his hands, he realised that the cave was like a tunnel and had no rooms or any resting place. After going two miles, he saw some light shining in the front. As he went closer, the light seemed bigger and when he reached close, he came across an exit.

Devi Singh came out and found himself near a small river. When he looked around, he found jungle and jungle all around. It was not clear where he had come and what was the way to the camp. The day had also advanced. He began to think that the old woman had badly cheated him and now it was very difficult to find out where she had gone and by which route. He had to return by the same route because he did not know how to reach the camp through the forest. He feared that he might go astray. He regretted that he had not followed the old woman in the cave but he had no knowledge that the tunnel had an exit on the other side.

Devi Singh was mad with anger but what could he do? He could not get hold of the old woman to settle score with her. At last, a helpless Devi Singh returned through the same tunnel and reached the camp in the evening.

He went to Kumar's camp and saw that several people were talking to Virendra Singh and Fateh Singh. Seeing Devi Singh, all of them left the camp except Fateh Singh. Kumar asked, "What's the news about that oldie?

Devi Singh, "She badly cheated me".

Kumar (laughingly), "How come?"

Devi Singh narrated the whole story what he had to suffer to chase the old woman. Kumar felt sorry to hear it.

Devi Singh asked Fateh Singh, "Where are our guru and Jyotishi ji? Fateh Singh replied that Kumar was very angry because of the old witch. In anger, he told Tej Singh that his *aiyari* had rusted. Hearing it, he felt angry and insulted and went away along with Jyotishi ji. He has not come back as yet".

Devi Singh said, "When had he left?"

Fateh Singh said, "A little after your departure".

Devi Singh said, "Guru's going off in a huff will not go in vain. He'll surely bring in good news".

Kumar said, "Let's see".

Immediately, Tej Singh and Jyotishi ji turned up.

Their faces were beaming with pleasure and smile, an indication that they had certainly achieved something. Kumar asked, "Now, what news?

Tej Singh said, "The news is good".

Kumar said, "Say without beating about the bush".

Tej Singh said, "What will you do hearing it?"

Kumar said, "Is it not worth my hearing?"

Tej Singh said, "It is worth your hearing, but I won't disclose it right now".

Kumar said, "At least say something".

Tej Singh said, "No, not at all".

Devi Singh said, "Arre guru, will you not tell even me?"

Tej Singh said, "Shall I, just because you addressed me as 'guru'?"

Devi Singh said, "You can't help telling me!"

Tej Singh said, (Laughingly) "First tell me, what credit have you brought?"

Devi Singh said, "Sorry, I've sullied your guruship".

Tej Singh said, "Then it's all over".

While such talks were going on, the chobdar announced with folded hands that the Diwan of Maharaja Shivdutt has come. Hearing it, Kumar turned to Tej Singh and said, "Okay, let him in, others to remain outside".

The Diwan of Maharaja Shivdutt turned up and having saluted, presented lots of jewels. Kumar touched them. The Diwan said, "I have brought this presentation on behalf of Maharaja Shivdutt. By the grace of God and your mercy, the Maharaja has been released. Immediately, he summoned court and announced that henceforth he has accepted the loyalty of Kunwar Virendra Singh and ordered that all his *aiyars* and staff will regard Kumar as their master. Thereafter, giving this gift and the letter, he has sent me to you. Please accept this presentation!"

Kumar accepted the presentation and handed it to Tej Singh and gestured the Diwan to take a seat. Giving the letter, he sat down.

As night advanced a little, Kumar summoned the court. When the full court had assembled, Tej Singh was asked to read the letter loudly. Tej Singh started reading. After an elaborate salutation, the words were —

"I got released from that cellar which can be ascribed to be the outcome of your mercy because it was you who had imprisoned me. Please don't think so. For certain reasons, I can't disclose the secret of my release nor can I be present before you. But when the occasion comes and you know the secret of my release, you will be convinced that I had not told a lie. Now I hope that forgiving all my faults, you will accept this presentation. Please also note that henceforth none of my *aiyars* and attendants will ever try to cheat you.

Yours,

Shivdutt".

All were pleased to hear this letter. Kumar ordered that the imprisoned Pundit Badrinath should be brought in. When he came at a hint from Kumar, his hands and feet were untied. Dressing him in ceremonial *Khilat*, he was handed over to the Diwan and was requested to be the royal guest for two days and then proceed to Chunar. Then ordering Fateh Singh to play the host, he dismissed the court.

□

9

It was midnight when the court was dismissed. Taking Diwan Saheb with him, Fateh Singh went to his camp. After a while, Tej Singh, Devi Singh and Jyotishi ji assembled in Kumar's camp. There was none except them.

Kumar said, "Tej Singh, the old woman proved true!"

Tej Singh said, "Yes sir, but the letter of Maharaja Shivdutt tells something else".

Devi Singh said, "His writing is dubious, he might be misleading".

Jyotishiji said, "This time we have to do something after proper consideration. Howsoever Shivdutt may show his sincerity, one should never trust a foe".

Tej Singh said, "You are an astrologer, just consider has Shivdutt written this letter sincerely or craftily?"

Jyotishiji said, (after considering) "He has written this letter with a sincere heart, but it is doubtful whether he will keep himself clean".

Tej Singh said, "These days such things are happening as they have no base at all! If he has written this letter with an honest heart, why has he not written clearly about his release?"

Jyotishiji said, "No sir, *ramal* doesn't work with *tilism* and that cellar is *tilism* in which Maharaja Shivdutt was imprisoned".

Tej Singh said, "It goes beyond comprehension".

Devi Singh said, "That witch seems to be a seasoned *aiyar*".

Jyotishiji said, "Never, I've considered, she doesn't know even the ABC of *aiyari*".

Kumar said, "Anyway, we'll see what happens. But from tomorrow we must resume breaking the *tilism*".

Tej Singh said, "Yes, we must start the *tilism* work tomorrow".

Kumar said, "Now you people should also go".

The three *aiyars* took leave of Kumar and went to their respective camps. Next day, Kunwar Virendra Singh took the three *aiyars* with him to *tilism*. He also took the *tilism* book and the lock. Reaching the *dalan*, he opened the lock to the cellar and removing the stone plate went down and passing through the room, reached the garden where they had previously dug the earth.

They started digging the same spot. After digging 8–9 feet, there appeared something like a box. Its upper flap was shut and the lock was covered with bronze foil to prevent rusting.

Kumar wanted to take the box out but failed. As they removed the soil from the four sides, the box appeared larger and larger. Howsoever they tried, they could not find how much deep it was buried in the earth. At last, being hopeless Kumar opened the book and began to read. It read —

Tying the lock with a rope, when you will drag it on, at one point, the lock will stick to the earth. There remaining a handful of earth, lift the lock and dig the earth so long as the face of a box does not appear. When the upper part of the box appears, stop digging because, in fact, that box is the door. Now, dig the earth exactly 7 feet east to the foundation in the middle of the garden. There you will see a pitcher which contains the key in it. With that key, open the lock to the cellar, you will see stairs, go down that way.

Inside that cellar will be very dark and full of smoke. Beware not to light a match or flare because the moment there is a fire or flare, the smoke will flare up and cause a heavy devastation and you will not save your life. Go down the cellar covering your face with clothes and fumbling your way, you must quickly walk on so that the smoke does not affect your mind. At a distance, there will be a shining chamber transparently showing the objects therein. The entire chamber is fitted with wires from top to bottom. You needn't investigate, just cut those wires quickly with a sword and come out.

Kumar stopped reading further. As written, he dug the earth seven feet east to the foundation in the middle of the garden. The pitcher appeared. He took out the lock and opened the mouth of the cellar. Devi Singh said, "Now wrap clothes on your faces. *Tilism* means risk, danger to life. Don't make a light, fumble in the dark, act like a blind man and walk quickly so that the smoke doesn't affect our minds".

Kumar burst out laughing to hear the words of Devi Singh. All wrapped up their mouths with cloth and reached the shining chamber inside. As far as possible, they cut the wires and came out of the cellar.

Though they had wrapped their faces, still the smoke had affected them and made them sick. Out of the cellar, the four men lay senseless for two hours. Regaining consciousness, Tej Singh asked Jyotishi ji. "How long is the day left?"

He said, "Still four hours to go".

Kumar said, "There's no time to work now. What can we do in four hours?" Jyotishiji had the same view. At last, all the four people moved out of the garden and passing through the room and the cellar came to the veranda of the ruins. They placed the rock plate over the mouth of the cellar as before and locked it before coming to their camp.

Having taken rest for a while, Kumar had a mind to enjoy fresh air walking in the forest. He told Tej Singh who also agreed and with the three *aiyars,* went out of the camp. Kumar rode his horse and the *aiyars* went on foot.

Kumar was riding slow. He might have gone a mile when he saw a piece of paper pasted on a thick *saal* tree. Tej Singh said, "Look, what's this paper and what's written on it?" Devi Singh went near that tree and read that paper. The words were —

"Now, have you realised what a nuisance I am! I told you to marry me and I would tell you how to meet Chandrakanta by breaking the *tilism*. But you didn't agree and I got Maharaja Shivdutt released out of my anger. Now what's your desire? Will you marry or not? If you agree, paste your reply on this tree and I'll immediately come to you and if you don't agree, give me your reply forthwith. This time I will satisfy myself by killing Chandrakanta and Chapla. I take no time to go to the *tilism,* in a day, I go and return a hundred times. Just consider your own welfare and my youth. Your *aiyars' aiyari* will not work before me. That day Devi Singh had chased me but what was the result? Be advised, listen to me and don't persist. Shivdutt has become your friend only on my advice. Be advised even now.

Yours – Suryamukhi".

After reading it, Devi Singh called all of them by the gesture of his hand and said, "You people also read it".

All people burst out laughing to read the word 'Suryamukhi'. Kumar said, "Look, how that witch has given herself a pompous name! Tej Singh told Jyotishi ji, "See, what's all this written here".

Jyotishi ji replied, "Whatever may happen, but take it from me that witch cannot harm Kumar. Don't take this letter seriously".

Kumar said, "You are also right but what she says, she does". Kumar proceeded further. While walking, he saw such writing on paper pasted on several trees. Kumar did not feel assured by the words of Jyotishi ji. A dejected Kumar returned with his three *aiyars* to his camp.

For some time, they talked about that Suryamukhi. After an hour at night, Tej Singh told Kumar, "Right now, we are going on vigilance. Maybe, we may come across something new". Saying this, Tej Singh, Devi Singh and Jyotishi ji took leave of Kumar and went on the prowl. Kumar too, after having dinner, lay down on bed. He had no sleep, thinking about the helplessness of Chandrakanta, the longing for the forest girl and the mischief of the old woman and longing for the forest spent half the night. Meanwhile, he sensed the presence of somebody inside the camp. Seeing Tej Singh Kumar asked, "Tej Singh, is there any news?"

Tej Singh, "Yea, I have chanced upon a good thing".

Kumar, "What's that? Where? Let me see".

Tej Singh, "Come along".

Kumar Virendra Singh followed Tej Singh out of the camp. He saw some light at a distance and a gathering of several people. He asked, "How come, this crowd?" Tej Singh replied, "Let's go and see, it's a happy thing!"

As Kumar reached, the crowd was set aside. Several flares were burning. Kumar saw that the blood-oozing body of Krur Singh was lying, a dagger still planted in his chest. He told Tej Singh, "Tej Singh, you've killed him after all".

Tej Singh said, "Do we ever kill anybody all of a sudden?"

Kumar said, "Then who killed him?"

Tej Singh said, "How do I know?"

Kumar said, "Then where did you bring the corpse from?"

Tej Singh said, "While patrolling, we went to the back of this *tilismi* ruins. From a distance, we saw three to four people standing. By the time we reached close, they all fled away. The dead body of Krur Singh lay there. Then through Devi Singh, I had a carriage and carriers and got this corpse brought here as it is. He is not dead yet, the body is still warm, but there is no chance of survival".

Kumar said, "It's very strange! Who killed him? Well, take out that dagger from his chest".

Tej Singh took out the dagger and washing it with water brought it to Kumar. When looked at it in the light of the flare, there was something engraved on it. When he scrutinised it minutely, he found the name 'Chapla' engraved in tiny letters. Tej Singh said surprised, "Look, it has 'Chapla' engraved on it, besides I recognise this dagger very well. Chapla always had it strapped to her waist, but how did it come here? Has Chapla killed him?"

Devi Singh said, "Poor Chapla must be sitting beside princess Chandrakanta in the cave. There wouldn't be any light".

Kumar said, "Then who brought this dagger?"

Tej Singh, "Besides this, we should also think why Krur Singh came here. He was with Maharaja Shivdutt and his Diwan is here who says that Maharaja has no enmity with you now".

Kumar said, "Send somebody to summon the Diwan of Maharaja Shivdutt".

Tej Singh asked Devi Singh to send for the Diwan. Devi Singh went immediately and waking him up gave him the message of Kumar. Then and there he came to Kumar. Fateh Singh also turned up. Seeing the dead body of Krur Singh, Diwan Saheb blurted, "The devil has met his fate but his accomplices Ahmad and Nazim are still at large. Had he met the same fate, it would have satisfied me". Kumar asked, "Is he not with you now?" Diwan Saheb replied, "No, the day Maharaja came on release ordered that none of his men would nurse any enmity against Kumar, Krur Singh fled away from Chunar with his wife and children as well as Ahmad and Nazim. Later, Maharaja ordered his search but there was no trace of him".

Moments later, Krur Singh made three or four hiccups and breathed his last. Kumar told Tej Singh, "Now that he's dead, dispose him of and keep the dagger with you, leave the rest for tomorrow". Tej Singh got the corpse of Krur Singh removed from there and all went back to their camps.

□

10

In the morning, after daily routine work Kumar decided to break the *tilism* and along with three *aiyars* entered it. Like yesterday, passing through the cellar and the rooms reached that garden. Sat down on the black rock and began to read the *tilismi* book. It read—

"Having entered the smoke-filled cellar, when you cut the wires, there will be no smoke in a short time. You might have noticed something written on the white platform placed on the marble seat in the black twelve-door room, a mere touch of which causes sensation in the body and the man who touches it becomes senseless, but such things will not happen by cutting the wires as they are connected underground to the twelve-door room. Next day again, go to the same smoky cellar, there will be no smoke. So, you will light a flare and fearlessly see immense wealth stored there for you. Take that out and keep at a suitable place. Until you exhaust all the wealth from the cellar, don't take up another *tilismi* work. Also take away the white square slab placed on the seat in the black twelve-door room. In fact, that is a box which contains unique objects. You will find key to it in the same *tilism*".

Kumar read the contents twice and then got ready to enter the smoky cellar. Tej Singh, Devi Singh and Jyotishi ji all three lighted their flares and entered the cellar along with Kumar. They reached that room in which they had cut several wires. Now, in the light, they saw that the disconnected wires were lying here and there. The room was large and spacious. Hundreds of iron and silver boxes lay scattered. On one side, a bunch of keys was hanging on the wall.

Kumar took away the bunch of keys. It seemed that they were the keys to those boxes. He opened a box and found full of royal diamond ornaments for women. He promptly shut it and opened another box and found precious diamond-studded wonderful swords and daggers. Kumar shut it too and with joy told Tej Singh:

"No doubt, there is tremendous treasure in this room. There is no need to open and check them, take the boxes out one by one and send them to Naugarh. We should lift them at the earliest".

Tej Singh replied, "Howsoever early we may try, it is difficult to take away these boxes from here in less than ten days. If you check each one before sending to Naugarh, it will take several days and the *tilism*-breaking work will be kept pending. Therefore, in my view, it is better to send these boxes to Naugarh without checking them. When we are free, we will open and check them. Thus, nobody will know what came out of them and the enemies will not be jealous. Nobody knows the amount of wealth in these boxes for the safety of which such a big *tilism* had to be built".

Kumar liked the idea and Devi Singh and Jyotishi ji also approved it. The four people came out of the cellar and through the same ruins and process, closed the top of the upper cellar with the *tilismi* key and came out to their camp.

Today they came out of the *tilism* in a short time. It was hardly mid-day. Kumar handed over the bunch of keys to the treasure and the *Tilism* to Tej Singh and instructed, "Now, you arrange to forward the boxes to Naugarh".

□

11

Tej Singh took several days to remove the boxes from the *tilism* and send them to Naugarh because he had to arrange security and surveillance. He would go to *tilism* everyday and come out an hour before dusk. So long as all the boxes were not dispatched to Naugarh, the *tilism* breaking work was put off.

One night, Kumar was sleeping on his bed. Half the night had passed but the memory of Chandrakanta and the forest girl did not let him sleep; he slept for a moment and awoke thereafter. At last, he was so badly overpowered by sleep that he lay sleeping till mid-day.

When Kumar woke up, he did not find himself in his own room, rather in a lavishly decorated room with precious chandeliers hanging from the ceiling. In utter amazement, he looked around. It appeared that it was a grand court having marble walls on three sides and big decent doors on the fourth side. The doors were closed. There were several candle stands on the walls and candles were still burning in the day. Enchanting pictures of beautiful women were hanging on the walls. In the middle of the long wall, a life size picture of a man was set in the door frame made of gold.

While looking at those pictures, Kumar fixed his eyes on that pig picture. He began to think rather mutter as if talking to a friend sitting by his side—

"Aha! Nothing in this court is more valuable than this picture and, no doubt, this is the picture of that woman whose love has intoxicated me! Wow! What a clean innocent face!"

Kumar got up with a start and stood beside that picture. The doors of the court were closed but on top of each door, there were small holes fitted with glass panes through which direct light was falling on that large picture. Kumar had got down from the bed just to see that. In fact, it was the picture of Chandrakanta.

Kumar stood near that picture and started speaking as if narrating something to a man—

"Aha! What a nice and clean picture. It shows the same height, similar eyes big and inviting. The glow on the pink cheeks is marvellous as is the red on the thin smiling lips, ear rings in the ears, nose ring and red mark on the forehead are all wonderful. The necklace is all the more artistic in the midst of which a shining emerald is set dexterously. Not to speak of the necklace, all ornaments are enchanting and see how Chapla on one side and Champa on the other are standing with their fingers on their chins".

"Alas, where is Chandrakanta!" With a long sigh, he stared at the picture.

Somewhere from above the tinkling sound startled Kumar. Upwards there were several windows, all closed. Where did the sound come from then? Who's that woman in this house! Till now, Kumar was not in control of his senses, but now he was puzzled and began to think—

"How did I come to this place? Who brought me here? He was kind to me to show the picture of Chandrakanta but I fear I may not be dreaming all this! It must be a dream, it's better to go back to bed".

Thinking so, Kumar went back to bed, closed his eyes but sleep was evading him. Meanwhile, the sound of anklets again startled him. This time as he got up, he rushed straight towards the door and thrashed all the seven doors. All doors opened. A small lush green garden came to sight. Almost three hours might have passed since sunrise.

This garden was full of wild flowers and bushes. A small pond in the middle was also visible. Kumar went straight to the pond which was made of stone. On one side, there were descending stairs, upwards there were two big blackberry trees on both sides of the staircase. Their shadows fell on all stairs and even extended to the water. Under those trees, there were small marble platforms. On the platform, on the left side, there were soft mattresses.

On a small silver desk, there were *dhoti-gamchha* and other valuable decent clothes to wear.

On the marble platform to the right, there was also a silver desk with worship articles placed on it. Several small ancestral worship paraphernalia were arranged neat and clean. A soft woollen sheet lay with a small stone fruit.

Kumar was thinking where he was and who had brought him there, the name of the place and to whom this room and garden belonged. Meanwhile, he looked at the tree under which lay the worship articles. A chit of paper was pasted. He went there and read the words on the chit—

"Kunwar Virendra Singh, all these things are meant for you. Take a dip in this pond and use these things as today you are my guest".

Kumar felt even more bewildered to think that in spite of such a big arrangement, there was not a single person to see. It must be the abode of fairies and they might be roaming in this garden, but are not visible to me. However, let me first take a round inside this garden to see what it has; thereafter, I will take a bath, etc. If I find an exit, I will go out but no, how can I think of going from here unless I know the owner of this garden and why I was brought here. Thinking this, Kumar entered the garden for a walk.

The room in which Kumar had slept was to the west of this garden. There was no building on the east side as the rising sun had clearly shown which must have climbed up. While walking, Kumar reached the north block attached to the eastern room.

Kumar wanted to step into that room also, but it was not possible because all its doors were closed. Hence, he moved on watching the wild flowers and bushes to the south of the garden. He saw a small room, the writing on the wall showed that it was a toilet. There was a *lota* (round metal jug) placed on a wooden stool nearby.

It was about forenoon and Kumar was worried. After thinking, Kumar lifted the *lota* from the stool and went into the toilet. Then he washed himself, had a bath, cleaned his teeth and finally put on the clothes meant for him. He also prayed sitting on the other marble platform.

Having disposed of morning routine, Kumar moved to that room in which he had slept and seen the picture of Chandrakanta. But all the doors of the room were closed and Kumar could not open them despite all efforts. There was broad sunshine outside. He felt uneasy because of the hot sun and wanted to take a rest in a cool shade. At last moving away from there, he went to see the room on the other side which was closed till sometime ago. Now the doors were open. Kumar went in.

Inside the room, the marble floor was neat and clean. It seemed that it had been washed just now. In the middle, there lay a Kashmiri carpet. In the front, several food items were arranged in gold and silver plates. On the seat, there was a letter. Kumar read the letter. The words were—

"Have no fear of any sort. This house belongs to a friend of yours where you will be hosted most warmly. Now, have your meal and take a rest in the adjacent room on the bed meant for you".

Reading it, Kumar began to think what to do next. He felt very hungry but in the absence of the host, he did not want to eat those things. Also he had no idea of the owner of the house and the person who was hosting him in disguise. It was not clear where the things came from, where they are prepared and where are the attendants, etc. If their desire was to remain unknown, why did they bring me here?

Sitting on the seat, Kumar went on thinking in different ways until at last he was upset with hunger. How long could he suppress his hunger? At last, he extended his hand towards the food articles but withdrew his hand thinking something.

Kumar's being ready to eat and then withdrawing his hand caused a loud laughter which baffled Kumar. He looked right and left but nothing was noticeable. There were windows above but no person was visible.

As Kumar was staring at the above windows, a voice was heard.

"Please don't take time to eat. This place is not dangerous at all".

Kumar felt extremely hungry. He began to eat. All items were sumptuously tasty. Having a full meal, Kumar got up. On one side, there was water in a pot ready for washing the hand. Having washed, he moved towards the adjacent room. As written in the slip of paper, an exquisitely beautiful bed lay in that room. Lying on bed, Kumar started thinking variously, who is the owner of this house, what is his interest in not appearing himself, how long I shall have to stay, what will happen to my caravan, etc. Thinking all this, Kumar fell asleep.

Till two hours in the night, Kumar kept sleeping. Thereafter, he heard the sound of violin and one's singing. He opened his eyes and looked sideways. He realised that it was not the same room in which he had slept after eating. Rather, it was another twelve pole room extraordinarily decorated. The sound of violin and singing was coming from outside.

Kumar got up from the bed and looked outside. The night was pitch dark but there was bright illumination, which showed that it was not the same garden in which he had taken a bath and eaten his meal.

This time it was not noticeable how big the garden was because its wall on the other side was not visible at all. There were also large trees in this garden. There was profuse illumination. A few beautiful and tender girls were seen singing and walking. Kumar stood watching the enchanting scene. The girls were laughing and exchanging banter among themselves passing from one flower bed to another. Kumar could not help himself and moving slowly stood near them.

Seeing Kumar, girls stopped and started talking among them, which Kumar could not understand, but from their gestures, it seemed that they were amazed at Kumar's presence. Meanwhile one of the girls came near Kumar and said, "Who are you and why did you enter this garden?"

Kumar saw her closely and found her very active and attractive. He replied, "I don't know whose garden it is. If possible, you please tell me who is the master?"

Woman said, "First answer my question, then I'll answer all your questions".

Kumar said, "I don't know at all why and how I came here".

Woman said, "What a fun! How innocent you are! (looking towards another woman) Sister, see how such innocent thieves enter into our garden, who don't even have any idea why they have come!"

At her call, all others came and surrounded Kumar and started questioning him, "Tell us the fact, who are you and why have you come here?"

Another woman said, "Pass your hand round his waist to see whether he has stolen something".

Third woman said, "Certainly, he must have stolen something".

Fourth woman said, "Look at his face, he has assumed the face of a prince".

First woman said, "First tell us, where did you steal these clothes from?"

Kumar was bewildered to hear the words of these women. He thought he had been caught in a mischief. Nothing is clear. Certainly it must be the mischief of these people to bring me here and now they are calling me a thief. Such thoughts came to his mind and the conversation resumed.

Kumar said, "It appears you people have brought me here".

A woman said, "We were not required to bring you here. What reward can you give us? No doubt, you have come with an intention to steal".

Kumar said, "I don't even know the way into this place nor the way out of here. If you tell me, I'll go from here".

Second woman said, "Oh, the poor innocent man! You came up to us and don't know the way".

Third woman said, "Sister, you don't understand this man. He wants to dodge us".

Fourth woman said, "We should arrest him and take him away".

Kumar said, "Where will you take me?"

A woman said, "To my master".

Kumar said, "What's the name of your master?"

A woman said, "Who can dare take my master's name?"

Kumar said, "Is there any harm in naming your master?"

Second woman said, "Harm? Your tongue will be severed as you name him".

Kumar said, "Then how do you people talk to your master?"

Second woman said, "We talk to master's picture. We are never face to face".

Kumar said, "If one asks who do you serve, what will you say?"

Third woman said, "We keep dangling from our neck our master princess' picture to show whom we serve".

Kumar said, "Are there several princesses other than your mistress?"

First woman said, "No, there are only two princesses and the same system prevails in both houses. No one can name their master. When we have to disclose our identity, we just show the picture hanging from our neck".

Kumar said, "Will you show me that picture?"

"Why not, see it!" Saying this one of them pulled off the picture sling and showed to Kumar. Kumar was taken aback to see it and exclaimed – "*Arre,* this is the picture of princess Chandrakanta! Well, then are all these her maids? No, no, not possible. How can princess Chandrakanta come to this place! Her kingdom is Vijaygarh. Well, let me ask, in what city is this house situated?"

Kumar said, "Tell me the name of this city".

A woman said, "The name of this city is Chitranagar because the picture of the princess is always hanging from our neck".

Kumar said, "When was this city named thus?"

A woman said, "This name continues for thousands of years and we have been wearing such a picture for many generations. First my great grandmother got it from the master and it rolled down to me".

Kumar said, "Has this princess been ruling it since then? Has she got no parents?"

Second woman said, "How do we know all this! We never see her to know who she is and how she looks young or old".

Kumar said, "Then who conducts the court?"

Second woman said, "We have a big picture of our master princess and the court is held in front of that picture. The orders come from that picture".

Kumar said, "Your words have bewildered me. You talk improbable things, things which one can neither believe nor understand. Now, can you take me to that court?"

Woman said, "No need to say it. After all, having arrested you, we will take you to that court and you will see things yourself".

Kumar said, "When you don't have a master rather than a picture, what harm have I caused? Why will you arrest me?"

Woman said, "Our princess roams about in her territory and her garden away from public notice and nobody ever sees her. We clean the garden and the rooms everyday as the bed, the floor and other articles in the room look like used. They are used and dirtied so that we understand that the princess roams about behind our notice who is thousands of years old."

Second woman said, "Sister, how long will you go on replying to his queries? This way he wants to save himself".

First woman said, "No, no, he must be the son of a king, it is fit and proper to answer his queries. We should take him to court arresting him with respect".

Third woman said, "Why don't you ask the names of his parents? Will you take him to be a prince without knowing the fact? (Towards Kumar) Well mister, what's your name and who is your father?"

Kumar said, "I am Virendra Singh, son of Maharaja Surendra Singh of Naugarh".

Hearing his name, all of them were pleased and started talking among themselves — "Wow, we must take him to court, we will surely get some reward because the administration had announced a reward on his head because he had caused a heavy damage by breaking the *tilism* and looting away the treasure. Now, let's not talk to him. Tie his hands and feet immediately and take him to court. The night has not far advanced and the court must be in session. If we delay, we will have to look after him the whole day tomorrow because our princess holds the court at night".

Kumar was bewildered to hear such words. Alternating between amazement, thinking and nervousness, he was in a strange state. At last, looking towards those women, he said, "Why do you make a fuss, I'm ready to go with you. Let me see the court of your princess!"

A woman said, "When you are yourself ready to go with us, then we needn't bother. Come on".

Kumar said, "Move on".

These nine women in all, four in front of and four behind Kumar moved on. One of them went ahead of the party to inform that they had arrested a notorious dacoit who is being brought by her companions.

Taking Kumar with them, they went to a corner of the garden which had an exit on the other side. A white cauldron was seen on fire. They entered with Kumar from that exit. At a short distance, there was another garden well decorated and profusely illuminated. A few attendants and guards with gold and silver swords were moving about. Apart from them, several others were seen moving about the place.

Nobody questioned those women. They went on boldly along with Kumar to a grand court, the magnificence of which startled Kumar.

First of all, Kumar looked at the big picture right in front, placed on an ancestral seat. It seemed that Chandrakanta was sitting on the seat wearing a crown with an umbrella overhead. There were live lions sitting on either side, who at times growled and roared. Moreover, big sardars in expensive clothes were sitting with their heads low in front of the seat. There was complete silence in the court; all were sitting silent.

Seeing the picture of Chandrakanta and the imposing court, Kumar felt bold. He stood silently, and the women who had presented him like a thief stood on his two sides.

A voice from behind the picture came – "Who is he?"

One of those women replied, "He has been arrested while moving about in the garden. On asking we came to know that his name is Virendra Singh. It is he who has destroyed the magical *tilism*". Another voice came – "If this is true, a lot will have to be considered about him. This time, keep him in safe custody. Then produce him in court on order".

Those women took Kumar to a nice room, which was well decorated but Kumar was absorbed in thought. The walk in the new garden and the picture court amazed him even more. He was thinking bending his head. He could not understand those miracles he had seen in the previous garden. Now the things were even more puzzling with a court being held in front of the picture of Chandrakanta. Engaged in such thoughts, bending his head, he followed the women knowing not where he was going, who was leading him and what a decorated room he was sitting in.

There was a carpet on the floor and high seats were arranged besides several pillows. Kumar sat on that high seat and for two hours, kept thinking so deeply that he was not conscious of his own self. When he felt thirsty, he opened his eyes to see a woman attendant in front who asked him with folded hands — "Your order, sir!" In reply, Kumar asked for water with gesture of his hand. She filled a gold bowl with water and handed to Kumar. Drinking the water, Kumar felt so much satiated that his head started drooping and gradually he became unconscious and lay on the high seat.

□

12

Kunwar Virendra Singh's disappearance caused an upheaval in his caravan. Getting nervous, Tej Singh and Devi Singh made a thorough search in all directions but found nothing. After the day ended, Jyotishi ji told Tej Singh — "From ramal, it appears that several women made Kumar unconscious with some anaesthetic drug and took him to a room in Naugarh. The rest is not visible".

Hearing the words of Jyotishi ji, Tej Singh said, "Naugarh is part of our kingdom, there can't be any enemy of Kumar. With the rule of Maharaja Surendra Singh, all his subjects are happy and even ready to sacrifice their life for his family. Then who can arrest Kumar there?"

After thinking for a long time, Tej Singh got ready to venture out in search of Kumar. Devi Singh and Jyotishi ji also accompanied him and the three started for Naugarh. While departing, they bade farewell to the Diwan of Maharaja Shivdutt who had come with gifts for Kunwar Virendra Singh on behalf of Maharaja Shivdutt. They handed Fateh Singh the *tilismi* book, which was found on Kunwar Virendra Singh's bed after his disappearance.

After midnight, the three *aiyars* started for Naugarh. They went on and on for five miles. At day break, they stopped in a forest and changing their faces, resumed their journey. Walking whole day without food and water, they reached Naugarh in the evening. They decided among themselves that they should not meet anyone, rather they should search for Kumar in disguise.

The three *aiyars* started their search separately. They searched in gardens, inside houses by talking to people but they found nothing. Next day, the three together in disguise went to the court of King Surendra Singh and standing in a corner started eavesdropping.

That very moment several spies appeared in the court who looked agitated and nervous. Tej Singh's father Diwan Jeet Singh asked those spies — "Why are you so nervous?" One spy came forward and said, "I have brought news of Kumar from *Lashkar*".

Jeet Singh said, "What's the matter? Be quick".

Spy said, "For two days there is no trace of him".

Jeet Singh said, "Has he gone somewhere?"

Spy said, "No sir, He was sleeping in the tent. Some women came and took him away. It is not known where she has kept him".

Jeet Singh (nervously) said, "How did you know some women took him away?"

Spy said, "After his disappearance the *aiyars* searched for him a lot. When they found nothing, the astrologer Jagannathji from his ramal found out that some women had taken him away and had kept him in Naugarh area itself".

Jeet Singh (with surprise), "In this Naugarh area? We don't have any enemy here!"

Spy said, "Whatever it may be, Jyotishi ji has said like this".

Jeet Singh, "Then where is Tej Singh?"

Spy said, "He has gone somewhere in search of Kumar. Devi Singh and Jyotishi ji are also with him. Just after their departure this misfortune has fallen upon us".

Jeet Singh (surprised) said, "What misfortune on our caravan?"

Spy said, "Finding an opportunity Maharaja Shivdutt mounted an attack".

Hearing of attack, Tej Singh and other *aiyars* in disguise who were standing in a corner became more attentive to hear further.

Jeet Singh, "Previously, you had brought the news that Maharaja Shivdutt had accepted the friendship with Kumar and his Diwan had come with gifts. What happened now?"

Spy said, "That news that time was correct but at last he betrayed and became dishonest".

Jeet Singh said, "What happened from that attack?"

Spy said, "For an hour, Fateh Singh fought bravely at last being wounded at the hands of Shivdutt, he was arrested. With his arrest the leaderless army ran hither and thither".

So long sitting silently, Surendra Singh was listening to all these matters. Hearing about Fateh Singh's arrest and his caravan's escape, his eyes shot red. Turning towards Jeet Singh, he said, "This time I have no army here except a few guards, but I will march on this very moment. It is not difficult to kill such a coward".

Jeet Singh said, "It must be so. Hearing of your leading the march, the frightened army will surely come back".

While such talks were going on, two more spies entered the court. They said, "Hearing about Kumar's disappearance, the *aiyars'* search expedition, Fateh Singh's arrest and the running away of the army, Maharaja Jay

Singh has attacked Chunargarh with his army. On the way, it was learnt that just two hours after the arrest of Fateh Singh, Maharaja Shivdutt was also missing and a chit of paper was found on his bed which read, "This rogue will be heavily punished, he will not be released from jail in his life time". Thereafter, it was heard that Fateh Singh too had been released and was near the *tilism* and Kumar's army was again coming together".

Hearing this news, king Surendra Singh turned towards Jeet Singh.

Jeet Singh said, "Whatever the fact, Maharaja Jay Singh has attacked after all. It is fit and proper that we settle the issue of Chunar forever. Such frequent disturbances are very bad".

King said, "You are right to say so. Let's do likewise. What can I say. I had wanted that Chunar should be won at the hands of my son, so that he felt bold but now it is not tolerable".

Hearing these words and the news, the three *aiyars* left the place and conferred among them.

Tej Singh said, "What should we do now?"

Devi Singh said, "Whatever happens, first we should search for Kumar".

Tej Singh said, "I ask you to go towards *Lashkar* and we two will search for Kumar".

Jyotishi ji said, "My advice is to first go to that cave in which Maharaja Shivdutt was arrested".

Tej Singh said, "The very door doesn't open".

Jyotishi ji said, "First let's go, perhaps we may open it by any means".

Tej Singh said, "You uselessly try to do so. Even if the door opens, what purpose will it serve us?"

Jyotishi ji said, "Let's go".

Tej Singh said, "All right, let's go".

The three *aiyars* made for the cave.

□

13

Gradually, Kunwar Virendra Singh became unconscious and lay on the bed. When he awoke, he found himself lying on a rock. Baffled he looked right and left. Lofty hills all around, a running stream in the middle, blackberries on the sides gave the impression that it was that very cell in which *aiyars* were imprisoned and Maharaja Shivdutt with his wife was imprisoned or where Kumar had seen Chandrakanta and Chapla but he couldn't reach there.

Kumar got up from the rock and started moving round the place and scrutinising each and every object to firmly recognise that cell. Now he had no doubt and was fully convinced that it was the same cell because he had seen the imprisoned Maharaja Shivdutt lying on a rock under a blackberry tree and his wife massaging his legs. They were, no doubt, looking the other way so that Kumar saw them but they couldn't see Kumar.

Kunwar Virendra Singh went running under that hill over which he had left princess Chandrakanta and Chapla before he had set out of the cell to break the *tilism*. Even now he saw the princess in the same tattered and dirty *saree*, grime covered body and matted locks of hair as on the previous occasion.

On seeing her, the frenzy of love overpowered him. His eyes were filled with tears as he saw the princess in that helpless condition, his throat was choked and with a blush stood behind a tree and began to think — "Alas, how can I face Chandrakanta and what shall I say? Shall I be able to say that I had gone to break the *tilism* to free you but I couldn't break the *tilism* as yet. Oh, I shall never be able to say it. What to do, I forgot to break the *tilism* for the love of the forest girl. I wasted several days in her pursuit. When the princess asks me how I came here, what shall I say? Even Shivdutt seems to be present here. At *Lashkar,* I had heard that he was released and moreover, his Diwan himself had come with gifts. What's all this rigmarole?"

As Kumar was thinking all this, he saw Tej Singh coming towards him. Devi Singh and Jyotishi ji were trailing behind. Kumar advanced towards them. Seeing Kumar, Tej Singh ran forward and fell on Kumar's feet who embraced him. Kumar also met Devi Singh and saluted Jyotishi ji. Now the four started talking sitting on a stone under a tree.

Kumar said, "Look Tej Singh, there in the front as on that day princess Chandrakanta is sitting sad in tattered clothes and by her side, Chapla is wiping her face with her scarf".

Tej Singh said, "Did you talk to her?"

Kumar said, "No, not at all, at the moment I was thinking whether I should go to her or not".

Tej Singh said, "For how many days are you thinking like this?"

Kumar said, "I have come to this valley scarcely two hours ago".

Tej Singh (surprised) said, "Have you come to this cell just now? Where had you been so long? You left *Lashkar* a long time ago. Seeing you suddenly here at this hour I thought that you had secretly come from *Lashkar* for the love of the princess".

Kumar said, "No, I haven't come from *Lashkar* on my own. I don't know who brought me here and how".

Tej Singh (astonished) said, "Oho, don't you know till now who lifted you from *Lashkar* to this place?"

Kumar said, "No, not at all".

Kumar narrated the whole story and the three *aiyars* kept listening to him with utter surprise. When Kumar concluded his story, Tej Singh asked Jyotishi ji, "What's the matter, did you understand anything?"

Jyotishi ji, "None at all. I can't imagine where Kumar had gone and who was enacting the whole drama!"

Kumar said, "We saw astonishing things while breaking the *tilism*, but I saw even more astonishing things during the last two-three days".

Devi Singh said, "A weak-hearted man would die of nervousness in such a situation".

Jyotishi ji, "No doubt about it".

Kumar said, "One more surprise, even Shivdutt is here".

Tej Singh said, "Where?"

Kumar (Pointing with his hand), "There, look under that tree".

Tej Singh said, "Yes, he's there. But what's the matter! Let's talk to him to find out something".

Kumar said, "There is princess Chandrakanta just in the front on that hill. First we should ask her. I find myself in a dilemma to think what she will ask and what I will reply".

Tej Singh said, "The lover has the same fate. It doesn't matter, I'll speak on your behalf".

The four people moved towards Shivdutt. First they went under the hill over which, in a small veranda Chandrakanta and Chapla were sitting. Kumar was looking the other way, Chapla saw them. She got up and started inquiring about the welfare of Kumar to which Kumar himself replied and inquired about Chandrakanta's welfare. Chapla replied — "Her condition is written on her face, no need to explain it".

Till now, Chandrakanta was sitting with her head low. Startled at Chapla's voice, she raised her head. Seeing Kumar she stood with folded hands and tears started streaming down.

Kunwar Virendra Singh said, "Princess, just wait for a few more days. The *tilism* has been broken, a little more needs to be done. I had to come here for other reasons, now I will start towards the same *tilism*".

Chapla said, "The princess says that in her heart, she feels that Kumar's love for her has diminished or someone else has usurped it. She has been suffering at this place for a long time and recently the new thought in her mind is torturing her".

Saying so much, Chapla kept silent. Smilingly, Tej Singh glanced at Kumar and said, "Oye, shall I expose the secret?"

In reply, Kumar said nothing, tears started flowing down and with folded hands looked at him. With a laugh, Tej Singh undid the folded hands of Kumar and on his behalf replied to Chapla —

"Convince the princess that she should have no misgivings about love for her in Kumar's heart".

Chapla said, "For what purpose have you come today?"

Tej Singh said, "We have come to see Maharaja Shivdutt. We had news that being released he had gone to Chunar".

Chapla said, "Some *aiyar* might have changed his face, I always find these two people here".

Tej Singh said, "Let me talk to him".

Maharaja Shivdutt was attentively listening to the talk of Tej Singh and Chapla. Now he came near Kumar, but seeing above Chandrakanta and Chapla, kept mum.

Tej Singh said, "Shivdutt, what did you want to say, why have you stopped?"

Shivdutt said, "Now I'll not speak".

Tej Singh said, "Why?"

Shivdutt said, "Perhaps my silence may save my life".

Tej Singh said, "Who will kill you if you speak out?"

Shivdutt said, "Do what you will but I'll not speak".

Hearing this, Tej Singh drew out the sword from his waist when Chapla from above shouted, "No, no, don't do so!" Tej Singh stopped and glanced at Chapla.

Chapla said, "Why this drawing the sword over Shivdutt?"

Tej Singh said, "He had come to say something but seeing you he stopped. Now, when I ask him to speak out, he keeps mum and says if he speaks out, he'll be killed. I don't understand what the matter is. You see, we were already worried for him, then his coming to us and keeping mum on seeing you and saying that his disclosure will kill him are all very baffling".

Chapla said, "These days he has gone mad. I often see sometimes he goes running and shouting. His condition is like that of a mad man. Don't mind his words".

Shivdutt said, "Funny! She calls me mad!"

Tej Singh said, (to Shivdutt) "What did you say? Say again!"

Shivdutt said, "Nothing! You talk to Chapla, I'm mad these days as you think".

Devi Singh said, "What a mad man!"

Shivdutt said, "Chapla says correctly, there is no doubt about my madness".

Kumar said, "Jyotishi ji, please consider this self-made mad!"

Jyotish ji, (laughing), "When it has been declared that he is mad, what remains?"

Kumar said, "Several misgivings crop up in the mind".

Tej Singh said, "It certainly has a big secret. We don't know when it will come out, we are helpless to do anything".

Devi Singh said, "Our lady *guru* knows this secret but she doesn't like to expose it".

Kumar said, "It's perfectly true".

Hearing the words of Devi Singh, Tej Singh laughed and kept mum. Maharaja Shivdutt also got up to his seat. Tej Singh told Kumar — "Now we should more to *Lashkar*. It is said that in our absence Maharaja Shivdutt attacked *Lashkar*, causing heavy damage. It's not clear who that Shivdutt was, again it was said that Shivdutt disappeared. Now, we are face to face with Shivdutt here!"

Kumar said, "No doubt, all these things are very surprising. Anyway, who told you, say frankly".

Tej Singh related the whole story how the three men went out of *Lashkar* in search of Kumar, how they heard in disguise in the court of King Surendra Singh the report of two spies, mounting attack on Chunar by Maharaja Jay Singh and King Surendra Singh, hearing which Kumar became agitated and got ready to move out then and there. Talking with Chandrakanta for a while and consoling her,

Kunwar Virendra Singh, with tears in his eyes, came out of the cell.

It was evening when the four men came out of the cell. Tej Singh asked Devi Singh to go to Naugarh and bring a suitable stallion from the royal stable for Kumar to go to the *tilism*. He also warned that nobody should know that Devi Singh has taken away the stallion.

Devi Singh said, "If it is known to someone, my going is useless".

Tej Singh said, "How long will you take to move?"

Devi Singh said, "Why should I take time, it's not a serious matter. I'll come back in two to three hours".

Saying this, Devi Singh made for Naugarh. After his departure, the three men sat gossiping under a tree.

Kumar said, "Jyotishi ji, will the secret of Shivdutt come out?"

Jyotishi ji, "There is no doubt that he was the real Shivdutt who on his release from prison had sent gift for compromise through his Diwan. From my calculation, it seems that the Shivdutt you have deposited in the cave is also real. But it is not known what happened in between".

Kumar said, "Father has attacked Chunar. Let's see its result. It would be proper for us to reach there earliest".

Jyotishi ji said, "No harm, who is there to object. You have already heard that Shivdutt has again disappeared or from the chit on his bed, it appears that he has been arrested again".

Tej Singh said, "Yes, there is no doubt about capturing Chunar because there is none to face it but there remains the lurking of his *aiyars*".

Kumar said, "It would have been better had Badrinath and others been arrested".

Tej Singh said, "Next time, I'll surely arrest them".

They spent two to three hours talking like this. Devi Singh came back with a stallion riding which Kumar made for *tilism* and the three *aiyars* walked on foot.

□

14

On hearing the news that after the disappearance of Kumar Tej Singh, Devi Singh and Jyotishi ji have gone out in search of him, Maharaja thought out a sinister plan. He called his Diwan and *aiyars* and told them in secret — "At present, Kumar has disappeared from *Lashkar* and his *aiyars* have gone out to find him out. It is a good opportunity. It comes to my mind that I destroy Kumar's caravan by mounting an attack and usurp that treasure which they have found in the *tilism*".

Hearing this, Diwan, Badrinath, Pannalal, Rammanayan and Chunnilal pleaded with Maharaja Shivdutt that he should not do so because he had already compromised with Kumar. Even if he won that caravan, it was nothing. It was not advisable to recreate enmity. But Shivdutt didn't listen to their advice. Among those, *aiyars* were Nazim and Ahmad who used to concur with Shivdutt and provoke him to attack.

At last, Maharaja Shivdutt attacked the caravan of Kunwar Virendra Singh and himself came into the open field and challenged General Fateh Singh to fight. He was also a brave soldier, instantly came out and fought fiercely for two hours, but at last got wounded at the hands of Shivdutt and was arrested.

As soon as the General was arrested, the army felt discouraged and ran away. Maharaja Shivdutt got nothing more than the tents. The *tilismi* treasure had already been dispatched to Naugarh. He got the *tilismi* book, no doubt, which pleased him and said, "Now I'll myself break the *tilism* and taking Chandrakanta out of the cell, I'll marry her".

Having arrested Fateh Singh, Shivdutt held a party. He got up from the dance court and lay on bed in his private chamber. On the same day, he got missing, nobody knows who took him where, only a chit of paper was lying on the bed. After his disappearance Commander Fateh Singh also got released and found himself in a jungle. It was not known who released him from captivity, rather his wounds were bandaged which gave him much relief.

Fateh Singh came to the *tilism* again where he met other men of his caravan and gradually the fugitive soldiers came back and gathered. Only then it was reported that Maharaja Shivdutt was taken captive.

On his own, with a few brave soldiers, Fateh Singh attacked Chunar. Hardly had he covered two miles when he came to know that Maharaja Jay Singh had also arrived. He abandoned his plan to go to Chunar and proceeded to accost Jay Singh and finding him like-minded both moved to Chunar.

The army of Jay Singh seized the Chunar fort. The army of Shivdutt blocked the gates from inside, mounted the machine guns on the terrace, collected some food stuff and started fighting from the minarets and terrace.

□

15

On an evening near Chunar between two hills on one side of a lane, Pundit Badrinath, Ramnarayan, Pannalal, Nazim and Ahmad sat talking among them.

Nazim said, "What can I say, our master went to heaven and we have been left to suffer".

Ahmad said, "Till now nobody knows who killed him".

Badrinath, "His sins killed him and you two will soon meet the same fate. You are called *aiyars* but you are dishonest and ungrateful".

Nazim said, "Are we dishonest?"

Badrinath said, "Certainly. It's obvious. When you were not loyal to your master Maharaja Jay Singh, who will you serve honestly? You were yourself defeated, got Krur Singh killed and ruined our king rather got him imprisoned. I just feel that I should kill you both by beating with boots".

Ahmad said, "Behave yourself, otherwise I'll tear off your ears".

Hearing the words of Ahmad, Badrinath was boiling with anger. He took up a piece of stone from the ground and struck on Ahmad's face so violently that he died then and there. Seeing him thus, Nazim ran away but Badrinath was after his blood. He placed a big stone in a *Chhaga* and struck him down with a shot. Then Pannalal and others came and finally killed him kicking. Having killed the two the four *aiyars* sat talking on the same spot.

Pannalal said, "Now the obstacle to our durbar has been cleared".

Badrinath said, "Maharaja will not feel otherwise".

Pannalal said, "Now we should try to protect the throne somehow. Maharaja Jay Singh has fiercely surrounded us and without Maharaja, the army cannot fight into the open".

Chunnilal said, "After all how long can we fight from inside the fort? We have just two months' ration in the fort, what will we do thereafter?"

Ramnath said, "We didn't get time enough to store food grains".

Badrinath said, "There's one thing, we should abduct Maharaja Jay Singh by any means from his caravan. If we have him in our clutch, it will not be a problem to defeat them".

Pannalal said, "Sure, we must do like this. It is our duty to be loyal to our master".

Ramnath said, "But our king is also bent upon dishonesty. What's wrong with Kunwar Virendra Singh?"

Chunnilal said, "Whatever it is, it is our duty to support our master".

Badrinath said, "Nazim and Ahmad were the evil stars for our king who are no more. Next time surely I'll get a compromise signed between them. Then we will have the opportunity to serve him. Wow, what a smart and promising prince he is!"

Pannalal said, "Let's go, the night has far advanced. By some *aiyari* trick we should arrest Maharaja Jay Singh and imprison him in the fort through the secret tunnel".

Badrinath, "I've thought out an *aiyari* trick, that will work".

Pannalal said, "What's that?"

Badrinath said, "First let's entrap his cook. I'll impersonate him and cook food and you people will entrap his attendants work with me taking on their faces. I'll mix anaesthetic powder in the food and serve it to Maharaja and later other attendants who will be on guard. And that's that".

Pannalal said, "That's right. You become the cook because you are a brahmin. If Maharaja eats food from your hand it will not pollute his religion; we must think of it. But we must see that there isn't a heavy dose of anaesthetic powder".

Badrinath said, "No, no, am I a fool, don't I know that the royalty eats only after tasting the food on others? I'll mix the drug in such moderation that for two hours they won't have any feel that they have eaten food mixed with anaesthetic agent".

Ramnath said, "That's fine. Let's move now".

□

16

King Surendra Singh, too, left Naugarh and helter-skelter reached near Chunar in two days. In the evening, Maharaja Jay Singh came to know about it. He immediately dispatched Commander Fateh Singh to receive the king.

King Surendra Singh heard the whole story from Fateh Singh. By morning, his caravan also reached Chunar and pitched tent with the caravan of Jay Singh. King Surendra Singh sent Fateh Singh to Maharaja Jay Singh to talk about their meeting.

Hardly had Fateh Singh gone a few steps from the tent of king Surendra Singh that Diwan Hardayal Singh of Maharaja Jay Singh with his generals was seen coming very perplexed. He stopped. His heart started beating fast. When they came closer, he asked, "What's the matter? Why are you so nervous?"

A soldier said, "Don't ask us. A great misfortune has befallen".

Fateh Singh said, (nervously) "What's that?"

Second soldier, "Let's go to Maharaja, there we will narrate everything".

Fateh Singh came to the tent of king Surendra Singh with all these people, saluted the king courteously and sat down as directed.

King Surendra Singh was also taken aback to see them so bewildered. On being asked Hardayal Singh said, "Very early in the morning today we heard machine gun shots coming from inside the fort. I went into the tent of the Maharaja to inform him. I was astonished to see the guards at the doors unconscious. Still I went further inside. There I found the bed of Maharaja empty. I was flabbergasted to see it. Seeing them, Kavirajjee found that they had been given some anaesthetic drug. Instantly, several spies were dispatched hither and thither to find out Maharaja but, so far, there is no trace of him".

Hearing it, Surendra Singh looked at Jeet Singh who was sitting on his left.

Jeet Singh said, "Had only Maharaja been missing I would say that someone might have abducted him by any means. But as several people are still unconscious it appears that particularly the Maharaja's food stuff has been mixed with some anesthetic. If we find his cook, he can provide the details".

Several attendants ran fast. They didn't have to go far. The tents of both caravans were pitched alongside. They soon came back to report that there was no cook present there. At the same time, some people informed that the cook and attendants of Maharaja were found outside the caravan, who are being carried to this place in a palanquin.

Diwan Jeet Singh said, "All palanquins must be kept outside. Only the palanquin carrying the cook should be brought in".

The unconscious cook was brought in. Jeet Singh brought him back to consciousness with the smell of *lakhlakha,* and asked him how he became unconscious. In reply, he said, "Past two to three hours in the evening, a confectioner came to us with a basket and started talking highly of his eatables. We bought something from him and ate the stuff. The very moment I felt dizzy, I didn't even pay him. I don't remember what happened thereafter".

Hearing it Diwan Jeet Singh said, "All right, we have understood everything. Now go to your tent". Then he gave *lakhlakha* to other soldiers to bring them to consciousness who were lying at the door. He also told Diwan Hardayal Singh to sit a bit longer.

All people were sent away only king Surendra Singh, Jeet Singh and Diwan Hardayal Singh remained.

King Surendra Singh, (looking towards Jeet Singh) said, "Let there be a plan to get Maharaja released".

Jeet Singh said, "What plan can we make! We don't have here even a single *aiyar* to deploy him. Tej Singh and Devi Singh have already gone in search of Kumar and so far there is no trace of them".

King said, "You yourself think out something".

Jeet Singh said, "You see what can I do. I gave up *aiyari* long ago. The day I presented before you, Tej Singh after giving him full training in this art, your good self relieved me from *aiyari*. Now, I am asked to do it again. I was sure that I wouldn't be engaged in *aiyari* till the end of my life. Therefore, I don't even keep the *aiyari* bag with me".

King said, "You are right to say that but at this time, it is not proper to cow down nor to refuse *aiyari*. And I'm sure, whether you keep or don't keep the *aiyari* bag with you, you certainly must have got something of it".

Jeet Singh (smiling) said, "When I am with your lordship and I know the art, why shouldn't I have something of it and that on a journey!"

King said, "Then what do you think? Now invoke your old mastery and free Maharaja Jay Singh".

Jeet Singh said, "Yes sir, you please do one thing. Keep our plan to yourself and after evening mount the attack along with Fateh Singh. Whatever may happen but the battle must go on throughout the whole night. You have to ensure it".

Hardayal Singh said, "Very well, so be it".

Jeet Singh said, "You please go and arrange the battle, I too, take leave of Maharaja and go to my camp. I have to do a lot in a short time".

Diwan Hardayal Singh took leave of King Surendra Singh and moved to his camp. Diwan Jeet Singh called Fateh Singh and gave him sufficient advice on warfare and went to his camp. After daily worship and dinner, he started arranging his *aiyari* paraphernalia.

Diwan Jeet Singh had an old attendant who was very dear to him. He kept his *aiyari* paraphernalia with him. When leaving Naugarh, he had entrusted this old man to arrange his *aiyari* paraphernalia. He had given up *aiyari* long ago, but when he saw that his king was going to battle and the *aiyars* were out in search of Kumar, he thought that he might be required to help. Therefore, he thought it reasonable to equip himself with all necessary things. He asked the same old attendant to fetch his *aiyari* kit and fill it with necessary things. He also put in the anesthetic oil sealed in a phial. Hours before dusk in the guise of a *zamindar,* he came out of his camp.

From his camp, Jeet Singh moved towards a hill to the south of the fort and at a distance, he sat on a big rock in the lonely field. He took out from his bag a pen, inkpot and paper and began to write which meant, "Your tricks fell flat and at last I entered the fort. You will see what a disaster I bring about. All the four of you are *aiyars,* whereas I am ignorant of *aiyari*, still you people cannot get hold of me. Shame on your *aiyari*!"

He wrote a number of such chits and prepared some gum and, finally, putting them in his bag, moved towards the fort. By the time he reached, it was evening. Hence he started moving around the fort. When it was sufficiently dark, he climbed a low damaged wall with the help of his lasso. Finding it lonely he started walking around.

Outside the fort, Diwan Hardayal Singh and Fateh Singh had waged a fierce battle, machine guns were booming, the fort army was also fighting from the minarets and hundreds of men were nervously watching the scene at the door. From this, Jeet Singh had enough opportunity to walk around.

The paper chits lying in the bag now began to be pasted on doors and walls. Whenever he saw someone coming, he hid himself and after his going away, resumed the work. Thus, all chits were pasted.

The battle is on at the gate, all *aiyars* and staff are engaged, nobody has any knowledge that the arch *aiyars* Jeet Singh has already entered the fort and is on with his *aiyari*. He wants to find out where Maharaja Jay Singh has been arrested in this big fort and then free him. He also wants to capture the *aiyars* of Shivdutt and see that not a single *aiyar* is left to try to get other *aiyars* released.

□

17

The brave General Fateh Singh humbled the fort army. It seemed that if the battle continued the whole night, the fort would be defeated and the gate smashed. In such a crisis, the nervous *aiyars* like Badrinath were moving about when suddenly a guard raised a hue and cry which frightened Badrinath even more. The guard was badly wounded and had too many wounds on the face, making it difficult to recognise him.

Badrinath (nervously), "How come, who wounded you?"

Guard said, "You people are singularly attuned to this side and don't care about other things. From the back side, several men of Kunwar Virendra Singh have entered and God knows what they are doing moving around the fort. I encountered one of them but he was so clever and agile that he wounded me so grievously that I lay unconscious on earth for two hours. I have with great difficulty come to give you this information. While coming back, I again saw him pasting paper chits on walls but didn't protest out of fear".

Pannalal said, "It's a bad news".

Badrinath said, "How many people did you see?"

Guard said, "They may be many but I encountered only one".

Badrinath said, "Can you recognise him?"

Guard said, "Yes, I'll surely identify him as I saw his face in full light".

Badrinath said, "I am going to find them, can you accompany me?"

Guard said, "Why not? He had half killed me, I can't rest without arresting him".

Badrinath said, "All right, come along".

Badrinath, Pannalal, Ramnarayan and Chunnilal, all four people moved towards the inner side along with the wounded guard. On reaching the lady's fort, they saw that a man is lying senseless, a flare is dimming at a distance on the ground. The oil pot indicates that the man is a lamp man. The guard burst out, "See, he has killed another man" Saying it, he picked up the flare and the oil pot and held the flare to the man's face. Badrinath recognised him as his lamp man. He put his hand over the man's nose and felt that he had been given the anaesthetic drug. The guard said, "You please leave him and first find out that rascal. I also go with you holding this flare, lest they should release Maharaja Jay Singh and take him away".

Badrinath, "First let us go where Maharaja Jay Singh is arrested". All agreed and they reached the place direct. They saw that Maharaja Jay Singh is lying handcuffed in the room. The guard very closely scrutinised the room and the door and said, "No, they haven't reached up to here, let's search in another direction". The four turned to another side. While moving they saw several paper chits pasted on doors and walls, reading which they were stunned. As they were thinking, the guard cried and, pointing to a room, said, "Look, just now a man has entered that room, he must be the man who has wounded me". He ran towards that room, but stopped at the door as the *aiyars* turned up.

Badrinath said, (to guard) "Move inside".

Guard said, "First you people hold a sword or a dagger, because he'll surely attack".

Badrinath said, "We are alert. You go inside as you hold the flare".

Guard said, "No, no, I won't go inside. My life was hardly saved once. Why should I go again to endanger myself?"

Badrinath said, "O coward! Do you serve the king on this very cowardice? Give me the flare, don't go in!"

Guard said, "Take this flare, call me a coward, I have suffered so many wounds and still you call me a coward! Had you suffered, you would have realised. I've done so much. That's enough".

Saying so, the guard handed the flare and oil pot to Badrinath and kept away. The four *aiyars* entered the room. Hardly had they taken a few steps, the guard bolted the door from outside. He took out the flint stone from his waist and struck the explosive-soaked rope. The fire spread inside.

The guard was, in fact, Jeet Singh, the arch *aiyar*. In the guise of a guard, he convinced the *aiyars* and took them on his side. Walking around with them he saw where Maharaja Jay Singh was arrested and then he played a trick and shut them inside the room already made of a special type.

□

18

Kumar came out of the cave with Tej Singh and other *aiyars* and moved to the *tilism*. Having spent a night on the way, next day on way they saw a man in disguise who was coming their way. When he came close, he got down from his horse and stood at some distance. Kumar reached there and found the *tilismi* book and a letter. Very happily he told Tej Singh —

"Tej Singh, what shall I do! This forest girl is again and again heaping obligations on me. There is no doubt that this man is from her who is standing at a distance keeping the *tilismi* book on my way. Alas! Her love has rendered me good for nothing! Let's see what's written in this letter".

Kumar read the letter —

"Somehow I got this book which I am sending you. Now, without making further delay free Chandrakanta, she is in dire distress. A battle is waging at Chunar, you, too should go and win laurels showing your bravery".

Kumar said, "Tej Singh, you, too, read it".

Tej Singh said, "(After reading), It's not clear whether this forest girl is a human or a spirit who does such strange things".

Kumar (Heaving a sigh) said, "Alas! It's not a single one to tackle".

Devi Singh said, "I advise you to stay here! First of all, I go to Chunar to see what's happening there".

Kumar said, "All right, now Chunar may be just ten kilometres from here. You bring us the latest report only, then we should proceed having done some brave deed".

Devi Singh proceeded to Chunar. Kumar was held upon the way for one more day. Next day, when Devi Singh came back and told about the battle at Chunar, the news of the arrest of Maharaja Jay Singh and praised the *aiyari* of Jeet Singh and said, "The battle is still on. Our army reached the fort gate several times but could not break it. The machine guns of the fort caused a heavy damage to us".

Hearing such news Kumar told Tej Singh, "It would be a big chivalrous work if we could enter the fort and break the gate".

Tej Singh said, "There is no doubt that this is a chivalrous work, we'll either open the gate or lose our lives".

Kumar said, "What other way is better for us than to risk our lives? We'll either win Chunar or ensure the throne in heaven, we have greatness on both hands".

Tej Singh said, "Bravo, no bravery can equal it! Let's go and enter the fort in disguise. But we can't do it in the day time".

Kumar said, "It doesn't matter, let it be in the night. We will keep hiding in the fort all night and when the battle is in full swing, we'll pounce upon the gate. All will be stationed on the terrace, it is not very difficult to open the door tearing into all fifty to hundred people there".

Devi Singh said, "Kumar's suggestion is perfectly all right but Jyotishiji must be left outside".

Jyotishiji, "Why so?"

Devi Singh said, "Because you are a Brahmin, why should we take you for *brahmhatya*. This is the task of the warriors' caste, not yours".

Kumar said, "Well Jyotishi ji, you don't go inside the fort".

Jyotishi ji said, "You would have been right to say so had I no knowledge of *aiyari*, but even the brave and adventurous bow down before an *aiyar*".

Devi Singh said, "All right then, we are to gain rather more".

Kumar said, "What gain?"

Devi Singh said, "There's no doubt that Jyotishiji is our fast friend, will never desert us and even if he dies, he will be born as a devil spirit and will serve our purpose".

Jyotishi ji said, "Shall only I be doomed? If it so happens, I'll never spare you! You're most dear to me".

Kumar laughed at their words and riding his horse proceeded to Chunar with *aiyars*. By evening, they reached

Chunar and finding an opportunity in the night, they sneaked into the fort with their lasso.

□

19

About three hours past morning, the army of Fateh Singh reached the fort gate fighting. The army of Shivdutt was bombarding from the terrace in a bid to repel them. Suddenly, the fort gate opened and four red flags came into view, seeing which king Surendra Singh with his army forced into the gate and soon the entire force entered the fort. Nobody had the guts to encounter. Everywhere there were supporters and supporters. Fateh Singh dropped the green flag of Maharaja Shivdutt from the mast and hoisted the red flag instead. Then he held the band stick and beat the drum vehemently three times. *'Krum ghum-fateh'* was heard which unnerved the fortmen and the love of Kumar Virendra Singh bore fruit.

Kumar had slashed the heads of forty men, but he was himself badly wounded with his *aiyars*. Hardly had king Surendra Singh entered the fort when Tej Singh and Devi Singh fell on his feet holding flags. Jyotishi ji blessed him. They could not endure any longer, because of the wounds, bleeding they fell down unconscious.

Jeet Singh bandaged the wounds of the four men, after their faces were washed, they were identified. After some time, they regained consciousness. King Surendra Singh embraced his son for long and was kind to the three *aiyars*. Maharaja Jay Singh enamoured of the bravery of Kumar showered praises on him. Kumar touched his feet and they met others cheerfully.

The Chunar fort was won. Both Maharaja Jay Singh and Surendra Singh seated Kumar on the throne and solemnised it. The party began and gifs were distributed among the poor and helpless. The party lasted seven days. The entire army of Shivdutt whole-heartedly accepted the command of Kumar.

None of the men entered the women's wing, as strict patrolling was arranged.

Several days after giving instructions to Kunwar Virendra Singh to break the *tilism,* Maharaja Jay Singh and king Surendra Singh happily moved to Vijaygarh and Naugarh. After their departure, Kunwar Virendra Singh with his *aiyars* and some force set out for the *tilism*.

□

20

Kunwar Virendra Singh pitched his camp at the gate of *tilism*. He had already taken out the treasure, what remained was to break two pieces of *tilism* — one that platform on which the stone man was sleeping and the other to break the door inside which the princess and Chapla were arrested. Kumar had got the *tilismi* book. Today he read the remaining pages of that book. He took note of all details which he had to perform to reach Chandrakanta but the book had no mention of the trick to break that platform on which lay the stone man. No doubt, it was written that the platform is a door to another *tilism* which is bigger than this one and there is unlimited wealth inside. There is one more amazing thing about it, which can perplex even the wisest. There is another trick to open the door and the key is in possession of that sleeping man.

Kumar pointed to Jyotishi ji, "Jyotishi ji, shall I not be able to break this *tilism* of the platform?"

Jyotishi ji, "We'll see it later, first you get Chandrakanta released".

Kumar said, "All right, it'll be done today itself".

With three *aiyars*, Kunwar Virendra Singh entered the *tilism*. He recalled all that was written in the *tilismi* book and started working likewise.

Going inside the cave, they opened the door to the head side of the stone platform. They went down through the room to the garden, where there was the stone cover of the royal seat and the treasure touching which Chapla had lost consciousness. It was described in the *tilismi* book as "a box containing something unique."

The four people swimming through the canal reached the other side of the garden as Chapla had gone out. Then walking along the canal under the hill, they reached the small veranda where lay the cobra into whose mouth Chapla had entered.

On one side of the wall, there was a life-size black stone set in the wall. Kumar kicked it forcefully; the stone slid like a panel and a flight of stairs was visible.

Lighting a flare, the four people stepped down. Here they saw the artistry of that cobra. Composed of several wheels and parts made from palm leaves, the bellows was placed underneath from which Kumar knew that when someone puts his foot on the stone facing the cobra, the bellows start heaving and its wind force forces the man into the mouth of the cobra.

On one side, there was a window which was closed. A key lay in the front. The four people opened the lock and went in. Then they went upstairs, which showed a cave looking like a lane.

From the book, they already knew that this very cave-like lane led to that veranda where Chapla and Chandrakanta lay helpless.

Thinking that he would now meet Chandrakanta, Kumar's heart started beating fast; the love of Chapla shook Tej Singh. Very happily they proceeded further. Kumar was thinking, "Today, I'll see Chandrakanta in a unique situation as never seen before. I'll myself arrange her hair, shake the dust off her body with my shawl. Alas! I've committed a blunder; she must be feeling sorry in her rags. I've not brought clothes for her. She'll certainly feel angry and will regard me as selfish. But no, she'll never be angry. She loves me immensely, she'll be excited to see me and won't mind the clothes. O, well, I'll wrap my shawl around my waist and give her my *dhoti* to wear for the present. (Startled) What's this! I can hear the footfalls of some people. Perhaps Chapla and Chandrakanta have fore knowledge of my coming and they are coming to receive me! No, no, how can they know that I have come here!"

With such thoughts in mind, as Kumar was going on, he heard the sound of two wolves fighting, hearing which Kumar felt discouraged. Looking towards Tej Singh, he wanted to say something but he kept mum. Walking on, he reached that veranda where he had seen the princess and Chapla from inside the cave.

He had high hopes to see princess Chandrakanta and Chapla here, but they were not visible anywhere. However, there were two corpses lying on earth, with faces disfigured, from head to foot only mangled bodies with little flesh left.

Only Kumar must know how he felt at this moment. His face looked mad, he started crying and prattling — "Alas Chandrakanta, who took you away! No, not took away rather killed you! Surely, those very wolves must have separated you from me whose voice I had heard just before I reached here. Yes, that wolf must be very foolish who in a hurry devoured you, for him I had turned up. He would have been very happy to drink my blood because it is full of love. What was there in your body, you were just a skeleton. But is it a fact that a wolf devoured you or I am mistaken? Isn't this a different place? No, no, see that wicked Shivdutt is sitting in the front. Alas, why should I live now, what's the use of my life? How shall I face Maharaja Jay Singh? Make no haste, take your time, I'm following you, I will not leave you even after death? Today the three states — Naugarh, Vijaygarh and Chunargarh have been humbled. I'm coming to you with some more people who will attend on you. Alas, this ominous *tilism*, this wicked Shivdutt and these wolves have reduced the big stalwarts to dust! That's the end, that was my world, no more now! *Arre*, why are you running! Lo! I follow you!"

Saying that and looking below the hill, he wanted to end his life and the three *aiyars* were looking stupefied when suddenly with a bang, the wall on one side of the veranda split open and an old gentleman caught hold of Kumar's hand.

Kumar looked back. About 80 years old, long, white cotton-like beard touching his nape, matted locks touching the ground, the whole body smeared with ash and big protruding eyes, holding a trident in the right hand, supporting Kumar with his left hand, trembling with anger looking like bronze Shiva spoke in a vehement tone — "Beware lest you should widow someone !"

The sound was so violent that the whole building shook. The three *aiyars'* hearts were fast palpitating. The agitated mind of Kunwar Virendra Singh became normal again. Looking at him from head to foot, Kunwar Virendra Singh said, "I've seen and understood that you are Lord Shiva himself or some yogi who has come for my welfare. Very well that you have come. My religion has been protected, being a warrior caste, I couldn't commit suicide. I'll fight you and sacrifice my life on this trident. You've surely come for this very purpose, but Mahatmaji, first tell me who will become a widow from my death? Being such a great soul, why do you tell a lie? Who belongs to me? Who have I married? Alas, if the princess would hear such a thing, she would certainly believe it. Who can belie the words of such a Mahatma?"

The old yogi said boldly, "Am I a liar? Are you a warrior caste? Is this the way of a warrior caste? Do they forget their promise? Did you not promise to marry someone? See, take it and read, who has written it?"

Saying it, he handed a letter to Kumar from under his matted locks. Kumar was startled to read the letter, "*Arre,* 'tis my writing. What's written in it? I agree to it". What's written on the other side? Well, now I understand; this is the letter from that forest girl in which she had proposed me to marry her and in reply I had agreed. But how could he find the letter? How is he related to that forest girl?"

After a while, Kumar asked, "Do you know this forest girl?" In reply again, the old yogi thundered, "Do you still talk of knowing her? Shall I present her before you?"

Saying that, he struck the earth with his foot and the earth split and the forest girl appeared and fell at Kumar's feet.

□

Part-IV

1

Kunwar Virendra Singh was taken aback as the forest girl suddenly appeared from under the earth and fell on his feet. For a long time, he kept thinking why did the forest girl come here and who is this yogi, who is helping her? After keeping mum for long, Kumar told the yogi, "I know this forest girl, she has obliged me a lot and I have also promised her but my promise cannot materialise unless I meet Chandrakanta. See, what promise is written in this letter which you have given me? She has written herself. I and Chandrakanta should be married the same day and I had agreed to it. But when Chandrakanta is no more in this world, I can't marry anybody. The agreement is to marry both of them together".

Yogi said, (Looking at forest girl) "*Arre,* do you want to prove me a liar?"

Forest girl said, (Folding her hands) "No, Maharaj, how can I prove you a liar? You please ask him how he came to know that Chandrakanta is dead".

Yogi said (to Kumar), "Did you hear! What the girl says? How did you know that the princess is dead?"

Kumar said, (Surprised) "Is the princess alive?"

Yogi said, "First give your reply to what I ask".

Kumar said, "Previously when I had come to this cave I had seen princess Chandrakanta and Chapla here, I had also talked to them. Today seeing in place of them two corpses, I knew that these two corpses belong to ....". (his voice choked with emotion).

Yogi said, (Looking at Tej Singh) "Had you also lost your senses? Seeing these corpses could you not recognise whether these are male or female corpses? Did you not consider their length and structure?"

Tej Singh said, (Looking at the dead bodies) "I was gravely mistaken that I didn't think over the two corpses; with Kumar I was also nervous. In fact, the two corpses are male bodies and not female bodies".

Yogi said, "What a matter of shame for *aiyars* to commit such a mistake! This tiny mistake had virtually killed Kumar? Look at that side between those two hills! So much is enough for you as you already know the details of this cave, you have heard of from your guru".

Tej Singh glanced at that side and his gaze was fixed. Kumar also started looking that way, Devi Singh and Jyotishi ji too looked that way. Suddenly, Tej Singh ejaculated in surprise, "O, what's happened?" Hearing the words, all turned their attention in that direction.

After a while, in order to talk to Yogiji, Tej Singh turned towards him, but he was not there. Even the forest girl was missing and they couldn't know which way they had come in and when they went out. So long as Yogiji and forest girl were here, their incoming path was open, there was a crack in the wall and a split in the earth, but now there was nothing anywhere.

□

2

At last, Kunwar Virendra Singh told Tej Singh, "Uptill now, I don't know what Yogiji showed you from the sign of his finger and where you had your gaze fixed for so long, what you were seeing and now where they have disappeared!"

Tej Singh said, "What can I say; where the two went away. I couldn't know anything clearly from them. Now we'll have to struggle a lot".

Virendra Singh said, "Tell me, what were you looking that way?"

Tej Singh said, "It will take a long time to explain what I was looking at and now I can't tolerate the stench of these corpses. Leaving them here, let's go out of this *tilism* there. I'll tell you everything. But before leaving this place, please see what I was looking at in amazement. The door between the two hills that is open now was closed previously; we have to come back here. This *tilism*i is situated on such a path that coming here from inside takes ten miles and from the outside path it will take thirty miles".

Kumar said, "All right, let's go now but I feel tense until I hear the details of the incident".

The way the four people had reached here through the *tilism*, they went out the same way. Today, it was midnight by the time they came out. The people of their camp were anxious that usually they came back an hour before sunset but why this delay today? When they reached their camp all felt assured. Tej Singh told Kumar, "This time you go to bed. Tomorrow I'll tell you what I have to tell".

□

3

It was known that Chandrakanta was alive but where she was, and why she left the cave, who was the forest girl, from where the Yogiji came, what he showed to Tej Singh were the things that Kumar spent the night thinking about, he didn't have a moment's sleep. Now it was not yet dawn when Kumar got down from bed and in a hurry went to the camp of Tej Singh. He woke him up from sleep.

Tej Singh got up and greeted Kumar. In his heart, he knew that Kumar had come to ask about that very thing and therefore he had come so early, still he asked, "Tell me, why have you got up so early?"

Kumar said, "I couldn't sleep the whole night. Now, tell me what you have to tell, be quick. I feel anxious".

Tej Singh said, "All right, please take a seat, I'll explain".

Kumar sat down and called for Devi Singh and Jyotishi ji. When they turned up, Tej Singh began, "Uptill now, I don't know who took away Chandrakanta or who that yogi was and why he was helping the forest girl, but whatever he showed me was so amazing that I was absorbed in seeing and couldn't ask Yogiji further and he went away without disclosing the details. That day, when for the first time I took you to the cave, I told you all that I had heard from my guru, don't you remember?"

Kumar said, "Yes, I remember very well".

Tej Singh said, "What had I said?"

Kumar said, "You had said that there is a massive treasure but there is a small *tilism* tied to it which can be easily snapped because your guru has told you the trick to snap it".

Tej Singh said, "Yes, it's true. I had said it. In that cave, I had showed you a door between two hills which the yogi had indicated through gestures. Seeing that door open, I knew that someone had snapped that *tilism* and took away the treasure. That very moment, it came to my mind that the yogi had indicated that the man who had looted the treasure by breaking the *tilism*, the same man had taken away Chandrakanta, too. Thinking this, I kept gazing at the door and yogi Maharaj went away".

Hearing so much from Tej Singh, Kumar kept sitting silent for long, he almost lost his consciousness, then he controlled himself and said, "Which means Chandrakanta has fallen into another trap?"

Tej Singh said, "It seems so".

Kumar said, "How to find it out? What should we do now?"

Tej Singh said, "First of all we should go to that cave. Going there, we should see that *tilism* which someone else has broken and taken away that treasure. Perhaps we may find something or some sign there. After that, we will decide on further step".

Kumar, "All right, let's go. But, at the moment, one more thing comes to my mind".

Tej Singh, "What's that?"

Kumar said, "When we had gone to arrest Badrinath in that cave and came back as we could not open the door, perhaps at that time he might have shut the door from inside who has broken the *tilism*. He might be there at that time."

Tej Singh said, "Your thinking is right, surely this is the truth, no doubt about it. Rather that very man must have freed Shivdutt".

Kumar said, "It's just possible, but after release Shivdutt was out on dishonesty and had attacked our camp, then had the same man put him in the cave again? And were those paper chits written by him that we had found on Shivdutt's bed after his disappearance?"

Tej Singh said, "May be."

Kumar said, "From this it appears that he is our friend. But if he is our friend, why did he take away the princess?"

Tej Singh said, "It is difficult to answer. I'm at a loss. Even after Shivdutt's release you had to go to that cave and, while searching for you, we, too, had reached that cave, that time Chapla didn't say that somebody had come to that cave who had released Shivdutt and again arrested him in that cave. She didn't mention it, rather said that she always saw Shivdutt in the cave. She also didn't say anything to be afraid of."

Kumar said, "The issue seems very complex, but you, too, did a mistake."

Tej Singh said, "What was my mistake?"

Kumar said, "Yesterday, yogi came out of the wall and prevented me from jumping down. Thereafter, he kicked the earth, it slit open and the forest girl came out of it. Now, the Yogi was not a god to kick open the earth. Surely, there is some secret under the earth. You could kick the earth in the same way and see whether it opens or not."

Tej Singh said, "You have pointed out very correctly, but what to do now?"

Kumar said, "Let's go again today. We may find something. What's the need to go to the cave just now?"

Tej Singh said, "All right, let's go."

Today again, Kumar and the three *aiyars* went to that *tilism.* Moving from the common path they reached the same veranda where the yogi had appeared. They saw that the two decomposed and half beast-eaten bodies were no more there. The ground looked washed clean. For some time, they stood surprised. Thereafter, Tej Singh kicked the earth vigorously where the Yogi had kicked.

Immediately, the earth split on that very spot showing small stairs downwards. Cheerfully, the four people went down. There they looked for another door in the dark room, but they couldn't find one. Helpless they came out but the split earth was not rejoined, it remained open. Tej Singh said, "It seems there is some mechanism to close it from inside, which is not known to us. Anyway, we got nothing, now without entering this cave from the outer side, we'll get nothing."

The four people came out of the *tilism.* Tej Singh locked the gate.

Kunwar Virendra Singh stayed there for a day and having appointed Fateh Singh Deputy, sent him to Chunar. Then he proceeded towards Naugarh and met his father there. At the instance of king Surendra Singh, Jeet Singh asked Kunwar Virendra Singh about the *tilism* when alone in the night. In reply, Kumar told him what had really happened.

On that very spot, Jeet Singh called for Tej Singh and told him, "Both of you *aiyars* go to the cave with Kumar and ensure victory over that small *tilism* at the hands of Kumar whose details were told to you by your guru. All happenings will come to light in between. But before winning the fort, do two things once, take some people with you and bring in Maharaja Shivdutt with his wife here. When you go inside the cave, you must close the door from inside. Now there's no read to see Maharaja and take instructions. You people march on here and now and take with you a palanquin for the queen."

Kunwar Virendra Singh set out for the cave with his three *aiyars* and some people. By the morning, they reached there. Leaving the guards at a distance, the four people opened the door of the cave and went in.

It was morning. Tej Singh took out from the cave Maharaja Shivdutt and his queen and entrusted them to the guards. He also gave instructions to send Maharaja Shivdutt on foot and his queen in a palanquin to Naugarh before they entered the cave.

□

4

The guards of king Surendra Singh took Maharaja Shivdutt and his queen to Naugarh. On the advice of Jeet Singh, they were given a nice house to live in. Their handcuffs were removed but strict patrolling was arranged around the house for safety.

Next day, having consultations between them, king Surendra Singh and Jeet Singh went along with Pundit Badrinath, Pannalal, Ramnarayan and Chunnilal to that house in which Maharaja Shivdutt and his queen were kept.

Hearing of the arrival of king Surendra Singh, Maharaja Shivdutt with his wife came up to the door to receive him and seated him in, then he sat himself face to face. The *aiyars* in handcuffs were also seated on one side. Maharaja Shivdutt asked, "Why did you take the trouble to come at this hour?"

In reply, king Surendra Singh said, "Till this day, at the provocation of Krur Singh, you did whatever you liked, cheated us, even fought us just to harm me. But, so far, God protected us. Krur Singh, Nazim and Ahmad were done to death thinking ill of us. Now what's your intention? Do you want to languish in prison or you have thought something else?"

Maharaja Shivdutt said, "There's no doubt about the bravery of Kunwar Virendra Singh and yours. No praise will be sufficient enough. May God grant you happiness and give you the pleasure of nursing your grandson in your lap and forgive me for whatever I have done. Now, I don't have any ambition for kingship. I know how you have won Chunar and all that has happened there. Now, I want just one thing and for the sake of your bravery and manliness please fulfil my desire." Saying this, he stood up with folded hands.

King Surendra Singh said, "Say whatever you have in mind. I'll fulfil it as far as possible."

Shivdutt said, "Please listen to what I want. I have no son to think of. Though in my fort at Chunar, there are several widows related to my family, who were maintained by me. Please make some suitable arrangement for them so that they may live comfortably. I have some people related to me but I'll not pray for them rather I'll not even name them because they are men and can earn their livelihood by any means and now please release me from captivity. I'll now go to forest with my wife and pray to God. I don't want to show myself to anybody. That's all, I've no other wish."

Surendra Singh said, "All women related to you in Chunar will be properly maintained and you needn't worry for them. But many issues are involved in releasing you".

Shivdutt said, "None at all (holding the sacred thread) I swear by religion, now I have no ill will in my heart, I'll never think ill of you."

Surendra Singh said, "So far, you are not old enough to practise penance."

Shivdutt said, "Whatsoever, if you are brave enough, free me."

Surendra Singh said, "I don't believe in your swearing in but as you say that if I am brave, I should free you, then I free you. You may go wherever you want to go and take as much as you need for your expenses."

Shivdutt said, "I don't want anything for my expenses rather I surrender all the jewellery of my wife's body."

Saying this, he looked towards his wife. She immediately took off all the jewellery from her person.

Surendra Singh said, "It was not good to get the queen take off her jewellery."

Shivdutt said, "When we want to live in the jungle, why should we carry such things? Shall we keep them to suffer at the hands of thieves and robbers and sacrifice our sleep at night?"

Surendra Singh (sadly) said, "Look Shivdutt, till very recently, you were the master of the throne of Chunar, today your going like this looks bad to me. Granted, you were my enemy but I feel pity for your queen. I have freed you. You may go wherever you want, but once again I tell you if you agree to live here, I can give you any work of your choice in my state, you live here."

Shivdutt said, "No. I'll not stay here, set me free. Withdraw all vigilance around the house. I'll go away in the night when I will."

Surendra Singh said, "All right, as you please."

The four *aiyars* of Shivdutt were listening everything silently. After the two kings concluded their conversation, looking towards Maharaja Shivdutt Pundit Badrinath said, "You are now going to practise penance, what's your order for us?"

Shivdutt said, "You do whatever you like. Go wherever you want, on my part I have given you liberty, rather it would be a good thing for you to live with king Surendra Singh because you will not find another king so brave and religious."

Badrinath said, "May God keep you safe and well! From this day, we belong to Kunwar Virendra Singh. You, with your own hands remove the handcuffs from our hands."

Maharaja Shivdutt with his own hands unshackled the handcuffs from the four *aiyars*. King Surendra Singh and even Jeet Singh didn't object to it. After the handcuffs were unshackled the four *aiyars* stood behind king Surendra Singh. Jeet Singh said, "Now, all the four *aiyars* stand in front of me, then you stand there — first you must perform the traditional ritual."

With a smile Pundit Badrinath, Pannalal, Ramnarayan and Chunnilal came in front of Jeet Singh and without being asked taking in hand the sacred thread and *aiyari* bag, swore in and said — "From today, I am the servant of Surendra Singh and his family. I'll discharge my duties honestly and sincerely. I'll regard Tej Singh, Devi Singh and Jyotishi ji as my brothers. Now, isn't the ritual complete?"

"No, that's all!" Saying this, Jeet Singh embraced all the four and then the four *aiyars* stood behind king Surendra Singh.

King Surendra Singh told Maharaja Shivdutt, "Well, now I take leave. Patrolling is being withdrawn. In the night, whenever you want to go, you may go but let's embrace each other."

Shivdutt said, (with folded hands) "No, I don't deserve to embrace you."

"No, you must do it." So saying, Surendra Singh forcibly embraced him and with a heavy heart moved to palace and ordered withdrawal of patrolling.

Along with Jeet Singh, Badrinath, Pannalal, Chunnilal and Ramnarayan, king Surendra sat in his court. For hours, there was regretful talk about Maharaja Shivdutt. Finding a good opportunity, Jeet Singh prayed, "We are happy that four more *aiyars* have come to our court. Now, it would be a good thing if this attendant is granted fifteen days' leave, I have something to do for the relatives far away from here. It is urgent."

Surendra Singh said, "These days you have taken one or two day's leave on several occasions."

Jeet Singh said, "Yes sir, I had some work at home but this time I have to go very far therefore I pray for fifteen day's leave. From today, Pundit Badrinath will work for me. There will be no harm of any sort."

Surendra Singh said, "All right, go but come back as soon as possible."

Taking leave of king Surendra Singh, Jeet Singh went home and took with him Badrinath and four *aiyars* to give them certain instructions.

□

5

Kunwar Virendra Singh with three *aiyars* went into the cave. Seeing some signs here and there, Tej Singh told Kumar, "Undoubtedly someone took away the treasure breaking the small *tilism* here. Surely that very man must have arrested Chandrakanta. I had heard my guru say that in this case there are many buildings and gardens worth seeing. We'll not be surprised if that thief comes across us."

Kumar said, "Now, we must hasten our work as much as possible."

Tej Singh said, "You just walk along and start the work here and now."

So saying, Tej Singh took Kunwar Virendra Singh under that very hill from where the water stream originated. Getting down from the stream he dug up the earth at a distance of forty feet from the stream.

Tej Singh had told Kumar that the mechanism to break this small *tilism* and getting the treasure was engraved on a metal plate buried in the earth about this place but at this time nothing came out of digging. No doubt, a letter was found there which Kumar read as follows—

"What are you digging now? There's nothing useful. Whatever was valuable, has been out, *tilism* was broken. You must regret now."

Tej Singh said, (looking at Kumar) "See, we have got all the proof of breaking the *tilism*."

Kumar said, "Now that the *tilism* has been broken, all its doors must be open."

"Yes, they must be open." Saying so Tej Singh took Kumar through upward hills to a cave which had an opening wide enough to allow a single person.

On Tej Singh's advice, the four people one by one entered that cave. Inside, at a distance, they found an open space so that the four people began walking together, actually just groping as it was pitch dark and even each other's hands were not visible. While walking, Kunwar Virendra Singh touched a closed door which on a push opened and showed bright light inside.

The four people went in, saw a small orchard which was clean on all sides, it seemed that it had just been swept clean, but it was not known where the tank was.

Loitering about in the orchard they felt that they were on a hill. When they reached a fountain something incredible came to sight. There was a pair of female bracelets on the ground seeing which Kumar soon realised that it belonged to Chandrakanta. He immediately picked it up, tears started rolling down his cheeks. He asked Tej Singh — "How come the bracelet here? What should we think about it?" Before Tej Singh could reply, he saw a chit of paper lying crumpled on earth. He immediately picked it up and read it — "Proceed very cautiously. *Aiyars* will chase you, lest they find you and inflict heavy damage to you and Kumar. I'll come tomorrow if an opportunity comes. The same one."

Reading the chit, Tej Singh started thinking – for long, he stood thinking. At last, Kumar couldn't help asking — "Why, what are you thinking? What's written in this letter?"

Tej Singh handed the letter to Kumar. He was also surprised to read the letter and said, "Considering what is written in this letter, it transpires that there is something disturbed about our forest girl, but it is not clear who wrote the letter."

Tej Singh said, "Your thinking is true, but I am thinking something even more perplexing."

Kumar said, "What's that?"

Tej Singh said, "I recognise the writing a bit, but I don't understand why the writer has written clumsily to conceal his identity."

Kumar said, "Anyway, leave this letter. Sooner or later the fact will come to light, now let's proceed with our work."

Again they started walking about. They saw on a corner of the orchard four small windows that were fitted closely side by side. First, the four people entered by the left window. At a distance, they found a door, beyond which there was no passage because down below there was a terribly dangerous hill.

Looking about and considering minutely, they came to know that this was the door which the yogi had pointed out to Tej Singh by gestures. From this point, that veranda looked clearly in which princess Chandrakanta and Chapla lay helpless for a long time.

They came back to the same orchard and entered the adjacent window which was very dark. At a distance, they saw some light and to the end of it there was a big gate open from which they came out and had full view of the surrounding.

They saw nothing more than the spacious field. Tej Singh wanted to walk around the field to know about it more, but couldn't do so for certain reasons. Firstly, the sun was hot and, secondly, Kumar did not permit it and said, "We'll see it when we have another chance. This time we should see from the third and fourth windows, what lies there."

The four people came back and entered the third window. As they reached an orchard they saw that the forest girl was walking around with a number of friends but as soon as she saw Kunwar Virendra Singh and others, she disappeared in a corner of the garden.

The four people chased her and moved around in search of her, but could find nothing rather where they had disappeared in that corner they found a closed door. They tried to open it by any means, but did not succeed.

On one corner of that garden, there was a small twelve-doored veranda. Being helpless along with his *aiyars*, Kunwar Virendra Singh sat there thinking — "How did the forest girl come here? Is it her abode of living? Then why did she run away seeing us? Does she not want to meet me now?" Thus thinking they spent the day but nobody could find the hang of it. There were several fruit trees in this garden besides a small stream. The four people ate fruits to their fill and drinking water lay down in that twelve-doored veranda on the earth. It was decided to spend the night in this veranda and to decide further course next day.

Taking things out of his bag Devi Singh lighted the flare and began to talk among them.

Kumar said, "I have been doomed in the love of Chandrakanta and more, there is still no hope."

Tej Singh said, "The princess is safe and sound and you'll meet her, there's no doubt about it. The thing which costs as much pain gives as much joy in life."

Kumar said, "What pains have you taken for Chapla?"

Tej Singh said, "What has Chapla herself suffered for my sake? She did everything for Chandrakanta".

Jyotishiji, "Why Tej Singh, does Chapla belong to your caste?"

Tej Singh said, "I don't know about it but when there is love, caste matters no more."

Jyotishiji said, "But has she got no parents and issues? If she does not belong to your caste, will her parents accept it?"

Tej Singh said, "If it happens like that I'll kill her and commit suicide."

Kumar said, "If you give me some reward I'll tell you the details about Chapla."

Tej Singh said, "In reward I'll hand over Chapla to you."

Kumar said, "Remember it, then Chapla will be mine."

Tej Singh said, "Yes, yes, she'll be, yours, yours."

Kumar said, "Chapla belongs to our caste. Her father

was a big *zamindar* and *aiyar.* Her mother died leaving her seven days old. Her father brought her up and taught her *aiyari*, only a few years back, her father, too died. He was very dear to Maharaja Jay Singh as he had worked a lot for him. At the time of death, he handed all his earnings and Chapla to Maharaja because he had no son. Maharaja Jay Singh regards her as his daughter and even Maharaja likes her. Because of companionship between princess Chandrakanta and Chapla since childhood, they love each other."

Tej Singh said, "Today you gave me very happy information. For long, I felt uneasy but thinking something I did not ask you. How did you come to know these things?"

Kumar said, "From Chandrakanta herself."

Tej Singh said, "Then it's all right".

They spent the whole night talking; they didn't have a moment's sleep. Got up early and after morning routine, bath and worship, they ate some fruit and went into that garden and came back by the same route and entered the fourth window to see what lay there. Going in, they saw again a flourishing garden which startled Kumar.

□

6

Tej Singh asked Kunwar Virendra Singh, "Why were you startled to see this garden? What strange thing did you see in it?"

Kumar said, "I recognised this garden."

Tej Singh (surprised), "When did you see it?"

Kumar said, "This is the garden in which I was lodged from the caravan. In this very garden when I opened my eyes I saw the picture of Chandrakanta, I was given food here eating which I became unconscious and was transported to another garden. Look, in the front there is a small pond in which I had bathed, blackberry trees on both sides are clearly visible."

Tej Singh said, "We had better walk round this garden".

Kumar said, "Let's walk, I can recall, the door of that room might be open in which I had seen the picture of Chandrakanta."

The four people started walking around that garden. The doors of the rooms were open. All those things, which Kumar had previously seen, were there. It was very neat and clean, no trace of dirt or dust.

When Kumar had come to this garden for the first time, he was in a different state of mind. He was all surprise, almost nervous, was facing a labyrinth of thoughts naturally. He could not enjoy this garden well. But, today, he is with his *aiyars*, has no care, rather there is hope of fulfilling his several ambitions. He started walking cheerfully with *aiyars*. Today no room, no chamber, no door is closed. He walks on showing and telling his *aiyars* that on a particular spot, he had sat, at another spot, had eaten and at a third spot he had slept and, thus, they reached another garden.

Tej Singh said, "After taking lunch in the daytime and sleeping for a while, the room in which you were, must be having the connecting path from this very garden. We should thoroughly search for it."

Devi Singh said, (to Kumar) "When you had come to this garden for the first time you were warmly received, you were given clothes to change after bathing, all materials for worship were well-arranged, you were treated to a sumptuous dish but today there is none to take care of, why so?"

Kumar said, "All this is due to you people."

While walking they went to another garden. Kumar said, "No doubt, this is the garden in which I had opened my eyes on the second occasion, when several women had arrested me, but it is surprising that nobody is here. What a funny world, it has changed from what it was yesterday. However, let's move and see the situation and find out that court of pictures and its splendour there. I well remember the path and can well lead the way." Saying that, Kumar led the way and the four *aiyars* with him made for the third garden.

□

7

Previously, Maharaja Jay Singh of Vijaygarh had got the information that even after breaking the *Tilism*, there was no trace of Chandrakanta. Thereafter, it was known that the princess was safe and sound and Virendra Singh had again entered the cave in search of her. Hearing such news from time to time, Maharaja Jay Singh felt unhappy. The condition of the queen in the palace was no better. In the separation from Chandrakanta, she had given up taking food and drink and had become a skeleton. All other women in the palace were unhappy and sad.

One day, Maharaja Jai Singh was sitting in his court. Diwan Hardayal Singh read out the urgent petitions and took orders from him. Meanwhile, a spy appeared, bringing in a written chit of paper in his hand.

The guard presented him. Diwan Hardayal Singh asked him, "What's this paper and it says what?"

The spy submitted — "This type of written paper is seen posted at many places in the town. At crossings, in the markets and streets, such chits are seen in abundance. I got it read by a man and his words caused fear in my heart and I plucked one and have brought to your court. In the market people have become panicky to read them."

Taking the paper from the spy, Diwan Hardayal Singh read it and read it out to Maharaja. The words were —

"The king of Naugarh and Vijaygarh must be enjoying themselves these days. Both of them may be boasting that they have no enemy now. In the same way, Virendra Singh also might be feeling puffed up with pride that he is enjoying himself in the cave. But it is not known to anybody that I, their avowed enemy, am still alive. From today, I'll initiate my mission. I'll kill the kings, sardars and selected big businessmen of Naugarh and Vijaygarh and reduce their states to dust and still evade arrest. Don't think that you have big *aiyars,* I don't care a toss for them. I am also a big *aiyar,* but I'll not arrest anybody, my business will be only to kill them. Now, if you want to save your life, run away from here. Beware! Beware!! Beware!!!

The guru of *aiyars* — Jalim Khan."

Maharaja Jay Singh became panicky to hear the words of the letter. Hardayal Singh also became nervous and all people present in the court began to tremble with fear. To console them, Maharaja spoke boldly, "I don't fear the words of such ruffians. No need to panic. Let it be announced in the city that the government wants to arrest Jalim Khan. He will not be able to harm anybody. Nobody should leave his home out of fear. After announcement, let there be strict vigil in the city and several spies be sent to search for that devil."

After a while, Maharaja dismissed the court. Diwan Hardayal Singh also wanted to go saluting the Maharaja but stopped at a hint from him.

Taking the Diwan, Maharaja Jay Singh went to the private court and began to think about Jalim Khan. After considering for some time, Hardayal Singh said, "We don't have any *aiyar* which is essentially needed". Maharaja Jay Singh added, "Right now you write a letter about the situation here to king Surendra Singh. Also attach that notice which the spy has brought."

As per the order of Maharaja, Hardayal Singh wrote the letter and, giving it to a spy, sent him towards Naugarh. Thereafter, Maharaja gave orders to intensify vigil around the palace and then bade goodbye to Diwan.

Having disposed of all these, Maharaja went inside the palace. He also told the queen about the situation. She also became very much afraid. There was wide excitement among women about it. Today, the whole day and night were spent in disturbance.

Next day, again, like yesterday, a spy presented a paper and said, "Today the whole city is seen with such chits pasted here and there." Diwan Hardayal Singh took the paper from the spy and read out to Maharaja —

"Bravo, bravo! You could do nothing and started begging help from Naugarh! Don't you know that I have also created havoc in Naugarh. Could your spy go escaping from me? I've killed him. Send somebody to take possession of his corpse. At a mile outside the town, you will find his corpse."

The same — Jalim Khan."

Maharaja started trembling to hear it. All people sitting in the court became panicky. Each one was worried for his life. By order of Maharaja, several people were sent to bring in the dead body of that spy. There was agitated excitement till the dead body was brought outside the court. Thousands of people flocked around. Everybody was talking of Jalim Khan. People trembled to hear his name. The head of the spy was missing and the letter he was carrying was tied to his arm.

Publicly, Maharaja consoled people but in his heart, he was afraid for his life. He told Diwan, "Let it be announced that whoever arrests this Jalim Khan, the administration will give him a reward of ten thousand rupees. He also asked to send a letter about the present situation to Naugarh with five horse-riders."

Giving this order, Maharaja dismissed the court. The five riders who set out for Naugarh with the letter were shaking with fear. They were sure of their death. They decided among them that outside the city, they would abandon the horses and run away, but couldn't succeed.

Next day, early morning, with a letter, a guard came to the court. Hardayal Singh took the letter and read —

"How could those five riders escape from me? Today it befell on them. From tomorrow, I'll create havoc in your palace. Now be most careful. You have announced that whoever arrests Jalim Khan will get a reward of ten thousand. And I say that whoever arrests me, I will give him a reward of twenty thousand!

— The same Jalim Khan"

Reading today's letter, Maharaja was hell-shocked. Now, he had no hope that his news would ever reach Naugarh. To send the entire army with a letter was below his calibre. To make matters worse, the spies brought the news that the whole city was trembling with fear of Jalim Khan and, no wonder, the public might vacate the city in a day or two. Hearing it, he became more worried.

Maharaja sent several men to bring in the dead bodies of those riders. People had no nerves to go, but had to obey Maharaja at any cost.

The five corpses came. Their heads were not cut. It seemed that they had been strangled as there were marks of rope around the neck.

Seeing this, Maharaja was sitting dazed. He was at a loss to think. Meanwhile, Pundit Badrinath was seen coming.

Today, the outfit of Pundit Badrinath was most remarkable. He beamed active from every inch of his body. He was well-decked with *aiyari* paraphernalia; rather more, having bow and arrow, wearing tight fitted under-clothes, bag and dagger hanging from the waist. The lasso hung over the back, the bag of stone around the neck and holding a small stick appeared in the court.

Maharaja had already got the news that king Shivdutt with his queen had gone to forest to practise penance and Pundit Badrinath, Pannalal and others had joined king Surendra Singh.

In such a condition, the arrival of Pundit Badrinath was like showering nectar on a dying person. He was overjoyed to see him. After greeting, he asked him to take a seat. Badrinath after wishing sat down.

Jay Singh said, "Today, you have come on a great occasion".

Badrinath said, 'Yes, now don't worry at all. I'll arrest the rogue Jalim Khan in a day or two."

Jay Singh said, "How did you know about Jalim Khan?"

Badrinath said, "I had this news at Naugarh itself, details of which I will share later. Having arrived here I found the city folk sad and trembling with fear. On way, whoever met me, I consoled him saying not to worry because I have came. I'll narrate the rest later on and whatever has to be done will be decided before you and Diwan Hardayal Singh at another time because till now I haven't even performed my morning chores. Only after performing them I'll do any other thing."

Now there was a little cheerfulness on the face of Maharaja Jay Singh. He ordered Diwan Hardayal Singh, "Take Pundit Badrinath to your house and arrange everything for his comfort, so that he has no inconvenience of any sort, now I take leave."

Badrinath, "Where will Maharaja be available in the evening? Because I want to talk."

Jay Singh said, "Whenever you choose, you can meet me."

Maharaja Jay Singh dismissed the court. Taking Pundit Badrinath, Diwan Hardayal Singh came to his house and arranged all necessary things for him.

For the rest of the day Pundit Badrinath thought of ways to arrest Jalim Khan. In the evening, with Diwan Hardayal Singh went out to see Maharaja Jay Singh. It was learnt that Maharaja was walking in the garden. They entered the garden.

At that time, there were many people with Maharaja. As soon as Pundit Badrinath came they were sent away, only, Badrinath and Hardayal Singh remained with Maharaja.

At the beginning, for some time, the talk veered around king Shivdutt of Chunar. Thereafter, Maharaja asked, "How did the news about Jalim Khan reach Naugarh?"

Badrinath said, "At Naugarh also, he has pasted this type of chits from, which I knew that he would create trouble at Vijaygarh. Therefore, my Maharaja has sent here."

Maharaja said, 'Hasn't this wicked Jalim Khan killed someone there?"

Badrinath said, "No, so far he has not succeeded there, our *aiyars* are also engaged very cleverly in arresting him."

Maharaja said, "Here he has killed many people."

Badrinath said, "I got the information on entering the city; anyway, we'll see it later."

Maharaja said, "Had you brought Jyotishi ji with you, with his *ramal* it would have become easier to arrest him."

Badrinath said, "Maharaja, just consider his audacity, giving notice he is doing with a bang! Such a man should be arrested in like fashion. Where's the need of Jyotishiji's help?"

Maharaja said, "Let's see, how he is arrested. The entire city is trembling with fear."

Badrinath said, "Don't worry, I'll arrest someone either in the morning or evening."

Maharaja said, "Are they several people?"

Badrinath said, "Must be many people. It's not a single man's work to have an account of things from here to Naugarh and have the design to cause damage on both sides."

Maharaja said, "All right, do whatever you want, from your coming, I feel somewhat assured. Otherwise, I was very much perturbed."

Badrinath said, "Now I'll take leave. I have to do a lot."

Hardayal Singh said, "Will you not go towards your camp?"

Badrinath said, "No need, I've come fully prepared and will go whichever way I choose."

A little night had passed when Badrinath, taking leave of Maharaja Jay Singh, left in search of Jalim Khan.

□

8

Badrinath set out in search of Jalim Khan. Nobody knew what he would do and how he would arrest Jalim Khan.

In his last notice, Jalim Khan had threatened Maharaja that he would rob his palace.

The notice had a very bad effect on Maharaja. The guards on vigilance were increased fourfold. He himself kept awake throughout the night, always had the hilt of the sword in his hand. There had been some assurance from the arrival of Badrinath but from the next day, he went out to arrest Jalim Khan. Again notices were seen pasted on road crossings. A spy picked up one such chit and presented before Maharaja and Diwan Hardayal Singh read out thus —

"Maharaja Jay Singh,

Beware, don't forget on the *aiyari* of Pundit Badrinath, what can that green chap do? Previously, Jalim Khan was your enemy, now I have joined. Within fifteen days, I'll destroy your city and on fourth day, from today, I'll reach your palace with the head of Badrinath at twelve o'clock in the night. Beware! Even then, whoever wants, may try to arrest me. Let me see, who dares? Whoever is the enemy of Maharaja and wants to see me, may see me at *'Teti Choti'* at twelve in the night.

— Aafat Khan Khooni"

This notice extremely baffled Maharaja. Desperately, he felt like leaving Vijaygarh then and there, but his manliness and bravery did not allow him to do so.

He immediately dismissed the court, went into private court with Diwan Hardayal Singh and began consultations about this new Aafat Khan Khooni.

Maharaja said, "What to do now? One had already created much trouble and now another Aafat Khan has shocked us all the more. If the two are not arrested, it will be a shame on our state."

Hardayal Singh said, "After the return of Badrinath, there was some hope to arrest Jalim Khan, but now even his life is not safe."

Maharaja said, "It would be better to send this news to Naugarh by any means. From there, we might get some *aiyar* to help Badrinath."

Hardayal Singh said, "Whoever is sent to Naugarh, will be killed. However, if the letter is sent with one or two hundred guards, it might reach there."

Maharaja (angrily) said, "We have over fifty spies here only in name, they are idle shirkers and can't perform a single task. Neither one brings in news of Jalim Khan nor is he able to carry a letter to Naugarh."

Hardayal Singh said, "Only one spy's death has humbled all."

Maharaja said, "Anyway, in the evening come to the garden with all spies, they will either perform something or will be arranged in front of the machine gun and shot dead. We'll see what happens thereafter. I will myself arrest that scoundrel."

Hardayal Singh said, "As you order."

Maharaja said, "That's all, go now. Remember what I've said. Diwan Hardayal Singh taking leave of Maharaja went to his house but was puzzled what to do because Maharaja was exceedingly angry. It was anticipated that the spies would do nothing and the poor fellows would be shot dead. Then he also thought that if Maharaja himself would set out to arrest those rogues, his own life would be endangered, now there was no hope of life left."

□

9

Kunwar Virendra Singh set out for the third garden, where he had seen the picture of Chandrakanta, who had taken him there arresting like a prisoner.

He knew the way to the garden. When Kumar reached the door that led to the garden, there he saw a tender girl coming towards him. She was good-looking, wearing expensive clothes. With a letter in hand, she approached Kumar. She handed the letter to Kumar. Quite surprised he read the letter. It was written —

"You have been in my locality for several days. Therefore, your hospitality is due to me. Today everything has been arranged. Come along with this poor girl and honour my cottage. I'll never forget your obligation in my whole life — Siddhnath Yogi."

Kumar handed the letter to Tej Singh. Reading it he said, "He is a saint and yogi. So, there is some royalty, in the letter". Devi Singh and Jyotishi ji also read the letter.

It was evening and Kumar had not yet given a reply to the letter. Tej Singh told that girl." We accept Mahatma ji's hospitality but we can't go with you just now; we'll go an hour later because it is worship time now."

Girl said, "I'll wait till then. You people perform your worship. If you order, may I bring in water and seat for the purpose?"

Devi Singh said, "No, there's no need."

Girl said, "Then how will you perform worship here? There is no canal, no pond in this garden."

Tej Singh said, "There is a pond in the other garden."

Girl said, "Why take so much trouble? I'll bring in everything just now. Then you accompany me. You will perform evening worship there, there's still time for that."

Tej Singh said, "No, we'll perform evening worship in this very garden. Anyway, bring in water. Immediately, the girl strode away to the third garden."

Kumar said, "If the sender of this letter is that very yogi who had prevented me from jumping, it is a good thing, surely the forest girl would be there. But why did you refuse? We would have performed worship in that very garden! I was going to accept that very moment, but stopped short thinking there might be some meaning in your refusal."

Tej Singh said, "Certainly, its' so."

Devi Singh said, "Why guru, what's the secret in it?"

Tej Singh said, "Look, it'll be known just now."

Kumar said, "Then why don't you say it? When will you say it after all?"

Tej Singh said, "I thought that Yogiji might cheat us by mixing anaesthetic drug into our food and when we fall unconscious, he might lodge us in the cave and close the outward door. If it so happens, all our labour will go in vain. Look, you, too, were made unconscious in this very garden. When you were brought here as a prisoner and the moment you drank water, you became unconscious and were transported to the cave. Had it not so happened, then and there, we would have received information about this place. Moreover, I think that if we go there and refuse to eat, it will not be proper because once having accepted hospitality it is not proper to refuse to eat."

Devi Singh said, "Then what have you thought about it?"

Tej Singh said (with a laugh), "Just that I will crush that *tilismi* rose flower and make you drink the juice and also drink myself. Thereafter, nobody can make us unconscious for seven days."

Kumar said, "Okay, but how clever that man would have been to cultivate such a wonderful flower."

Tej Singh said, "Perfectly true."

Just then, the same girl was seen coming. Behind her three maids were carrying, water, seat and pot, etc. in their hands.

In that garden under a tree were several stones fit for sitting on. The maids arranged the goods on those stones. Thereafter Tej Singh told them, "Now, for some time, you people go to your garden because we don't perform evening worship in the presence of women."

"I have spent my whole life serving people like you. Why do you talk like this? Why don't you say plainly to go away! Lo, I am going." So saying the girl went away with other maids. Hearing her, they laughed and said, "She must be some *aiyar's* companion!"

After evening worship, Tej Singh crushed the rose flower and, mixing it with water, gave them to drink and also drank himself and began waiting for the maid.

After some time, the same woman came and asked them to follow her. They were already prepared to go, so immediately got up, and following her, reached the third garden. The *aiyars* hadn't seen it yet, but to Kunwar Virendra Singh, it was well-known. He had been brought to this very garden as a prisoner and had seen the picture of Chandrakanta, but today, the garden was not so, neither it had that light nor so many people. No doubt, 5 to 7 women were seen loitering here and there and there was also light under 2-3 trees, which was necessary.

It was evening, rather a little dark. That girl took them to that room in which Kumar had seen the gallery of pictures. Kumar went on thinking, "Today, whatever happens, I will not let go yogi without knowing all the secret. Today, it will be clear who the forest girl is, how and why she gets the *tilismi* book, why she is so kind to me and where has Chandrakanta gone away?"

He reached the court. Today, there was no picture gallery, rather it was the court of the same yogi, who had prevented Kumar from jumping down the hill. A wide carpet with deer skin on it and the yogi was sitting on it. On the left a little behind the forest girl was sitting and on the front side stood four to five maids with folded hands.

Seeing Kumar coming, Yogiji stood up. Coming to the door he caught Kumar's hand and seated him to his right on the deer skin. The forest girl got up and stood at some distance staring at Kumar with loving eyes.

Kumar also set his eyes towards the forest girl. At this moment, love, sympathy and shame were oozing from the eyes of both. The four eyes were linking together. Had there been no sense of the presence of the yogi the two would have met with open hearts but both of them were cautious that the yogi should not understand their loving looks. After sometime Kumar and the yogi began to talk —

Yogi said, "Are you and your company happy?"

Kumar said, "From your kindness they are all happy but...".

Yogi said, "But what?"

Kumar said, "We are restless because the secret of certain things is still unknown but we hope from your kindness our such anxiety will come to an end."

Yogi said, "By the grace of God there will be no anxiety left and all your doubts will melt. This time you people please accept our simple dishes. Thereafter, we'll be talking all through the night. You may ask whatever you have to. God willing hence you will not have to face any trouble and your happy days will begin hence forth."

These pleasure-soaked words of yogi gladdened the hearts of Kumar and his *aiyars*. After a while food was arranged. All the dishes were such as only to be available in the houses of kings and emperors. After dinner in the middle of the garden a carpet was laid on the beautiful floor of stone. Spreading deer skin over it, yogiji sat down and seated Kumar by his side. At a distance, the forest girl with her two companions, sat down and others were sent away.

More than three hours at night had passed. The moon was rising spreading its beams. Cool breeze was blowing which carried the sweet scent of flowers. Yogi asked Kumar with a smile —

"Now, you may ask whatever you have to ask. I'll give reply to all your questions and I will help you accomplish all your works pending till today."

Kunwar Virendra Singh had several incredible things in his mind. He was at a loss what to ask first. After all he sat carefully and began to ask yogiji.

□

10

Whatever daytime was left, Diwan Hardayal Singh spent in collecting the spies and briefing them. In the evening, along with spies, he presented himself before Maharaja Jay Singh in the garden.

Maharaja Jay Singh himself asked the spies, "Why can't you find out Jalim Khan yourselves?" In reply, they submitted, "Maharaja, we try to the best of our ability and hope to find out."

Maharaja said, "Aafat Khan has emerged as a new Devil! In his notice, he has written his meeting place. Then why don't you meet him at that place and arrest him?" The spies replied, "Maharaja, Aafat Khan has written *'Teti-choti'* as his meeting place. We don't know where *'Teti choti'* is, which locality it is or what place he has called by this name. We don't know where to go."

Hearing it, Maharaja himself was puzzled over *'Teti Choti'*. He could not understand anything. Regarding spies as innocent, he did not blame them, just threatened them and with a warning sent them away.

Now Maharaja had little hope of his survival. Out of fear, he kept awake throughout the night with a sword in hand because the only thing he could depend on was his bravery.

Next day, another notice was found pasted in the city, which the guard presented. Diwan Hardayal Singh read out the letter thus —

"Beware, keep cautious! I've arrested Badrinath. As per my previous promise tomorrow at twelve o'clock in the night, I will appear at your palace with some men carrying the head of Badrinath. I'll see how you arrest us!

— Aafat Khan"

□

11

Four people in police fatigue are sitting on a rock in a fierce forest near Vijaygarh. On another rock nearby, two people are talking slowly. There is clear moonlight, so that their faces and clothes are clearly visible. One of the men sitting on another rock might be about forty years old. Black complexion, tall figure, black beard wearing pant and tight *kurta*, having bow and arrow, sword and shield, the man is sitting resting a knee on the ground. Long black, taut moustache is pointing upward, the grey and fierce eyes are sparkling, the face proclaims a robber. His name is Jalim Khan.

The other man sitting to his opposite in a warrior position is Aafat Khan. Moderate stature long beard, wearing tight *pajama* and *kurta* with a scimitar in front and a bag on the left side is keenly listening to Jalim Khan and responding to him.

Jalim Khan said, "You are a big help to me."

Aafat Khan said, "Same to me! Look, this scimitar will chop off thousands of people. I don't keep any other weapon than this. It is treated with poison, a slight scratch with it is fatal."

Jalim Khan said, "You've met me after a long search."

Aafat Khan said, "It was a must for me to meet you, therefore, I got notices pasted because you don't have any fixed place where I could find you, but I was sure that you must have known *aiyari*, so I wrote my address in *aiyari* language so that others may not understand the meeting place."

Jalim Khan said, "I had learnt just a bit *aiyari*, but you seem to be an expert in it. Only then you could arrest Badrinath so soon."

Aafat Khan said, "I'm not an expert at all, but I am too much for a boy like Badrinath."

Jalim Khan said, "Whatever you may say but I consider you as my guru, just show me Badrinath."

Aafat Khan said, "Oh sure, see it. I have buried his trunk but the head is tied in a bundle, but don't touch it because it has been treated with spice, so that it doesn't rot till tomorrow."

Saying this, Aafat Khan opened another bag, which contained the head of Badrinath. The cloth was profusely blood soaked. All of his comrades present started dancing overjoyed to see the skull of Badrinath.

Jalim Khan said, "This man was a rogue."

Aafat Khan said, "But how could he escape me?"

Jalim Khan said, "But my guru, it is odd to hear you that we will have to take on the fort at twelve in the night."

Aafat Khan said, "What's odd, see the drama."

Jalim Khan said, "But guru, because of your notice many people would be present at that time, let's see that we are not arrested!"

Aafat Khan said, "Who has the guts to arrest us?"

Jalim Khan said, "Then what's the gain to endanger our life! Why not alter the time?"

Aafat Khan said, "You're a big dunce, have you any idea why I have done so?"

Jalim Khan said, "You're to know it."

Aafat Khan said, "Now listen, I tell you. My intention is that as soon as possible we should finish the matter by beating and killing them. You must regard all men present there as just dead bodies. You'll see how I finish them off without a hassle."

Jalim Khan said, "But guru, how is this possible?"

Aafat Khan said, (taking out a ball and showing it) "Look, I have prepared a number of balls like this one and I'll give each one of you such a ball. You will just throw them into their mob, who will be present to arrest us. These balls will explode with a thundering sound and emit lots of smoke that will cover them. The smoke will make them immediately blind and suffocate them."

Hearing Aafat Khan, all people were overjoyed. Jalim Khan said, "My guru, just explode one ball in our presence. If we see it, it will boost up our morale."

"All right, see "saying it Aafat Khan threw the ball on the ground. The ball burst with a loud noise and spread lots of poisonous smoke seeing which Aafat Khan, Jalim Khan and their comrades moved away from there, even then their eyes got swollen and heads were dizzy. Seeing it, Aafat Khan took out from his bag a balm and applied it to each one's eyes and also rubbing the balm on his palm, made them to inhale it. They felt relieved and began to applaud Aafat Khan.

Jalim Khan said, "Wah guru, you've made a wonderful thing!"

Aafat Khan said, "Now, have you got the guts to go to the fort?"

Jalim Khan said, "Thank God who sent you to me. What we could do in a year, you can do in a day. Wah guru! Cheers!"

Now we will go to the fort jumping and dancing and send all to hell. Now, give a ball to each one and all.

Aafat Khan said, "Why just now, I'll give when we proceed, we have a whole day to spend".

Jalim Khan said, "All right, but guru, why did you give the notice of a long period? Had you scheduled it for today it would have been a pleasure."

Aafat Khan said, "I thought Badrinath to be clever and not an easy catch. So, I gave time but he proved a total nincompoop!"

Jalim Khan said, "What should we do now?"

Aafat Khan said, "Nothing at the moment, but we must be ready to take on the fort tomorrow at twelve in the night."

Jalim Khan said, "No need to mention it. Now you and I are together, I'll do whatever and whenever you ask."

Aafat Khan said, "All right, then it is advisable to shift from here and take a rest. Let's see what God wants. I have taken an oath that unless and until I kill everybody in the fort I will not eat at all."

Jalim Khan said, "Guru, you shouldn't do like this, you will become weak."

Aafat Khan said, "That's enough, hold your tongue, no harm will come to me if I don't eat."

They all left the place.

□

12

The appointed day came when Aafat Khan would come to the fort, holding the head of Badrinath. Today, the whole city was agog with excitement. Ever since evening, Maharaja Jay Singh himself was making all types of arrangements. Big gallants and stalwart fighters were being roped in inside the fort. All were highly spirited. Maharaja himself with a sword in hand was walking around praising his fighters and advising them to arrest anybody unknown to them. And the brave people were giving themselves airs of their bravery, saying that they would arrest strangers like this and kill them like that. The vigilance around the fort was tightened because Maharaja was sure that Aafat Khan would be arrested then and there. He also felt that if the vigilance outside was not tight Aafat Khan would easily enter the fort. Otherwise, he would go back just killing one or two guards. Profuse lighting was arranged inside the fort. The whole fort was shining as in the daytime.

It was about midnight when from the roof on the eastern side, six people jumped down and stood in the midst of the crowd, where a number of brave stalwarts were sitting or standing. In front of them, all Aafat Khan had was the head of Badrinath hanging from his hand.

□

13

In the cave inside *tilism* garden, Kunwar Virendra Singh and Yogi were talking, which was clearly heard by the forest girl and her *aiyars.*

Kumar, "First tell me, is Chandrakanta alive or dead?"

Yogi said, "O God ! Who can kill Chandrakanta? She is safe and well in this world."

"Can I see her again?"

"Sure."

"When?"

(Pointing to forest girl) "When she wills." Hearing it, Kumar turned towards the forest girl. At the moment, he was in a peculiar condition. His whole body was shivering, looks were frightened. Seeing Kumar's condition, Yogi threw a hard look and she became alert. Kunwar Virendra Singh also noticed it clearly and said —

Kumar said, "If you will, I will surely see Chandrakanta."

Yogi said, "No, (showing forest girl) she is the incharge but she is under my command. So, why do you worry, ask whatever you have to ask, then you will be told the way to see Chandrakanta."

Kumar said, "All right, tell me, who is this forest girl?"

"She is the daughter of a king."

"She has been very kind to me, what does it mean?"

"It simply means that there is fond love between Chandrakanta and her."

"If it is so, why does she want to marry me?"

"There is no need to marry you nor does she love you. She is bound under the insistence of Chandrakanta because she wills so."

Hearing the last words of Yogi, Kumar felt very happy in the mind and told Yogi, "When there is so much intimacy between Chandrakanta and her, why does she not bring her before me?"

"The time has not come."

"Why?"

"When you bring king Surendra Singh and Jay Singh, here she will bring in Chandrakanta and entrust to them."

"Then I leave this place now and as early as possible I will come back bringing them together."

"But first reply to my query."

"What's that?"

Yogi said, (Pointing to forest girl) "This girl has helped you so much and you and your *aiyars* have seen it, too. Who else knows about it and who except you and your *aiyars* have seen her?"

Kumar said, "None other than Fateh Singh and I have seen her uptil now. No doubt, today *aiyars* are seeing her."

Forest girl said, "Once he (pointing to Tej Singh) visited me, but perhaps he did not tell you about that because I had made him swear not to divulge it."

Hearing it, Kumar looked at Tej Singh. He said, "Yes sir, the matter is related to that period when you had told me that my *aiyari* had rusted. Then I tried my best to see her and told her, "Until you tell me everything about you, I will not go and never abandon my pursuit." Then she told me that a day would come when Chandrakanta and she (forest girl) would be known as belonging to Kumar. But, for now, you don't pursue me otherwise it would harm your mission. Then I said, "If you swear that Chandrakanta will meet Kumar, I'll leave this place this very moment." She said, "You also swear that you will not disclose to anybody what has passed between us today till I am not face to face with Kumar." Both of us took an oath to this effect. This is the reason that even on being asked I did not disclose the matter and today finally you and she are face to face and therefore, I am disclosing everything."

Yogiraj said, (to Kumar) "It means that except you and your *aiyars* nobody else has seen this girl but the people of your camp must have known that a new woman has come who is helping Kumar."

Kumar said, "No, nobody knows about it because except *aiyars*, I don't tell anybody about her and even *aiyars* why should they talk about it to others than their group? No doubt, my campmen have seen her horsemen in disguise on several occasions and whenever somebody came to me carrying her letters, my campmen might have guessed something."

Yogiraj said, "That's no harm. Well, tell me. Have king Surendra Singh and Jay Singh heard from you anything about it?"

Kumar said, "No, but I told Jeet Singh, the father of Tej Singh everything about it and, perhaps, he might have passed it to my father."

Yogiraj said, "No, Jeet Singh can never pass it to your father. But now you must take care that whatever you have done with the forest girl is not known to anybody."

Kumar said, "I will never divulge it, but please tell me what advantage is there if I don't disclose the matter? If I disclose things it will be a praise to her."

Yogiraj said, "It may be a matter of praise between you people but when her parents come to know about it, they will be very angry. Because it is disgraceful for a girl of an aristocratic family to meet a third person male and write letters to him and send marriage proposals etc."

Kumar said, "You're right to say so. However, who are her parents and where they live."

Yogiraj said, "Even this thing will be known to you when king Surendra Singh and Maharaja Jay Singh come to this place and Chandrakanta is handed to them."

Kumar said, "Then you please order me to set out this very moment to bring in both of them."

Yogiraj said, "Is this the proper time to go from here? Is this a city? Stay till the night and start in the morning. Take a rest as only a little night remains."

Kumar said, "As you please."

It was too hot. So, Kumar preferred to sleep in the open. Arrangements for their sleeping were made immediately by order of Yogiji. Thereafter, Yogiji made for his room and the forest girl went her way.

The remaining part of night also passed as they talked on. The sun had not yet risen when Yogiji alone came to Kumar and said, "I forgot to tell you yesternight which I tell you now. When king Jay Singh gets ready to come to the cave; rather your father and Jay Singh come upto the cave, then leaving them outside you come with your *aiyars* to me and then you will bring them here. Now be done with your morning routine and worship before you go." Kumar did likewise but he was surprised at the last part of his advice to see him before bringing in king Jay Singh and his father.

Food was arranged. After treating them properly, Yogiji disposed them of.

Previously, as Kunwar Virendra Singh and his *aiyars* had come to this garden, in the same manner from one garden to another and then to third and, finally, came out of the cave. All were seated under a thick tree and Devi Singh set out for Naugarh to fetch a horse for Kumar.

A little before sunset, Devi Singh came to Kumar with a horse on which Kumar made for Naugarh, with his *aiyar*.

Having reached Naugarh Kumar saw his father and going inside the palace met his mother. He did not say anything to anybody about himself. No doubt, from Pannalal and others he came to know that a new enemy Jalim Khan had emerged who had killed many people in Vijaygarh and the people there were trembling to hear his name. Pundit Badrinath had gone to arrest him and after his departure, it was learnt that another man Aafat Khan had come up who had given the notice that, on a particular day he would come to the palace with the head of Badrinath. He had also challenged that none could arrest him.

Hearing such things, Kunwar Virendra Singh, Tej Singh, Devi Singh and Jyotishiji, all felt afraid and began to think that they must reach Vijaygarh by any means because at this time, if they did not help Maharaja Jay Singh and protect the subjects from the clutches of the devils, Chandrakanta would find an excuse to taunt him and he would always feel demoralised.

Thereafter, it was also known that Jeet Singh had gone on fifteen days' leave. This news baffled Tej Singh. He began to think where his father had gone because among his relatives nobody had any business for him to attend. Then why did he go making such an excuse?

Tej Singh asked his mother where his father had gone. The poor mother replied, "My son, are the women in *aiyar*'s houses considered suitable to be told where her masters go?"

Hearing it, Tej Singh kept mum. Next day, on being asked by king Surendra Singh, Tej Singh just said that he had gone into the cave in search of Chandrakanta, where they met a yogi, who told them that if they brought Maharaja Surendra Singh and Maharaja Jay Singh to him he would call in Chandrakanta and surrender her to her father. For this purpose, they had come to take him and Maharaja Jay Singh.

Being pleased, king Surendra Singh said, "I am ready to go just now but Maharaja Jay Singh is involved in such a problem that I can't describe. Pundit Badrinath has gone on the mission, let's see what happens. You might have heard about that!"

Tej Singh said, "I have heard everything, it is desirable of us to go there and cooperate."

Surendra Singh said, "I myself was going to say so. What's Kumar's opinion, will he go or not?"

Tej Singh, "You yourself know that Kumar is not afraid of death, Jalim Khan is nothing to him."

King said, "That's true, but it is our duty to accept the challenge of brave people and to counter the thieves, robbers and *aiyars* is your duty. Nobody knows, he might attack Kumar in cognito!"

Tej Singh said, "It is true that it is Kumar's duty to face brave fighters but no thief, robber or anybody else has the guts to harm Kumar so long as we are there."

King said, "Nothing is valuable to us against reputation, but it is also advisable to guard against rogues. Though there will be no difference if Kumar doesn't go, anyway you people go and help Maharaja Jay Singh. When Jalim Khan is arrested, report to Maharaja everything and bring him here. Then I, too, will go for the cave together."

Thinking of king Surendra Singh's unwillingness to let Kumar go to Vijaygarh and not proper for him to insist, Tej Singh kept silent and took orders from Maharaja to go to Vijaygarh alone and taking a letter from him set out for Vijaygarh.

At a distance, he took shelter in the shade of a tree in a forest and then resumed his journey. They reached the palace at Vijaygarh exactly at the time when a big horde of brave men had gathered and every man was cautiously watching around. Suddenly, from the roof on the eastern side six people abruptly jumped down and stood in the middle Aafat Khan carrying in hand the head of Badrinath.

Nobody had seen Tej Singh till then, now he asked challengingly, "Arrest these rogues, fast." Saying this, he himself threw the rope towards them. A number of people attacked then and there. They started throwing the balls from their hands, but to no avail. It was a damp squib, an eyewash. They could do nothing and all of them were arrested.

Now everybody saw Tej Singh, Aafat Khan also looked at him and said, "Tej I'm Badri." Hearing it, Tej Singh held the hand of Aafat Khan and separated him from the crowd and removing the fetters from his hands and feet, embraced him. All people started shouting, "No, no, what are you doing? He is a rascal; he has killed Badrinath. See, he is carrying the head of Badrinath, what has happened to you to shower your favours on him?" But Tej Singh said menacingly, "Keep silent, do you know who this man is? Is it a fun to kill Badrinath?"

All people respected Tej Singh. Nobody had the guts to oppose him. Aafat Khan had to be handed to him but the other five men were tied tightly.

Tej Singh freed Aafat Khan and taking him together, moved to Maharaja Jay Singh. There was excitement all round. Even after the arrest of Jalim Khan and his men, people were trembling with fear. Maharaja was looking at the drama from a distance. He was unnerved to see Tej Singh with Aafat Khan coming towards him. He quickly took out the sword from the sheath. Tej Singh called loudly, "Don't be afraid, we two are not your enemies. The man with me who you think is someone else, is in fact, Pundit

Badrinath." Saying it, he pulled out Aafat Khan's beard making him recognisable.

Now, Maharaja Jay Singh felt relieved. He asked, "How come Badrinath with him?"

Badrinath said, "Maharaja, had I not become their companion, who could bring them here to get arrested?"

Maharaja said, "Whose head is dangling from your hand?"

Badrinath said, "It's a wax model!"

Now there was great excitement that Badrinath got Jalim Khan arrested. He was surrounded on all sides. People were pushing and jostling against one another. With great difficulty, Badrinath was separated from that crowd. Jalim Khan and others also understood that Aafat Khan was none other than Badrinath, who duped them into the trap, but what could they do now? Everyone's hands and feet were tied and, thus, were totally helpless. In helplessness, they started abusing Badrinath. It's true that when one's life is in danger, he talks anything.

Badrinath did not mind their abuses; rather he looked towards them and laughed. Many people along with him, even Maharaja started laughing.

By order of Maharaja, all people were sent out of the palace; only a few distinguished people remained. Jalim Khan and his associates with their hands and feet tightly tied were shut up in a room inside the palace. Water was ordered and Badrinath's hands and feet were washed. Thereafter, sitting in the court, Maharaja asked him in full detail about the arrest of Jalim Khan. Tej Singh was also very eager to know it all.

Badrinath spoke, "Maharaja, to meet this devil Jalim Khan, I devised the first thing to change my name Aafat Khan and published the notice writing my address in such a language, which no other than him and his *aiyars* could decipher. It was already known to me that there was not any *aiyar* here to decipher my writing."

Maharaja said, "Yes, all right, you had written your meeting place as '*teti-choti*, what does it mean?"

Badrinath said, "In *aiyari* dialect, '*teti-choti*' means a terrible drain."

Thereafter, Badrinath narrated in detail the story of his meeting Jalim Khan, showing the ball show and giving them the fake ball ensured their roping into the palace, etc. hearing which, Maharaja was overjoyed and wanted to give him some real estate as reward, but he declined and said that without permission from his master, he could not accept anything. The work he was assigned by his master, he had done to the best of his ability.

Badrinath made some more submissions like this hearing which Maharaja was further pleased and made up his mind to give Badrinath much more and he would not be able to decline.

While the talks went on, it was day break. Tej Singh and Badrinath took leave of Maharaja and came to the house of Hardayal Singh.

□

14

Very happily, Maharaja summoned the court in the morning. Tej Singh and Badrinath were also seated with due respect. By order of Maharaja, Jalim Khan and his four associates were brought to the court in fetters. As ordered, Tej Singh began to question Jalim Khan —

Tej Singh said, "Well mister, is your name really Jalim Khan or something else?"

Jalim Khan said, "I will reply to it later. First tell me is it the rule to kill an *aiyar* in your court or not?"

"Not to speak of our court, throughout India no religious Hindu king will ever kill an *aiyar*. No doubt, the *aiyar* who goes beyond the rules, will surely be killed."

"Then shall he be killed?"

"That depends on the will of Maharaja! But why do you ask such things, are you *aiyars*?"

"Yes, we are *aiyars*."

"Fi-Fi! Why do you stigmatise *aiyari*! You people are seasoned dacoits, you have nothing to do with *aiyari*!"

"We have been *aiyars* for several generations. We are not green ones."

"Your ancestors may have been *aiyars*, but you people are the samples among dacoits."

"When you have called us dacoits, how can there any hope of our survival?"

"Whatsoever, tell us, who are you?"

Jalim Khan pleads, "When we are on the block, why should we earn notoriety by disclosing our names? And why should we give out the details about ourselves? But if you promise not to kill us, I will tell you all."

Tej Singh, "We can't ever commit such a thing and you will have to give out the details under compulsion."

"Never."

"Then we will hurl shoes on your head."

"Whatever may come."

Badrinath said, "What a shameless man!"

Jalim Khan said, (to Badrinath) "Guru, you have cheated me, you have proved my senior."

Badrinath said, "Your admission will serve you no good. Today or tomorrow you people are sure to be beheaded."

Jalim Khan said, "I'm sorry, could do nothing."

Tej Singh realised that there was no gain arguing with him. Whatsoever they do Jalim Khan was not going to disclose things, therefore it was better to devise some plan. Thinking so, he told Maharaja, "Let these people be sent to prison and that man (pointing to one) should be retained here." It was done under the order of Maharaja.

As per Tej Singh's instruction, barring one of these dacoits, the rest were forwarded towards the prison. While going, Jalim Khan looked towards Tej Singh and said, "Guru, you are very clever. There is no doubt that you know the real man by seeing his face. You have retained a good coward, now you will win."

Tej Singh replied with a smile, "First he should be taken to task, thereafter all of you one by one will be brought to this very place."

Jalim Khan and his three associates were sent to prison, but one of them stayed. In fact, he was a coward. He become afraid to see his associates leaving him behind. His face showed even more nervousness when Tej Singh asked a guard, "Fill the fire pot with coal and bring in two or three iron rods with wooden hands just now."

All people in the court were flabbergasted to think why Tej Singh had ordered fire pot and iron rods. And it is beyond words to describe the nervousness of that dacoit present there.

Four-five iron rods and coal filled fire pots were brought in. Tej Singh asked a guard, "Light the fire and heat the iron rods." Now that dacoit couldn't help asking with fear, "Tej Singh, what will you do by heating these rods?"

Tej Singh said, "By heating them two will be inserted into your eyes, two into your ears and one through your mouth into your stomach."

Dacoit said, "You people are known as kind-hearted, but killing somebody by torturing him like this will it not be a blot on your kind heartedness?"

Tej Singh said, (laughs) "Sparing you people is a serious matter. So long as you are alive, you will be killing thousands of people. It is better to finish you. By giving as much pain you will be killed, your dacoit associates will feel the same amount of fear."

Dacoit said, "Then can't our lives be saved by any means?"

Tej Singh said, "Yes, it can be saved by only one means."

"What means?"

"If you tell about your associates correctly, you will be released right now."

"I will tell everything correctly."

"How to know that you are truthful?"

"I'll prove that I am truthful".

"Then tell us."

"Now listen."

Everybody was eager to know why Tej Singh ordered the fire pot in, what was to be done with the iron rods, etc. All eyes were set towards the dacoit, who was going to talk about his associates.

As that dacoit got ready to narrate the story and opened his mouth, a young man from among the crowd drew his sword and rushed towards the dacoit and, in a flash, chopped off the head of the dacoit. Brandishing that blood soaked sword and injuring others the man went out.

Out of fear, nobody came forward to catch him but how could Badrinath resist himself, he ran after the young man.

Hundreds of people followed Badrinath, but Tej Singh did not follow him. He directly ran towards that prison in which Jalim Khan and others were kept. He had the suspicion that somebody by practising *aiyari* might have released them but no, they were caged in. Tej Singh strengthened the vigilance and came back to court immediately.

The crowd had thinned out to one fourth. Some people voluntarily ran along with Badrinath and many people followed at the instance of Maharaja. When Tej Singh came back, Maharaja asked, "Where had you gone?"

Tej Singh said, "I was worried whether Jalim Khan and others had got free. Therefore, I ran towards the prison. But they were found in."

Maharaja, "Let's see when Badrinath returns and what he has done."

Tej Singh, "Badrinath will return soon because he runs very fast."

Today Maharaja sat at court longer than usual. Though Tej Singh pointed out, "Today, Maharaja was unusually delayed." Maharaja replied that so long as Badrinath did not return or anything was known about him, till then he would be sitting like that.

□

15

Two hours thereafter, they heard noise coming from outside the court. All people turned towards that side. A guard came to inform that Pundit Badrinath was coming carrying that murderer.

Pundit Badrinath came along with that killer tied with rope.

Maharaja said, "Badrinath, have you found out who he is?"

Badrinath said, "He doesn't say who he is and will never tell."

Maharaja said, "Then?"

Badrinath said, "What then? I think he has changed his face." His face was washed with water and a totally different face came to view.

There was a big gathering, they became excited, it appeared that he was known to everybody. Maharaja was taken aback and looking towards Tej Singh, said, "Lo, it's clear. He is Nazim's brother-in-law. I think Jalim Khan and others, who are in captivity, they too must be relatives of Nazim and Ahmad. They should be brought here."

By order of Maharaja, Jalim Khan and others were brought to court.

Badrinath said, (looking towards Jalim Khan) "Now you people have been recognised as relatives of Nazim and Ahmad, your associate has told it."

Before Jalim Khan could speak in reply, that killer, who was arrested by Badrinath burst out. "Jalim Khan, don't get cheated by Badrinath, he was very timid, I sent him to hell. Whatever way we are killed, we should never disclose our identity.

Jalim Khan said, (Loudly) "Surely."

Maharaja felt very angry to hear them. His eyes turned red, his body started trembling. Looking towards Tej Singh and Badrinath said, "No more, we don't need to know their identity, whatever may come, chop off their heads right now in my presence."

The entire city was thirsty of their blood. On the spur of the moment, the overenthusiasts brandishing their swords killed all of them. Their dead bodies were thrown away. Maharaja got up. Tej Singh appealed with folded hands — "Maharaja, till now, I did not get the opportunity to say my purpose of coming here and even now, there is no time for it."

Maharaja said, "If the matter is urgent, follow me to the court!"

Tej Singh said, "The matter is really very urgent, but I would not like to say it now because Maharaja is in a tantrum and I am also in a bad mood. But, at present, I find it reasonable to say that I want to tell you what will really please you."

The last clause of Tej Singh dampened the anger of Maharaja and showed happiness on his face. He caught hold of Tej Singh's hand and took him into the palace. At a sign from Tej Singh, Badrinath also joined them.

Along with Tej Singh and Badrinath, Maharaja went into his special chamber and then asked Tej Singh the purpose of his coming.

After laying bare all facts Tej Singh said, "Now you and Maharaja Surendra Singh should go to the cave and by the grace of Siddhnath Yogi, come back cheerfully along with the princess."

Hearing the words of Tej Singh, Maharaja was beside himself with joy. He came forward and embraced Tej Singh and said, "Now you ask Hardayal Singh to make arrangement for my journey and you people also perform your daily routine and eat something. I am going in to communicate this happy news to the mother of the princess."

Today three, fourths of the day was spent on anger, bother, disturbance and joy, nobody ate anything at all.

Taking leave of Maharaja, Tej Singh and Badrinath went to the house of Diwan Hardayal Singh and the Maharaja going inside the palace assured Chandrakanta's mother of the hope of her recovery.

An hour earlier, the palace bore a dismal look. Now everybody looked happy. From mouth to mouth, the news spread across thousands of houses that Maharaja is going to fetch Chandrakanta.

It was also decided that a little before day break, Maharaja Jay Singh will set out for Naugarh.

Now, the time has come for the reader to feel happy and share in their joy of Chandrakanta and Kunwar Virendra Singh. As planned, Maharaja Jay Singh was to go to Naugarh and from there along with king Surendra Singh and the prince, they would go inside the cave in the hope of meeting the princess. Siddhnath Yogi had already instructed Kumar to meet him first while going into the cave with his father and Maharaja Jay Singh.

First let us go to that garden inside the cave in which Kumar had seen the court with the gallery of Chandrakanta's pictures and Siddhnath Yogi and forest girl had met. The setting sun is shining over the tree tops presenting a spectacular scene. The cool breeze is casting around the aroma of fragrant flowers. Look, on the marble platform in the middle of this garden, there are three beds and beautiful girls are spreading exquisitely fine sheets on them particularly the bejewelled bed is the centre of attraction for all people. On that side, there is a fine bed of green grass, mowed symmetrically.

On the other side, there are dense trees and a small nice bungalow in their midst surrounded by multi-creepers. On the west side, there are croton plants showing a variety of colour and shapes. Their leaves with white lines and curled like curly hair add to the charm. The scene is so eye-catching, spectacular and dreamy.

But, our attention gets stuck at the sight of three women, who are plucking henna leaves and collecting them in their bags. One of them is the super-heroine of this story, the forest girl and the others are her attendants.

The forest girl has put on white clothes while her dear attendants are in green and red clothes.

Haring plucked henna leaves the three girls are coming towards the other end of the platform. May be, they want to sit on those three beds.

And so it happened. The forest girl deposited the henna leaves on the ground and in a mood of languor lay on the bejewelled bed in the middle and the two attendants sat on the beds on either side and keep talking slowly.

Forest girl said, "Oh, I feel tired."

Attendant in green said, "Walking is no less tiring."

Attendant in red said, (to other attendant) "Are you also tired?"

Attendant in green said, "Why should I be tired? Even while walking ten miles I was not tired. After all, Kumar's *aiyars* could not trace us till now."

Attendant in red said, "Even the Jyotishi ji was puzzled who is regarded as an expert in *ramal* and astrology, not to speak of others!"

Forest girl said, "The *ramal* of Jyotishi ji has been nullified by these machines which Siddhnath Baba has hung around our necks and does not allow us to put it off till now."

Attendant in green said, "We don't know what is there in this machine which obstructs the functioning of *ramal*."

Forest girl said, "Once I asked Siddhnath Baba the same thing in reply to which he spoke a lot many things. I don't remember all that he had said but I remember this much that the metal ramal is made from the metals that affect attendant stars, planets, satellites, all of them are mixed in this machine. So, one who has it nobody can know about him through *ramal*."

Attendant in red said, "No doubt, it is very effective, just see I went dressed as sunflower, still Jyotishi ji could not say from his ramal that it is *aiyar*."

Forest girl said, "Kumar must have been greatly outwitted".

Attendant in red said, "Don't ask anything, he was awfully nervous to think who was that devil settling her terms what she wanted."

Attendant in green, "A short while ago, I had gone as a messenger to obtain reply and had made Devi Singh my disciple. Nobody could recognise."

Attendant in red, "That's all right, but destiny is also a very important thing. Remember, when the *aiyars* of Shivdutt stole the *tilismi* book and were burying it, by chance we saw it from a distance and after their departure dug out and found the *tilismi* book."

Forest girl, "Ough, Siddhnath gave us permission to walk after much difficulty and over and above he gave us the vow to see Kumar from a distance and not to approach him".

Attendant in red said, "It was in your interest, he didn't mean any personal gain."

Forest girl said, "All this is true, but what to do there is no satisfaction without meeting."

Attendant in green said, "Both of us were given the instruction to help Kumar walking around. How we had been saved from Badrinath in the guise of a flower girl!"

Attendant in red said, "Were the *aiyars* not trying their best to find out? But here we had the guru of gurus Siddhnath who was on his toes all the time to help us, they could do nothing. Look, while approaching our boat in the Ganga, how were Tej Singh, Devi Singh and Jyotishi ji befooled, we even took away their clothes."

Attendant in green said, "We had knowingly brought them with us."

Forest girl said, "Howsoever clever they may be, but they can't equal our Siddhnath. No doubt, among them Tej Singh is very clever."

Attendant in red said, "What if Tej Singh is clever, our Siddhnath is Tej Singh double."

Forest girl said, (laughs) "You know him better!"

Attendant in green said, "In fact, Siddhnath badly cheated Kumar and his *aiyars*. They did not even get the hint that Siddhnath Baba was getting the *tilism* of this cave won over by us."

Attendant in red said, "When locking the door of this cave from inside we were breaking the *tilism*, Tej Singh came carrying Badrinath in a bundle but finding the door closed, went back."

Forest girl said, "They must have been puzzled to think who had shut the door."

Attendant in red said, "Sure, sure! Not only here in some other matters too, we had cheated Kumar and his *aiyars*. As Surajmukhi, I told them that I would free Shivdutt and then taking a word from Shivdutt not to nurse enmity against Kumar, I myself released Shivdutt. They must have thought that Surajmukhi is very wicked!"

Forest girl said, "Still that bastard Shivdutt betrayed us and was bent upon nursing enmity towards Kumar, he is not at all reliable."

Attendant in red said, "That's why we arrested him again and getting the *tilismi* book we gave it to Kumar. No doubt, Krur Singh once recognised us. I thought that if he was left to live, all our secret would be exposed. So, I fought and killed him."

Attendant in green said, "That guy was determined to possess all the wealth by winning the *tilism*."

Forest girl said, "I am happy that the victory of the *tilism* of this cave was credited to me."

Attendant in red, "It was so easy, over and above the help from Siddhnath Baba."

Forest girl said, "That's true."

□

16

Maharaja Jay Singh left for Naugarh along with Tej Singh and Badrinath from Vijaygarh. He had a train of only five hundred people. They spent one day on the way and next day, they camped near Naugarh.

King Surendra Singh got information of the arrival of Maharaja Jay Singh. Then and there along with his generals and courtiers, he proceeded to welcome him and brought him along to the city.

The house was already well-furnished for Maharaja Jay Singh. The king ordered his lodging in that house and Maharaja Jay Singh was requested to be the royal guest, but he refused and said that for several reasons, he could not accept his hospitality and also requested him not to insist on it as well as not to ask the reason why he refused."

King Surendra Singh understood the purport of it and felt very happy.

At night, Kunwar Virendra Singh and the *aiyars* met Maharaja Jay Singh. Maharaja embraced Kumar cheerfully and seating him by his side and asked him the details of *tilism.*

During the previous night it had been decided that before day break, they would go to see Siddhnath Baba in search of the *tilismi* cave. Accordingly, next day, while the stars were still shining Maharaja Jay Singh, King Surendra Singh, Tej Singh, Devi Singh, Pundit Badrinath, Pannalal, Ramnarayan, Chunnilal and others started for the *tilismi* cave with a retinue of one thousand people. The cave was not far off, they reached there by day break.

Kunwar Virendra Singh with folded hands appealed to Maharaja Jay Singh and king Surendra Singh, "When Siddhnath Yogi had sent me to fetch you people, he had cautioned me that when you people reached near the cave, I had to see him alone leaving you people behind. Now, if you please, I'll go to see Yogiji."

Maharaja Jay Singh and Surendra Singh said, "Yogiji must be obeyed. You go and meet him, till then, we'll have our camp here in this very forest."

Kunwar Virendra Singh, taking only Tej Singh with him, went into the cave. Opening the gate of the cave and passing through several rooms and houses and gardens both of them reached that garden in which Siddhnath lived i.e., the garden in which Kumar had seen the gallery of Chandrakanta's pictures.

As they stepped in the garden, they saw Siddhnath Yogi who was already standing at the gate. Seeing Kunwar Virendra Singh and Tej Singh coming, he moved towards them and called, "You have come?"

They greeted him and replied —

Kumar said, "As per your instruction, I have come to see you leaving behind Maharaja Jay Singh and my father outside the cave."

Siddhnath said, "You have done the right thing to bring them. Today you people will surely meet Chandrakanta."

Tej Singh, "By your grace, so will it happen."

Siddhnath said, "Tell me, is the rest all right? Has there been no disturbance of any sort in Vijaygarh and Naugarh?"

Tej Singh said, (looking towards him with surprise) "Yes, there was some disturbance; someone called Jalim Khan had cropped up as a new enemy of the two kings."

Siddhnath said, "Yes, I know that. No doubt, Pundit Badrinath is adept in his art, he arrested him very cleverly. It was good that they were killed; now their associates will have no courage to nurse enmity towards the two kings. Come on, let's talk walking."

Kumar said, "Very well."

Tej Singh said, "When you know all this, you must have known who was this Jalim Khan!"

Siddhnath said, "It is not known who he was but I guess that he might be one of the relatives of Nazim and Ahmad."

Kumar said, "That's right, it must be what you think."

Siddhnath, "Has Maharaja Shivdutt gone to forest?"

Kumar said, "Yes, he has told my father that he will practise penance."

Siddhnath said, "Whatsoever, but we should never believe an enemy."

Kumar said, "Will he again nurse enmity?"

Siddhnath said, "Who can say?"

Kumar said, "Now if you please, I'll fetch my father and Maharaja Jay Singh!"

Siddhnath said, "Yes, but first let you hear why I called you before them?"

Kumar said, "Say, please."

Siddhnath said, "The fact is that if a man loses something which he loves most and then one day suddenly gets that back, he is drawn to that as much as a hungry eagle is drawn to its prey. I know that there is deep love between you and Chandrakanta. If, in the presence of the two kings you suddenly see her or she sees you, no wonder, you or Chandrakanta may behave in an unseemly manner out of excess zeal. Even if you approach her, it will not be desirable. Therefore, my suggestion is that you meet the princess before they come. Come on, follow me!"

Aha, it was what Kumar wanted. After a long time, he will see princess Chandrakanta by the grace of Siddhnath Baba, for which he was pining day and night, on whose one meeting he had offered his kingdom, even lost his life. Today, all of a sudden, he will see at a time when there will be no doubt, no resentment or regret, no enemy left. At such a time, Kumar's joy was definitely boundless! His heart started beating fast. Being overjoyed, he could not even reply to Siddhnath Yogi and followed him.

Hardly had they gone a few steps towards the room when they saw a maid plucking flowers. Yogi Siddhnath called her and said, "Just now you go to princess Chandrakanta and tell her that prince Virendra Singh is coming to see her. She will sit in her room with her friends."

Hearing it, that maid went running one way and Yogi Siddhnath started walking here and there in the garden along with prince and Tej Singh. Prince Virendra Singh and Tej Singh both were engaged in serving their interest. Tej Singh was happy at the prospect of meeting Chapla. Both of them began to think in what state they will meet their love, what they will say, what they will ask and if she complains, what will be their reply? In such thoughts, they were so much engrossed that they did not talk further to Siddhnath Yogi and silently kept on walking behind Yogiji.

After walking along with these two men, Siddhnath Yogi reached near that room in which they had seen the gallery of Chandrakanta's pictures. There, looking towards Kumar, Siddhnath said, "Go inside this room and meet Chandrakanta and her friends, meanwhile I do something else."

□

17

Kunwar Virendra Singh entered that room. He saw princess Chandrakanta at a distance along with Chapla and Champa standing with her eyes fixed towards the door.

On seeing instantly, Kunwar Virendra Singh ran towards the princess and Chandrakanta towards the prince. Though some distance away from each other, both of them fell on the ground and became unconscious.

Tej Singh and Chapla also had their eyes fixed on each other. Seeing the condition of Kunwar Virendra Singh and princess Chandrakanta, Champa went running into her room and came back carrying an earthen vessel of *bedmushka*'s juice in one hand and a sod of dry smooth earth in the other.

She sprinkled the juice over their faces and pouring a little over that sod, made *lakhlakha* and held it before their noses.

After some time, Tej Singh and Chapla came to their senses and they too, seeing the condition of Kumar and Chandrakanta, started making efforts to revive them.

Kunwar Virendra Singh and Chandrakanta both regained consciousness, both of them began to see each other, neither was able to utter a word. In their heart of hearts, they were thinking what to ask, what to complain, where to begin talking, etc. The words started from their belly, but got stuck in the neck. The throat swelled because of the volume of words, their eyes were teary and even tear drops began to slide.

Hours passed away, the two were so engrossed in meeting each other that they were not conscious of their presence. They were not mindful of the place, the work and the immediate environment.

If somebody has knowledge of the heart of Kunwar Virendra Singh and princess Chandrakanta, it is Tej Singh and Chapla themselves. Who else can gauge the depth of their love as the two were not themselves, no doubt, poor Champa got flustered to see their love of the highest order. She began to think that they might not lose their mind in such intimate meeting. She began to think of some plan to improve their condition and let them talk to each other. At last, holding the hand of the princess, Champa said, "Princess, you used to say that the day you met Kumar you would ask who he had named forest girl? Who was that girl? What had he promised her? Who did he want to marry? Have you forgotten these things, will you say all this to him?"

A person's love towards somebody lasts so long as another man does not hit his mind and disturb his concentration. Therefore, the yogis have to sit in solitude. The love of Kunwar Virendra Singh and princess Chandrakanta was not ordinary, the two were becoming one. They expressed the pang of separation through each other's heart, they understood each other but others standing around could not see it because the two were not speaking. No doubt, the words of Champa startled them. Their four eyes were mingling into one. They stirred, lowered their eyes and began to talk. Nobody knew what they spoke and understood only they could know. Disjointed sentences and not-clear-words were not for others to understand. Neither princess Chandrakanta could help complaining against Kumar nor could Kumar ask her about her grievances.

Had they been sitting for hours, then perhaps they could open their hearts, but here after two hours, Siddhnath Yogi separated them. The maid came in and said, "Kumar, Siddhnath Baba has called you immediately. Come on, don't delay please."

Kumar had no guts to disobey Siddhnath Yogi. Getting nervous he got ready to go then and there. The feelings of the two hearts remained encased.

Leaving Chandrakanta in the same state Kumar got up, before he wanted to say something to the princess another maid came to make haste. At last, Kunwar Virendra Singh and Tej Singh came out of that room. Standing at a distance Siddhnath Baba called Kumar to him and said, "Kumar, I did not ask you to sit along Chandrakanta whole day long. It is about midday, they must be waiting for you whom you have left outside the cave."

Kumar said, (looking towards the sun) "Yes, the day...."

Baba said, "The day what?"

Kumar said, (feeling subdued) "There has been some delay, no doubt, now if you ask I will fetch my father and Maharaja Jay Singh immediately."

Baba said, "Yes, go and bring them in here. But tell the two kings on my behalf to bring along with them only those who can see Chandrakanta or before whom she may appear."

"Very well."

"Go, no more delay now."

"I bow to you in salutation."

"No need of it as you will be back today."

Tej Singh said, "I bow to you."

Baba said, "You will have the opportunity to bow all your life, but now make it a point that you do not disclose the story of your meeting the princess to those outside the cave and while returning if it is too late, don't return today."

Tej Singh said, "No sir, why shall we disclose anything?"

Baba said, "Now go."

Both of them taking leave of Siddhnath Baba came out walking through the same path.

More than midday had passed. Till then Kumar had not performed daily routine and worship, etc.

Going to the camp Kumar met king Surendra Singh and Maharaja Jay Singh and conveyed the message of Siddhnath Yogi. Both of them asked why Babaji had called them earlier. They replied whatever they thought proper and went to their camps and performed the daily ritual and had lunch.

Sitting aloof king Surendra Singh and Maharaja Jay Singh began to consider who they should have along with them inside the cave.

Surendra Singh, "Yogiji has instructed that we should have within the cave only those people before whom the princess may appear".

Jay Singh, "I, you, Kumar and Tej Singh will surely go, take others of your choice".

Surendra Singh, "No need to take lots of people. But we must take the *aiyars* because nothing can be hidden from them and more, it is not desirable to maintain secrecy from them".

Jay Singh, "You are perfectly right. Except these *aiyars* nobody else is fit enough to carry with us to the cave!"

While talking and deciding the day was about to end. Surendra Singh called Tej Singh and asked, "How much time does it take to reach Babaji?" Tej Singh replied, "If we go direct then in two to three hours we may reach that garden in which Babaji lives but my advice is not to go at this hour because the day is about to end and we will have to walk on rugged path in this cave. If it gets dark we may not be able to walk a single step further".

Maharaja Jay Singh was very impatient to see the princess but at this hour he had to accept the advice of Tej Singh and decided to proceed next morning.

□

18

Early morning Maharaja Jay Singh, king Surendra Singh and Kumar with all their *aiyars* came to the gate of the cave. Tej Singh opened both the locks seeing which Maharaja Jay Singh and Surendra Singh were very much puzzled. Going inside the cave they were even more puzzled, they moved around astonished and admired things.

Taking them around showing the astonishing things and explaining them, Tej Singh reached the gate of that garden in which lived Baba Siddhnath. Before they arrived, Siddhnath was there at the gate to welcome them.

Pointing with his fingers, Tej Singh told Maharaja Jay Singh and Surendra Singh, "See, Siddhnath Baba is standing at the gate."

Both the kings wanted to reach the Baba quickly and bow to him but before that Babaji said, "Beware, nobody will prostrate before me, otherwise you will regret and fail to meet."

Their desire remained unfulfilled, nobody had the courage to ask why they were forbidden to prostrate. Then approaching him they wanted to shake hands but Babaji did not permit it saying, "Maharaja, I am not equal to it, your stature is much higher than mine."

Surendra Singh said, "Nobody's stature is higher than that of sadhus."

Babaji said, "You are right to say that but you don't know what type of a sadhu I am".

Surendra Singh said, "Whatever type of a sadhu, he is venerable."

Babaji said, "Whatever the type provided he is a sadhu."

Surendra Singh said, 'Then who are you?"

Babaji said, "No one."

Jay Singh said, "Your words are such as not to understand and again and again aggravate surprise, guess and nervousness."

Babaji (laughs) said, "All right, come, let's walk in this garden."

Taking all along, Siddhnath went inside the garden. Walking along with Maharaja Jay Singh, king Surendra Singh, Kunwar Virendra Singh and their *aiyar* Babaji reached that court in which Kumar had seen the court of the princess or say the room in which Kumar had only yesterday met Chandrakanta.

The way this court has been decorated today, Kumar had not seen it. In the centre, there was an expensive carpet, Babaji seated king Surendra Singh, Maharaja Jay Singh and Kunwar Virendra Singh on it and the *aiyars* on their sides and himself sat in front of them on a deer skin — which was already lain there. Then the conversation started.

Babaji said, (looking towards Maharaja Jay Singh and king Surendra Singh) "Are you fine?"

Both kings said, "By your grace, everything is fine and having met you today we are very happy."

Babaji said, "Excuse me for the trouble you had to take on the way to this place."

Jay Singh said, "The very idea of coming here resolved our troubles. Had you not bestowed your grace and there was no chance of coming here, nobody knows how long we would have been suffering the pang of separation from Chandrakanta."

Babaji said, (smilingly) "Now you will have no trouble to see the princess."

Jay Singh said, "We hope by your grace we will surely see Chandrakanta."

Babaji said, "Maybe, for some reason if you could not see the princess today, then tomorrow you will surely see her. This time having performed your daily rituals have your meal and then we will talk further."

Babaji called a maid and asked her to arrange things for the guest's bath in that garden with the pond.

Babaji led them all to that garden. All of them took a bath and, having meals in the northern room, sat in that room in which Kunwar Virendra Singh had opened his eyes. Even today, that room was as decorated as Kumar had seen earlier. The only difference was that today princess Chandrakanta's picture was not there.

When all people sat comfortably, king Surendra Singh asked Yogi Siddhnath, "This beautiful hill having several small gardens is part of my territory. But, till today, I had no chance to visit it. Is there any other way out above this garden?"

Babaji said, "The path to this garden being secret nobody could come in or go out, no doubt, one who has knowledge of this small *tilism* may perhaps come here. Its one path is the one by which you have come, the other path to go out passes through this garden but that is even more secret."

Surendra Singh said, "For how long have you been living on this hill?"

Babaji said, "I have come very recently to this cave and even then I have not come on my own rather on my master's service."

Surendra Singh, (surprised) "Who is your master?"

Babaji said, "This too will be known to you very soon."

Jay Singh said, (pointing to Surendra Singh) "From your words it appears that this interesting hill may be in his kingdom, but he is not aware of it and the place is not such as it may not have its owner. You are not a native of this place, then who is the master of this beautiful hill and fine houses and decent gardens?"

Before Siddhnath Baba could reply to the words of Maharaja Jay Singh the forest girl was seen coming. On her two sides were her friends and a horde of 10-15 maids behind.

`Babaji said, (pointing to forest girl) "She is the master of this place."

Hearing the words of Siddhnath Baba, both kings and *aiyars* started looking at the forest girl with wonder. At this moment, Kunwar Virendra Singh and Tej Singh were also looking at the forest girl in utter amazement. Hearing form Siddhnath that she is the master of this place, Kumar and Tej Singh were reminded of the past incidents. Lowering his head, Kunwar Virendra Singh began to think that undoubtedly princess Chandrakanta is a prisoner of this forest girl. When that poor girl came through the *tilism* path, she was enmeshed in this cave and they arrested her. That's why, she had written that letter that without her help, we can't see Chandrakanta and even Baba had said the same thing that only when she willed we could meet Chandrakanta. No doubt, she has imprisoned Chandrakanta. We can never regard her as our friend, rather she is our enemy; she unnecessarily put Chandrakanta to prison and made her suffer besides us.

Lowering his face and thinking such things, Kumar got angry and raising his head looked at the forest girl.

Howsoever love may Kumar have got in his heart for Chandrakanta, but his love for the forest girl was no less. No doubt, there was one clear difference that when he was absorbed in thoughts of Chandrakanta, he did not think of the forest girl but on seeing her love overpowered him. The same thing happened just now. Thinking that she has imprisoned the princess, he got into a tantrum, but for how long? Only till he was thinking lowering his head towards the earth, but the moment he raised his head and saw the forest girl, all anger dissipated, the very thoughts changed. Previously, he thought something, and now he was thinking something else.

"No, no, she is not my enemy. O God, I don't know why such a thought crossed my mind! No better friend is there. Had she not helped us, it was impossible to break the *tilism* and the hope of seeing the princess would have vanished; rather I would have fallen into the hands of my enemies."

Not only in Kumar's mind, rather in the minds of all people, the same thought prevailed that if she was the master of this hill and the garden, then surely she must have imprisoned the princess. At last, Maharaja Jay Singh could not help asking, "Getting entangled in this cave, was Chandrakanta her prisoner?"

Babaji said, "No, when Chandrakanta got entangled in this cave, at that time, nobody was the master of this place. She got this hill, garden and the house thereafter!"

The second part of Baba's statement confused them. Even Kumar started feeling ill at ease. Had there been no Maharaja Jay Singh and Surendra Singh present, Kumar might have cried, but he kept mum out of courtesy.

Maharaja Jay Singh and Surendra Singh could not help themselves. They looked towards Siddhnath and gave a hint to the forest girl to come to them. The forest girl came to Siddhnath with her two friends, one wearing a red dress and the other green. Babaji snatched away from her face something like a filmy layer attached to the face and holding her hand, led her to the feet of Maharaja Jay Singh and said, "Here is your Chandrakanta!"

Shorn off the film from her face, everybody recognised Chandrakanta. Raising her head from his feet, Maharaja Jay Singh kept her close to his heart for a long time, feeling overjoyed.

Siddhnath yogi also stripped off the film from the faces of the two friends of Chandrakanta. Now the one in red dress was recognised as Chapla and in green dress as Champa.

Everybody's face was glowing with radiance. Nobody had ever enjoyed such happiness as today. At the instance of Maharaja Jay Singh, princess Chandrakanta put her head at the feet of king Surendra Singh who blessed her raising and stroking her head.

For hours, everybody was beside themselves with joy. It is beyond words to describe the mental state of Kunwar Virendra Singh. Had Siddhnath not made him meet the princess, this time surely he would have committed something unseemly regardless of shame and courtesy.

Looking at Maharaja Jay Singh, Siddhnath Baba said, "You please ask the princess to roam about with her friends or go to some other room and, then, I will narrate to you the strange story of this hill and the princess."

Jay Singh said, "I have seen her face after a long time. Now how to part her from me lest something unseen happens and it becomes difficult to see her again."

Babaji (laughingly) said, "No, no, she can't be separated from you now."

Jay Singh said, "However, don't separate her from me and please narrate the full story now."

Babaji said, "All right, as you please."

□

19

Siddhnath Baba began to narrate the story of this interesting hill and princess Chandrakanta.

Babaji said, "I already knew that this hill is a small *tilism* and there is also a *tilism* in the Chunar area. One who breaks this *tilism,* and who he marries, this *tilism* stands as dowry and the would be bride will be its master."

Surendra Singh said, "First tell us what is *tilism* and how it is made."

Babaji said, "*tilism* is made by one who has lots of wealth but no heir. Then he consults prominent astrologers and foretellers to know whether in his or his brother's line, there will be a powerful and competent man or not. The astrologers or foretellers declare that after a certain period a son in his clan will be illustrious, they also prepare his horoscope. In his name, they deposit money and valuables and tie *tilism* over it.

These days, they tie *tilism* by depositing some wealth, they sacrifice one or two for safety and that man is reborn as snake or ghost and guards that property and does not allow others than the declared person to touch it. But, previously it was not so. In old days, when kings were required to tie *tilism*, great astrologers, foretellers, physicians and artisans were gathered. According to their advice, the earth was dug. And keeping the treasure inside the *tilism*, building was constructed. The astrologers, artisans and foretellers to the best of their knowledge tried to conceal it, but they also considered the would be owner's planets and stars for whom the treasure was meant. Kunwar Virendra Singh has broken a small *tilism*. He will tell you himself the details and then think deeply over each and every move and you will yourself understand what those astrologers, artisans, foretellers and philosophers were able to do."

Jay Singh, "Anyway, we have learnt a little about it and the rest will be clear when we hear the details from Kumar. Now, tell us about this hill and my daughter and also tell us why Maharaja Shivdutt escaped from this cave and was imprisoned again."

Baba said, "Now listen, I tell you in detail. When having entangled in the *tilism* of Chunar, princess Chandrakanta came to this cave, she spent two days in trouble. When I got information I reached there on the third day and freed the princess where she was enmeshed which I will show you."

Surendra Singh said, "We have heard that breaking the *tilism* requires strength."

Baba said, "That's true, but in this *tilism* the princess did not have to face any trouble nor required strength because it was related to that *tilism* which Kumar had broken. If that *tilism* or its part was not demolished, this *tilism* would not have been broken."

Kumar said, (looking towards Siddhnath) "You did not say by which path you reached the princess. When we came to this cave and saw the princess helpless we saw no way to reach the princess and free her."

Baba said, "Only by thinking you cannot know about *tilism* ? I had also heard that princess Chandrakanta was enmeshed in this cave and you were trying to free her but were unable to do anything. I could go there and free the princess but I did not like it because I wanted that this wealth should go to the princess."

Kumar said, "You are a yogi, you can reach anywhere but what could I do!"

Baba said, "You people shouldn't think that I am a yogi. I cannot do what man or *aiyars* are unable to do. Now listen, which way I reached the princess and what I did."

□

20

Siddhnath yogi said that opening the door of this cave first he went inside and above the hill in a pass he saw the princess lying helpless there. He had heard from his guru that there were several small gardens in this cave that had a passage through the stream that was flowing in the cave. They must have seen them as they came in because the beauty of that stream was worth seeing.

All nodded in agreement. Siddhnath Yogi continued, "Wearing loin clothes, I went down the stream and started moving here and there. Suddenly, on the eastern side something like a door was felt, so I dived inside. For 8 to 10 feet, there was even water then gradually it was less and less to the waist line. Then I realised that this was a tunnel which was going up.

After walking for half an hour, I found myself in the west and north corner (where you are sitting) and walking around come to this room. (Pointing with hand) look, the cupboard in the wall is not really a cupboard rather it is a door, it opens as you kick it. I kicked it open and went inside. It was totally dark inside. After about 200 steps, I found the wall. In the same manner there again I opened the door by kicking and reached exactly where princess Chandrakanta and Chapla were weeping helplessly. By my side, there was another path leading to the Chunargarh *tilism* a part of which Kumar has demolished.

Seeing me both of them got flustered. I told them, "Don't be afraid! I have come to free you". Saying this I came back to this garden by the same path along with Chandrakanta and Chapla. I knew all this path and beyond that I did not know anything. It was not difficult for me to take the princess and Chapla out of the cave or reach them home but I wanted that the small *tilism* should be demolished at the hands of the princess and all the property should belong to her.

It is known to all that Kumar was breaking the *tilism* of Chunargarh just to free princess Chandrakanta from this prison, he had no temptation for wealth and property. Had I taken the princess out of this cave and sent her to you, Kumar would have stopped breaking the *tilism* and all the treasure would have remained there. I am your well-wisher. How could it be acceptable to me that so much wealth was rendered useless and did not go to Kumar or princess Chandrakanta?

I told my innermost feelings to the princess and Chapla and also told them that if they did not accept my advice I would go away leaving them in the same garden. At last being helpless, the princess accepted my advice and promised not to do anything against my advice.

I was not at all aware how the wealth of this cave could be obtained and where the keys to these locks lay but was convinced that the princess would surely be the mistress of this *tilism*. My dilemma continued for two days. The condition of these gardens was very wretched, but there were two to four such fruit trees that satisfied our hunger.

The third day was full moon. Sitting by this pond, I was thinking something, the princess and Chapla were roaming about, just then Chapla came running to me and said, "Hurry up, there is something strange in this garden."

Instantly I got up and reached there with Chapla where princess Chandrakanta was standing by the eastern wall gazing at something. Seeing me the princess said, "Babaji, look, there is a hole in the bottom of this wall and big size white ants are coming out of it. What can it be?"

I had heard from my guru that the presence of white ants indicates the presence of a treasure or the key to that treasure. Thinking so I pulled out my sword from the waist and handing it to the princess asked her to dig the earth around. Thus, as directed the princess dug the earth. Just a foot deep a glass urn appeared with its mouth sealed. I got it broken from the princess. It was filled with some oil which spilled out as the urn was broken. Inside there was a bunch of keys which made me very happy.

Next day handing the bunch of keys to princess Chandrakanta I told her, "Look carefully walking around the place and wherever you see a lock, apply one of these keys. I will also be with you."

The bunch had thirty keys. Searching several days we opened for all the thirty locks. We also came across three passages through which we could go out from above. We found four gardens and twenty-three rooms full of wealth and goods and food containing all kinds of aristocratic goods and immeasurable wealth.

When I found the way out of the *tilism* from above I went home and brought in a few maids and some necessary things for the princess. All locks were opened in a few days. But after prolonged stay the princess felt uncomfortable and one day said to me, "I want to walk around beyond the *tilism.*"

On hard insistence I agreed. I changed their faces with my skill and arranged two to three horses for them to ride on and see things out of the *tilism.* I cautioned them to keep their identity hidden so that nobody recognised them. They agreed and kept themselves hidden as much as possible. Meanwhile these gardens were also improved.

Kunwar Virendra Singh got the treasure of that *tilism* and all the treasure and goods went to the princess. (looking towards Jay Singh) Till today, Chandrakanta was my daughter and master, now I hand over to you your property.

Having mercy on the queen of Maharaja Shivdutt the princess released both of them and made them swear that they would never nurse enmity towards Kumar. But that wicked man did not honour his pledge and meeting old friends he got ready to harm Kumar and harass his camp in his absence. At last, I was compelled to arrest him and put him in this cave at the same place where Kumar had imprisoned him. Now ask me whatever else you have to ask. I will clear all your doubts and confusions."

Surendra Singh said, "We had a lot to ask but at this hour we are so happy that I have forgotten them. What to ask? Anyway, I'll ask you some other time. Why did you help the princess?"

Jay Singh said, "I also have the same question because so long as we do not know the details from you, the confusion persists. Moreover, you have said again and again that you are neither a yogi nor a mahatma. Hearing this we are all the more confused. If you are not what appears from your face, then who are you?"

Baba said, "Anyway, you will come to know that".

Jay Singh said, (towards Chandrakanta) "My daughter, don't you, too, know who is this Yogi?"

Chandrakanta said, (with folded hands) "I know everything, but why should I disclose? He has made me swear severely so that I can't say anything."

Baba said, "Why are you in a hurry? In a short while, you will know the reality about me. First, please go and see those things that Chandrakanta has got in this *tilism*."

Jay Singh said, "As you please."

Babaji got up and led them to another garden.

□

21

With Jay Singh and others Babaji reached another garden and walking around started showing them all the gardens, buildings, treasure and goods which the princess had got in this *tilism*.

At first sight, Maharaja Jay Singh exclaimed, "Wah, wah, those people were blessed who had amassed so much wealth. Had I wished to raise a dowry selling my whole kingdom, I would not have raised even one fourth of it?"

The biggest treasure and jewel safe was seen in that garden and cellar where Kunwar Virendra Singh had seen the gallery of princess Chandrakanta's pictures.

In two to three days, Siddhnath Baba made them travel the whole area. When they were free from such works and sat at court Maharaja Jay Singh told Siddhnath Baba, "We will remain grateful to you for the whole of our life for all the help you rendered to save the life of Chandrakanta. Today, by any means, please tell us about yourself and relieve our tension, our patience is breaking down."

Hearing the words of Maharaja Jay Singh, Siddhbaba spoke smilingly, "Just wait, I am going to disclose my identity just now." Saying this he sounded a whistle loudly. Then and there three to four maids came running and stood by his side. Siddhbaba commanded, "Bring me immediately water for my bath, clothes to wear (real) from the box and put them in this room. Today I will give up this skin coat and my long beard."

Immediately his order was carried out. Meanwhile they were talking at random. Siddhbaba went into that room in which water and clothes etc. were just arranged for him.

In a short time, Siddhbaba came out of that room in a new avatar. Now he was no longer Siddhbaba. So long he was called Siddhbaba, now he was really Jeet Singh.

Now there was no need to ask for the details! Immediately recognising Jeet Singh Maharaja Surendra Singh got up and embraced him saying "You are a thousand times more than my brother." He said further. "When there was a battle between Maharaja Shivdutt and Kumar, you had helped Kumar with only five hundred cavalry force. Today, you have earned better reputation than Kumar and indebted both Naugarh and Vijaygarh states for generation after generation." He kept embracing him for long. Thereafter, Maharaja Jay Singh regarding him as of equal rank embraced him warmly. Tej Singh, Devi Singh and others cheerfully applauded him.

Now it came to light that it was Jeet Singh in the garb of Siddhnath Baba Yogi who was the saviour of the life of princess Chandrakanta, the preserver of the prestige of Naugarh and Vijaygarh, the well-wisher of both the states, the deceiver of big *aiyars*, the big showman before Kunwar Virendra Singh and the saviour of the life of Kumar when he was about to jump down the hill to kill himself.

Now, everybody was overjoyed. Kunwar Virendra Singh had got utmost happiness to be reunited with princess Chandrakanta. At the moment, the mutual love between Maharaja Jay Singh and Surendra Singh had reached the climax. Then and there, Maharaja Jay Singh held the hand of princess Chandrakanta and deposited her at the feet of king Surendra Singh and wiping his tearful eyes said, "Please allow me to take this girl to my home and in the presence of my relatives and clan and the pundit declare her to be the maid (wife) of Kunwar Virendra Singh."

King Surendra Singh lifted the princess from his feet and very lovingly embracing Maharaja Jay Singh, said, "As soon as possible take the princess to Vijaygarh because her mother must be pining in the absence of her daughter."

Thereafter, Maharaja Surendra Singh asked, "What to do now?"

Jeet Singh said, "Now everybody should go from here, but in my opinion there is no need to take along the treasure and other goods because the things belong only to princess Chandrakanta as they are her dowry and also because the keys are already in her possession. There is no need to lift them from here and then send them with her to show others. Moreover, the princess likes the climate here very much. I think, princess Chandrakanta will surely come again to stay here for some time. So, now we should just go away along with princess Chandrakanta."

Everybody endorsed the suggestion of great Jeet Singh and they all got ready to set out for Naugarh.

Jeet Singh asked the maids who were brought into serve the princess, "You clean your faces and in your real form bring the palanquin here which I have already got ready for the princess."

Obeying Jeet Singh's order, the maids, around twenty, went into another garden and, in a short time, in their original form, came back carrying on their shoulders a unique ancestral golden palanquin.

Kunwar Virendra Singh and Tej Singh now recognised these maids. Tej Singh said, "Wah, wah, I did not recognise the maids of my house. Even my mother did not share the secret with me."

□

22

The passage through which Kunwar Virendra Singh and others used to frequent and even Maharaja Jay Singh had come, was not good enough for one to pass on an elephant or a palanquin and the passage above leading to the cave was a roundabout passage. Therefore, Jeet Singh called for a palanquin for the princess, but he would have to think what will Maharaja and Kunwar Virendra Singh ride on.

In the cave, there were two horses brought in for the princess. Jeet Singh considered them fit for Maharaja Jay Singh and king Surendra Singh and called for a palanquin for Kumar, but Kumar declined it and preferred to go on foot.

To the south of the same garden, there was a big gate the two sides of which had two beautiful iron puppets. Jeet Singh approached the left side puppet and inserted his finger into its right eye, immediately its stomach split open like two panels and showed a silver handle. Jeet Singh began to turn it round. As he turned it round, the gate started sliding into the earth and finally the entire gate sank underneath and a beautiful green garden came to sight.

After the gate opened Jeet Singh came to these people and said, "We will go out by the same passage."

Within half-an-hour, Maharaja Jay Singh and Surendra Singh, riding on horses with princess Chandrakanta's palanquin in the front, came out of the gate. Between the two kings holding the reins of the horses and talking in between Jeet Singh set out followed by Kunwar Virendra Singh with his *aiyars* moving towards the gate of the cave.

Walking for three hours, they reached that camp which was stationed at the gate of the cave. They spent the night there and resumed the journey next morning. In fine and expensive dresses, the bearers lifted the palanquin of the princess and made for Vijaygarh with Maharaja Jay Singh as also those maids, who had been till today with the princess and had borne the palanquin here, out of love and under orders of Maharaja Surendra Singh went along with the princess, too.

Along with Kumar, king Surendra Singh reached Naugarh, Kunwar Virendra Singh first of all met his mother inside the palace and after worshipping the family, goddess came out.

Now the days were passing in cheers. On the eighth day, the *tilak* from Maharaja Jay Singh reached and the ritual was performed with great pomp and show.

On an auspicious day and at auspicious hour, the marriage party of Kunwar Virendra Singh with a lot pomp and grandeur made for Vijaygarh.

At Vijaygarh, preparations were on for the grand reception of the *barat* party. Festivities had already begun even before the arrival of *barat*. The *mehfil* was full of beautiful and renowned female singers and dancers. But, when the *barat* arrived there was a ruckus.

Leading the *barat*, Maharaja Shivdutt on horseback, well-dressed, wearing the ceremonial dress, saddled with double sword at the waist and holding a flag in hand reached the gate of the reception. The procession followed slowly. Kumar in the garb of the bridegroom got down from the horse and went inside the reception.

As Kumar Virendra Singh entered the reception, a big ruckus was caused outside. Everybody saw that two Maharaja Shivdutts were fighting each other. Both were wielding their swords swiftly and both were calling, "Don't come near us, enjoy the scene from a distance." One Maharaja Shivdutt was the same who had just come in ceremonial dress, holding a flag in hand riding a horse and the other Maharaja Shivdutt was in plain clothes, but both of them were fighting bravely.

In a short while, our Maharaja Shivdutt (who had come holding a flag on horseback) had time enough to pull out the rope from his waist he tied the other enemy, Maharaja Shivdutt and dragged him into the reception. Following them, a crowd of people entered eyeing in utter surprise.

Our Maharaja Shivdutt tied tightly the other Maharaja Shivdutt in plain clothes to a pole and taking a flare from a lightman, handed it to him and himself sat by the side of Kunwar Virendra Singh. He took up a golden ceremonial pot filled with rose water, wetted his handkerchief with it and wiped his face with it. Now, it was the same dress, the same outfit but the face of Tej Singh!

Seeing it all, people burst out laughing. There was laughter and laughter for some time.

In fact, it was Tej Singh looking like Maharaja Shivdutt in his outfit, holding a victory flag was leading the *barat* and, on the other hand, the real Maharaja Shivdutt who had on a pretext gone to forest to practise penance also came to attend the *barat* of Kunwar Virendra Singh. Tej Singh loved fun and frolic by nature.

When the real Maharaja Shivdutt saw somebody in his own image holding a flag on horseback, he understood then and there that it was the trick of some *aiyar*. His valorous blood ignited his anger and he fell upon his adversary. The fake Maharaja Shivdutt had to play the light man and Kunwar Virendra Singh and princess Chandrakanta were married very happily.

□

Glossary

Khanjar — carved dagger

Aiyar — a person skilled in spying, transmogrification and warfare

Diwan — a post like minister or secretary

Maharaja — literally great king or the king of a bigger state

Maharani — great queen

Lakhlakha — anaesthetic powder

Chobdar — mace-bearer

Hukka — a device for smoking tobacco through water

Chilam — a clay bowl with or without stem in which tobacco is filled and smoked. It's a part of hukka

Miyan — a term of address for a Muslim

Bhai — brother

Guruji — teacher

Sutaka — the thirteen-day condolence

Wazir — minister

Munshi — clerk

Sadhu — holy man

Tilak — vermilion mark on forehead

Maharajadhiraj — king of kings, honorific term for great king

Prithvinath — lord of the earth

Birha — a song of separation

Tikka	—	a round ornament worn on the forehead
Bhairawi	—	a form of music/song
Mirmunshi	—	head clerk
Hujur	—	an honorific term of address
Kripanath	—	literally the lord of gratitude. An honorific term of address
Kshatriyas	—	warrior class in the Hindus
Brahman	—	priestly class in the Hindus
Saree	—	a dress for an Indian woman usually five-metre long cloth to be worn by wrapping around the body
Lopanjan	—	a herb that is said to have properties to make someone invisible
Yogini, bhutani and dakini	—	witch or female spirits/ghost
Patra	—	almanac
Pyjama	—	man's lower garment, cut either very loose or tight
Dalan	—	courtyard
Khilat	—	a robe of honour presented to an office-holder
Dhoti-gamchha	—	a piece of cloth worn round the lower body,one end of which passes between the legs and is tucked in behind
Lota	-	round metal jug
Lashkar	—	military camp
Chhaga	—	a piece of cloth cut out for throwing stones
Zamindar	—	landlord
Brahmhatya	—	killing of a Brahmin
Mahatma	—	saint
Yogi	—	exponent of yoga
Sardars	—	leader of a group/clan

Kurta	—	man's upper garment
Bedmushka	—	a herb used for making anaesthetic powder
Babaji	—	an old holy man
Barat	—	bridegroom's guests in a marriage
Mehfil	—	assembly

□□□